CW00516448

The Zoo

Book 1: The Beast, The Boy and The Zoo

John Regan

The Zoo: The Beast, The Boy and The Zoo

First Edition published in 2023
John Regan asserts the moral right to be identified as the author of this
work.

Copyright © John Regan

The Zoo: The Beast, The Boy and The Zoo

For Diane

Preface

Many zoos today are no longer menageries or stamp collections of animals exhibited for human entertainment. They share a higher purpose – to halt the decline of species in the wild. Some zoos are better at this than others, but at least the concept of zoos contributing to nature conservation is widely known now. Sadly, there are zoos that pay only lip service to that goal, and worse, there are still menageries where animal welfare and conservation are unheard of.

It is clear that John Regan has been thoroughly immersed in this very world for many decades, and so this is one of the fundamental themes of The Zoo – Zoos good? Zoos bad?

It is difficult to pigeonhole this book. It is a sort of phantasmagorical eco-fable for readers aged about ten to a hundred. Tweens and teenagers will be mesmerised as the characters Seth and Sam grow from childhood to young adulthood, whereas we older folk will get a brain workout dealing with conundrums as old as time – humankind vs nature, truth vs lies, right vs wrong. John Regan deftly combines overtones from nature and natural history with undertones from religious and classical works in a counterpoint that races along in a cracking good story. The setting is in what seems to be a mainstream zoo, but on another level it is the backdrop to dramas of universal significance. Cliff-hangers abound, and gory battles alternate with tender moments. Good triumphs over evil….and sometimes evil triumphs over good. But what is good and what is evil? The story is not finished, and I can't wait for Book Two!

Dr Lee Durrell MBE

Foreword

John thinks differently to anyone else I know! I find that intriguing.

After reading an early draft of 'The Zoo', I said I would not be at all surprised to find out that he had actually lived a former life as a fish! Or for that matter a bat, or a lion cub. Certainly 'The Zoo' brings us right inside the head of animals in a quite startling manner; whilst at the same time stressing the impossibility of ever truly understanding a non-human mind.

I have known John for about thirty years, starting out when we worked together at Chester Zoo, and then through his activities on behalf of many other zoos and similar organisations in the UK and around the world. His particular work has as a matter of course required him to think deeply about everything that zoos do mean and might mean in all kinds of contexts.

Now he has gone off and, within this work of fiction, turned that very idea of a zoo into a symbol for so many different questions that affect the lives of us all. The adventures of the twins Seth and Sam lead us into all kinds of fundamental divisions: between the human and non-human; between the wild and the tame; between male and female; between truth and lies; and so on.

The best stories are those that keep us thinking about them long after we have heard or read them. This one certainly does that.

Dr Mark Pilgrim OBE, Director Zoos Victoria (Werribee Open Range Zoo); Former Chief Executive Officer, Chester Zoo

Note for the Reader

'The Zoo' is set in a world and continuum that is similar, but *not* quite the same as our own. As seemed to suit the story I have played fast and loose in terms of the state of development of the society within which our characters live their lives and the technology to which they might therefore have access.

Although I have naturally been influenced by many of the zoos, wildlife parks and other wonderful organisations with which I have the privilege to work over so many years, the story, all names, characters, and incidents portrayed in this novel are entirely fictitious. No identification with actual persons (living or deceased), places, buildings, and products is intended or should be inferred.

Contents

Prelude

"To discover our father was not after all our father at all was a bit of a shock..."

That sentence above is how this story will begin. How it must begin.

But not just yet.

No. Not yet. Please allow me a few minutes first.

You see right here, right now I really am at my ease.

And I would like to remain that way for a little longer.

Of course I can see you over there, my long expected visitor slowly approaching. And you certainly have no intention of leaving me in peace, have you? You are coming here to drag this story out from me, to rip it word by word from this fuzzy old brain of mine.

You could not – even at my advanced age – you simply could not bear to leave me here in comfort in my *own* study; at the top of my *own* house; in my *own* armchair (Father's chair once of course); and surrounded by all my *own* books; looking out of one of the four windows that give north, east, south and west over the Zoo. It was, it seems, too much to ask that a few days before Christmas I might as an old man simply sit here staring into the fire. Or that I could spend time just gazing at the snowflakes wafting down, or losing myself in the million motes of dust dancing up there in the shafts of winter sunlight?

I *do* like the smell of this room though, you know.

Some faint hint of vanilla over the mustiness of so many volumes piled up high.

At least... At least I have been able to enjoy myself a little. Enjoy myself watching you struggle to get here.

I have patiently traced your coming to our appointment, making your way slowly but surely through the piles of winter snow, past the Rhinos, over the Otter bridge, across the Wallaby woods.

Your steps then ringing out up the grand staircase.

A single knock and there you are, sitting opposite me. You smile. Quite a nice smile, considering. A bit condescending perhaps. You switch on your so modern looking recording device, and you open that mouth of yours to say:

"Begin then, Seth."

And I oblige. *"Alright. But tell me, man to man - where exactly? Where should I begin?"*

"At the beginning," you say.

Then in a tone I neither like nor understand.

"Well, as near to the beginning as you yet know Seth."

Something within me shakes itself vigorously. It clears its throat and it squares its shoulders. Grudgingly it steps out into the limelight.

And so I do indeed reluctantly begin.

^^^

Part One: Seth's Telling of the Tale

The Zoo: The Beast, The Boy and The Zoo

Chapter One: Our Father

Our father..?

To discover our father was not after all our father at all was, well, a bit of a shock, yes. But not, you know, an especially unpleasant one.

We had always vaguely considered Gogol in that sense without really thinking about it very much at all. Most people who had anything to do with us made such an assumption anyway. So that day crouching high up there hidden in the rafters learning that he wasn't really; it did not seem to matter so very much. It was something of interest certainly. It was a surprise undoubtedly.

But mainly - it was a relief.

That is at least how I recall my feelings. What precisely might have been going on within Sam's head I absolutely did not know. People make a rather foolish assumption that twins, especially when they looked as alike as Sam and I did back then, can somehow read each other's minds. You know, like that Corsican Twins nonsense? If you really want to know the truth: I have never had any inkling whatsoever as to what Sam is actually thinking.

Unless that is I am actually told.

That entire affair with animals, the alarming manner Sam had with creatures. All the very strange business that so much of this story is actually about. No, no, I never understood that about Sam. For me as a young boy, animals were good to eat. I would hunt them, kill them, trap them for sport, yes, certainly; but that was where it began and ended.

The Zoo: The Beast, The Boy and The Zoo

I do recall once I fashioned a trap for Sam to catch birds - who then naturally insisted we had to let the blessed things all go again. For hours we each sat taking turns to hold the end of the piece of string. My sibling would sit there so very quietly and just stare at the animal. When I asked what was going on, I would get some absolute twaddle about 'feeling for the animal's soul'.

As for whether in those times my dear twin knew or cared how I felt about things either; well back then I always assumed us to be as mirror images... So no. Not really. Sometimes true enough Sam did baffle me in seeming to be aware of certain things, things about me. But I always supposed that this was just guesswork or pretension.

Sam blowing Sam's own horn really.

The one certain thing (and now I appreciate it was pretty extraordinary) was that we always had a sense of the other's physical presence. We always knew that the other was there, and specifically where they would be.

Well, no, that is not quite right either, is it? I have not explained it properly.

Where am I? Wait a moment... Yes. We knew that - *if* and *only if* the other twin wished it. So Sam would always know where I might be at any given time; and I knew where Sam was. Unless either of us was to choose to switch it off. Unless we chose to hide from one another.

Which we never did.

At the time I certainly did not fully appreciate it, but there was a unique background bliss in all of that. All of my young life, I knew there was this other, my Sam, whose constant friendship and companionship I could always feel. So despite whatever quarrels might bubble up between us, there was that abiding sense of peace and security on which I could always depend.

Always.

Until the day that I could not.

The Zoo: The Beast, The Boy and The Zoo

Ah...! Wait.

(....)

Oh yes, there it is, a certain expression across my inquisitive visitor's face sitting there across from me. Impatience. I am not, it seems, proceeding quite fast enough for him. And perhaps I am not being clear enough on certain matters. Let us look sharp then. I shall need to move on quickly and cleanly with this story.

My visitor will excuse me though if I now turn my words away from him. I must instead address a very different audience - those people who may just one day read all of this. Let me clear up any confusion for that supposed reader on a critical score, the important matter of where and more importantly 'when' this tale unfolds. These memories concern a world and times similar and familiar enough in some ways to the one which you all know; but in others they will seem *very* different indeed. You will soon see what I mean. As to whether you can get from your kind of place to this kind of place, that I am afraid would involve a much longer telling.

And please can we also understand that as a matter of practicality, I need to lead you forward in this tale. My twin Sam will not be saying that very much. Not to begin with at least. You will need to know specific things that Sam said at given points.

Don't be concerned. *I* will tell you that.

I will speak for Sam.

I shall also make my best endeavours to tell this story with the thoughts I had and the kind of words I might have used at the relevant period of my life. I will use the knowledge and reactions most natural to me back then too.

Yes, I shall do what I can there, but the truth is, the older me, this forgetful figure sitting here in this armchair right now shall likely leak in from time to time.

The Zoo: The Beast, The Boy and The Zoo

Some of the terms I will use, especially as to the names and details of different kinds of animals (and there will be plenty of these), I owe to my later career and experiences. I suppose for that matter some ideas and attitudes of mine that I certainly didn't have back then, these too will intrude. So on that front you may have to just put up with things getting a bit mixed up.

I apologise in advance.

As I say, I took it as my place to look after Sam when we were young. I am the elder. Someone once told me by a *full* half an hour. When we were children I was a little bigger too, certainly quite a lot stronger and more robust in frame. The Seth of that period regarded it as quite natural that he should lead, and that Sam should follow.

Even when we were youngsters with a little effort people could tell us apart. That word 'identical' did not seem quite appropriate in our case, but people will be that way, cleaving to their clichés. They like to keep things simple. We did though both have the same silky coal black hair, shoulder length and very unkempt. And of course our bright blue eyes, frequently remarked on as unusual in children with dark coloured skin. Sam's eyes were that bit brighter than mine, ever darting around, fixing on one object of interest after another. 'Little Hawk' was a nickname that began to naturally emerge until Gogol stomped on it with his scowls and threats. We were dressed very much alike too in trousers and tunics, hand me downs or cast offs from wherever or whenever or whoever.

So, I will tell this story.

And Sam will be...?

Well, Sam will be the special one. Sam will be the one with 'that little secret'. I felt it my duty to protect Sam on that subject. Do you know - in an odd sort of way I still think it is.

Some things never really change.

The Zoo: The Beast, The Boy and The Zoo

But you must, despite everything that will follow in these pages, you must be sure of one very important thing.

I. Love. Sam.

I love my twin.

****

We can forget with any idiocy about mind reading then. But it was easy enough through conventional means for Sam and me to know exactly what the other was thinking. You must picture twins balancing there side by side and staring at one another. An exchange of glances and widened eyes between excited ten year olds, skinny, ragged children, spies precariously perched up on those thin rafters. We were high above the adult world, way over the old people's heads. I so well remember the smell of resin, the tiny splinters from our too tight clasp of the beams, the tingle of smoke in our nostrils from the fire below, and the dusky light filtering through. We were intent on overhearing yet another (but oh, by far the biggest!) of our father Gogol's many dirty dealings.

Up to then such secret goings on had one way or another been to do with cheating or stealing from his customers, the various travellers that came to the Vague Lands to exchange goods or occasionally information.

This was what occupied so much of that old man's time and thinking. How could he best extract value from others?

There was a straightforward pilfering element within this. We had been ruthlessly requisitioned into this practice from being tiny children. Old Gogol had long ago schooled us up to a truly impressive set of skills in looting. Carefully though it was never beyond that level where the resulting suspicion would be counter-productive. Small objects only then (handkerchiefs, rings, brooches, bracelets). He had even got us to practise our pickpocket skills on himself. "Go on. See if you two can slip my wallet out of my pocket - without my feeling a thing."

Although any especially interesting items acquired would find him crooning with delight, there was little if any praise for us in securing this bounty. A vivid, competitive spirit nonetheless motivated Sam and me. More importantly we spied, if only gradually, the possibility of redeploying these very thievish skills back onto Gogol himself.

This time though it was different.

This time, whatever legerdemain was in play, it was on a much grander scaler.

This time his guest below our feet was clearly someone very special.

And this time it was someone who seemed to want something to do with *us*.

But before I go further and my visitor chides me, you my readers are going to have to know a bit more about where and how we lived then. Only that way can you properly understand so much of what was to happen afterwards.

***

Chapter Two: A Fistful of Sand

Nowadays, I would describe it as scrublands; more technically 'a semi-arid region. In those times though we only had the most general notion that there might be anything much else at all anywhere, or any other ways of living in this world. It was not as scientifically interesting, nor as uncompromising in its extremity as an actual full-on, proper desert; but no glimmer of lasting green nor fertility was anywhere to be found.

We also assumed that this had surely always been the way of it.

Now I know that is very far from the case.

No, that place had once looked very different indeed.

So for us Gogol's trading post and watering hole was simply our home. It was also known as the 'Vague Lands'. I am not sure that represented any kind of official name. I think the expression had just gradually welled up from the visitors who provided Gogol's livelihood.

We had the honour of being the very last thing, the furthest point west before everything ended completely: the final watering hole, the very last place possible to stop and, under the sweltering sun, to take a deep breath between two different kinds of world. Looking to the west even the very occasional remaining splash of struggling green soon perished into a sea of sand, where lines and distances blurred and everything swam and swarmed beneath the heat. Looking to the east, first there were just a few other settlements; then just more scrub like us where there might be just a little water; beyond that a gradual smudge of brownish hills; and there finally, barely to be seen, taller, green and eventually blue mountains.

And somewhere, some place much further east yet again, according to those few random notions which had filtered through to us during our childhood, there was... the rest. The rest of the country. The rest of the world. On that our ideas were at best hazy, based on contradictory stories spoken half laughingly by travellers. We had a handful of books to go on too, or in some instance just pages torn from books left behind or stolen. But we had a sense that the travellers might be lying, probably simply amusing themselves by gulling ignorant children with fantastic tales.

We could never be sure. Certainty on anything here was as if forbidden. Nothing here was allowed to be fixed.

Everything in this place was vague.

There were a few other homesteads distilling a meagre living from the Vague Lands. A handful of men and women who seemed bitter and lonely; a couple of small mining operations; and before you got to Gogol's, some other trading posts dealing in different supplies.

And that was it.

A sparse desperate population spread over a sparse desperate land.

Travellers came regularly from the east and, after stocking up at Gogol's place, they passed on to disappear into the western ocean of dunes. Very, very rarely others emerged back out of the western desert, nut brown, and sand mad; and, once they had relieved themselves in different ways, they too processed on back towards those blue mountains.

No one ever really spoke at all of what lay beyond the western desert. There must have been something there surely, somewhere. On the one hand we were the 'end of the world'. Yet clearly it was not really the end of the world at all, was it?

The Zoo: The Beast, The Boy and The Zoo

Some of that tiny minority who did return from the desert, were they ever the very same people who had previously passed through Gogol's trading post?

Yes, I suppose I do remember thinking that, asking about it. Sam and I sometimes spoke or certainly *tried* to speak to those who had returned; but if they were the same people, then they were changed.

Almost not the same people.

Who could tell anyway? Everyone who came to the Vague Lands looked pretty much alike. Everything in the Vague Lands looked the same, bleached out, colourless, savourless. No sooner could you get a fix on something, on somebody, on some idea, on some feeling, but it would suddenly seem to have shifted. It would have become something else entirely.

There were no very discernible seasons. The heat bore down with no change day after day. A numbing, boring heat that sapped the body and the mind.

And everything and everybody spent an awful lot of time covered in sand. Not that lovely rich red sand I was to encounter and run my hands through later, but a kind of browny-grey - a nothing colour. Most events in the Vague Lands somehow or other seemed the same, 'nothing events'. Most days too were nothing days.

Except that day.

***

Our home was a spiral of small conical buildings, clustered around a well that was the place's reason for being. A single dead tree bleached white, standing next to the well in the very centre splaying its bare branches up towards the sun. In my childhood there was at least that tree to inspire some affectionate memories. I can still find it in my mind's eye as part of a scrabble of broken images of the Vague Lands.

The Zoo: The Beast, The Boy and The Zoo

Yes I liked that tree. Shame it gave no shade.

The tree and the well were altogether my favourite items at Gogol's trading post. No matter how hot it would get, the water was always there and normally right up to the surface. I would stare down into it; and it would reflect the limitless blue sky back up at me. No sound of running water though. Just the monotonous chirrup of crickets.

Sam would seek out any kind of animal life, however scarce it might be. For me, besides the well and the tree, the sky was the thing. If I could ever hide and snatch a moment from our constant labours, I might lie on my back looking right up into it. I would escape in my mind up there and try to imagine other things and other places; to think of entire other ways of being.

The blue sky during the daytime was alluring enough, but the *black* sky at night spangled with stars, now that for me was a beguiling of a very different nature.

Surely there had to be different ways of living. Other lives and experiences beyond this cursed, dead place.

Sometimes too I would reach down, dig my hand deep and pick up a handful of the grey, featureless sand. Bringing it to eye level I would stare deeply into it for long minutes. Millions of little grains, so countless. Then I would let them stream smoothly back to the ground from where they had come.

The stuff of nothingness?

Or an infinity of possibilities?

Oh, and yes, I nearly forgot. I liked smelling things too! The air in the Vague Lands was hot and dry. So especially at night it carried many kinds of scents: wood smoke; plant smells like sage, the creosote bush; and once in a blue moon, the smell of rain would float into our nothingness.

Smell has always been a special thing for me.

The Zoo: The Beast, The Boy and The Zoo

Simple, spare functional buildings, each and every hut spire had been gradually bent back towards the east by the wind sweeping in off the desert. From the distance visitors said this looked like the hats of a whole coven of witches set in a spiral.

When I am challenged like this to think back on it, it occurs to me that so many separate important incidents from my childhood happened in one or other particular witch's hat.

The thing for instance that time with Sam and those Mice.

***

Chapter Three: Rat magic

Sam was up to something, I could feel it. The twin thing in my head seemed to call to me from one of the outer huts at the edge of the spiral, the smallest 'hat'.

In the middle of clearing out the least used stock room I stood up. Gogol had ordered both of 'you two boys' to do this before driving off in his battered, open-top jeep on business or perhaps to go hunting, but Sam as usual seemed nowhere to be seen. But then of course Sam did always disappear several times through the day anyway.

The room was full of stuff Gogol has not been able to sell for ages. So I had dutifully categorised those items still worth selling, put most aside to throw away, brushed up, and cleaned all the shelves and boxes.

Now I was tired. And I was fed up. And my back was hurting. And why wasn't Sam helping?

Off skiving and dreaming. Lazy little pig! No doubt doing what neither of us should be doing. Doing *that* forbidden thing. Doing what we had specifically been told not to do.

"Come here." Sam's presence in my mind summoning me.

I would go. At least I would go to give Sam a damn good thump. I dropped the broom, and made my way to where the voice seemed to be coming. One of the very farthest witch's hats. It was the one without much of a roof, more or less decrepit. Half submerged, lost in the invading sands; it had not been used since before I could remember. I swept the entrance hanging aside.

The Zoo: The Beast, The Boy and The Zoo

Looking back, it was strange, ironic even how much Sam liked animals then, given that there weren't any really, well hardly any at all. The occasional Bird as I said flying in lost from the east. And if you scoured the stones (as Sam would do) you would perhaps find Snakes, Reptiles and some Insects. Gogol himself - to find anything really worthwhile to track and kill with his crossbow - had to drive some considerable distance to the east.

That young me pretty much saw all the crawling, creeping and flapping things wherever they might happen to live as vermin. But all the more so when they invaded and infested our buildings: Fleas and Flies and Cockroaches. A constant fight against them. And normally there would be a plenitude of Mice in our home in the Vague Lands. Most of the time there were too many to do anything about. In killing a lot of them you just made room for more. A losing battle. So our orders were on the whole to ignore them. But sometime there were Rats as well.

Rats!

They ate our food.

They damaged stock.

They gnawed holes.

They bit people

They carried plague.

So Rats did not get ignored. On them we visited war. We used poisons. And snap traps. And glue boards. A further weapon was Sandy our chief cat, another animal that inevitably drew Sam's rapt attention.

Then there was one of my favourite pursuits. There were no special materials available of course, so one just had to make do. But I became very skilled nonetheless in using whatever was at hand to render an arsenal of catapults and sling shots.

My word, did I get become proficient in their use. I learned how to choose and stockpile just the right kind of stone. Not too big, not too small, and of just the right constituency and shape. You had to understand how to whirl the sling around and around up to exactly the right speed, and let go at precisely the right point in its orbit. In that way that you could hit and kill a small animal with quite devastating accuracy. Woe betides the Scorpion, or Snake or Pigeon or Rat that let me get anywhere near them. When Sam wasn't looking I am afraid the young me would even have a go at Sandy once or twice.

Just, you understand, to scare him.

There could certainly be no objection to my targeting the Rats. Rats were the enemy. Gogol has told us that time after time. Rats ate his profits. Mice? They were a nuisance, but also an inevitability and simply not a major concern.

Even so, you certainly were not supposed to make friends with them.

Sam was sitting in the middle. A circle of Mice, on their hind legs, all around.

Some were clearly still timid. Still wild Mice running around in confusion. hating and fearing any human. But Sam was doing something, doing something to them. Singing to them all in low, soft, slow hum of a voice. Right hand circling slightly and slowly in the air above the Mice host. Many were already entranced, on their legs and staring back at Sam.

"Look Seth. Isn't it great? Look what I am doing. Aren't they wonderful?" Sam excitedly broke off humming, but didn't look up, eyes fixed, glowing a little, on the adoring subjects.

In that era small scurrying, furry things repelled me with a quite instinctual intensity. But for a second I too was lost in wonderment. And, just briefly, I could see what Sam was seeing.

Gingerly I walked around the circumference of the hut, just about avoiding crushing the hundreds of quiescent little grey and pink bodies all intent on my magical twin, completely ignoring the clumsy newcomer.

Then I remembered that I was the older brother here. I was in charge. We were supposed to be growing up and acting like it. We had to help Gogol and do what he said. And maybe if we did, we would earn his respect; he would treat us a little less harshly; life would be better.

So we should not be playing with Mice. More importantly, Sam should really know better that to let anyone see this special 'gift' with animals.

Why anyway should I have been left to clean out the store room all by myself, while Sam messed about with Mice?

My innate disgust was flooding back. All animals were filthy things that should just be cleared out of our world. Most of the diseases we humans get come in the beginning from animals, you know.

This thing that Sam had and that was denied to me; this way with vermin of which my twin was so damn proud. It was *not* a good thing.

No, how could it be, if just like Sam's other secret, we had to hide it?

And Gogol would be back soon.

"Stop it, Sam, if Gogol catches us. Stop it now! I am warning you Sam."

My slender twin looked up at me just briefly, still smiling, still humming; and then back preoccupied with the entourage. A shaman absorbed in a trance.

"I'm serious. Stop now. Let them go and we can get back and be working before Gogol gets home."

Sam ignored me. The smile got broader. The hum just got louder. And now it was less pleasant.

I walked over and I put my hand on Sam's shoulder. I shook hard. "Come on."

The Zoo: The Beast, The Boy and The Zoo

Sam didn't even look at me. The hum and the broad smile were irritating now. Louder, penetrating, insolent.

The room had become fuller and fuller of Mice. There must have been hundreds, maybe a thousand. You could hardly fit any more. If I moved at all, I could not help but crush dozens. All perched on their legs, paws in the air, some almost pirouetting, some facing Sam, twitching, sniffing, absorbed in Sam. An adored celebrant before a devout, rapt congregation; their combined presence now giving off a distinct pungent odour, reminiscent of the bleach we used to scrub the storeroom floors until our hands bled.

We were going to get into real trouble for this. Exactly the kind of thing we were not supposed to do. Exactly the kind of thing that Gogol called 'nonsense', which made his face take on that twisted, furious look provoking serious punishment. Sam knew this, just as well as I did and normally took care to hide anything of the kind. Certainly the least little thing that either Sam or I did that showed any interest at all in animals seemed to send Gogol into such a special rage, far beyond his normal irritability.

"Sam!" I grabbed my twin's long silky, dark hair. I was pushed petulantly but roughly away. "Go away Seth, you are spoiling it! You always do that. I hate you!"

That push was much stronger than expected from Sam's smaller, slighter frame. I was really slammed against the hut wall. If the shock and surprise had let me, I would have been hurt.

The old hut shook. The rotting walls threatened to fall.

Many but not all of the Mice scattered.

Then two things happened. Almost at once

From a hole in the wall a large dark shape emerged. Sam's Mouse congregation was infiltrated by a giant Black Rat, as fully entranced as its smaller kin, prominently taking its place in a front pew and staring at my twin with devotion, its long naked pink tail writhing rapidly in rapture from side to side.

And a Man's loud steps coming up the path to the hut. Angry steps hammering the ground.

The scattering of Mice was a thing to behold. Vertically up the walls, down holes and other escape routes I would not have even guessed of, disappearing into bags, dozens of criss-crossings of the floor. Three ran up and back down my leg. Uggh!

All gone now, leaving just Sam and me and one large, filthy, immobilised, twitching, disgusting, enchanted Rat.

And Gogol surely just outside the hut.

Sam looked at me. I looked back. Our stomachs clenched in equilibrium.

We both knew what we were in for. Shirking our work. Doing that 'animal thing' that was forbidden. And with, out of all the beasts, a plague carrying Black Rat.

This time we were really going to be in trouble.

Sam was still immobile, but all the humming, and smiling and gesturing had gone now.

I reached, almost faster than I knew I could. I grabbed Sam's only remaining and non-resisting audience member by the neck and twisted savagely, rising to my feet in the very same motion. I had not especially intended to, but my panicked strength had yanked its head completely off from its body.

The Zoo: The Beast, The Boy and The Zoo

The hut flap was swept aside and Gogol entered his face red with angry expectation.

"Look," I said, turning, with blood and viscera trickling slowly down my arm, and proudly holding in my two widened hands the severed elements of my limp, dead prey for him to see.

"We have been killing Rats for you."

***

Chapter Four: For God's sake will you go to sleep!

"Do you think we ever had a mother, Seth?" Late at night in bed long after dark, an unexpected whisper. "Seth? Seth!" Sam persisted even though I pretended to be asleep, shaking me hard to get a response.

"I don't know. Go to sleep Sam."

"What do you think she was like..?"

"I don't know. Shut up. Why are you asking now?"

"The traders' children... I saw them being picked up, and pressed into the arms of their mothers and fathers. And they smiled and laughed. And there was kissing and jokes. Is that what fathers and mothers are like? Is that what they are supposed to be like?"

"I don't know! I told you to be quiet Sam."

"Did we ever have a mother? Was she like that...? Do you remember Seth? Sometimes I pretend in my mind we have a mother and father to ourselves like the traders' children? Do you do that Seth?"

"I don't know. And you shouldn't be talking like that. You could draw attention to yourself. We don't want that, do we! It doesn't matter anyway. Best not to think of such things. It is weak. If you can't have something, it is better to stop wanting it."

"Now if you do not shut up and let me sleep, I will wallop you."

And there was silence.

But now *I* could not sleep. Dimly I did remember Gogol had a woman, but we had both been tiny.

More silence for quite a long time. Then.

The Zoo: The Beast, The Boy and The Zoo

"I bet our mother was beautiful." Sam's voice began again. A dreamy tone this time. "And you're wrong Seth. It is *not* best not to think of things like that. You are wrong."

"But then, you are wrong about *everything*, aren't you!"

I sat up and leant over to make good on my earlier threat of violence, but Sam had turned over and was mysteriously fast asleep.

I did not sleep for a long time.

***

Chapter Five: The shortest distance between two points

I would guess Gogol must have been around fifty years of age at that point, the day the visitor arrived. Long, straggly, greasy hair. Thin, a little stooped. The eyes watery and of a pale, colourless grey scanning the horizon frequently for god knows what. Looking back, his features remind me vaguely of a Baboon. The only physically unusual thing was about him were his hands, long and thin and, I suppose, rather beautiful.

There are two particular words I always associate with Gogol. Two words that tell you most of what you need to understand about him. They are 'no' and 'nonsense'. His overriding motif for almost everything.

Sometimes he muttered this mantra to himself quietly but feverishly, over and over again as he wandered about.

Or sometimes he would spell it out very slowly over three long, languorous and accentuated syllables, those skilful piano player's fingers intertwining in delight and a broad grin gradually climbing over his face. This would be invariably when he had concluded some kind of especially profitable deal. Or, even better and more so, when he felt had successfully put one over on someone.

Then again it might be addressed approvingly to one or other of his collection of bows. Crossbows of many types and eras, objects of ultimate desire for old Gogol. Displayed in pride of place over his fireplace. Or slung over his lap as there he sat in the evening contentedly oiling, polishing, and frankly sometimes drooling. Whilst caressing his

The Zoo: The Beast, The Boy and The Zoo

particular favourite, the 'Excalibur Assassin Crossbow' Gogol would exult out loud to nobody in particular: "See this here? This here is the shortest distance between two points. The straight arrow. No nonsense here. This is precision engineering. Any problem you might come across at all, this here will put it right, a no nonsense solution."

The longbow by contrast, although it had its uses, played second fiddle in Gogol's affections. It needed to curve its arrow in its trajectory. It took longer to arrive at its target. Some might find it more pleasing to the eye in its form or that the way it discharged its function was more elegant. But in Gogol's estimation that involved just too much fuss.

Once or twice we also heard his favourite phrase whispered as he drew his hand along the chassis of his old jeep. A classic army brown two seater. On the rare occasions when he could not avoid our travelling with him, Sam and I had to cling on for dear life perched on the back shelf. His beloved car was provided with every kind of loving care. He was so wedded to that automobile, a passion for an otherwise passionless man, so dependent on it, that is was almost difficult to see where the jeep finished and Gogol began. Sam and I giggled behind his back that he wasn't entirely human himself.

He was half man, half car.

And sometimes, I am afraid; he would be repeating his little chant over and over again rhythmically as he wielded his favourite cane on us. Gogol was knocking the nonsense out of us – for our own good, of course. Yes, in his mind some kind pernicious and dangerous folly hovered there insolently, just out of reach, but ever threatening to invade. This bothered him so much that he made it his mission to beat it well and truly out of his whole world. And especially out of us.

We had got away without being beaten by Gogol after the Rat thing. Or had we? Despite all of Sam's wilful self-indulgence? And thanks to my cleverness?

The Zoo: The Beast, The Boy and The Zoo

Well maybe. Did he know all the same what had been going on, but had, for some reason of his own, decided not to do anything?

Another maybe.

You never just knew with Gogol. That was the thing. Perhaps he was indeed some kind of machine mixture of cross bow, jeep and low life trader. If so he was a mixture whose inner mysterious mechanisms defeated us entirely.

Those hooded eyes. How could anyone ever really hope to divine what was happening behind them. Always this feeling that somehow Gogol was playing a longer game than anyone. Whatever that game might be, the one thing for certain was that the clicking and whirring within was in pursuit some form of personal profit. Perhaps immediate and out in the open. Or perhaps into a some far flung, strategic future.

All plainly there in his day to day dealings. Day in day out the machine moved on. No thoughts, no emotions, no joy beyond business, driving and hunting. He traded in whatever he could: food, drink, equipment, weapons and just occasionally people. Other beings existed solely in terms of the greatest value Gogol might extract from them.

Sam was repelled by his frequent drives out into the desert. His determined slaughter of the few remaining forms of life clinging on there.

Me, I was entranced.

If he had let me I would have gone with him. The thrum and thud of Gogol's various bows was one of the few exciting things in that nothing of a place. I lusted intensely after Gogol's armoury. How I wanted to get my hands on that Excalibur Assassin in particular. Something just so seductive about the burnished wood, the subtle, enticingly perfect bend of the bow, the perfectly matched tension in the string, and the way, carefully and slowly drawn back, the whole fitted perfectly into Gogol's shoulder, his long tapered fingers securely wrapped around the grip. And, best of all, oh by far best of all, the letting go. I could just imagine myself holding that bow and seeing the arrow fly straight and true from my own body.

Naturally I never got anywhere near it.

No, when I killed animals I had to be content with my stones and my slings.

What else do you need to know about old Gogol back in the Vague Lands?

Well it was clear we were there solely to work. To benefit him. But he didn't trust us to do so. The merest suspicion that in some indefinable way we might be cheating him out of the maximum labour value, this was designated as 'giving him nonsense'. It would render him white with confused fury.

That alone however was never enough of a trigger to beat us.

No, there was something that made him far angrier. Something deemed a much worse form of 'nonsense'. That was any sign at all of a curiosity in or empathy towards animals. In practice, this meant Sam. Because I, pretty much like Gogol himself saw animals as dirty things, unnecessary unless of some practical use, such as for target practice.

Finally, there at the very summit of Gogol's potential to suddenly flare into righteous ire, were those few occasions when we tried to run away.

The notion that we might have the insolence to seek something and somewhere other than here; that was the very greatest 'nonsense' that could possibly be conceived.

Then he would seek out his whip with a certain determination.

"You children are ungrateful little pieces of shit. I will tan your hides. Run from me?! Run to all that crazy nonsense out there? I will tear your backs into strips!!! What are you anyway, but guttersnipes that nobody ever wanted? If I had not taken you, what do you think would have happened to you!"

We were sore for a week.

The Zoo: The Beast, The Boy and The Zoo

So why, as we both flickeringly wondered at the time and more substantially considered in later years; why, if he didn't want us to think about the outside world, if he did not want Sam to think at all about animals; why had he taught us to read?

Why had he allowed us access to books at all?

Given the way Sam insisted on reading out large chunks aloud, or else later regaling me with the knowledge so gleaned - I almost wished he hadn't.

And why, when as inevitable, we fell ill from time to time, did he tend to us with such care? Showing such consummate skill and clear knowledge of remedies and treatments of all sorts? At those moments Gogol the hunter, Gogol the tyrant slave driver and Gogol the machine would disappear.

Just for a small time Gogol the healer and Gogol the carer would appear.

Then finally just now and again, in such brief flashes that one could never be quite sure, Sam or I would catch him staring at one or other us with an expression that was neither fury nor greed nor calculation. When he looked at us like that, I had the strangest conviction, born from I know not where, that he wasn't really looking at *us* at all. He was looking *through* us. He was striving to see something or someone within and beyond Sam and me.

I can honestly say at least that Gogol never visited any cruelty on us just for the sheer sake of it; for his own pleasure I mean. And nothing else happened to us either for his own pleasure. Oh yes, we knew, if only dimly, about *that* thing too. We knew that it could happen to other children. It never did to us.

He hardly ever called us by our names, Seth and Sam. In front of others he sometimes seemed to go out of his way to use the specific expressions *'my sons'* or *'you boys'* and with a feigned tone suggesting some vague sense of paternal emotion.

But in private we were usually just: *'Hey you'*.

We always had enough to eat, but since we could remember we had to work hard every day. We children were for work. That was just the way it was.

Sam had, despite myself, made me think on whether there had been a woman once. If there had, she was gone long before we could remember properly. I have no memories of any cuddling or that kindness or warmth of any sort. Nobody never ever used the word 'mother' around us.

Somehow, it had never seemed a relevant concept.

Then there were those few, scarce hints (old clothes, older graffiti, objects that might have passed for makeshift toys left around the place) that others might have lived here at some time. Other children like us? Perhaps once. But it did not seem especially healthy to speculate on what had become of them.

And that is really all I have to tell you about old Gogol.

Not a father, nor a parent, nor a guardian in any abiding sense. No, when it came to anyone caring for anyone else, it was always just Sam and me, me and Sam. Mirror images glued together, squabbling, working, surviving. And always, in a ferocious devotion, looking at and looking out for one another.

^^^

"Seth, forgive me, but you are doing it again."

"Eh...?"

"Oh... Sorry. I had almost forgotten you were sitting there listening to this. "Doing what again?"

"You are drifting a little in the story. Taking too long. So that they will later understand matters, you need to tell them now about the... you know..?... the..."

"The...? The...?"

"Just think hard, Seth."

"Oh...the Lions?"

"Yes, very good, Seth. Tell the reader about when you both went looking for the Lions."

^^^

Oh the Lions. Yes, of course. The reader must forgive me. I had almost forgotten, just before I get to that day with Gogol's guest - the day everything changed. I need to make one more diversion. Just one more honestly.

You do really need to know about the Lions.

Chapter Six: The Lost Lions of Barbary

Sam was really annoying me again.

"There is nothing there, I tell you." My finger stabbed down, almost knocking away the tatty, dusty old map carefully balanced on Sam's lap. We had carefully slid this out of Gogol's 'secret' chest. It was only one of many such purloined books and documents over time. But this scrap of parchment had become an object of special fascination.

Mainly for Sam.

"You don't know that, Seth. You don't know that at all. You just say things like that to look big. You always say things like that."

" You never want to believe in anything interesting."

"Look Sam. This is the *Vague Lands*. We have Rats. We have Flies. We have Scorpions."

"We don't have Lions*!*"

"We don't have anything interesting here. It's just... not allowed." I continued. "Stop dreaming. You will only ever be disappointed. Me, I am just trying to help you."

We had at least an idea of what Lions supposedly were; from the pictures in our pilfered or abandoned books: unfeasibly big Cats that could eat a whole person.

In one way or another, those few books informed a good deal of our young lives. So much flotsam and jetsam, random and at first sight on the whole meaningless to us, washing up somehow here at the end of the world.

The Zoo: The Beast, The Boy and The Zoo

But the effort alone to make sense of some of the words often drew us in. Yes, even the young me - just a little.

All of them must have all originated from that big wide world out there to the East; so this motley collection of volumes was almost our only way to form any notions, however fuzzy and fragmented, of anything at all beyond the Vague Lands.

There were works on history, science, music, and painting. Books with fictional tales and books with real things. They spoke of truly weird sounding places with weird sounding names, none of which we had ever heard. These places must, we supposed, be other trading posts like Gogol's?

So much I didn't understand. So much I just threw to one side.

But I did at least rather like looking at the *pictures* before doing so. And so, however unwillingly, unwittingly and gradually, random bits of knowledge began to stick within me.

Two of Sam's particular favourites were *"The Care and Husbandry of Exotic Animals in Captivity"* with the writer's names cut out of the pages; and *"Man and Animal in the Zoo"* by someone called Dr Heini Hediger. Those in particular didn't come from any of the visitors, but had, like the map, been stolen from Gogol's own bedroom.

That was strange in itself you know, as the truth was we had never seen Gogol actually reading a book himself. And to have one above all about animals?

If he had ever caught either of us looking at that very same material, then the nonsense word and the fury it provoked would be quick to make an appearance.

Nor had he ever complained they were missing.

These books were about running something called a 'zoo' where all kinds of animals lived together. A zoo seemed to be a bit like a farm. We knew well enough what that was, but where there were lots more

The Zoo: The Beast, The Boy and The Zoo

kinds of animals - some very strange ones indeed. And a zoo it seemed did not exist just to have animals to eat, or make eggs or milk.

No, a zoo seemed a very odd thing indeed. Whatever it was about, the very idea clearly enthralled Sam.

One of the zoo books was wide open right now on Sam's lap next to the map. My twin read aloud, eyes flicking in animation back and forth from one to the other. Loudly. Enthusiastically.

Very irritatingly.

My cold water comments bounced right off this particular duck's back.

"They are not tame Lions, nor ordinary ones you know, Seth. The ones near here are not African Lions found most frequently in zoos." Sam read bits out in a bright, enthusiastic tone and in a silly, put-on voice which succeeded in galling me. I was pleased though by the way unknown words were faltered over. "Not even the very rare Asiatic Lions now confined to In... In-dee-a. The Bar-bar-y Lion with its distinctive black mane, native to North Af–ree-ka is a race apart, about which scientists know little. They have been gen-et-ic-ally separated from their southern cousins by the... um... Sa -h-ar–a desert for thousands of years."

Where on earth were all these bizarre sounding places!?

"And here," Sam's hand trailed across the paper, fingers tapping down vivaciously. "Look, this bit of Gogol's map is exactly the same as the one in the book on zoos."

Sure enough, the rough sketch in the book with the rubric 'Valley of the Barbary Lions' looked an awful lot like the hilly area of desert only two miles to the north of our home.

For days, Sam and I continued to argue. There was no point, I insisted, in risking time from our work to explore that wilderness for the so called 'Lost Lions'. If Gogol caught us we would be in for a beating.

Anyway, it was all nonsense.

The Zoo: The Beast, The Boy and The Zoo

And if, if by any remote chance they were real, I really did not want to actively seek out nasty looking, smelly, scary brutes. Animals that could actually eat me.

But day after day Sam pored over the section on Lions, eyes gleaming with fervour. My twin was happy. And however incomprehensible and indeed exasperating I found this driving enthusiasm, secretly I was glad.

Perhaps it was because of that.

Or perhaps because in the end, despite myself, I had become just a tiny little bit interested to see these 'big, scary, fierce things' - as long, that is, as we could keep our distance.

So I told Sam that I had decided we would after all go.

The first practical question though was how to get far enough from Gogol's encampment without simply being seen walking away. There was no cover of any sort to cloak anyone stealing off from the post. In fact for some time, irrespective of any cockeyed notion about 'Barbary Lions', this issue had figured large as to our longer term future.

Our prior attempts to flee Gogol had been half-hearted affairs, triggered when things had got pretty bad. You could even really call them proper escape attempts really. More a case of our running away on impulse, full of tears, fear and anger.

We always ran together. We always got caught. We were always beaten. Never more furious, Gogol hurt us far worse than for anything else.

But Sam's obsession with those damned Lions led ultimately to a solution to the great escape problem. I was extraordinarily proud that it was *my* solution.

By clever use of one of the hats used for storage, we could get away to the north without being spotted at all. It was hat number seven, the same I had been tidying the day the Rat thing happened. Oddly enough, it was the Mice and Rats who had given me the idea.

The Zoo: The Beast, The Boy and The Zoo

You see I had dug a tunnel. I even got Sam interested and involved in helping. Well a little and only for a few minutes. But soon motivation dwindled and my twin was off again 'animal day dreaming'.

So it definitely was *my* tunnel and *my* invention.

"That's not a tunnel! Not a real tunnel. It is just a sort of trench." Sam's petulant reaction first time I had shown off my achievement.

Well, whatever it was, it worked. You went into the hat. You moved a couple of carefully positioned boxes. Then, if you were a skinny ten year old, you could just wiggle through my tunnel under the hat wall and underneath the adjacent perimeter fence. Only a few yards further and the dug tunnel met up with a natural gulley between the small hills to the north. From outside there was no way to see what was happening in the gulley, not unless you actually climbed right to the top of one of the hills. From there you could be away into the wilds within seconds. So Sam and I could saunter into hat number seven quite casually, and to all intents and purposes, completely disappear.

In the end Sam did admit it was clever. "You know Seth, that's exactly what a Rat would think of."

As if I didn't know. I can learn from other things. I was just as good as any Rat.

I think in all over a period of months we made three reconnoitres to the north. Sam was mainly looking for the Lions: I was mainly working out our final escape route. We even established a kind of hideout half way between Gogol's home and where the alleged Lions on the map. It was nothing more than a large abandoned wooden crate, but could function as somewhere to catch our breath. And we would not have to carry all the provisions from the trading post with us for a longer journey.

Gogol watched pretty carefully how much we ate. There was never very much extra. But stretched over months we could sneak small amounts of our rations to build up a stock of supplies for the big day.

The Zoo: The Beast, The Boy and The Zoo

Talk of running away before had been just that, only talk: now we had plan. When the time came, we could just vanish. We could run to the Valley of the Lions.

And then where?

Well somewhere to the east I suppose and to whatever was to be really found there. I am afraid we had got no further in our thinking than that.

We were after all only children.

***

So now, here we were at Sam's insistence flat on our stomachs and lying in the dirt. Almost at the very summit of the ridge which would give onto the last unexplored area in the so called Valley of Lions. The indication on the faded map 'Here be the Lions of Barbary' was badly obscured. There were so many creases and marks that it was hard to pinpoint. Our attempts so far to do so had only ever resulted in dust and dirt and... Scorpions. Each failure had spring boarded from Sam's greater confidence that *this time* a slightly better interpretation of the clues would yield up the lair of the fabled creatures.

And still Sam was resolute that the decrepit old map, almost falling part completely now, was finally about to surrender its secret.

I knew of course that there would be nothing. Almost face down in the dust we edged forward slowly and uncomfortably. "We mustn't scare them Seth." A nearly inaudible whisper. "We are downwind so the Lions won't be able to smell us. But the least little sound..."

"Oh for goodness sake Sam, you were wrong the last few times." I was not whispering. "There is nothing good here. All these things we read about in those books including your Lions, if they exist at all, or ever did exist, we won't ever find anything like that here. Not in the Vague Lands."

The Zoo: The Beast, The Boy and The Zoo

"I keep telling you nothing exciting will ever..." A finger pressed firmly onto my lips stopped me in mid flow.

"No." Sam's whisper took on a new and commanding tone. "I know it now. There *is* something over this ridge."

Something new in Sam's tone forced me glance sideways. Sure enough Sam's eyes had taken on a certain recognisable gleam.

"Something... there is *something* there, but... I don't know... It is not quite 'right'."

"What do you mean - not right?"

"I don't know. I cannot explain. Like there is an animal there, a big one. But there isn't as well. Let's get right to the top of the ridge and take a look. But quietly Seth."

We began crawling the last few inches. Then all too abruptly we stopped once more.

The noise had begun.

All these decades later I know only too well what Lions sound like, but back then neither of us had anything to go on at all. The 'roaring' noise we were now hearing, I would nowadays compare it to an old car refusing to start.

I froze. Sam moved forward over the crest and for a second was lost from my sight. I could not see my twin. Somehow, even though I could still feel Sam's presence, I really didn't like that. So I too crossed the frontier.

Nothing very exciting to see from the top of that hill. The depression in front of us was very much like all the others through which we had so tediously trudged, except... Except that it reverberated with this 'roaring sound'. Down we moved, our eyes adjusting gradually to detail. Transfixed by the unearthly sound, we were fit to run at any moment. Yet there was still nothing remarkable at all to see.

I was carefully scanning the wider surrounding horizon for any danger from that direction. So it was Sam peering straight forward that spotted it first. There in the rock on the far side of the valley a small opening, a narrow little cave. Now that it had our attention, this was clearly the source of the strange echoing sound.

"Let's get out of here Sam. Whatever that is in there, it is something bad!" My scepticism as to the Lions of Barbary had entirely evaporated.

"No I am not going back Seth. You go if you want to. I've not come this far to run away now we have found them."

I was inclined to linger as Sam edged nearer, but my hand was firmly grabbed and tightly held. To reassure me? To drag me forward? Both?

Together now we moved towards the cave, our hands intertwined; sweat trickling narrowly down my neck.

The sound seemed to grow louder, as it would, as we got nearer. But curiously it lacked natural variation in its real volume, in its pitch, in its frequency or in any other way.

Very nearly now at the mouth of the cave, we stopped. We exchanged glances. We stood immobile, waiting as if for the cave itself to give us a clue to their secrets. To offer some indication as to what we should do next.

Finally our hands loosened and unlinked. Sam reached into a canvas shoulder bag carrying the map and the book and produced one of Gogol's torches.

"What *is* inside there Sam? What do you know? Your special thing... You know with animals... What does it tell you?"

"I don't know. I still don't know! Usually when some kind of animal is about, I can feel it thinking. Or feeling. Or being. And it will be clear and sharp and sweet."

"This has got traces of the same thing..."

"But god, it is so dull!"

The Zoo: The Beast, The Boy and The Zoo

We were inside the rock corridor now, Sam's torch flashing on the ground, the roar so loud as to deafen. How big could these Lions be to make such a terrifying noise.

But ten or twenty feet in, the narrow corridor widened into a much larger area. All fell silent. The roaring of the Lions was replaced by a rush of air. It raised our hair. It passed beyond and over us, and on out the through the corridor by which we had just passed.

Puzzled, I walked back down the corridor towards the daylight. Meanwhile Sam had penetrated deeper into what was a large chamber, the torch scanning about to examine the ground and walls. The moment I was back in the corridor, the roaring also returned.

Then advancing again into the chamber, once more it vanished with the rush of air taking over.

"Sam, it's just the wind! Triumphant I ran back eager to share the news. A relief for me: a disappointment surely for Sam. "There are no Lions. It's just the air whistling through the tunnel."

Too bad for Sam.

But my twin was kneeling on the ground, absorbed in some new discovery, the torch carefully deployed. Hearing me at the back, Sam left the torch propped up shining into the air, stood and turned to slowly reveal an object needing both hands to hold it up.

"You see Seth, they *were* here. The map was right after all. They were here. Once."

Strange how the teeth on a Lion's skull seem almost bigger and more fearsome than on the living creature. Dozens of Lion skeletons or parts of a skeleton lying around the cave. Some were so old they had partially dissolved into dust.

So both us then?

Sam and I had both up to a point been right. The two of us, as ever, in perfect mirror symmetry: Sam's romanticism; my scepticism.

The Zoo: The Beast, The Boy and The Zoo

But in my young head I felt it was I who had really won. A long dead Lion is after all surely no Lion?

'The Lost Lions of Barbary'..? Yeah, *lost* was right. As we slogged through the sand back towards Gogol's, again reaching and cresting the so called Valley of the Lions, I turned for a last long look back at the scene, the cave and all of it.

I grinned to myself in quiet victory.

I picked up the largest stone I could find, the heaviest I could manage and in contempt and triumph I hurled it back at the valley.

I had won.

***

Chapter Seven: A Visitor to the Vague Lands

And now at last, without any further digression at all, I need to get back to that day with Gogol's guest. I need to tell you how our lives changed forever.

It took place in yet another of the witch's hats. The very biggest, right there in the middle besides the well and the tree. This largest, central hat was Gogol's place for meeting his 'guests'. His place for tricking and cheating them. *Our* place for spying on him in that very act.

At the top the outside was formed, like all the other hats, entirely from layered palm fronds. There was a kind of platform ceiling that cut off the working area from the very apex of the building. Sam and I (actually you know I think it was just me) had long ago found out how to climb up the outside and, like Squirrels, to wiggle through a small hole near the top to perch up on the main rafters.

There we would be still and there we would listen.

You could not always hear everything of course.

Sometimes just bits wafting up with the smoke. But usually our young minds could sew these together well enough to distil the gist of whatever intrigue was playing out beneath our feet.

In our young, grey Vague Lands experience we had no friends and little time off work. There were few diversions other than Sam mucking about with Mice and suchlike, my staring up vacantly into the sky, smelling things and killing the odd innocent creature. So this eavesdropping was superlative sport.

The Zoo: The Beast, The Boy and The Zoo

Lodged securely and silently up there beneath those sloping roofs the things we learned, and at such a green age, about human nature!

And all the better that it involved another one of our own secret places.

Hideouts, hideaways, dens... these were the only places free from Gogol's gaze. As per the non-existent Barbary Lions, they were essential for a concerted attempt to get away from him for good.

In fact secret or more accurately protected places seem across a whole lifetime to have become very special and very necessary for both Sam and me.

The light was only beginning to leak into the sky from the east. It was earlier in the morning than anyone might reasonably expect to be receiving a visitor. But if the time had been chosen intentionally to avoid anyone's notice, that very intention had been foiled.

Gogol had lit a cedar wood fire. The smoke tingled in our noses pleasantly and stung our eyes unpleasantly.

Now Gogol was speaking to someone. In our experience, that probably meant he was lying to them. We waited to hear that slightly strangulated, false tone Gogol adopted when in bargaining mode; the way his voice automatically moved to a familiarly higher register once the cogs started turning and he started lying and tricking and deal making.

It did not come.

If anything Gogol's words were lower in pitch than usual. It was as if he had become a *more* authentic version of himself rather than the very opposite. Though, god knows, the things he was saying were patently untrue.

"You cannot take them. They were entrusted to me. They are my life."

Yes, most *definitely* lying.

The Zoo: The Beast, The Boy and The Zoo

"You have been rewarded Gogol and you will be far more so now…" The voice of another and the chink of coins coming to the fore. Something was being bargained over.

"All the years that you have had them…"

Magnetised, we leaned in.

The voice of this visitor was a thin, strange thing, a very different accent and overall way of speech to anything we had ever heard. We had no points of reference. So it was hard to decipher the kind of person to whom such tones might belong. But even to our untutored ears the stranger's words did carry the ring of one used to be being in charge.

And in the tone of Gogol's replies, however odd this sounded to us, we could sense that he too knew this only too well. There was some kind of defiance though there. Certainly an overt resentment. Very much at variance to the cajoling and flattering voice he normal offered for these encounters

As to what was being said, we were still only getting fragments drifting up from both adults through the middle of the hut.

We were perched directly above Gogol's head. His guest though was sitting on the far side of the hut, so more difficult to hear.

"But now they must return with me."

"…to their real home."

"…real family"

"…as agreed years ago."

"I *never* agreed!" That was Gogol breaking in. "The twins are my life." The stranger seemed to neither hear nor care, and continued.

"…work for them."

"…hard tasks eventually before them."

"…trivialities sought of them as children."

"…full burden of their heritage."

"…leave tomorrow and they *will* leave with me Gogol."

The Zoo: The Beast, The Boy and The Zoo

Although we could only get parts of the discussion, the tone and thrust was clear. This was about us! This was a sales negotiation, a haggle. Gogol was selling us to the stranger. We had been puzzled at first that he was not his usual wheedling self. But now we understood it. He was only making a show of resisting.

'The twins are my life.'

Good grief! Come on now.... These dramatics were only to raise his price. Gogol would be quite content to send us away forever. But there was the crucial matter of extracting as much for himself in the process.

I shivered a little. I glanced over at Sam swaying slightly on the other beam. Beyond tight attention though I could see no specific reaction on my sibling's face as to what was playing out beneath our feet.

The feelings that now overtook me were both complex and unexpected.

Gogol was *not* our father. We had never really felt him to be so, in so far at least as we had any conception of what a father should be. He beat us. I certainly did not love him. And yet...

And yet here the only thing we had remotely *like* a parent was betraying us. There was a definite pang. I didn't want this one. But I didn't want this new one either!

The Vague Lands were a depressing vacuum of a place, a place we both wanted to leave. Yet it was the sole home we had ever known, and we had only ever sought to leave it on our own terms. To be taken away to suit the unknown purpose of unknown people? That did not feel right.

We could not see the speaker clearly. The top of his head was covered by a large black hood. The stranger did speak in the same tongue as we did, but the cadence, the tone and some of the words were very different indeed. From slivers and clues gleaned elsewhere, we sensed this was the tongue of someone with wide experience and knowledge. The kind which Gogol would typically disparage as belonging to 'a stuck up type'.

But wait...

There was a third participant within this conversation, unnoticed until now. We could hear it panting softly, its breath steaming gently up to us. Something was lying next to Gogol's guest. Straining carefully so as to make no noise nor fall off the rafters, we could just about make out part of its head and shoulders, with its snout facing away from us. A large spotted dog of some sort.

Things were totting up within our two heads.

We knew now definitively that we were not Gogol's children.

He had then been paid for us to live here.

This stranger below us must be our real parent.

So was this therefore what a real father should be like? Presented for us just feet beneath our dangling feet was a brand new model of a parent. A strange, exotic prospect, something for two feral children intimidating if not terrifying in its novelty and sophistication. Something that yet lacked any face. Something forced on us. Something, someone whom we would be compelled to get to know. Someone who would demand from us new, difficult ways and new, unaccustomed manners. Perhaps like Gogol he would beat these out of us. And this would all take place within some strange new place and amongst strange new people.

Sitting beneath us was a threat.

I looked at Sam. Sam still did not bother to look back at me. The expression on my twin's face was one I had never seen before. It was rigid. It was unblinking. It was determined.

"We have to get away." A whisper came. "This is the time, Seth."

I nodded silently, and began to lead us noiselessly down the outside.

The Zoo: The Beast, The Boy and The Zoo

And certainly we would have fled quickly there and then, but for what we heard next.

***

Just as I began, quiet as a Mouse, to turn to leave, Sam grabbed my hand and drew me back. Sam's eyes were still glistening but now with a new different form of intent on the continuing dialogue below.

"Blah, blah, blah…" It held no further interest for me, just business talk surely? Yet Sam was riveted.

Slowly I realised why. They were talking about animals.

The words coming mainly from 'New Father'.

"…Elephants, Crocodiles, Ostriches, Eagles, Rhinos…"

This dialogue smoked its way slowly up towards us. Sam's face was illuminated with extraordinary excitement.

"…Tigers, Leopards, Monkeys…"

New Father's voice drifted and swirled indistinctly from below. Neither of us could catch full sentences. Sam's eyes large as an Owl's, body taking on a new alertness. We slightly adjusted our stiffening arms and legs to maintain the tricky balance.

More wisps….

"Did not think it would be so long…"

"…Snakes…"

"But it is *still* dangerous for them both!" That was Gogol breaking in again, almost screaming at New Father. "From what you say even *more* dangerous now!"

"Stop Gogol. Stop resisting. Stop claiming to be something you are *not.* Stop pretending to rights over these children which you do not have."

"…Crocodiles…"

The Zoo: The Beast, The Boy and The Zoo

"…troubled times at the Zoo…"

The Zoo?!

"…affairs have encountered complexities…"

"…Ostriches…"

"…arguments amongst our colleagues, the authorities above…"

"…Eagles…"

"…the Rhinos… "

"…the night time thing…"

"…It…"

"…our unique nature…"

"… the Enemy…"

"…the Elephants…"

"…twins out of the equation…"

"…Safer for them…"

Sam leant forward so as to hear better. I twisted and crouched behind, listening as well. Sam suddenly tottered. I reached quickly, snatching at a handful of tunic. Now we were both off balance. Sam grabbed back towards my arm.

The moment froze.

Surely we should both fall. We would be discovered.

But somehow through a sequence of minute recalibrations back and forth, we two twins managed to rebalance one another.

Then time started again. We were safe and stable once more. No one below had noticed a thing.

The discussion continued, but the mood had changed. New Father's voice, speaking to Gogol was now more imperious, cold, almost threatening. He stood up and angrily strode across the floor He was standing directly beneath us now. He was much louder. We could hear every word.

"That is the way it is to be, Gogol, whatever you say. I will pay what you are owed, and the deal will be done. Their service is mine. I

The Zoo: The Beast, The Boy and The Zoo

needs them now. I have no time for your old resentments. No matter who said what to you and when they said it, you have no rights here. As I said, there is work for them to do."

"It is time for them to begin to shoulder their burden."

"It will be time soon for their childhood to end."

I looked again at Sam's face, a set mask. An expression I knew well. A mind made up.

It did not matter how much interest had been sparked by all this talk of animals and the magic word 'zoo'. It was not relevant that we had been resolved to one day find an escape from Gogol. That was always to have been in a way and at a time of our own choosing.

We were not going to allow ourselves to be sold on to a New Father. Not to someone who, especially given those last words, we might expect to be even sterner than Gogol; would work us even harder and would treat us even worse.

My twin said nothing, but gave a single, curt nod.

And I knew what we would do. The time for fathers of *any sort* was over. The time to take charge of our own future was here. We would run. We would use the Lion valley.

I am pretty sure it was my decision. Sam moved first. And I followed

***

Chapter Eight: Fleeing

We moved as quietly and as efficiently as only we could, slithering silently down the outside of the witch's hat. Having so many times spied on Gogol's conversations without either he or his other guests ever having any clue, this was an accomplished manoeuvre on our parts.

Sam and I casually skirted the other witch's hats in a pre-determined pattern. If anyone were watching they would have no reason to think that either we were in any particular hurry nor going to any particular place.

We were all the same a little breathless in reaching hat nineteen, slowing down and entering as nonchalantly as we might. Once within we sped up, ducking under the flap that led to my tunnel and wriggling like two Snakes out under the perimeter wall and into the gulley.

From this angle nobody could see us. Not that is, unless they performed the inhuman task of scaling the hills surrounding the gulley. No sounds of pursuit behind us.

We were away.

Yet we kept running until completely out of breath. By the time the daylight was full, we were at our crate hideout, where food and water was safely stashed for a longer journey.

Done running and refreshed a little, we trudged on in some triumph. Until beside me Sam suddenly put a palm on my chest and stood, hand shading eyes, peering at the crest of the hills on our right. Surely there could be nobody following us up there? It was far too difficult to climb those hills from Gogol's place.

The Zoo: The Beast, The Boy and The Zoo

Then I too caught a flash.

A streak of yellow hide with black spots bounding effortlessly amongst the boulders high up on that eastern ridge. New Father's spotted dog. We had left it out of the equation. It threw its head back and it called. But not a bark nor a howl. A strange noise something half way between a dog and a cat.

There was an immediate answering chirping call from the hills flanking the gulley on the west. Our twin heads swivelled as one. Were there two of them? Before we knew it this second 'dog' had bound down and was sitting on a low boulder a little ahead , staring back at us, nonchalantly licking his lips and barring our way.

And now noise behind us too. Human footsteps coming quick. Still out of sight around the bend.

Gogol with his whip? No, worse. The form appearing was the cloaked and hooded one of New Father. Panic consumed us. We ran stumbling over the broken scree that littered the gulley floor.

The spotted cat-dog things, or whatever on earth they were, sprang forward with impossible litheness and speed. I saw two heavy paws thump heavily into the middle of Sam's back, who was slammed face down into the sand. The beast sat pinning my helpless twin to the ground. Snarling it twisted its neck into a striking position, stretching its jaws to an impossible width as so bite down on Sam's defenceless nape. Within a gaping triangle of crimson and black, two unbelievably long and wickedly cruel upper scimitar fangs were poised to clamp and close with an equally vicious phalanx of waiting lower teeth.

For only a split second, visceral terror vied with protective fraternal fury. Then instinctively I sprang at the brute that dared to endanger my other self, my twin.

I never got that far.

I too was hurtled flat into the dirt by a dappled blur from my right moving at a speed far too great for any evasion. I wriggled in a vain

The Zoo: The Beast, The Boy and The Zoo

attempt and with desperate moves to fend the damn thing off. But my hunter simply sat calmly on my chest. It used its paws and weight to cease my struggles. I could at least see that its ever so smaller pair, also still poised securely pinning down Sam's slighter body, had not yet struck down with those barbaric looking jaws.

If ever there was the time for my twin to do some more of that uncanny animal stuff, as with the Mice and the Rat, this was it.

Come on Sam! I thought. Get us out of this. Make that blasted weirdness of yours useful for once.

But nothing happened. I could not even see Sam's face from here.

New Father's threatening figure was right upon us now. From our position, completely supine and each with a heavy animal pressing down on our chests, we could only see his boots slowly approaching.

His pace slowed.

Slower…

And slower again…

And stopped. His dark thin figure cloaked bending down. Towards both of us. No, it was to me specifically.

"Hello Seth my love, it has been so long…"

The hood was thrown back, and I was staring up into a smiling face. It was a face flanked with long silky, silver hair.

It was by any yardstick a pretty old face.

It was the face of the most beautiful woman I had ever seen. An opinion on which I remain firm to this very day.

***

Chapter Nine: Leaving Home

"It is called an E-Type," she said. "An E-Type Jaguar car, the four seater version." Proudly she ran her hand over its gleaming blood-red body.

I have already spoken of Gogol's prized if battered jeep. And Sam and I had been in other people's vehicles before. But not often. Mainly just beaten up old trucks.

This was something else altogether. Something from a different world. A beautiful shiny thing, its vermilion hide glinting conspicuously in the Vague Lands' midday heat. Hard to resist actually stroking the metal and caressing the bonnet as if a living thing. Surely nothing was ever so vividly out of place in this most vapid of places.

"It's like ... some kind of Cat coiled, ready to spring," said Sam, circling slowly in wonderment. Inside the cream coloured seats smelled of leather. All too easy to think of sinking into them, and of dozing off.

Sam has said it was like a Cat? It would only be much later of course that either of us would become directly acquainted with an actual Jaguar, an acquaintance that would carry a special significance in this tale. So my twin's thoughts would have surely have been going instead to the Sand Cats, which we just very occasionally knew from the desert around us.

Yet when I think back now and with my experience of so many different kind of animals, I cannot help but think of that car as almost more like a thoroughbred mare or stallion, one possessed of great speed, dexterity and power, but by the same token a certain fragile vulnerability.

The Zoo: The Beast, The Boy and The Zoo

A steed fit for its owner.

The first thing we learnt about that owner was her name - Lilith. Not of course our new father. Nor, equally plainly, mother. But just eighteen hours or so after our failed escape bid, this strange, beautiful and aged woman was driving us away. Taking us away forever from everything we knew.

At the outset we had asked no questions. It was all too strange. Too sudden. We were too young and too frightened. And Lilith just did not seem the kind of person of whom on first meeting you could ask questions. Or at least who would answer them. A quality of hers that would be slow to change.

But the questions were all there all the same. And as we drove, she herself chose to answer at least some of these. Some gaps were filled in, and many, many others opened up.

A jigsaw with only a few of the pieces provided.

So Sam and I had been born at this place - 'the Zoo', but had been taken away when very young, and given to Gogol to raise as his own. Now we were going back to live with our real father at the Zoo, where he was the 'Director'. That, it seemed, meant he was in charge. Lilith was the 'Curator'. We did not understand what that meant, but it sounded important.

After these many years, if you were to ask as to the exact sequence of events between being caught in the Lion gulley, being taking back to Gogol's trading post and now being driven away in Lilith's car, I am afraid we would come across all kinds of blanks in my memory.

Did we get punished by Gogol for running away? I cannot for the life of me remember. I imagine Gogol would have wanted to. I expect Lilith would have forbidden it.

Were there further exchanges or arguments between Gogol and this extraordinary woman? Probably. If so. Lilith won.

The Zoo: The Beast, The Boy and The Zoo

Was there any kind of leave taking between ourselves and Gogol? Certainly no such memory is lodged in my head. But then that is not only the fault of my aging mind. As I have said, clear or consistent memories and the Vague Lands, even in the best of times, never went together anyway.

But I do remember the bit where Gogol produced the book.

Before we left, when Lilith was out of sight for just a moment, he gave us that small book. Well, clearly giving it specifically to Sam. He did not really look at me at all. "Here. You had better take this." He said with an unpleasant smile and tone, staring intently at my twin. "Where you are going, and with what is in store for you, you will probably need it one day". I barely glimpsed the title before Sam twisted from me and spirited Gogol's unexpected gift away. It was just two words: 'The Zoo'.

So just another bloody animal book for Sam to obsess on.

"But don't let *her* know you have it. And don't open it until you really need it," Gogol added in completing the transaction.

I would have dismissed the whole incident wholly from my mind, except that was the only thing I remember Gogol ever giving anyone.

As we drove away I turned round to look out of one of the two square rear windows. Sam on the other hand was already solely focused on what lay ahead of us. To my surprise Gogol was still standing there. Was that a hand raised as if in some kind of farewell? Is my memory right about that at least? It may just as easily been a fist raised or a rude gesture. That is the Vague Lands again for you. But for whatever purpose, until he was a dot in the distance, Gogol did stay there looking after us for such a long time.

***

Sam and I were sitting in the back either side of one of the 'Cat-Dog' things. The second, bigger one was up front with Lilith. Their

The Zoo: The Beast, The Boy and The Zoo

names were Sinister (the one in the passenger seat) and Dexter. These it seemed, were actually not Dogs or 'Cat-Dogs' at all, but something called 'Chee - tahs'. Sam had identified them in his book, without waiting to be told by Lilith.

"They are part of the Cat family, although they have e-volv-ed characteristics more commonly associated with the can – ines."

Oh god, shut up Sam, I thought. All this to deal with and still you are wittering on about animals. What a silly, unimaginative bore my twin was.

And so the sleek little E-Type sprinted onwards. Miles sped past. Miles of landscape, of places and people we had never seen. The countryside gradually changing into a greener and more vivacious place, something well beyond the grey, two-dimensional world of our knowledge. The cream seats were soft. The smell of the strangely familiar leather was good. The car was pleasantly warm. And we were very, very tired.

But Lilith was still talking, still telling us, just a little, about where we were going. Sam interrupted her.

"Will we meet our mother at The Zoo as well?"

Lilith utterly ignored Sam's question, continuing fixedly on her own separate track. "It is actually by far the oldest zoo in the country. There are others better known of course found in other places far from here."

"How far?" Sam piped up again.

"Oh, so very far as that, for you at least, to be quite unreachable. Many of these other zoos there are quite wonderful too, make no mistake. But in the end, and whether they know it or not, these are just shadows of *The* Zoo, the *real* Zoo. You see your father's Zoo is the very idea of a zoo. And all those other places derive themselves from it."

Then there was something about some man Lilith knew. At least I thought she meant she knew him. He was called Plato, and she was

The Zoo: The Beast, The Boy and The Zoo

talking about 'plat-on-ic forms' (?). I switched off straight away. Sam stayed listening trying to follow it all, but was soon clearly lost as well.

So neither of us really knew what she was speaking about; but both of us rather liked the fashion in which she spoke, so different to the way we or anyone we had ever known. It was so calm, and now that she was talking to us and not Gogol, she sounded so kind. Above all she was entirely certain of herself.

One last time I looked back over my shoulder, but the Vague Lands were long gone now, lost in our past. So for reassurance instead I looked over at that single familiar thing left to me. But Sam still peered ever forward, eyes bright and full of questions and since the second we had left not one single glance backwards.

Our attempt at a great escape, so long planned, so many times discussed, it had failed.

Yet it hadn't exactly, had it? We had 'escaped' after all.

We would never see Gogol again.

Or Gogol's trading post.

I would never see the dead tree nor the well. I would never smell those smells. Never look up at that particular sky. We would never see the Vague Lands again.

We were going to meet our father.

We were going home.

We were going home to a place called 'The Zoo'

***

Chapter Ten: A snowbound pursuit

I had been asleep.

I woke to a comforting, if odd, mixture of smells, sensations and sounds: the leather seats; the smell and warm soft muscled feel of a Cheetah wriggling between Sam and me, all three of us under a thick woollen rug; and the reassuring drone of the car.

It was Sam's voice and sharp elbow that woke me.

"Look Seth, it is snowing!"

Snowing? What was snowing? I looked out the window.

But yes. Something there, half remembered about a story with 'snow' swirled back into my head. Two children, a woman and a sleigh. Who on earth could had told me such a story to me? And why? And when?

The landscape was so different. Now there were fields, woods, streams, houses, even small villages. Warm enough in Lilith's car, but outside really, really white.

"Why is it like this? Why is it so different here? How come it has all changed again so quickly?"

Lilith absent-mindedly scratched the head of the Cheetah sat beside her. "In the Vague Lands you had no such things as seasons. But whilst you slept we moved deep into the heart of the country. Here we have spring, summer, autumn, and now winter. In fact in the Zoo and its wider Domain the coldest winter we have had for a hundred years. All the same you are right to be surprised. It should not be as white, nor

The Zoo: The Beast, The Boy and The Zoo

snowbound, nor suddenly upon us as this. This is not an entirely natural thing."

"How long before we get there?" Sam was excited again.

"About an hour or two."

A hesitation, then, "..if, indeed, we do get there."

"What do you mean?"

"I mean..." Her hand tightened on the car's austere steering wheel. "I mean that Something might try to stop us." Her gaze steadier than ever now on the road ahead. "There are those who may not be too keen to see you return safely to the Zoo. Not you two of all people. And not now of all times. But don't be frightened. I am only telling you because you need to be prepared. This unnatural weight of winter brought down on us is only one weapon in Something's will to frustrate our passage. I do not doubt but that there will be others."

Seth and I turned to stare at one another. The snow became thicker. The world became ever whiter and ever stranger.

The compact vigour of the E-Type ate up the miles. The air was fluffy now with slowly falling globules of snow, hanging in the air almost motionless. It was hard to see any distance at all out of the windows. All sounds, even the drone of the svelte, low slung car, a crimson streak breaking through the colourless landscape, was muffled. I shivered just a little.

Lilith sped on.

Now there were snow laden trees dotted all around us, completely white. Nothing could be more different to the Vague Lands. Nothing could be more beautiful. Sam and I were struck dumb with the wonder of it all.

Bump! The car shook violently.

"What was that?!"

Our driver did not seem to notice.

The Zoo: The Beast, The Boy and The Zoo

Sam and I stared ahead. Suddenly and just for a split instant an immense fan of white feathers spread all across the windscreen. The car's view forward was completely blocked. We were driving blind. Then, just as quickly, whatever it might have been, it was scraped off the screen. Only a trickle of blood remained to obscure our view.

Then something on the left hand side where Sam was sitting? Something flying, something flinging itself furiously at the car. A huge, screeching white bird with a large, round head.

A snowy owl, as I was to learn later.

And now on my own side another kind of bird. A massive, white seagull smashed itself head first into my window, leaving feathers, blood and entrails over the glass.

"They are actually killing themselves to stop us, Seth. Such an odd tone in Sam's voice, more of reverence and admiration than of fear and loathing.

More white birds of different types colliding with the car from all angles. Dozens, perhaps hundreds of kamikaze attacks. Every second another crash shook the car. That perfect fuselage of the E-Type must surely now be a mass of dents. The road behind was strewn with bits of feathers, bones, and dying white birds twitching in agony.

For a few moments I was staring on my own side straight into the face of a flighted something. Very different this time to a bird, a large splay-faced, white thing clinging on to the wing mirror on the side of the car, chittering its hatred at me through the window. Leathery wings, a snub yellow noise and pointed ears. How filthy this creature seemed to me then. They all were.

Then mercifully, it too was swept away. The blizzard of white suicides ceased.

The eerie, snow-damped quiet reigned again. Everything silent save the ever present noise of the motor. Then, thirty heart beats or so later and the still was broken again by *that* noise.

The Zoo: The Beast, The Boy and The Zoo

It is a noise which has stayed with me down all these years. A noise all too familiar across history to frightened human huddles, people of all types in all places and in all times. The lonely howl of a wolf.

It came from the near to the left side of the car. A few seconds. Then an answering howl a long way off to our right.

"Look!" Sam pointed out the window. I turned in time to see a white tail disappearing on that side of the car. The Cheetahs tensed and pivoted their heads in synchrony, Dexter to the left and Sinister to the right. They gave a long slow purr-y growl in unison.

"That was a Timber Wolf, Seth. A huge white Timber Wolf."

The snow had stopped falling. We could now see clearly some distance again around Lilith's E-Type. For the first time I saw the Wolf distinctly running alongside Sam's window.

Then we saw a third. And a fourth. An entire pack padding along, keeping pace with car at cruising speed on both sides. Some close beside us. Others further away at first, but all gradually arrowing in, converging in a tactical 'v' shape on our path ahead.

"Hmmm," Lilith was speaking to herself. "Friends or foes, I wonder? These days could be either. Well then, let's find out, shall we?"

She revved the little E-Type. It seemed to leap forward. The Wolves easily increased their speed to keep up.

"Seth, Seth... look!" Sam grabbed my hand and pointed. "Do you know what that is?"

Another big, white thing lumbering towards us now. Certainly not a Wolf. Four or five times bigger, but with stubby little ears. No I didn't know what it was. And I didn't bloody care. Some other horrid, frightening animal. I just wanted to be in another place calm, safe, warm and away from all these horrible, revolting creatures. But bloody Sam..? No, no. Sam of course was enjoying this!

That you see was always been the problem. That foolish, rash, dangerous enthusiasm coming on top of the little secret that both of us needed to hide. That at base is why, not only in our young lives but so much later as well, I was forced to be always on lookout for my twin. A habit that I have never, irrespective of all that was to come, been able to entirely lose.

Am I my sibling's keeper? Yes, definitely.

"I think it is a Polar Bear... an actual Polar Bear." Sam rose a little in the seat to see better.

I began to tremble. Not with fear of course, you understand, but out sheer frustration, indignation and anger at being put in this position at all. At least that was the impression I was keen to give at the time.

Lilith leaned backyards. "Now listen to me, both of you." She was almost whispering. "You both must calm down. We are not so very far from the Zoo now, not far from home and from safety. Within our domain, our rule still holds strong - for the most part anyway. Hold on tight, this little car is more than it seems. It can go a lot faster if it needs to. And a lot faster than these beasts certainly. These particular animals are not especially clever, you know. They are merely blunt tools in the hands of Something else. They don't really know what they are doing nor what they are up against. Look ahead - do you see there?"

We had left the dotted trees behind and were now surrounded by smooth white plains. These gently sloped down towards our road which pointed into to the thick black forest lying before us.

To this day I have never seen taller, wilder, more ancient trees of so many sorts all clustered together. Our road was straight into that deep, dark place, a peculiarly inviting place.

No, wait. There was something else first. Something in the way. A thick oily black line of some sort curving and undulating between us and the forest.

"There." She pointed. "That is where we are going. That is safety. That is where our power holds sway. That is home."

The Zoo: The Beast, The Boy and The Zoo

Then the red maw of a Wolf snapped up at my window, bashing its snout against my reflection. Trying somehow to stupidly bite through the glass or metal, succeeding only in leaving saliva and blood on the triangular panes.

"They are trying to force us off the road."

Now there came was a truly sickening sequence of sounds: the agonised yowl of a dog-like thing; an instant of conflict between metal and flesh; and the mechanical grind of a skeleton crushed under the car wheels.

One Wolf the less.

More white things, more different sorts of creatures emerging from all sides. Each one so perfectly camouflaged against its snowy background that it was as if they had, mere seconds before their assault on the car, popped into existence for the first time. The white-out that surrounded us had clearly and cleverly been conceived to work to the advantage of our colourless assailants. At the same time it had placed a clear, bright red target on our own backs.

So many new animals encountered for the first time in our young lives; only later in life would they all become too easy to identify.

Some smaller, yappy little dog like things with big ears - Arctic Foxes.

Stocky, wild eyed white ponies - Przewalski's Horses.

Deer of various kinds charging us with vicious antlers - Elk, Reindeer, Fallow Deer.

An army of blanched malevolence, screaming, neighing, bruiting their hatred toward the car and its cargo.

One after another they slammed into the Jag or into its path. With each huge impact we careened from side to side.

But that was a very special car, a very strange little car. If it looked like a pure bred Arabian Stallion, there was an armoured Carthorse in there somewhere. The way the frame of the E-Type held up seemed more akin to that of a Sherman tank than a sports car.

And such a very strange and special driver too. The animals always came off worse. Sometimes Lilith seemed to exactly gauge the angle and speed of attack, veering the car to ram the beast in advance and send them hurtling off back into their snowy nothingness. For others she was somehow able to coach yet more speed out of the E-Type and show a clean pair of back wheels to our enemies, baying in frustration. In short moments between repeated shocks and alarms, I found myself staring in a kind of baffled wonder at the nape of our driver sitting in front. This was a kind of adult entirely new to us, caring, competent and simply beyond comprehension.

Compared to the battlefield scenes of dead and wounded in our rear window the carnage caused by the first wave of bird attacks seemed now as nothing. Despite all their vicious intent, nothing the white animals could do was stopping us getting nearer and nearer to the forest. And before us, this strip we had to cross. Now that we were nearer, I saw it must surely be a river. And if it was river, there must then be a bridge somewhere?

I had several times nearly been sick, but, as we got nearer, the panic in the car fell away. We were leaving the white horde behind. In a few short minutes we were going to get out of this. It was going be okay. Well, it would have been. But for that damn Polar Bear.

That and Sam.

***

Chapter Eleven: Cheetah versus Polar Bear

Suddenly there it was standing in the middle of our road. Another one of them. Had this been the pack's plan all along? Rather than really trying to stop us, had they been driving us forward towards this second Bear? What kind of mind indeed was behind it all? Cleverer perhaps after all than even Lilith had reckoned with.

Again and again this second Polar Bear, a male reared up on its hind legs. A repulsive, roaring monster just waiting for us to come within its range. So much of my later life and career has been about protecting our fellow animals, preventing entire species from sliding off the edge. But to my mind in that very moment, this was an ugly thing of no value of *any* form. Right there and then, I must confess I was wishing that all the Bears, of any sort in all the world, might be slaughtered and that their type should vanish for good from the face of the Earth.

There could surely not be space to get past that monster on an ice laden road, ten times the weight of a grown man.

Mere feet away from the brute Lilith suddenly slammed on the brakes. But instead of just stopping, the E-Type skidded smoothly in an elegant clockwise circle on the ice. Wham! Just at that a moment when the front of the E-Type was facing back where we had come from, the whole rear of the car slammed into the Bear, knocking it for six.

The car continued skidding slowly but smoothly on its wide circle; ending up in a position that once again faced roughly forward.

Lilith gunned the E-Type to get out of there. For a split second we could feel the car strain forwards. Then it jolted back and I suddenly felt cold air in my face. I looked to where it was coming, where Sam was sitting. The very top of Sam's window was six inches open! My idiot twin had opened it. Why? For a better look? And the Bear had jammed his paw through the slit. Hitched to the car and with his massive strength and bulk, he was easily able to hold the whole car back.

Our wheels spun. We didn't move an inch.

Lilith gave a piercing whistle and the command: "Dexter! Sinister!"

The two Cheetahs sprang up through the driver's car doors which their mistress cracked opened and slammed shut again almost in a single motion. And they were on the Bear in a flashing, curving sickle of limbs, fangs and claws.

Maybe the young me was not one for admiring animal kind, but by god, in that instant there was something truly magnificent about those two. The joyous noise they made as, caught in my memory in almost slow motion, they tore gloriously into that big white bastard. Not anything as loud as a roar. Yet much more exciting than any growl. A 'yowl' is the nearest I can manage.

Cheetahs are pretty slight animals when it comes down to it. They do not at all have the power of those other spotted cats like Leopards or Jaguars. The Bear, even alone, outclassed the pair by far in strength, size, jaws, claws and sheer killing ability. But it did have one disadvantage, one paw uselessly jammed into our car. It could not move away from the E-Type nor turn very much at all. Dexter and Sinister used their incredible speed to good advantage to bait the great beast, tearing in on it one after the other, first left flank, then its right. The Bear swaying back and forth in rage, and no little pain, seemed baffled that it could not easily deal with these little creatures.

A howl to our rear.

The other white animals were catching up again.

The Zoo: The Beast, The Boy and The Zoo

With a wrench from either party, both besieged Bear and becalmed car were free. The odds had shortened. The game had changed. Lilith gunned the car forward.

All three of our hearts thumping, we put distance between ourselves and two balls of black-spotted yellow, now fast dwindling in the rear mirror. Vivid, vicious spots of colour valiantly whirling amongst a snarling on-rolling phalanx of white fur and feather which slowly engulfed them.

No emotion on Lilith's face. Only much later did we come to appreciate that Sinister and Dexter had been her constant companions, reared from being cubs.

We had been motionless for a good two or three minutes. The E-Type was only slowly picking up speed again: but the relentless white army had never ceased advancing. The river and the welcoming forest were perhaps only half a mile away now, but the Wolves and all the rest were getting closer with every second.

The car moved on. We looked to see where and how the road crossed the river. But neither bridge, nor other means of crossing was visible. The road simply led directly into the river. A river, edged with ice but not reliably frozen over, one that was clearly deep and wide and fast flowing.

A great white bull of some sort (now I would know it as an Aurochs) paced us on the right hand side of the car now lowering his head in preparation to charge. Certainly just as powerful and as capable of overturning the E-Type as the Bear, if not more so.

Three or four huge Wolves on the left side, jumping at the car.

We were almost at the river. Lilith would surely have to stop.

She drove straight into the river. Both Sam and I screamed.

The water rose quickly around the E-Type.

***

ςςς

Excerpt from 'Man and Animal in the Zoo',

Dr Heini Heddiger, Director of Basel and Zurich Zoos 1944

Without doubt rats are the most dangerous animals in zoos all around the world, a fact every keeper should constantly bear in mind. It is not even necessary to be bitten by a rat to receive a fatal infection; it is sufficient if a drop of urine from an infected rat – dead or alive - gets into small wound or abrasion of the human skin. Occasionally even the white laboratory rats which are generally regarded as harmless turn out to be carriers of infection.

Mensch und Tier im Zoo Pg 80
Albert Muller Verlag, Zurich.

ςςς

Part Two: Sam's Telling of the Tale

"So, it seems, I have an unexpected visitor..? Well whoever you might be exactly, you are very welcome, my friend. You say you have already been to see my brother Seth?"

"Yes, I saw Professor Faraday previously at the Zoo. And he began to share the start of your story, Sam. Now I would have you continue it."

"..?!"

"...Sam?"

"......"

"Sam...?"

*"Oh yes...Sam! That **is** what I was called back then. You must forgive me. It has been so long. Hmmm... how long exactly? Since our childhood back then? Forty years, fifty, sixty... a thousand? You have to understand that I have since lived in so many places, I have done so many things, been dragged into other people's stories so often, had so many different names. That time and space, and even identity can all get a little blurred."*

"So, okay, I am to take the same story on now then? I suppose what you are looking for is a sort of... another perspective"

"Yes, Sam, that's it. A sense of balance"

"Balance!"

"Oh my god, that bloody word over again after all this time! Well, yes, I once knew someone who was quite obsessed with 'balance'. As you can see, I am more the glorious off kilter type myself. I find the whole idea of equilibrium, of things meekly staying in their correct places, a trifle drab - a little vulgar even."

"But yes, yes, fine, I am happy to help. And especially so since you have come such a long way. Let me get us both a drink first."

"There, now. Tell me, before we begin, what you think of my home."

"It is lovely Sam. So peaceful. And the weather is perfect. "But... I am not sure I would myself like to live on an island."

"No... Not for everyone. But it suits me. I have always been drawn to one sort of hideaway or another, places where one can do what one pleases and far away from those who disapprove, those people who want to impose their own sense of order – and of balance. It suits certain others too that I should be way out here".

*"Not too many animals on my island either. Well, not ones that have **always** been animals, at least. Good few pigs trotting around though."*

"Now, tell me about Seth, tell me about my brother. I can imagine him there holding forth dressed in that smelly old tweed jacket of his, a pipe in one hand in that revoltingly cosy room at the very top floor, the one with all his precious books lined up in orderly ranks on all four sides? The one that used to be our father's study?"

"Yes, that is about right Sam."

"Aha! Nothing changes too much with dear old Seth. Not like me. I never seem to stop changing. I imagine I am quite different from what you know of me, what you think you know anyway."

"But what about you, mysterious stranger demanding that my brother and then I, we all of us lay our stories before you. Nothing seems to have been said at all yet as to you. How do you fit into all this. Not so much as even your name?"

"It is not really important to know anything about me, Sam. This is just about Seth and yourself."

"You are a puzzle then? Someone who evades easy classification - a little of the wild in your soul. I like that! But I sense also something of a manipulator. You are pulling all

our strings. I like that less. But let it pass. For the moment at least"

"Right then, my curious young gentleman from far, far away, let us pick up the tale. But first of all, you will please stop calling me 'Sam'! You will stop confusing the readers.

My name, as you very well know, is <u>Samantha.</u>

Sa –man –tha.

It is, and it always has been.

Chapter Twelve: Truth and Lies

I have to say I took little pleasure in being addressed just now and after all these years as 'Sam'. No! Ugh, it made me positively shudder. Such a vulgar, tame little syllable.

And just to avoid any confusion or embarrassment around these things, I have *always* been a Samantha and never in any sense a Samuel.

But I believe you, such clever people; well come along, you will have most certainly already deduced something of the sort for yourselves? When you look back at what my brother set down so far, so many strangely missing third person pronouns, that will have made you a bit suspicious? You will have guessed that I am not exactly as my dear little brother has depicted me.

Yes, I know Seth is half an hour older than me. What a ridiculous thing to be proud of. But from time to time, I call him 'my little brother', because..?

Well, just because I want to.

So the shared puzzle before us must be: has Seth purposely led you astray on this; and, if so, why? Why should a brother do such a thing? Then you will wonder whether there might be other details in Seth's tale to consume only with quite a pinch of salt. I am afraid on that I am going to be of limited use. But it should not pose you such a problem. After all, each one of you who might be reading this, you will have lived a full, rich life yourself. So let us suppose that you have drunk deeply of the cup of experience, it will then follow, as reliably as night does day, that...

The Zoo: The Beast, The Boy and The Zoo

You. Are. All. Bloody.Liars.

Forgive me. I was not just being rude for the sake of it. You see the human is after all that especially pathetic animal who can stand very little truth. So we lie. All of us. Oh, we lie *a lot*.

So we are clear. We the various parties serving up this story are liars of one species: you who are consuming it are highly experienced liars of another species.

Whether Seth's overall tale so far is then on the whole honest? Since you are such experts in the telling of tall tales yourselves, let me leave that to your own discernments. But on *certain particular* things, on those I would wish to set down the truth here.

Now to that substantial issue of my girlhood. The truth was that in those early times, if Seth and I did not look *exactly* alike, and were not identical twins in the technical sense, we were certainly very similar in looks. So people tended to immediately categorise us as a single item; and so conveniently dispatch us from any further consideration.

We were dressed alike as twin boys. Gogol's exploitation and lack of care was dispensed entirely even-handedly. Most of our days were spent beneath a camouflaged layer of work related filth and the grey sand that got everywhere; all serving to further blend two unique and special individuals into a very unremarkable and anonymous one. Anyone visiting the Vague Lands simply had no inclination to pay us a close inspection. There would be no reason at all to assume we were anything but a filthy pair of urchin brothers.

Gogol himself would have known of course perfectly well what he was getting in Seth and me. In my early times though, I assumed that he simply didn't *care* that I was a girl. I imagined anything special or extra he might have had to do to distinguish me in that way, that would have been too much extra effort. It might have cost him money.

I was wrong though, wasn't I?

The Zoo: The Beast, The Boy and The Zoo

Only a lot later did I realise that, on the contrary, he - and others too I suppose - must have gone actively out of their way to create this 'disguise'. So that, if some character were to show up one day looking for the daughter and son of Professor William Faraday, and with the massacre of the innocents on their minds, they would hardly start sniffing around an obscure and slightly repellent pair of identical male twins.

Simplest you see all around that Seth and I might just be and grow up as 'those two grime-ridden little boys over there in the corner'.

What about the impact, the confusion visited upon on a young, delicate and pliable little mind? To be raised from birth to hide who and what I was. To need to develop all kinds of clever stratagems to be away from company several times each day without aggravating suspicion. To be forced to almost be *ashamed* of what I was.

To be contrite to be a girl?

Oh, yes, I will have plenty more to say to you on that! On Gogol too. Such a strange man. And I need to fix a number of other things in Seth's version.

But not just yet. I can see the impatience building up in my visitor's face. He wants to be in control of my tale. As far as he is concerned, my only duty right now is to move along smartly with this story itself. So I will be dutiful. I will play along. I will accompany my gentleman caller along the path *he* has chosen. For the moment. He needs to be careful though. He needs to watch me closely. Take his eye away at the wrong moment in this story and this particular character may all too easily slip her collar.

***

Chapter Thirteen: The Zoo Domain

I have to agree with Seth's so vivid description at the point where his own narration left us.

He and I did indeed scream. We screamed long and hard and embarrassingly loudly as that strange car drove straight into the river. We turned and burrowed our faces in each other's arms.

The expected feeling however of plunging down into the river or being swept sideways by the force of icy waters never arrived. Instead Lilith's sports car just forged forward in a beautifully straight line.

It was all the same only once we had safely got back to the road proper on the other side of the river, that we dared slowly to lift up our faces and look around again with widening eyes.

Our chauffeur was nonchalant about it all. She let matters slide long seconds further, until Seth and I had clearly got it a little together again, before she could be bothered to explain what had just happened.

There was it seemed a bridge after all. Well 'a bridge 'if you were pretty relaxed about the definition. We had been saved by a causeway or an underwater bridge; exactly where it was and how to use it kept a secret; its surface hidden two feet beneath the level of the waters.

The vehicle had continued to move forward along the exact course set where Lilith knew the bridge lay. The jag (let me admit it was a fabulous piece of engineering) had been built to be both waterproof enough and powerful enough to plough on through the water and straight on up the other side.

The Zoo: The Beast, The Boy and The Zoo

The ancient towering forest began slowly to close around and behind us. It seemed to enfold the car in a protective embrace. The white beasts either could not follow or maybe they chose not to. Seth still sat shaking with his head hidden in his hands. I twisted round to look out the back window.

You might have thought I would see a scene of rage and mass frustration. But those magnificent animals only seemed to turn around calmly and fade slowly back into the snowy landscape from which they had come, as if they had never truly existed.

They had lost: we had won. We had reached the safe place. And that was all there was to it.

***

I wish my demanding interviewer drawing these memories out of me did not seem in such a hurry. I could otherwise have given you a lot more detail about the hour we spent driving through those strange woodlands. My god though, but they were beautiful. My lord, they were beguiling!

But so be it. I shall discipline myself.

This was to be my very first encounter with the 'Old Forest', the bewildering tanglewood that encloses the Zoo in varying thicknesses on all four of its sides. Yet another completely new and strange kind of place for both of us. I was awestruck. Up I stared at those giant trees, more like the buttresses of some great green cathedral than mere plants. My neck craned through the E-Type's little window panes.

Some of those trees are nearly a thousand years old. The forest itself is much older again. It has not changed from its basic form since the very first human apes wandered into this land.

The Zoo: The Beast, The Boy and The Zoo

At some points, the afternoon light barely filtered through the leafy pavilion at all, but every so often we motored through large open glades gloriously drenched in winter sunshine, rays which then dappled on through the trees on either side, gradually thickening on into total darkness again. In clearings like these, the forest floor itself seemed every bit as alive, if not more so than the surrounding trees. It was blanketed with decaying leaves, twigs, moss, fungi, and fallen wood.

Seth drew back, wrinkling up his nose at death and decay. I leaned forward grinning and rejoicing; taking in great draughts of this fertile life-bringing mulch.

Many people these days find little use for old woods like these. Places that are gradually decomposing so new things can arise. But then those very same people often find little use for old people either. Especially for annoying old women like me.

Then, where the light was strongest, grasses, ferns, wildflowers, bushes, brambles all pushed up and around the smaller, younger trees. It was as if they were desperate to become as big as the grownups and fill in the canopy beside them.

Since that first blissful first rendezvous, I have often in my spare moments stolen off to those same woods. I have lain there surrendered, flat on my back and, tingling with desire, simply stared up all along those great stout, straight columns to the point where they vanish into the sky.

Yes, this wild, full place made me tipsy with lust. Something seeded in my soul that day. Something fierce, something wild and lucky. Something that would slowly grow.

Eventually the newness of it all began to recede just a little. Seth began bombarding Lilith with a torrent of questions. And my gaze was reluctantly wrenched away from the window.

The Zoo: The Beast, The Boy and The Zoo

Who were the white animals on the other side of the river? Why had they attacked us? Why would anyone wish to stop us from reaching where we going?

All fundamentally ignored.

"You are safe now. That's all you need to know." The woman who had taken control of us shut him down firmly.

"Nothing will dare attack us here. Inside the perimeter river, we still have most of the power. And when in a little while we will arrive within the Zoo proper, then the only thing that matters a wit there is the Zoo's own rule." A flicker of her eyes and lips accompanying this last assurance forbade the further questions which it itself implied.

Dark was falling when the ancient trees finally began to give way. They unveiled glimpses of strange manmade structures of varying shapes and forms. At that first encounter we could make neither head nor tail of these weird little buildings - enclosures, aviaries, pools - all sizes, shapes and designs.

I did find the edifices themselves interesting. But I was so much more excited when I was lucky to get a glimpse of their astonishing inhabitants. It was annoying that the fast fleeing light made it so hard to see these.

Those first memories of the Zoo itself that evening are all a little blurred. Yes I am sure as well that many later remembrances will be heaped on top. But I seem to still clearly picture myself glued to that left hand window as we passed by one tableau after another of exotic creatures. Slowly we penetrated deeper and deeper into heart of this most seductive of places, the Zoo.

Seth, whose interest in those days began and ended with his own dull species, had little idea as to the name and nature of most of these new beings. But I whispered each word to myself, sweet as nut, my tongue rolling in delight around every welcome syllable.

The Zoo: The Beast, The Boy and The Zoo

For some, a mere whisper was simply not enough. I am sorry, but simply to see for the first time in the flesh creatures that I had only been able to thrill to in books; for it to truly sink in that that the prehistoric-looking, thoroughly unlikely concoction that is a Rhinoceros was actually real! For it to sink in that that here was I looking at this startling being; and more, that the same startling thing could look back at me.

No, this was too much for any restraint left to this girl.

One by one, at the very top of my lungs I yelled their names out.

"Ostriches!"

"Giraffes!"

"Brown Bears!"

And finally, as the car seemed to be slowing down to a destination, "ORANG UTANS!!!!" That last one in particular was very far from a quiet whisper.

Lillith made no comment as to my excitement, but my zest visibly irritated Seth. Hmmm... did I in fact shout out the names of the animals quite that loud, in part at least to vex him?

Possibly.

Probably.

A good way to think of the Zoo in its overall shape and layout is as a rough series of concentric circles. And there at the very centre of this great winding, and as the E-Type finally purred to a halt, was a house.

The house. The house where Seth has already entertained our shared interrogator. 'Edensor', our home for so many years.

By now those young bodies of ours were sleep ridden. A busy little woman whom we come to soon know as Maria appeared from nowhere. Carefully she helped Lilith bundle us up that wide, rickety wooden stairs. All the way nearly to the very top.

Up, up, up.

Four stories in total within this structure. It was so alien in type to us, taller by far than any we had ever known.

The Zoo: The Beast, The Boy and The Zoo

She opened the door to the huge room I remember as our old bedroom, just below the final uppermost storey. We were ushered into beds softer than any substance we had thought possible; and two exhausted children fell immediately into a dreamless sleep.

You will learn more about Edensor the house later. But if you please not just now. I must, as you know, obey my orders to get on with the story: orders from my interesting but implacable visitor sitting there opposite watching me, and taking all of this down.

So on that basis let me first recharge both his and my wine glasses. Then I need to press on to a most important part in our tale. That next morning, when for the first time, we met our father.

***

Chapter Fourteen: Interview with a Father

He didn't even glance up as we were ushered into the study.

Not in the least bit interested to see us; too busy sharpening his pencils. It is such a sign of a well-tempered life to have properly whetted writing implements, don't you find?

The current Professor Faraday, my brother, will, I would guess, still be using that very same room as his office. He will be surrounded by shelf upon shelf of well-ordered and carefully classified, impressively entitled volumes.

There were lots of books back then too. Many of the same ones, I should not wonder. But that first time they were not all up on the shelves. Piles strewn at random on tables, on chairs, on the floor. Papers scattered everywhere as well. No room to sit, nor barely to even walk across the floor. A spicy, musty, fetid smell, not entirely unpleasant, emanated from the overall compost of our father's study.

A small grey headed Parrot suddenly flew in a flash of grass green and tangerine orange from father's shoulder squawking across the room. Seth ducked in alarm. Sparking in delight, I ran over immediately to where it had climbed into the safety of its cage.

Poison Arrow Frogs in primary blue, red and yellow glared out from glass vivaria strung all along the wall at the intruders who dared enter into this holy place. All manner of jars and receptacles for bits of plants or animal organs, mysterious looking scientific devices, and what might be half-finished experiments ranged across a mantelpiece over the fire. A set of animal skulls, large and small alike, were lined neatly along the shelf behind a big desk.

Wasn't it curious that the only objects in that room with any sense of arrangement at all were these last dead things?

A tall man, clearly caring very little at all for what he wore: faded chinos; a check shirt; green cardigan full of holes. Snow white hair badly dishevelled. Two or three day's stubble on his chin. Not the kind of person in my social circle these days.

But, when he finally turned to look at us, we caught the force of those eyes. Now *they* were remarkable. Piercing, crystal blue irises around coal black pupils at the centre of large unblemished whites. This man's fair skin and hair were very different to our darker hues. But his eyes were our eyes.

 It was such an expressive face.

No, let me put it better, it was a *potentially* expressive face. As if there were a hand grenade sitting there about to go off at any time.

In all the time I knew him a certain something frequently danced around our father's mouth and eyes, as if some profound revelation was about to come forth; and that he might be on the verge of doing something truly extraordinary. That he might suddenly make a pronouncement that would fundamentally capsize every understanding around him.

But what that intensely interesting thing might precisely be? What the mutinying word might be? No, never any clue.

In the moment when he finally did look at us, the overwhelming expression in those eyes could well have been of pained embarrassment. Or could it be irritation, or just plain bafflement? It sure as heavens wasn't one of any kind of pleasure.

Then a long, drawn out sigh.

 "So... Yes, yes, here you are." Such a limp greeting.

The Zoo: The Beast, The Boy and The Zoo

To a degree both our father and Lilith shared an accent, a vocabulary and demeanour stunningly different to the tones and manners we knew from everyone we had ever met in the Vague Lands Different therefore too from the way Seth and I both spoke then. Gogol would have dismissed it as 'stuck up'. He would certainly say that of the way I speak today. But whereas Lilith's speech was always measured, her sentences perfectly formed, the thoughts therein complete and the cadence finely balanced, our father's delivery was cracked, his utterances tense, his phrases mostly left unfinished.

At the instant he began to speak, he once more turned his gaze away from us.

"Very well..."

What exactly had we expected? What did we think a father would be like? I am not all sure. After all, Seth and I had very little to go on.

I had tried once to get Seth to join in imagining what a real mother and real father might be like. He refused to do so, pretending that it was because he did not care to enough. Pretty sure the truth was he cared too much.

Shame, it would have amused me to play that little game with him.

So possibly the off handedness we now saw was after all just the way fathers and mothers were 'supposed' to be. The way they all were?

Yet no words at all of greeting or welcome for his own returned offspring? On any scale that seemed strange. Did he have no notion what we had been through to get here? Had no one told him? Did he not care that his children might have died in the Old Forest and in an especially horrible way?

"Now that you are here," He continued at last. "You must *not* get in my way. There is important work, you know. Very important work."

The Zoo: The Beast, The Boy and The Zoo

Another sigh. Mumbling aloud he strode about the room for no particular reason.

So many questions tumbling around in my head if only it had seemed possible to ask him. Why had we been sent away? And why to Gogol of all people? And I did so very badly want to ask him about our mother.

Lilith discretely gestured me back across the study from the Parrot's cage. For some long seconds we both stood a little behind her. A kind of shared, gauche embarrassment reigned as to what, if anything might be next said. Then I broke ranks.

"Perhaps we can help..?"

"Help..?!" Father was uncomprehending.

"With your important work..."

"No, no, you couldn't possibly understand what is at stake. She... she never really understood either, you know" He broke off as if he had said something he had not meant to. He strode over to the window. He stared out distractedly and silently until I spoke again.

"But we could help you run the Zoo. Help look after the animals." I persevered.

Seth glowered at me, annoyed and embarrassed by what he would consider my pathetic eagerness. Our father swivelled. "Look *after* the animals!?" Suddenly he was quite furious with me. "They don't need looking after, those bastards, they need *stopping*!!"

The earnestness and anger on his face faded as quickly as it had arrived.

His eyes met Seth's and softened again. "You... are... *Seth..?* " He seemed wonderingly and falteringly for the first time to be recognising his own child. He bent down, gently touching Seth on the shoulder. Their matching azure eyes locked.

"Seth and..." Turning to me now. "Sam".

The Zoo: The Beast, The Boy and The Zoo

My own father touched my hair, and something akin to electricity flew through me. As if memories were about to surge back. Except, you see, no actual memories did; but rather it was a more general, haunting recognition. Jumbled scenes, sounds, tastes and smells.

And there was something about the way he smelled when he was near; something that was 'right', something that opened a door in my head.

"Sam and Seth... Seth and Sam...." He seemed to weigh and savour our twin names and to rock us back and forth for a long second or two. Then a note of actual joy seemed to flow forth freely from him. "Oh, it was so good in those early days!" The words rushed out. "Just after you were born. Your mother and I! And the Zoo at peace. Whole. Happy. Healthy!!"

The weird, distracted half mad figure of a few moments ago had melted entirely away.

"There was none of this... none of this suspicion then. Just the natural order. Just your mother and I. And then later you two. We didn't know how good it was then. Well, how could we? Didn't understand that just as it was, this was arcadia. Already perfect."

"We didn't know what was coming. We didn't really know 'It' could come. No hatred. No fear."

"That was before It got in." He stopped for a beat or two as if something had just occurred to him. "...Or did It actually '...*get in*'? Maybe It somehow started here inside the Zoo? Do you think It was here all along..? I don't know... I don't know. That's one of the things I must find out." He was becoming feverish in his speech again. And it was unclear to whom exactly he might be speaking. He started pacing about once more.

"I don't think, Director, we need to go into all of that quite at the moment, do we?" Lilith had intervened "But the twins should be given some kind of duties. They can help in that way at least, surely? And that will help them gradually learn about how the Zoo works."

"What..?" He turned to her, gradually registering her words and even her presence. "Oh yes, yes." It was baffling how yet again he quickly calmed down once more. "Good idea." Hugo certainly needs help down at the Elephants, there, see, down in the south Zoo."

He strode over now to a huge map taking up almost half of the study wall, a layout depicting the whole Zoo.

That map will be still there, I should guess? I suppose by now a lot of the detail will have changed, but the outline will surely the same: the great flattened oval of the Zoo bisected and then surrounded by the river; all the ponds and canals and lakes towards the centre, and the high cataract at the very northern most point. Always so much water across the Zoo.

I used to think just how clever that artist, whoever they might have been, had been to fit in those perfect miniature illustrations of hundreds of species, all with their correct locations, radiating out from the centre.

I ran over immediately to get as close as possible. I felt like I could almost step into that map.

"And you see up there to the north," The map had started him off again. "Those Gorillas, well they at least are still happy. They stay in their homes at night where they should be. But the Chimps right next to them! Hooligans! In open rebellion. They move all over the Zoo at night. And they name the Gorillas collaborators. They have slaughtered several already. Horrible! Quite horrible!"

"And down here." He gestured to another part of the Zoo, largely along the path we had travelled from the west the evening before. "The Giraffes? Well, as long as they have enough to eat and can mate when they feel like, those animals are not interested in debates about the worth of human beings. The Rhinos though..." Now he was pointing to the lower left hand side in the south west. "They are majestic to look at and so endangered, but when you try to talk to them? To reason with them? Forget it. Just angry, stupid 'tanks'."

"Oh, it is all fine during the daytime of course. The visitors just see the Zoo in all its ancient glory and beauty. But at night..."

Father stopped pacing and stared at us both again in penetrating distraction. Then he turned and stretched out an arm and a hand to point directly at Lilith.

"You..." a cresting growl of irritation.

"You!" He was shouting at her now, "Damn you. Oh, you shouldn't have brought them back!!! I shouldn't have let you persuade me."

"Always *you*. Always interfering. Always taking it upon yourself to.... to...." He trailed off for a second,

"I told you, didn't I? Just like I said. It will get to them too now. They were safe with... with..." His own failure to finish sentences seemed to overcome him with exhaustion.

Our father stood bent leaning on the desk, head bowed.

Lilith drew us gently out of the room.

***

Chapter Fifteen: In the Beginning

I was annoyed that that on very first full day of our presence a storm had visited the Zoo. Torrential rain hung around for most of three days. I had arrived plumb in the middle of this glorious place only to be locked up inside Edensor.

I made no attempt to hide how frustrated I was.

At least we were given free rein of the house. And its extensive library. I consoled myself that the second best thing to a zoo full of animals is a 'zoo of books', many of which proved to be, one way or another, about animals.

I became especially wrapped up in one large old leather backed volume. It was simply, if portentously, just called 'The Book'. With delight I dived into its stories, I enjoyed the strange way it stirred in me certain curious ideas on this outlandish place that was our new home.

Then there was a bonus in being able to goad Seth a little. So in front of him and Lilith I took it on myself to read a few passages out loud. I adopted what seemed to me to be an appropriately solemn tone. I expect it was hampered by my childish and, I suppose, still uncouth Vague Lands' accent.

"In the beginning the Earth was... barren. And the Stars looked down upon the world, and said.... 'Let There Be Living Things'"

For a second Seth pretended not to be annoyed.

"And that which was alive arose up from that which was not alive. And life begat life unto the hundredth generation. The forms of the beasts on the Earth multiplied and spread out into all the lands."

The Zoo: The Beast, The Boy and The Zoo

"Oh shut up Sam! "

Ha! It had worked. A spoon flung in my general direction was easily ducked, as were various following missiles. Interesting that only a few years back when we were, say - seven, Seth's skills in play fighting would have so outmatched mine that he certainly would have scored a hit. But I seemed, almost without thinking, to do much better these days in dodging his projectiles and fending off occasional attempted blows.

The wooden spoon clattered down the wall harmlessly. I missed not a single beat in my declamation. I had the floor. I continued.

"But there was dissension amongst the nameless kinds of creature and a great tumult reigned across the Earth." I tried to make my voice rise and fall in what seemed to me to be an appropriately rhythmic effect.

On those rare and deadly occasions when these days I have to deal with some poor soul who still labours with the crude accent that Seth and I shared then, I reflect on how ridiculous I must have sounded. At that moment though and to myself at least I seemed very grand indeed.

"So the Stars said we shall create a Garden, flowing with good things. We shall call forward one animal and name him Man and he shall be the Namegiver. Man will rule as Lord over the Garden, and give names to all the other Beasts. And the Lord Namegiver shall say that the Behemoth shall dwell in this place; and that the Sparrow that shall dwell in this other place..."

In the corner Seth was muttering something, not quite audible, but surely very rude.

".... and that the Lamb and the Lion shall lie down with one another. Man shall be the steward of all the beasts and the birds and the fish and the fowl and all things under the sun that crawl and creep and fly and swim. To each the Namegiver shall assign its role and its place. "

Finally I snapped the book shut. My eyes gleamed along with pronouncing those sententious and rather ridiculous last words: *"And peace shall dwell in the lands."*

The Zoo: The Beast, The Boy and The Zoo

"How about some peace and quiet right here?" Seth growled in response.

Even though I had in part been only been trying to irritate Seth, I must confess I had genuinely got a little carried away by this passage. With those last words, I looked straight at Lilith and demanded of her. "'Is that right? Is it all true?"

Her own eyes had been elsewhere, but now were summoned back to mine. She left aside whatever she had been reading herself, waiting a second or so before replying. "Well, some think so, but..."

Aha! the famous Lilith *'but'!* Or her classic *'on the other hand'.*

Even on a few short days acquaintance I had begun to note how often Lilith would hedge her bets. Rarely would she definitively favour one thing over another; her answer to any question always carefully laying out two sides to everything.

She continued: "Some others think that is just a foolish story. Different people have different versions of how things started. Others again think that stories like this are really good symbols to understand it all, and that you do not need to take it all literally."

At that period neither Seth nor I had any concept of what either 'a symbol' was, nor what 'literally' might mean? I could see though that was an unhelpful quibble.

I thought I might needle her in pursuing the point. "So is 'the Garden' in this book the Zoo? And is Father the Namegiver?"

This was intoxicating stuff. I was clearly putting this annoyingly opaque old woman under some pressure. I leaned eagerly into whatever I might force from her.

But Lilith just smiled back benevolently at me. "The stories in that book are long, long ago. Now come on." She nodded to the adjacent bay window where oppressive rain had, as we had been reading and talking, gradually been replaced by a bright blue sky. "You have been cooped up long enough in here." She stood up abruptly, seized our hands one on either side. "It is high time for you both to get to know the Zoo a little." How skilfully she had blunted my questions by redirecting us to what she knew was by far my greatest interest.

So the three of us walked down the metal stairs from the main door of Edensor.

We walked through the small, cultivated front garden. We unlatched the little green gate.

And on a cold, but brilliantly bright winter's morning as the clock was bolding striking ten, we walked out into our Zoo for the very first time.

***

Chapter Sixteen: A Step into Technicolour

All of you following our little story here will surely be citizens of the big wide world. You will be used to having many different, varied and highly coloured experiences at your disposal. They will be all stored neatly up there and accessible in your memory.

I have to ask then that you strain your imaginative sinews. I need you to imagine how this was for us; for two half-wild brats who, in our washed out Vague Lands home, had, in our lives up to then, still seen very little of... Well, of anything much at all.

Two grayscale waifs, two blank sheets, two unsuspecting little sponges unwittingly plunged into the most vivid thing on earth.

And that very brilliance, that same resplendent vigour is of course is why, I might well guess, most of you deep down inside harbour an intense early remembrance of your own adults taking you that very first time on 'a trip to the zoo'. A trip to the Zoo! Can you still conjure up the almost unbearable excitement? The way thereafter you would thrill to just the word 'zoo' itself?

Such a good word, isn't it? There isn't any other much like it or with which it might be confused. No, that short, sharp little noun finding a rhyme with almost every other letter in the alphabet: 'zoo' is out there by itself. Not only is the sound electrifying, but also the way those three stirring little letters stand out before you on the white page.

What is there after all that is more exotic, more simply overflowing with the weird and wonderful than a zoo? An explosion of the extraordinary and exceptional injected into the midst of the very

The Zoo: The Beast, The Boy and The Zoo

ordinary and day to day. And *the* Zoo. *Our* Zoo burned so much more brightly than all those other zoos you may have visited yourself.

So, decanted unceremoniously into this wonderland, the impact for me was a flux of sheer delight and astonishment. The snippets from Lilith, the sneak preview in the dusk drive to Edensor, the details on the brightly coloured map on Father's wall, all these tasters were as nothing at all compared to the reality of our walking out in the bright sunshine that first day.

Only now did it sink in that this is where Seth and I had begun our lives. This panorama unfolding around me, this was what I had been born to. Drinking in this landscape overflowing with life and the living, I knew now I was home.

Our route from Edensor through the Zoo that first day with Lilith was more or less south. We walked past wonderfully busy, lightly scampering creatures called Meerkats. After too short a moment we were dragged away from the slippery, svelte, contours of the Short Clawed Otters. What would it be like to actually *be* one of these sublime little animals splashing and dashing away in their pool? But Lilith pulled us ever onward.

Then we were mounting the bridge that divides the home of the Flamingos from that of the public's favourite zoo bird – the Penguins.

From the corner of my eye, I could see Seth's gaze was not in the least enlivened by these wonders. Nothing in his own features to match my giddy elation at each non-human rendezvous. As far as my brother was concerned these would be no more than things that could infect him, make him sneeze, sting him, bite him, or claw him. For Seth, you see, animals basically divided into those who were disgusting, those who were terrifying and those you could eat.

No, it was something else entirely that swung his head from side to side. Another kind of interest caused him to lag curiously behind us. He might even, had Lilith's firm grasp not pulled us inexorably onwards, have begun to wander off on his own. It was not the animals that entranced Seth: it was the people.

And, as I would one day come to understand, a growing fascination for the thoughts buzzing away inside people's heads.

On that December day the Zoo was packed with visitor. Typically these, as we grew to know, would originate from towns, cities, villages and countryside, hundreds of miles apart in every possible direction. And the way people dressed and spoke and even moved betrayed these very varied origins. Not at all like the dull, sullen, undifferentiated human handfuls seen in the Vague Lands. Young; old; quiet; loud. Strange ways of dressing; different coloured skins. Clothing in many different shapes and materials and shades. People smiling; people talking; people discussing; people *frequently* arguing.

Mostly in families.

Oh and above all there were children.

Children everywhere, children running, laughing, crying, and squealing with delight. Mothers and fathers smiling at and happily playing with their offspring. I may have been chiefly pre-occupied with the new furred and feathered phenomenon found around every corner, but this new variety of our own species, this sheer human warmth struck home for me as well as Seth.

Again the same gnawing question arose within each of us.

Was *this* then how were parents supposed to be? Was this what one might expect from a mother or a father? Very different answers would gradually lead us to very different places

Now Lilith was leading us into the Butterfly House. I am told it is still there today in the exact same form? A soaring glass house packed with magnificent planting.

As we walked in my senses were overwhelmed by so many different fragrances combined in a single splash. I loved being at once engulfed by all these new odours, by all the plants and their blooms. But most of all I was thrilled by the host of radiant 'flying flowers', the Butterflies themselves.

Seth, clearly dismayed by this fresh hell of flapping pests, entered only slowly and grudgingly.

"Air and earth," said Lilith. "They start off crawling on the ground and over plants as Caterpillars. They become wrapped in their magic cocoons. And then, just briefly, they become creatures of our skies. All things in nature change eventually."

One especially large Butterfly shimmering in bright blue tones hovered directly ahead of me. I recognised the species from one of the books I had plunged into on these last few rainy days. Unchecked excitement once again squealed embarrassingly out of me. "That's a Morpho!"

I looked over my shoulder for Seth. He had hardly advanced beyond the entrance. My new Butterfly friend circled around me as if inviting me to play with it. It drew me on. I followed its darting deeper into the indoor rainforest. It came back and circled my head. It was like we were dancing together. Then it was off again ahead of all three of us, intent on guiding us through the maze of the glass house, drawing me into its jungle.

Perhaps we were not progressing fast enough for the liking of this wild thing. For now it returned yet again and gently landed on my arm. Finally Seth walked forward to join us, and for a moment to my surprise he stroked the Butterfly's velvety wings.

Then the silence was broken. My brother spoke in a tone I did not recognise. "Earth is better than air." He grabbed the Morpho. He laughed.

And he tore its wings off.

"Seth..? Seth!! What did you do that for! You pig. That poor little thing was harmless..."

The Zoo: The Beast, The Boy and The Zoo

He stood looking down at the dismembered pieces in his hands with a helpless and dazed expression. "I don't know." He shook his head in what seemed genuine puzzlement and reverting to his normal, dull Vague Lands tones. "I... I don't really know why I did it."

And I knew he was telling the truth.

The tall, strange, white haired woman who had all this while been happily leading two compliant children by the hand through this extravaganza, smiling and chatting serenely enough, stiffened. She took two steps back from both of us. Then Lilith carefully picked up the crumpled wings. Forcefully and meaningfully she shoved the Butterfly's cadaver deep down inside my brother's shirt pocket.

"There. You can carry that around now to remind you of what you did!"

I watched his face fall further, the twin thing inside me telling that Seth has just then felt an almost physical slap of pain. Much more interestingly, his *real* distress was not so much at the poor old Butterfly's fate in itself.

No, little Seth was utterly despondent about something else entirely - at letting Lilith down.

This was the moment, the earliest glimmer that, for first time in our lives, he and I were slowly parting company.

Once back in bed in the Vague Lands Seth and I had argued long and deep into the night whether it was better to wish that one day we might have a father and mother, or to shut such futile thoughts away. It had been he who said we should not to wish for things we would never get.

But, you know, I do not think he had not really been telling the truth.

We had together grown up knowing that there was only one other person in the entire universe whom you could *really* trust. One sole being whose opinion fundamentally counted and about whom, when it came down to it, you really gave a damn. It was Seth for me: it was me for Seth.

And that was fine. That was enough. That *should* have been plenty.

But as I watched Seth that same day, I knew that when he stared up wide eyed at Lilith, lonely little Seth was seeing the wonderful, lovely, magical lady who had come all the way to the Vague Lands with her Cheetahs to rescue him. The little boy saw someone to whom he could at long last reach up with arms outstretched in trust.

Me? Oh, I saw something completely different.

But then came that so stern rebuke from Lilith. And my brother's crestfallen features. A sudden denting of his absurd puppy dog love. A reversal which, I am afraid, I personally found quite delicious.

Behind Lilith's back, a brief but broad smirk suddenly crossed my face. It happened every bit in despite myself as Seth's murder of the Butterfly had been despite himself.

It only lasted for a split second.

It was still long enough for Seth to see.

***

The icy silence with which we three left the Butterfly house threated to hang over us for a long time. Yet, as we followed down the winding path, the sunlight, the screams of childish laughter, cacophony of animal noises and other warming notes within the Zoo's symphony all colluded in a gradual thaw. Once again Lilith began one by one to name the animals we encountered. She patiently explained how each fitted into a greater pattern. This thing was another's food. That animal served a purpose that helped others survive. This one cleaned up the mess that those left behind.

The Zoo: The Beast, The Boy and The Zoo

Now we were near to the southern extremity of the territory of the Zoo proper. Finally we turned a corner. Suddenly there before us, there were the Elephants.

What to say about Elephants?

What to say about our reaction? Well for me of course it was a straightforward surge of pure glee. And the contrite and disconsolate Seth? Up to this point, his morning had been a gauntlet of smelly, disgusting or alarming phenomena. On first sight, the Elephants I am sure they also stirred a kind of fear. Yes, definitely. I mean, the truth is you would need to be a little crazy not to take a step or two back at your first sight of these mighty giants. I certainly noted his nose creasing up a little for a second too at that so pungent smell.

But the slow change (far *too* slow), as regards the other living things with which we share the world, that was over many years to creep up on my brother; that gradual sloughing off of his cruel carapace, if I had to take a guess, I would say *this* was the moment where it began. There he stood, with a dead butterfly in his pocket, gormlessly open mouthed before the unlikely and magnificent titans that are the Zoo's Elephants.

After all these decades I am still find quite inexplicable those who stand utterly dismissive or askance as to the animal world. But even the most vulgar, sour and soul dead amongst that tribe tend to dully recognise that these prodigies at least clearly cannot be shrugged off as '...just some animals'.

Elephants are simply so unlike anything else: the great grey dome of a head; that spiralling trunk waving out in front of them; the deep mystic rumbling noises that that day vibrated through our entire bodies. And there they were ...playing! Splashing about in the enormous pool set out for them. A joyful mother and her two calves.

Yes, it was the Elephants. Those happy, living things. I am sure, now I think back on it; it was the Elephants that day that began the footdraggingly slow change in my brother. Yes, as sure as here I am sitting on this couch pouring out my memories together with another drink, I think you should put it down to the Elephants.

***

Chapter Seventeen: Someone with some answers at last

"So the heirs to the kingdom have returned?" Hugo, Master of Elephants looked Seth and me slowly up and down. Hugo was a well-built man of around fifty. He was balding and with a matter of fact grin on his face. He spoke in a deliberate fashion and down to earth accent that we came to know well. I confess, even now after so much that was to happen, to a continuing, if ambivalent respect for Hugo and Keepers of a similar ilk.

Lilith dutifully made introductions and after a few minutes conversation, left us in Hugo's hands. We had instructions to be back at Edensor by six pm sharp for supper.

He spent a little while proudly showing us around his fiefdom. The large outdoor paddock and indoors home to his herd of eight elephants. Four cows, three calves and the bull, alone at the moment in his musth pen, red eyed and furious.

Then he put his hands on his hips: "Well I suppose you two had better make yourselves useful then."

If we had any doubt as to what he meant by that, this vanished when he produced two large shovels and a wheelbarrow. He gestured over to the yard, where large piles of steaming dung lay strewn over a wide area.

I do not suppose looking at me now, you would guess that I began my zoo working life shovelling excrement. Actually I am rather proud that I did.

The Zoo: The Beast, The Boy and The Zoo

Working alongside Hugo, as our young backs became sorer and our limbs became heavier, we learnt a lot about the Zoo that first time. Especiallyabout how he felt about the visitors who came in every day.

I should explain that the keepers had a confusing and perhaps unfortunate habit of referring to some of the daily visitors as 'the Saints'.

At least that is how I heard the word in my mind when first encountered. It seemed a very strange thing to say. Many of the visitors were far from saintly. Later it sounded more like 'the Cents'. So perhaps was it some kind of reference to money then? Or maybe it was 'Scents'?! It was only after some considerable time that Seth and I came to understand the full background to the term and how through the keepers' gossip, it had gradually arisen.

We finally worked out what it was short for.

It was clear right from the start though that it was definitely a derogatory term. In some instances there was an outright sense of disdain on the part of those who worked with the animals towards the hordes of paying customers who poured into the Zoo day in, day out.

Only *some* of the time, mark you; and it tended to be directed only at the most extreme examples of visitor vulgarity.

But Hugo would have none of it.

"That is downright disrespectful, that is."

"I don't want to hear that word! You should never lump people together like that."

"So you *do* talk to the visitors a lot then, Hugo?"

He rubbed his face. "Well... yeah, you know... when I can... I talk to some of them, anyway." A wry and rather bashful grin now. We were not quite sure Hugo really did talk to his visitors that much. Perhaps he too despite himself had some reservations?

"I mean some of the others..." He meant his fellow keepers. "Well they do get grumbly when the visitors misbehave, or just don't understand what the animals really are, or what the Zoo really is. So they use that word. But you shouldn't tar everyone with the same brush. Talking to visitors is in the job description. And they serve their purpose, don't they? I mean the Zoo could not survive without them."

He wiped the sweat from his brow as the three of us worked side by side piling up bales of hay as high as we could.

"Yeah, they shouldn't call them that. It is not a nice thing to call anyone. But most of the keepers don't mean anything nasty by it. They are just different from us, that's all. And people like to grumble about other kinds of people you know. Anyone who is different. Just the way it is."

"And what about you Hugo? What do you think?"

"Well I do worry that for some of them, the outsiders - and not all by any means. The thing is they are not what the Zoo is about, you see. So many of them just don't 'get it'." He ran his hands over a balding pate. "They don't really *see* the animals. Or, don't see the 'real' animals. Don't see their true nature. And of course they have no idea what they are like at night after the visitors leave."

"What is the Zoo 'about' then? " Seth asked, his eyes brighter with curiosity than I would have expected.

Hugo stood up straight to stretch. Then sat down again on a hay bale, motioning us to stop working too and sit beside him.

"Well in my opinion, this is the place where we work it out, see? Where we all come together. Or at least that is what it should be. The Zoo is where humans and other animals start working out where we all fit in together. Working out what our shared story is."

"What do you mean - the story? What story?" Seth clearly misunderstanding what Hugo was saying.

"I don't mean a real, actual story. I mean the way we can and should all live together in the world. The Zoo is the place where that lot," he gestured at one particular gaudy, raucous family (definitely 'Saints') passing by outside the Elephant house. "Where they get the

The Zoo: The Beast, The Boy and The Zoo

privilege of being in the same space for a little while with all these wonderful creatures and have the chance, if they take it, to dive deep into their strangeness, to understand just how special, how alien, how dangerous and above all how fragile they all are."

"But of course, no, most of them just see 'funny looking animals'. They cannot but help dress them up in their minds as really being people in animal suits. For them a day at the Zoo is just some way to shut the kids up for a bit. A bit of fun. That is *not* what is should be, and *not* what it really is."

"What is then? What is the Zoo, Hugo?" It was my turn to probe eagerly.

Hugo did not reply immediately. Instead he sat there staring at me with a steady, seemingly meaningful gaze. It went on so long that Seth's eyes started to dart back and forth between our faces as if excluded from some secret.

Finally Hugo broke his study of my features and said slowly and carefully: "It is one of *the - most - important - experiences* in their short, silly lives.

"Oh, some of them may just get a glimmer of it all when they visit perhaps at the weekend. But as soon as they go back into their day to day world outside, their ordinary working lives, it all vanishes again. And that's just not right. It is downright unhealthy. We people need to know and understand and respect animals. And animals need to be satisfied with the way us people run the world. We need to 'do a deal'. When the way we humans live and the way the wild things are, when that all fits together, when these two things are in balance, well that's okay. But when it goes lopsided and unstable, then you can feel the world going wrong, you can sense things slipping away, becoming.... sick."

Off balance? Do a deal? I was intrigued. Hugo was putting my lifelong passion for animals and my feelings for how we should treat them into a kind of framework, far wider than any I have ever considered. I wanted to know more about these ideas. Then Seth elbowed in and took the conversation off in a different, but still interesting direction.

"What's this about the animals being different at night?" Hugo was clearly a good source of answers for so many questions.

"Ah...,"he scratched his head again. "Well, see, half the time most of the animals think like the keepers about the visitors, they just cannot be bothered with them. So they don't waste their true nature on the people in the day time. *'If they think we are just funny looking animals, cute furry versions of humans, then that is what we give them.'* "

"That's how they feel, you see. Only at night, do these animals let it drop and become their true selves."

Was that a wink with which he finished? Was he pulling our legs? Surely he could not be serious?

With Hugo of all people at the Zoo it was so hard to tell.

"Of course in the old days, long before you were born, even though they dropped back into their real selves at night, they stayed in their own areas. They might come truly alive, but there was no rebellion against your father and mother. There was no violence. Not like what those Chimps did to those poor Gorillas."

"Can some animals really speak, Hugo?" Some of the stranger things that our father had said or seem to imply had been cycling in my head. It seems wise to press our advantage whilst the going was good.

"Well yes sort of... Maybe. In a sense, and at the right time, but only for those... well..." And here once again he gave me a peculiarly intense look from which I knew Seth felt subtly excluded. "Those who know how to hear them."

"And our father spoke about *Something* getting into the Zoo, Hugo? Something bad..?"

The Zoo: The Beast, The Boy and The Zoo

Now he stood up abruptly. This was, it seemed, one question too many.

"It is getting dark and you were to get back for six o'clock?" We had clearly pushed our luck. "So you had best be off."

And so we did. We remembered quite clearly that Edensor was in the very centre of the Zoo and to the north of the Elephants. So all we had to do was simply retrace our steps, by way of the Butterfly house, the Penguins, the Flamingos, the Otters, the Meerkats and the other animal areas we had traversed on our outward path. We had been careful to remember the route. Then we would be back at the house. It would be easy.

It wasn't.

Was it just that the light was beginning to weaken? Or perhaps it was because we were tired physically and mentally?

The spire of the house was clearly visible. In addition to remembering our outward route that offered a further to navigate our way home. But all the pathways seem to have changed.

I swear that coming out we had not passed this island full of Macaque monkeys. Or this wading birds aviary. Or the little hill where the Coatis live.

And yet..?

We may have been pretty tired when we set out from the Elephants. But we were well and truly exhausted when a long time later, as the light was about to be lost entirely, we finally stumbled back into Edensor.

Clearly this place, this Zoo our new home, was not, even in its simple physical layout, something to be easily tamed.

And what by the way *did* 'Saint' or 'Cent' or 'Scent' mean? Why was it used for those visitors for whom the Zoo and its animals and the animal world as a whole seemed to be just some trivial, passing entertainment?

What did it abbreviate?
It was short for 'adolescent'.

***

Chapter Eighteen: A quarrel at the Tapir house

The next morning we were sent off to work with Maxim (slicked back hair and sly cigarettes) on the Parrots. The day after it was with Dee (oh, those oppressively cheerful cheekbones) and the small Monkeys. Then it was the Sea Lions where Tasso (immaculately coiffed but ever stinking of fish) was in charge.

And so it would go, each morning we would work in some part of the Zoo. Each afternoon though was time for lessons from Lillith. She seemed competent in every single little thing we were obliged to learn. My favourite subject was science. And zoology of course. The other subjects - of which for my taste there were frankly far too many - I tolerated well enough, but just with no particular enthusiasm.

Seth has ever only rarely upset the apple cart by surprising me. In the Vague Lands I had always led on eagerly stealing what few books we ever had. So I had not anticipated the way Seth's interest in learning suddenly grew and grew before my eyes.

First it was it was only geography that attracted him. Then anything to do with cities in particular. Then within that subject area in turn how people behaved in large groups. Finally the whole question of how people thought and had thought across history.

The brother, who had been previously chiefly interested in killing things, in trying to get his hands on Gogol's crossbows and in unsuccessfully telling me what to do, was slowly turning into something of a scholar.

A stuffy sort of scholar, but a scholar nonetheless.

The Zoo: The Beast, The Boy and The Zoo

To my utter contempt we were sometimes given work assignments that had nothing directly to do with the animals at all. On such days, dreaded by me, we might be obliged to work on the main entrance in the south east corner. There we would take the admission money off the visitors. Or show them where to park their cars.

Or we might be ordered to the animal supplies section and have to deal with great clunking deliveries of cabbages, bananas or fish.

On each and every occasion I was quite desperate to get back to my friends, the animals. I made no secret of my disdain for this...'Scent work'.

Seth would tease me about the difference between my features lit up with delight around the animals and the sour, sulky glare I turned on the visitors. Hugo may have resisted use of the 'Scent slur, but to me the word seemed to fit them perfectly.

Every seventh day was free, available for us to explore wherever and whatever we wished. As long, that was - and we were warned on this *over* and *over* again - as long as we did not either range into the Old Forest beyond the Zoo proper, or stay out at all after dark.

These first days blurred quickly into weeks, into months, and then longer. We thought we had worked hard at Gogol's, but the tough and varied physical tasks demanded by the care of so many stunning and complex creatures, some very big so both eating and excreting in large amounts, impacted fast to grow and tighten our muscles.

Our minds were given quite a workout too.

Looking after our array of charges, beasts, birds, insects, fish, required the building up of a vast treasury of knowledge. This in turn seemed to be having a seemingly almost physical effect on our brains themselves. It was perhaps to be expected that I should soak up all this lore. But slowly Seth too, I could see, was becoming something more than he had been.

The Zoo: The Beast, The Boy and The Zoo

We barely saw our father after that first day at all. An occasional pass on the stairs. Or we might hear him taking loudly to himself in his office. Lilith's early attempts at all four of us eating together were soon abandoned due to the inevitable awkwardness. That sudden glimmer of recognition and affection when we first met in the study never returned.

Father was actually gone quite a lot of the time anyway. Where precisely and exactly why was vague. Our questions there remained unanswered. So eventually we learned simply not to ask. But we would often glimpse him striding off at dusk beyond the Zoo itself towards the Old Forest.

The very two things specifically forbidden to us.

And all the while Lilith stood and watched us both. And watched us watching others.

***

Early one particular morning Seth, I and a number of the other zoo keepers were all at the Tapir house. I do love tapirs! But then I love them all. Did you know that if you tickle a Tapir on both of its flanks, it will lie down and go into a kind of ecstatic trance? My fool of a brother said that to him they looked a like an unappealing cross between a Horse and Pig.

A small striped calf had been born there in the last few days. The inexperienced and clumsy black and white giant that was its mother had trampled and kicked her new born baby. She wasn't suckling it either. The poor little creature forlornly cowered in one corner.

It was at least not actually badly injured as such. So to be on the safe side, Seth and I had been instructed take it away and bottle feed it overnight.

Well actually I did all that. And with great gusto. All Seth did was to fend off the mother with a broom, all the time cursing it for a stupid animal. I carefully gathered up the calf in my arms.

The Zoo: The Beast, The Boy and The Zoo

Hand rearing any baby animal takes up lots of time. And if you do it for too long, it can risk forgetting what it is. It comes to think itself as a human. Difficult if not impossible then to get it back with its own type. So the aim is always to reunite them with their own type as early as you can.

In the early morning, as gingerly as possible, I popped the little fellow back. We both stood back, as in inconspicuous as possible.

The mother just continued to ignore her offspring, greedily munching on her mixture of browse, apples and bananas.

This calf looked to have no better fortune than Seth and I with parental care and affection.

Several of the old hand keepers including Hugo had now gathered at the Tapir house to discuss what to do next... Constanta, the Zoo Vet was there too.

You might be forgiven for thinking that as youngsters and still relative newcomers, and even considering we were the Director's children, we two would be drowned out by all of these other older, wiser and louder voices.

Well, that I am afraid was not something I was about to let happen. I had plenty to say and I said it. Seth, poor lamb, he tried to make his words heard too. He had after all a special motivation on that day and in that particular company. But I will tell you about that in a minute.

It is curious thing, don't you find, the way one person's voice seems to naturally command respect and attention, and another's none at all? Can you guess how that worked out respectively for Seth and me?

Ah-ha, but now I get to tell you about Constanta! Constanta, the vet. Or more accurately to tell you about Constanta and Seth.

I think I am really going to enjoy this bit. I would be interested to see how Seth himself might have told this part of the story. My guess is squirming with embarrassment.

The Zoo: The Beast, The Boy and The Zoo

My brother had already fallen'for someone of from that very first moment when Lilith's hood felt open.

More fool him.

But that was only in a specific and rather rarefied way. Now we are talking about something quite different. We are dealing here with good old lust. The first spark of that in my twin was in the general direction of the thirty year old figure of Constanta, the Zoo's veterinary surgeon.

With a mixture of amusement, contempt and something else, I watched as Seth made such fool of himself.

Was it despite or perhaps because of the age gap? Maybe it was her cool blue veterinary scrubs or the pristine white scientist's coat. Perhaps it was those rather severe looking glasses. Or her overall professional and no nonsense crispness, sprinkling a little extra allure.

Yes, I know all of the above of course amounts to the most ludicrous heap of clichés. But my silly little, hormone bubbling brother simply did not see it that way. Admittedly Constanta with that long black hair, green eyes, and those coltish contours, was by common assent of the chattering male - and some female keepers, a very desirable young woman.

Why, I might not, in the right circumstances, have been entirely immune to her charms myself. Had it not been for the fact that I could not stand the sight of the stuck up cow.

And of course she drew him on. Sometimes, just sometimes when their paths crossed, I saw her sneak Seth a special sidelong smile. Never smiled like that at me. And he would always beam back at her like a moonstruck idiot.

The gossip, which I did explicitly seek out, was that she had resisted all attachments to date. Perhaps the boss's son would be a sufficiently appealing career prospect to change that.

The Zoo: The Beast, The Boy and The Zoo

There was tension as well between the official zoo vet and many of the zoo keepers. Constanta, you see, was a 'pro – fess – ion - al'.

Over the years I have often mused on that over used word. Is 'being professional', I might ask, quite the same thing as being actually any good at your job? It certainly does not always seem to be the same as being a decent person.

At any rate she was keen that everyone knew that she was a scientist. You might assume that all those who become vets do so because they like animals. Because they want to help them when they become ill? Quite a few of them probably do. But in the case of the lovely Constanta, I was not so sure. Sometimes she seemed more interested in the cure or in the treatment than in the patient. I always suspected that what Constanta could learn from a case, or how she could show off what she knew, or how this particular matter could somehow advance her professional status or career, those things seemed more important than the welfare of the creature she was treating? A dispassionate detachment that didn't make the slightest difference to Seth's passionate attachment.

Most of the keepers, on the other hand, just straight out loved their animals. Just so with me. They could be quite desperate to make them better. If that was not possible, they looked to remove their pain. The 'greater good' or the overall advancement of science was quite meaningless to them, and to me.

Quite a lot of different and interesting tensions then to be playing out that morning all around the fate of this tiny and otherwise insignificant looking stripy being.

Constanta was intent on the potential to study at very close quarters the behavioural and physical development of a young specimen of an unusual species. I on other hand, I confess, was smitten by continuing to have a baby tapir to look after. She turned up her nose at that suggestion as selfish, childish and of course... 'unprofessional'.

The Zoo: The Beast, The Boy and The Zoo

But there was Heinz in the mix here too. Heinz was the head keeper in charge of the Tapirs, Rhinos, Okapis and a number of the other large grazing animals. Heinz raised himself to his full six foot two height and wagged his finger towards the crux of the matter. "That mother will accept her calf, *if* ... *If* we just give it enough time."

His posture and tone were laden with forty-five years of practical husbandry experience. "We only need to show a little patience and..."

"No." Constanta cut across him, her tone and body language carefully sculpted to convey a superior level of professional authority and competence. "She is not giving out any behavioural maternal signals at all, and even her lactation is not as it should be. I am going to take the calf into the laboratory for veterinary observation."

Heinz moved directly in front of his dependents. "You're *not*, you know!" Then one slow step towards Constanta with the merest, yet real hint of menace.

Voices began to be raised, and went higher and higher. I was about to join in and make my own feelings loudly known when the door to the Tapir House creaked open.

Some kind of scarecrow thing shambled in. An exhausted, bedraggled, dripping skeleton of a figure.

It was our father.

Apparently returning from one of his night time 'hunts' into the outer wood, seeking god's knows what or god knows whom. The distinguished Professor Faraday, Director and Chief Executive of our entire organisation, the largest of its kind in the land, stood before us with a baffled and almost frightened expression. As if a stray and hungry cat might have been drawn to a lighted building, attracted by random sounds of life.

Was our father here in some dilute and unfocused sense of vague directorial responsibility?

The Zoo: The Beast, The Boy and The Zoo

The squabbling voices all shut up at once. Respectfully standing back in expectant silence. Someone to take charge and settle the dispute then? One by one he stared blankly around at each of us, not especially lingering on either of his children. Then strode over at the Tapirs, saying nothing all this time.

"So..." swivelling uncertainly back to the assembled group, and raising his palms upward in a pointless fashion, our father seemed to be groping for something vaguely purposeful, something suitably authoritative to say. "So... err... How, how are things going on this section?"

Some meaningless and embarrassed murmurs in response. Nobody on any side of the dispute had any motivation whatsoever to draw our father into the row over the baby Tapir.

He was still reaching to fill in the silence. Pushed by some hazy need to explain himself. "I, erm... I was out.... over there..." Pointing vaguely towards the Old Forest. He shook his head, as if his thread had been lost again. Then, with some returning vigour, speaking quickly and excitedly: "Need to sort it all out, you see. We need to get things back in order. Keep us all together. The whole Zoo..." A gap of some seconds. Then he stumbled on.

"Well, good, good... Carry on."

Nobody said anything as he left. The boss's children were after all right there before everyone. But the quickly exchanged glances spoke loudly and clearly enough. I saw Constanta, ever the politician, scanning faces so as to usefully pick up the reactions of others; Seth gave her one of their special shared smiles.

She did not smile back.

I am afraid the baby Tapir died three days later. The Zoo's chief vet got it to herself after all. To dissect at her leisure.

The Zoo: The Beast, The Boy and The Zoo

None of which of course made the slightest difference to Seth's infatuation. You see, the problem in that area with my brother is that he has always been attracted to....

...Absolute bitches.

***

The Zoo: The Beast, The Boy and The Zoo

ϚϚϚ

Excerpt from 'Man and Animal in the Zoo',
Dr Heini Heddiger, Director of Basel and Zurich Zoos 1944

When passing the baboons one day with one of the vets he advised me to get rid of all the animals with the "extreme prolapse"; he was referring in fact to a completely normal phase in the sexual cycle of female baboons, which can of course to the uninitiated give the impression of being pathological. Other vets wanted to know whether the elks were ruminants or whether otters hibernated. (The elk is of course a ruminant like all deer; the otter is a mustelid and like all other members of this family it does not hibernate.) If the advice of a veterinary surgeon had been followed a sick Capybara (*Hydrochoerus capybara*) – known in German as a "water pig" – would have been kept cool corresponding with the treatment for domestic pigs. The capybara, however, is a tropical rodent, for which the recommended cool conditions would have meant certain death. (The German name "water pig" for the largest of all rodents is of course very unfortunate and in the circumstances misleading.) On one occasion I was told by a veterinarian that the hibernation of marmots is caused by a parasitic worm, which of course is certainly not the case.

Mensch und Tier im Zoo, Albert Muller Verlag, Zurich

ϚϚϚ

Part Three: Seth's Telling of the Tale

The Zoo: The Beast, The Boy and The Zoo

Chapter Nineteen: The Map of the Zoo

It lies with me one again then to retrace much of the next seven years. The seven years before everything came crashing down around Sam and me; the seven years in which we grew up at the Zoo; the seven years in which we became strangers.

The details are all rather jumbled up in my memory, but I will try to draw out the important strands one by one.

First you must have some better, fuller sense of this strange place we now called home. In the first few weeks we explored it widely. We fooled ourselves that we were actually getting our bearings, a misconception that now seems almost surreal.

Sam's face was shining in almost perpetual delight at this living playground unfolding around her. Every day we would be confronted by weird new animals one after the other such as we had not formerly even imagined to exist: anteaters, mongooses, hippopotami, musk ox, seahorses, conger eels, chevrotains, birds of paradise, oscellated turkeys. In response, my skinny, somewhat withdrawn, slightly younger twin, this deeply loved sibling, for whom I have always in so many different ways been the protective shield, now bloomed in bold delight and in sturdy confidence before my eyes.

Yes, I was so pleased to see my sister no longer dependent on me.

Despite my early disdain for animal kind, I could not help but be drawn in here too. At least a little. But every exoticism presented by the

The Zoo: The Beast, The Boy and The Zoo

zoo collection and the very variety of its visitors made me think that, if the Zoo were effectively a metropolis of animals, what might a city teaming instead with my fellow humans feel like? At night in my dreams, I walked with relish, not amongst fabulous beasts, but through the imagined streets of wonderful cities, all as yet unknown to me, all spread like jewels across the earth.

In our shared daytimes though the sheer brilliance of this contradictory place and the many puzzles it laid at our feet threatened to frustrate and even overwhelm. In the Vague Lands, we had of necessity become skilled at quietly excavating the secrets of others. So here, whilst on the surface compliant children meekly and gratefully playing along and accepting all on offer, at a deeper level we determinedly sharpened our tools. We got to work to understand that which was hidden from us.

Our first order of business was to understand the Zoo as an actual physical place. Before we finish here I will make sure you have a full map in your mind, but let me now paint you a picture in words.

First of all this place is big. You may consider you have visited very large zoological collections yourself, but let me assure you, they would seem as piddling pet's corners compared to the vastness of *The Zoo*. All the facts and figures, once unwillingly imbibed from Sam's obsessive recital in those early days, are still firmly implanted in my head. Two hundred acres of enclosures, paddocks, fields, glass houses, herbaria, aviaries, apiaries, aquaria, gardens, vivaria, pheasantries, penguinaria, insectaria, herpetaria, serpentaria and ophidaria. Outdoor and indoor animal houses of every possible size, shape, description and species.

And everywhere water! Waterways and canals criss-crossed by bridges and walkways; ponds, pools, large lakes surrounding small islands, small waterholes in the middle of those islands.

Each one home to some extravagant creature or other.

The Zoo: The Beast, The Boy and The Zoo

There was however nothing anywhere at all in the Zoo that could really be described as 'a cage'. One way or another there was some way to persuade various animals that this was *their* area and not to go wandering off. Distinct homes for each species then, but no bars; each group content of its own to stay in their given accommodation.

At least, that is, during the daylight hours.

30,000 individual animals, comprised of 3,000 mammals, 2,500 birds, 500 reptiles, 1000 amphibians, 12,000 fish and 11,000 insects; all belonging to over 600 particular types or species of living creature.

My own eye was drawn to the human animals, the visitors and their astounding variety: the long, the short and the tall, the good, the bad and the ugly (some exceedingly so); all pouring in to our Zoo every day of the week; a huge haul of souls across a whole year.

What with its physical size, the number of animals, the broad range of species and the number of visitors, it was - as you would *surely* be informed within five minutes of a conversation with anyone proudly working there - by far the largest and best zoo in every sense in the whole country.

You must imagine the Zoo's overall shape (if, that is, you were somehow magically able to view it from above) as something like a squashed circle, not quite an egg. The outer perimeter is entirely swaddled by the Old Forest. It is some miles thick over there in that western part through which we had travelled that first day. It dwindles though to a thin fringe on all other sides where it separates the great encircling river from the Zoo proper.

The estate's topography is characterised by an underlay of volcanic rock periodically surging up through the soil in crags of savage, bare white rock. This affords caves and crannies and grottos of all sorts. Many of these had been commandeered for various animal accommodations. The Baboon hills or the Vulture aviaries are two

The Zoo: The Beast, The Boy and The Zoo

examples but the Bat cave a truly enormous underground natural gallery was by far the most impressive.

However, the Zoo's single most important feature is its great river the Helicon. This shows up 'in disguise' at the far north amongst the forested foothills found there. It tumbles into our lives in the form of a shimmering waterfall from a crag that is the highest vertical point in the whole estate. There, it is simply known as 'the Stream'. After this brief dramatic entrance the torrent flows out of the massive pool that has been eroded, carved out by its violent impact over millennia to quickly disappear again, this time underground.

On the map you will not find any acknowledgement that 'the Stream' is the very same water course known as the Helicon that later re-emerges at the centre of the Zoo. In the north it is indeed pretty much just a stream: but by the time it resurrects, not more than a hundred yards from where we are sitting right now, it is most definitely a river. From there it flows almost due east, severing the north east and south east quadrants of the Zoo. Then the Helicon enterprisingly spirals outwards clockwise and south. Picking up volume and strength all the time, it finally almost encircles the whole Zoo and the clinging areas of the Old Forest.

When you look at it as depicted up there on the map it looks almost like a giant encircling Serpent or Dragon, one savagely seeming to try to bite its own tale. One might imagine it constricting and crushing the Zoo within its coils. Then look at it another way, and it is embracing and protecting that which is within from that which lies outside?

On the west, east and south, the river constitutes the Zoo's official boundaries. The only parts of our domain that actually lie beyond its great loopings of water and include land on the far bank are in the north around the Stream. If you happened to be walking up there, you would

The Zoo: The Beast, The Boy and The Zoo

not necessarily know when you were officially in the Zoo and when you had wandered beyond its reach.

It was over the Helicon and by way of its underwater causeway that we had on that first day fled the white horde. The question of when you were within the Zoo's estate and when outside its protection would one more time prove of life and death importance.

The river appears as if fixated on winding closely around itself, devotedly 'hugging' the Zoo close to itself. But at that last possible moment there in the south east, it abruptly changes its mind; and, with an uncaring shrug of its shoulders, it flows off fast and free. It escapes away to the wider world in south.

Perhaps, like me, it was at first pulled in helplessly but finally reached for its freedom.

There is one small gap left from the river's encircling, almost the only place where you don't need a boat or a bridge to get into the Zoo. So that is where, so many years ago, they placed the magnificent baroque iron entrance gates. Ever since these have swallowed the eager crowds of 'Scents visiting our Zoo.

If you go a few further miles to the south beyond those main gates and into the countryside you will find 'Zooville'. Not of course the real or original name, given to this small purpose-built and self-contained village where most of the people who worked at the Zoo lived. But an obvious expression had simply grown and stuck through long, casual usage.

My sketch of the Zoo's geography has left out one important detail. This was that, as Sam and I had discovered that first time walking back from the Elephants, that very geography seemed, from time to time, and within certain broad parameters, to change.

The shortest distance between two points, old Gogol had said, is a straight line? And 'no nonsense' about it?

Not at the Zoo it wasn't.

The Zoo: The Beast, The Boy and The Zoo

Not always.

Puzzled that pathways and minor elements of the site's layout seemed to fluctuate almost wilfully, we went to Lilith. She muttered something we did not understand about the Zoo lying in a 'Dodgson Wrinkle'. Something about non-Euclidean geometry or some such thing. Otherwise she batted away our questions.

Once again we learned not to bother asking. After a surprisingly short time we got used to it anyway. It became second nature to often have to re-navigate well known routes. We always got where we needed to all the same. Often this was to our benefit and we ended up seeing and encountering all kinds of things we had not anticipated.

This particular place clearly refused to submit for very long to any very specific form imposed by the silly little humans crawling over its surface.

Perhaps the truth is that straight lines are overrated anyway.

***

Chapter Twenty: Edensor

From the outside our home was grand enough. A great old thing of stone and wood almost as high as the beech trees that hid it away from the rest of the Zoo. A cluster of castle like turrets graced a steeply pitched roof. The arched windows, some with coloured glass and many with broken panes, lent an almost church like feel to the structure.

A church? Well if so, an apostate's church where the congregation had long since abandoned their faith and vanished. Most of the windows were shuttered, some of the brick and plasterwork crumbling. Much of the fabric inside seemed to be almost rotting. The preponderance of rooms lying behind those heavy and tightly drawn curtains benefitted from only rare wafers of sunlight, their bulky contents disguised beneath dust sheets. They looked to have been that way for a very long time.

Only a fraction of the building was actually used: the great sweep of the double staircase which dominated the whole structure; this study here at the very top. Sam's and my bedrooms; Father's room on the floor beneath; the library and Lilith's room on the first floor; and one formerly rather grand space that looked to have been a large family living room at some point. That was kept up to scratch for Zoo management meetings. Finally there was the downstairs kitchen, where under Lilith's supervision we were fed by Maria who came in every day.

Beyond that, someone had decided it best to pretend that the rest of the house simply did not exist. The huge, forgotten dining room was padlocked, though we managed to slip in through the narrow gap between the doors. Sitting rooms, parlours, winding staircases, narrow corridors, all kinds of spaces often lined with shelf after shelf of cobweb strewn books, but otherwise unused, unloved, abandoned.

Those parts of the house still under employment were kept tidy and spotlessly clean. The denied areas, strewn with dust, dead insects and mouse droppings were evidently untouched by human hand for years, perhaps decades. Together these constituted three quarters of the area of the overall house.

Edensor had gardens of course. Well it *used* to have gardens. The small lawn in front of the house itself was neatly maintained. Beyond that, nature had reclaimed all the flower beds and shrubs. A once carefully designed network of paths was a sad echo of some former glory throttled with weeds and grass. Roots and branches of untamed bushes and trees would trip you if you did not carefully navigate your feet or else brutally break your way through. Still though, here and there one detected hints of someone's former care and attention, peeking through where the roses had gone wild; or walls and fences once lovingly maintained were now overwhelmed by ivy.

The abandoned outhouses (old storerooms, potting sheds, granaries, chicken coops, kennels, etc.) became our private places. This is where Sam and I, still stuck within engrained and irrestibly enjoyable habits of childhood stealth, made our secret lair. And made our secret plans.

Now that life has opened up experience to me, I realise that the food at Edensor was not of the highest standard. But for two ragamuffin children used only to the gruel of the Vague Lands, it was as nectar from paradise. No matter that, as we gradually realised, there was a complete lack of any animal product in all were served. There was plenty of it. That's all that mattered.

I am sure, if we had not had to work so damnably hard, we would have become fat. Indeed the rabid enthusiasm with which we wolfed down all that was set before us prompted Lilith to introduce us to a

The Zoo: The Beast, The Boy and The Zoo

brand new concept, that of table manners. No matter that dinner normally was just the three of us. And on the back of how to negotiate one's knives and forks there came further lessons in etiquette. How to stand. How to speak. Even how to dress. With some subtlety and almost without our noticing, Lilith was instilling a certain sense of status, of duty, of expectation.

The children of the Director of the Zoo were not allowed to be 'ordinary people'.

And certainly not 'Scents.

For work clothing around the Zoo though, she was not too fussed. She made for one of the locked rooms and opened up the first of a series of ancient looking wooden chests boxes banded with iron. From here she produced a variety of t-shorts, trousers, shorts. All too big for us really, but still quite serviceable.

I remember one particular blue t-shirt. I could not but help going back to sniff at it time after time; some faint, lingering, musky scent determinedly tugging there away at me.

Sam and I secretly returned to the chests and opened several more. One contained a series of truly strange clothes, like nothing we had ever seen, but all clearly for a woman. There were dresses and skirts that surely seemed too short to have ever been actually worn? They carried bizarre geometric patterns. Then there were zipper laden leather jackets in the kind of unnaturally bright colours we have only ever seen in fireflies and glow worms; one piece suits clearly designed to cover the body, arms and legs from neck to ankle and made from some kind of bizarre, shiny, rubbery stuff; and last of all a pair of blue boots seemingly made to fit all the way up to above the knee.

Who on earth could these all have belonged to?

The surprising answer lay in the framed photo at the very bottom of the same chest. It showed a bright red Jaguar X-Type, and a young woman proudly leaning on the bonnet.

The Zoo: The Beast, The Boy and The Zoo

Who, when, where and why? Our eager queries flowed immediately. No help forthcoming from Lilith of course. This was the woman keen to provide the answers to all our practical needs and absolutely none at all to the questions that really mattered.

These we would have to all deal with by ourselves and in some other way.

***

Chapter Twenty One: Getting the gossip

I have lived long enough now that I know that if you want to find out what is *really* happening within a given place of work, or at least what everyone thinks about what is happening, or what happened of some particular interest in the past, then you go the canteen.

You shut up. You listen. You listen to the gossip.

Plenty of gossip at the Zoo. Much of it was disapprovingly centred on Father.

When Sam and I first arrived everyone was pretty tight lipped. As time passed, and as they saw that their Director wanted to have even less to do with his children than he did with his workers, this reserve dissolved. Tongues loosened.

So many different questions bounded within us: about the animals at night; about them being able to talk (?!); about the conflict festering within the Zoo; and of course about our mother.

And one other gnawing question

Lilith and Father were both non-starters. So our faces shining with innocence, we worried relentlessly away at anyone else at all who would talk to us. Odd scraps of narrative were our rewards. As old fashioned photographic film might gradually develop into a recognisable picture, the dim outlines of the mystery of the Zoo began hesitatingly to surrender themselves.

The different stories on offer however did not always fit together at all well. In other circumstances I might have gone through these each one by one. I would guess that my less than patient visitor drawing all

The Zoo: The Beast, The Boy and The Zoo

these memories forth would be unhappy with that though. So I will put together a kind of composite version. I will warn though that there will be gaps and contradictions in what we told.

Perhaps the reader will though see nothing wrong with a little ambiguity in a story?

Right then. Let me see now. Everyone certainly agreed that many years back (but had it been twenty, thirty, a hundred, or a thousand?), the Zoo had unequivocally been a place of harmony. They also agreed that Father had run the place well then. Although some insisted that was really only because our mother had helped him so much. That she had always been the real brains, so to speak. Others said, no, no, he was a really good Director all by himself. It was just time and events that had changed him, made him a lesser man.

Everyone at least came together around the fact that now it was all very much for the worse. Perfectly entrancing on the surface for the visitors, but beneath that, the Zoo was degenerating into something else. And in everyone's memory the past, even though for each a very different past, was always so much better.

What had happened to our mother? The only absolutely consistent information was that one day she just wasn't there. As to the cause? Plenty of angles. Even more hints. Nothing definitive whatsoever. By some it was something that Father had done. That there had been a row. His fault? Her fault? Someone else said no falling out at all. She had just never been well and she got worse. There was no consensus as to in what way she might have been unwell.

Nobody actually said for certain that our mother was dead. The turning away of faces and the lowering of tones simply drew us in that general direction.

You are beginning to see what I mean about inconsistencies and incomplete fragments?

The Zoo: The Beast, The Boy and The Zoo

And then one particular character came up with an alternative scenario for it all. An especially nasty one. I will tell you about that quite separately in a couple of pages.

What did she actually look like, colour of hair and so forth? There at least we had some clarity. She was, like us, dark in both hair and complexion. In fact it was right there in the way they referred to her. Sometimes they would speak of *'the Director's wife'* or *'the Lady*. But on the tongues of others our mother was *'the Dark Lady'*.

Sam of course wanted to know if she had been attractive. Whatever the truth of that, nobody was likely to be blunt if she had not been. Insinuations seemed to range from a strikingly beautiful woman through to a quietly pretty one.

According to some we looked a lot like her. But half of those who made this claim insisted the resemblance was to Sam, much more than to me; and the other half declared the complete opposite! Given that we are twins, and even granted that by now Sam and I had begun for obvious reasons to look entirely distinguishable, that was puzzling. In the same context we noted as well that nobody ever volunteered that either of us took after Father in looks.

They certainly never dared suggest that we were more generally *like* Father.

When we first charily ventured onto that other burning subject, that of the animals being different and able to talk, we sometimes just got a guffaw, others a patronising smile. Someone then had after all been pulling our leg? But from a small handful of sources, and significantly these tended to be those keepers we most trusted, another story distilled itself. I cannot say that it was one which we really entirely understood nor which seemed remotely satisfactory. It was at least a beginning. It went something like this.

Yes, of course the animals all had their own languages, or at least each species certainly had their own way of communicating with their

The Zoo: The Beast, The Boy and The Zoo

own kind; and to some degree if needed to other types of animals too. But in the daytime they hid their true nature and this ability. Anything that could make them seem weak or weakened or vulnerable; or even just to stand out, to be 'too interesting', this was something the animals would hide.

Now there was a familiar enough idea for Sam and me; and one that we could understand only too well.

So they only will speak, or only *can* speak after dark. A wise attitude. And not just to anyone. You had apparently to have the gift. You had to be able to 'hear'.

This was a delicious morsel served up by the canteen talk. It stimulated but was nowhere near fully satisfying. There must surely be more here. We needed another source of information, something more nourishing.

I suggested that we resolve to try Lilith once more. At first Sam did not seem keen on that suggestion and simply looked away. Her eventual mumbled reply came only after a long gap: "Well if *you* want to Seth." She offered no more at all. As time went on, Sam seemed to have less and less to say about or to Lilith.

We knew of long experience how skilfully our guardian could parry most of our questions. So I planned our attack strategically. I was careful to beard her only when the three of us were in the middle of dinner, so we knew there could be no distractions. No excuses for her to simply avoid the subject. After all as Curator of all the animals in the Zoo if anyone knew about this surely she did.

Her response was a long drawn out sigh of irritation and a roll of the eyes. "Oh very well, I suppose we *must* talk about this. However I explain it, you won't really understand. It is far too early for you two to get in this deep. But you will just keep coming back, won't you!"

So she pushed her chair back from the table, paused and then, in that careful and considered wording and slightly patrician style which I had over time begun to know well (and frankly rather enjoyed), she slowly began. "First of all you have to know that people, we human animals, we are not really built to get into our heads that other animals *cannot* speak. We can never really stop ourselves thinking, deep down inside ourselves, not only that Dogs and Cats have ideas and thoughts and wishes and loves and hates just like we do (and the words to express all these things), but that even stones and trees and rivers and the moon and the sun and the stars do all those things as well. Somebody once called it 'the face in the clouds' syndrome."

"Stones have thoughts and souls?" Sam suddenly forsook the detached pose now generally adopted around Lilith. On subjects like this it was never hard to get Sam excited; and this in particular was certainly not a topic she could resist.

A second, longer even more pronounced sigh from Lilith signalled a deepening irritation. I suddenly felt a little embarrassed and even regretful that we had pushed her on this. If she had really wanted to avoid this conversation, there must be a good reason. Now she was being dragged in deeper and deeper; two silly, little children insisting importunately on going where they really should not.

Lilith was after all wise enough to know herself what knowledge was best for us and at what stage. I shuffled uncomfortably in my chair, whilst Sam was upright   All attention, she now led the offensive. Lilith was looking back at us both severely as if to think how ungrateful and childish we both were.

I was sure she was going to close the subject down. We had gone too far. I looked down at my feet. So it was to my surprise that she went on and answered Sam's earnest demand.

"Well perhaps they do. In a way. Some people have gone far into this and think they may. But the really important thing to remember is this: if that willow tree outside the window over there has a mind, what is certain is that it is a very *different* kind of mind. So different in fact that

The Zoo: The Beast, The Boy and The Zoo

we human beings might not see it for what it is nor recognise it nor think of it as a mind at all, and, even if there were interesting signs of something like its feeling and thinking, and yes of 'its language' if you like, we are such poor things, such blockheads, creatures so blind, we wouldn't appreciate it for what it is, or even notice it."

"And above all," she continued. "We definitely should not think of it as somehow a person 'dressed up in a tree suit'."

"So we shouldn't think that our Tigers are just people dressed up in Tiger costumes." Sam's eyes reflected inwardly. It was an utterance that may have started out as question to Lilith but ended as a confident affirmation back to herself.

"Exactly." Lilith's tone was if anything appreciative now. "On the one hand there are those who want to relegate other animals to just being objects, black boxes, things without any inner life at all. On the other, we are tempted to dress them up as humans and pour our own foolish clichés into their souls. The great thing is to understand and value animals as wonderfully *different* to us, fascinatingly alien, and not to take the boring, unimaginative route of seeing them as second class humans."

"But you can forget trying to get people to think that way." She flicked her hair back from her brow in resignation. "As I said, when we were first made, somehow something got stuck, jammed fast in our brains. So when we look not only at other animals but pretty much anything, we cannot help but see our own selves looking back."

My own confidence and comfort in feeling able to pursue matters was returning; and I realised she was not really answering the core question, was she? "So Lilith, *do* the animals really speak at night, or not? " I gambled that this did not come over as too impatient. "Or is it all in our heads?"

"Which *one* of those is it really?"

The Zoo: The Beast, The Boy and The Zoo

She restrained herself from returning to languorous sighs. But the way she straightened her comportment and clothing, eyes focused downwards before proceeding seemed equivalent.

"To understand that you need to look at it from our animals' point of view as well. If they need to tell us anything, to explain what they want and what they do not want. If, as your father and others think, we need in some sense to engage in some great negotiation with them, and they with us. If we need to arrive at a new 'covenant' for the whole Zoo. Well, they just *have* to speak, don't they? We have to *make* them speak. Otherwise there is no way forward, no discussion at all. No point. This whole story will have to stop right here."

"Throughout history, when push comes to shove, when they have something really important to say, animals - and nature as a whole - have always found a way to make their voice heard. And loudly. In fact sometimes when things become really bad, the means that nature chooses to speak out truth to humans is absolutely ear splitting."

"But what about all this as to needing to have the gift." Sam was now again pursuing the point. "If you don't have it, the animals won't talk to you. And if you do, they will?"

"It is not a gift. Not exactly. It is more an attitude. If you cannot see what the animals really are, or you don't honestly and really want to. And by the way it doesn't really matter whether it is night or in the day. If you are unable to get away from the attitude that they are 'just animals'; or if you think people and animals are fundamentally such completely different kinds of things that they belong in utterly separated universes, places mutually unreachable; if fundamentally you don't look *really* look at animals and when you do, are not transported by their sheer wonder, then again I am afraid you will never have a proper 'conversation' with a non-human."

She hesitated for a moment as if to find better words. "Listen, there are all kinds of made up stories with animals who can talk and those who cannot, some in strange and fantastic places. But actually here it is the other way around. On the one side, we have 'dumb humans' who don't really see animals for what they are, and so cannot talk to them, even after dark. So that includes most, but not absolutely all of our visitors. And on the other, there are other humans, 'hearers' who are able to truly and honestly enter the animals' world to hear and understand what they are saying."

So I was a dumb human then. While my sister was a hearer?

She stood up. That finally was it seemed enough. "Now, all three of us, we have work to do, don't we?" Shaking crumbs off her clothes. "Beyond that," looking specifically and almost in accusation at me. "As to whether as you say Seth our animals speaking at night is a real or all a made up thing in our minds, you will just have to decide for yourself."

Sam broke in again loudly as Lilith moved to leave the room, sticking a hand urgently into the air. "I know which was the very *first* animal to get a voice and to learn to speak. And it spoke because it needed to persuade a human being to do something!"

However taciturn she had become around Lilith, it seemed my twin would miss no opportunity to show off what she had devoured from Father's library.

Lilith turned back for a second towards her but said nothing.

"It was a *snake,*" pronounced Sam confidently.

"A serpent. It was a serpent."

"Wasn't it?"

***

Finally we must turn to that last question: the one I have been holding back on; the one that is obvious; the one that began with our father's ranting that first day here in this study. An item which Sam and I were so desperate to get to.

The Zoo: The Beast, The Boy and The Zoo

This 'Thing' that Father said had got into the Zoo; and which Lilith had point blank refused to discuss. And what was Its connection to the violent incidents bubbling up all across the Zoo? These events only ever at night, were sporadic but increasing in frequency; each immediately hushed up. The visitors had not the least inkling, seeing only the carefully manicured, daytime Zoo.

Answers to that came tumbling out from the keepers' chatter alright. Eventually. Gradually. An initial façade of reluctance crumbled soon. Nobody in the end, nobody but Lilith was silent on that subject. Everyone and their brother had some story. They even all shared a foolish little rhyme:

> *Whatever you fear most It may be;*
> *That indeed is what you shall see.*

But here I think I am going to stand my ground. On this one point alone I am going to ask my interviewer visitor our tale to indulge me a little.

Because whatever he may think, for at least this aspect of our tale in particular, I really do believe it will be better for the readers to relish the way it unfolded gradually for Sam and me. Let me now relate one at a time one each individual version of what we were told by our eager gossip mongers. About It.

About the True Beast.

***

Chapter Twenty Two: Testament of the Keepers

Witness I

Yes, I saw it once. A long time ago. It or Him. Sort of. In the distance. All at night. In a glade in the far west of the Old Forest.

I had been working too hard. And too late. I have a bad leg. See, here. It hurts a lot, so I have to rest quite a bit. I fell asleep. And when I awoke. There it was. This figure. A shape. It was singing. To our animals. Yes, singing. Loads of them in a trance. All in a circle. Loving it, they were!

An animal or man? Well. Not sure. Something in between. Maybe in between a man and an ape? I think it had little horns. But the face of a person. Oh and I remember the smell. The smell and the music. Something like music anyway. I felt like I needed to follow that music.

But my leg hurt again badly. I tried to stay awake. Really I did. But eventually I fell asleep again. Didn't want to, but... Such a deep sleep! And when I woke up seemed like ages later, damp in the morning dew and covered in slug slime and the like, It was gone. No sign it had ever been.

The smell? The smell was sweet. Smelling that smell was like... well, it was like if you could get really drunk or stoned, but in just a few seconds. The music was just wonderful.

Our animals loved Him.

No. I didn't think there was any sense of harm in It. It...He was just reminding the animals that they are ... after all animals. And that us people, we are animals too. It was really amazing. I will never forget it.

The Zoo: The Beast, The Boy and The Zoo

I would give anything to see the True Beast again.

And I wish I had gone away with It.

Witness II

Oh, He comes into to the East of Zoo regularly. You hear him coming from afar. But YOU MUSN'T ACTUALLY LOOK AT HIM! If you lay eyes on him as He passes, that's it. It's all over. You will die. Either that or something else bad will happen. Horns, like the Devil in people's books? No, no, not horns. The True Beast has antlers, not horns. He has these two really massive antlers on his head. He rides a great big black horse with red eyes. The smell that comes with Him is awful. It turns your stomach inside out. You puke worse than anything. He blows this thing like a trumpet. The sound shakes down right inside you. And it never leaves you. You never forget it. He works our animals up into a frenzy of hatred... Against us and against each other. It was Him that made those Chimps kill the Gorillas. Oh, the horror of it all. He hates us people. He will destroy the Zoo. He will kill us all. Kill us.

He is chaos.

Witness III

No, no, no. None of them understands. The True Beast isn't a person, nor an animal, at all. It is an 'It'. Not a He. Because It is an *idea*. A way of looking at things. An idea that jumps from person to person, and species to species. Once the Lady, the Director's wife was out the picture, It leaked slowly from the South into Zoo. Such a lovely woman, she was... I do miss her. She kept It at bay. She was so graceful and powerful. Before that It only really made sense, as an idea out there. It could only survive out there in the Old Forest. In the really wild places. But once she left, and things between us and our animals began to break down, It was free to spill over into the Zoo itself. It is a greedy thing. It knew there were minds in here to feed on. Fat minds. Weak minds.

Why do some of the others think it is a single being? I don't know. Perhaps they are confused. Perhaps it is easier to think of It that way. Or maybe some people are a bit mischievous and like to take the piss. Especially out of you two. His children. Lots of the animals and us keepers like to play games with you, you know.

Witness IV

Of course he is a man. He hangs out in the North of the Old Forest, Yes, I know he is called 'The True *Beast*' but that is just a code name, see? I spoke to him once. He is seven foot tall, long hair and green all over. So he can blend into the trees.

Nice bloke. We had a cigarette together.

Witness V

It's not a man. And it is certainly not 'just' an idea. Oh, It is definitely flesh and blood alright. In fact there has never been anything more flesh and blood. It is not A predator. It is THE predator.

This is the creature that has always haunted the wild woods since time began, since before people came to this land.

We people gradually recognised different animals. We separated out the Wolves from the Bears, the Lions from the Tigers, the Crocodiles from the Alligators, and the Dolphins from the Whales. We classified them all. Flattered ourselves that we understood how each one was different. We gave each one a name and assigned it a nature. We fettered them all down.

But not this one.

This is the one that got away. The one that escaped our knowing. The one that was never named. The beast that truly stayed a beast. The TRUE Beast. Now do you get it?!

The Zoo: The Beast, The Boy and The Zoo

The thing that hunts and devours because it is the predator before and beyond all others. What does it prey on? It preys on Man. And on those animals who submit to Man. It is the wild itself. It is the rebellion.

It is quite simply The Beast.

Witness VI

Your father had met with It. Yes, many times. That's where he goes, you know. That's why he goes into the Old Forest. Every time he wanders away, he is just trying to work it out. He wants to know. To know where do we go from here? The first story of the Zoo was so good, so compelling. It made perfect sense. A perfect picture. Before the True Beast became part of it all. Then it was as if a beautiful mirror suddenly had an ugly crack across it. The Director thinks that maybe if he can just talk to the True Beast and to the animal tribes who are so taken with It, in negotiating with them all, he can maybe agree a way to put it back together. Carry on the story somehow. Trying to wrest everything into a single tale that all can join in on.

That is what this whole damn thing is about.

Thing is, the mirror wasn't just cracked. It was shattered. And the True Beast doesn't *want* to go back to the old story. Or anything remotely like it. Your parents in charge of the Zoo. Everything in its place. People in charge of all the animals, and then animals happy that they should be. The Lion lying down with the Lamb!

No, the True Beast has always been around. All across human history in one form or another. That is why It knows everything, all the ideas and stories we have told ourselves as people. It isn't interested in the tale the Director wants to start telling all over again.

No, no. The True Beast wants a very *different* kind of story altogether.

Witness VII

The Zoo: The Beast, The Boy and The Zoo

The True Beast...?

Don't you know who He is? What He did? Who He did it *with*? Come off it. You two of all people. I know you are only kids still, but...

Cannot you guess? Why your old lady left? After all those years with that old fool, your father. And then It or maybe He entered the Zoo. That music. That smell. The most virile thing that ever walked this Earth.

Stuck here with a bunch of stinking animals, married to Mr Straight and Narrow and then laden down with two squalling brats... What was that like for that lovely young woman?

It was a lot like being buried alive, I can tell you.

And on other hand the True Beast looked like... Excitement. Temptation. Disobedience.

It looked like... Sin.

***

Chapter Twenty Three: Our Roads Diverge

It did not of course take all of those seven years for people to stop constantly referring to Sam and me as 'the twins'. That term identical (never correct anyway from a biological perspective) had dropped away long before. By seventeen we looked very different to one another. You might not even have judged us to be brother and sister. Only Lilith, in treating us with a scrupulous even-handedness, continued to consider us in some undefined sense as a single proposition.

I was pleased to have shot up in height, but less gratified that no real development of muscles accompanied this. I was as scrawny as a scarecrow, and frequently on the receiving end of that very term. As in so often with her sex, Sam's blossoming had been much a more satisfactory affair. At the same time though, there was an unexpected tightness within her sinews, an impressive purposefulness in her stride and an unsteadying directness in her gaze; none of that especially typical of a young woman of that age. If anyone were foolish enough to designate my sister as 'girlish', they would be quickly disabused.

I strongly suspect that Sam has in her telling already regaled you as to my infatuation with Constanta, our vet? If you want more on that from me here though, well... carry on wanting.

But I saw signs that Sam too was now attracting interest in the very same area. I didn't like this. I said so. But Sam, ever a combination of wilfulness and naivety, would do exactly whatever Sam chose to do. In a very straightforward manner she told me so.

The Zoo: The Beast, The Boy and The Zoo

All of this was part of a gradual and regretted distancing in general between us. So much that had formerly bound us together now lay back unravelled there in the past. Our co-conspiratorial need to at least survive, if not escape from the Vague Lands; our serving in that nothing of a place as each other's main source of stimulation; the back-to-back vigilance we instinctively adopted on being transplanted into this exotic new life, so suspicious of what might be being slowly woven around us; our determined quarrying of the Zoo's many secrets. All of these couplings, formerly so necessary, began to take on the distinct patina of another time.

A shared, wide eyed curiosity had certainly dominated our first days here. But the blaze of colour that was and to this hour remains the Zoo, topped off by the package of many beguiling mysteries that had been dropped so neatly into our laps, all of this began, as the months melted into years, to assume a certain familiarity. The conflicts, tensions, unresolved questions were slowly muted by the weight of days and of multiple distractions.

The compulsion to get to the base of matters did not of course actually diminish as such. No, not at all, but now, rather than something that demanded an immediate and urgent resolution, it was more an accepted part of the background to our lives.

The weird had alchemised into the everyday.

Our deep linking, that 'twin thing' was still there. If both of us wanted and needed to, Sam and I could feel each other's presence. But childhood and childish things were, one by one, being put away. We were no longer engaged on a united if squabbling front within one grand joint enterprise. Our innocent bindings had come lose. My sister and I were now firmly on separate tracks.

We no longer, in a single word, *exulted* in one another.

***

The Zoo: The Beast, The Boy and The Zoo

In those first few years my instinct to look out for Sam had remained strong. We had, when all said and done, been dropped right in the middle of some truly weird surroundings and some even weirder goings on. I was, in particular, concerned lest Sam manifest her special talent with animals. It seemed to me that the Zoo was the very last place to reveal anything so 'interesting'.

To the best of my knowledge, this had never taken place; but then, if there had ever been a time for that, it would surely have been when Lilith sent her cheetahs after us? Or when the white horde pursued us?

Perhaps I concluded, when you are as frightened as we had certainly been on those occasions, this kind of thing simply does not work. Or perhaps this was another thing left behind in childhood. Or then again perhaps another example of our ingrained training to not attract attention.

***

And Father...?

Well our use of that particular word became only very occasional, and even then, especially in Sam's case, it carried an ironic undertone.

Normally he was 'The Director'. Though there was irony enough there too.

Lilith's had made further futile attempts to find ways to bring the four of us together. Her efforts, I noted though, never concerned just the Director and we two. One might perhaps have thought it natural and to be expected that a father and his two children would have some family time alone. But no, Lilith took care that she too should always be present. All rather academic, as any such junctures that happened at all were excruciatingly embarrassing. They fell away fast in the first twelve months. Our only really close physical encounters with him thereafter were on the broad staircase within Edensor. Very occasionally we might also find ourselves passing in relative proximity in some highway or byway outside in the Zoo. Even those meetings seemed to always involve Sam and I going one way and he in the very opposite direction. I cannot recall a single instance when we were all travelling in the same direction.

He did not exactly ignore us completely. Not quite. Nothing as straightforward. At first, when absolutely obliged to pass us, there were mumbled attempts at some kind acknowledgement that, if not his very own children, we were at least other human beings. Then, even these tailed off to be replaced by a quick and silent flickering of the eyes in whichever direction left or right we were to be found.

Embarrassment? Fear? Regret? The triggering of some specific memory? I had no idea. Only the stars above knew what was happening within that the black box. And finally, as the years mounted and as he descended further into his wide eyed dishevelment, his disregard became total. As he either strode quickly or ambled distractedly, past his only family and the people with whom he continued to share a home, Professor William Faraday stared straight ahead. 'Professor *Faraway*'. Was the sniggering nickname that had grown up behind his back.

Father did not seem to see us at all.

No, what he was seeing was something very different indeed.

***

Chapter Twenty Four: A change in Father

All these seven years he had ignored us. All Father's energy relentlessly focused either inwards lost in his memories and forebodings; or very much outwards through his questing into the Old Forest and towards the more rebellious parts of the Zoo.

As Sam and I approached the threshold of adulthood in my respect little had changed. He continued to be largely oblivious of my existence. But as for my sister, behind our father's watery blue eyes, some old thing seemed to be slowly awakening.

It was late September after certain of his wilderness forays that the direction of his gaze and interest seemed substantially to move.

From every one of these expeditions he would usually come back quite exhausted, absolutely filthy, and normally so cast down that for days he would lock himself into his study. On this occasion, the first two expectations held well; but the third decidedly did not.

"So what have you two been up to, hey?" These words, pretty much the first addressed to us in years, jolted into our early morning minds as he suddenly strode up to where we sat in the kitchen breakfasting with Lilith. It was the day after his return. This jovial tone was a reasonable facsimile of that of an older, wiser person who is casually and benevolently interested in the activities and general wellbeing of his younger charges. Thrown into confusion, Sam, I and even the never off balance Lilith, could only stare at him dumbfounded.

Father's eyes shone with a preternatural light. His silver hair and beard gleamed with a new vitality. This was somebody with a tale to tell. A tale that he *needed* to tell and to share. To share with someone in particular. It was Sam whom he stopped as she made a hasty move to tidy away the dishes. It was Sam's shoulder which he grasped with his skinny hand.

After a pause Lilith spoke for us. "The twins have been working hard, sir. They have been on the Bush Dogs, the Sulawesi Macaques and today the Giant Tortoises. They are very accomplished nowadays in their husbandry skills".

A gap. Then. "Excellent, excellent... well perhaps, you would care to come and have a cup of tea in my study sometime later this morning, and we can, eh, compare notes, as it were?" This again was directed at Sam alone, conspicuously not to me at all. And again Lilith chose to be our spokesperson. The two of us exchanged baffled glances, entirely thrown by this sea change in our father. It was almost as if the bizarre old apparition now confronting us was someone raised from the dead.

"Seth and Sam will be out all morning on the Giant Tortoises, I am afraid, Director".

Father's face tightened. His eyes flickered once, and then twice, an expression swiftly swept away by a smile which did not quite reach his eyes. Then slowly.

"Very good, very good. Well.... perhaps I will see you all for dinner." And he strode off resuming that mumbling to which we had become so accustomed.

Little surprise and considerable relief that he wasn't there for dinner. But one afternoon three days later, passing on the stairs on our way to eat, he caught us again. "Aha. There you are now. Come on. We really must have a chat." He put his arm around Sam and pulled my sister towards his study.

The smell of lentil stew wafted deliciously towards me from the kitchen. I was tempted to just let Sam go with him to discuss whatever 'zoo stuff' he wanted to indulge in. But no, I would not give up my place at the family table just for the sake of a little soup. Neither specifically invited, nor explicitly excluded, I trailed along.

Since our very first day that room had retained its unique character. With its chaos of books and papers, bones and skulls, maps and notations, dust and disorder, parrots and mice, it was hard to resist the notion that this was Father's own head turned inside out. He motioned us to sit. He sat back in his old battered chair, stiffly crossed his legs, interlaced his fingers and bared his teeth in what was no doubt intended to be a smile. "So, you have been here quite a while now, haven't you? How long has it been? Over three years?"

"Nearly *seven* years." It was I who corrected this ludicrous mismeasurement. His attention vigilant on Sam, he ignored me.

"Now that you have got to know it, tell me, what do you make of it all? This place, that is, the Zoo?"

This was definitely a different man.

Despite the freakishness of the situation, Sam was as ever thawed by any invitation to talk about the Zoo and the animals. She began to gush. "It's wonderful! It is so big. There is just so much. Why you could be here a thousand years, and not get bored." Privately I disagreed. "Not see everything there is to see, not get to know all there is to know about all the animals."

"A thousand years?" Father's thoughts for a moment were not in this room. "Yes, that *would* be a long time, wouldn't it?" His eyes slanted sideways back to Sam. But what would *you* do with the Zoo if you were in charge? You will be one day, you know." All these remarks including those last words exclusively pinpointed on Sam.

"I would make things better for all the animals. Even bigger and better homes. More environmental enrichment. You know - things for them to do." Sam streamed forth eagerly.

The Zoo: The Beast, The Boy and The Zoo

"Yes, yes, that is all very well, but what do you think the Zoo is *for?* Is it for the day visitors? Or for us, for our family? Or for the animals? Or for something else entirely?"

The question threw us. Hugo had once said something on the matter, but we had not really taken it in nor understood. We had never thought of it like that. The Zoo was just there. We had never thought of it as being 'for' anything. In face of our silence he just carried on. "Do you know where I go when I go into the Old Forest? Do you know to whom I speak there? Of what we speak?" Still no reply from his rather gormless children. A gap. He stared ever more intently at Sam.

Then slowly. "Why don't you come with me next time, and find out?"

And once again, I might as well have not been in the room. Or on the planet. Rage ignited within me. I was the oldest. Sam may have been the one passionate about animals and with the special though still secret gift, but *I* was the one who had spent time and effort educating myself on the wider world. And I was the only one of we two who took any interest in the more prosaic aspects of operating this place. *My* Father ought to be talking to *me*. All that business about running the Zoo one day. Heirs to the Kingdom. Well that was me; I was the elder, not Sam. This was my heritage, being given away here.

"Yes!" my voice cracked uninvited into the room. I spoke up in such a way and in such a tone and with such a voice that I could not and would not be ignored. "Yes, I will come with you Father."

And our father turned and stared at me.

It was possibly the first time, since that day years back when on our arrival and he touched my shoulder, that he had looked at me properly

There were several fathers really, weren't there? There was the distracted mumbling old man who had no interest in either of his children. There was the recent development with all this feigned bonhomie. Now there was this other third one, the one beneath all those other layers, a man whose clearly sharp intelligence was suddenly spotlit on me.

At the time, carried away with my own indignant bravado, I gave it no thought whatsoever. Only later rerunning that scene over and over again in my mind's eye was I to consider what could in those next few seconds have been playing behind those startled, vivid eyes of his. That look was certainly one of surprise. But did it also carry some kind of recognition? Gratitude even. Or perhaps sudden calculation. All of these together?

I may have been imagining it, but it seemed as if I might be momentarily glimpsing the young man he once had been. A William Faraday of long ago before we were born. Before so much had gone wrong for him. Before so much weight had been loaded on his shoulders. The encrusted strata of worry, regret and strife for a moment scabbing off and falling away.

A knock at the door that did not wait for answer. Lilith striding in, taking things in with a single scan and ending in an accusatory glare at Father.

"Bill, what are you doing?! What have you being saying to these children?" My bridling at the unwonted word children was fleeting; there were deeper matters at play now. Despite the fact that she worked for Father and normally maintained a varnish of deference, hers was an outright demand, if not accusation; use of his first name only one of the signs. But who was this Tigress springing forth to protect? The father. Or his offspring. Or both.

It didn't really matter. She was too late. The old man relaxed further into that old armchair that seemed almost a part of him, folded his hands, and smiled a certain kind of smile.

The Zoo: The Beast, The Boy and The Zoo

"Nothing to be concerned about at all. Seth has simply agreed to come with me on my next expedition. It will be good for him, you know. We will be leaving together. At sundown."

I could not help letting a little smile flitter across my lips.

I couldn't help letting Sam see it either.

***

Chapter Twenty Five: Father and Son

As we strode away from Edensor that dusk, we left behind us both a sulking Sam and an extremely tight lipped Lilith. How quickly the tables had been turned on two people of such strong, if quite separate wills.

Objections and pleas of every possible size and shape had, during the remainder of what was said in the study, been comprehensively strewn in our path. From Sam's *'that it wasn't fair'* to Lilith's *'that it wasn't safe'* and *'that I was far too young'* and *'that I wasn't ready.'*

Ready for what?

At one point Sam and I were swept from the room to hear Father and Lilith arguing furiously within. We could not hear the actual words. Somehow from the shape of the sentences and sounds, I got the impression that it was not just any dangers for me that exercised Lilith. Something other and something deeper was at play. Did she dislike the idea of Father isolating me all to himself in the wilder parts of the Zoo, by some means drawing me into his own obsession?

As for me, I chose not to dig too deeply into why, despite his clear, prior focus on Sam, Father had assented that I would be the one who would accompany him. The sheer strength of my own personality alone might have won the day? Quite simply our father had finally seen which of his children; his first born was the natural leader.

A small quiet voice whispering that this seemed very implausible was even more quietly strangled somewhere in the dark.

The Zoo: The Beast, The Boy and The Zoo

In any event all complaints and whining were to no avail. The Director of the Zoo was unrelenting. And I, well, I was just rather pleased with myself.

Father had given detailed instructions as to our provisions. We had been properly kitted out. We were in for a long trek. To be out at least all night, if not longer. He made no explanation as to where we were going, nor exactly why. And, although my head was full of all the strange things we had been told about the Zoo at night, it really did not somehow seem a good idea to ask.

He led us through the failing autumn light with an eager, light hearted step of a type I had never noted in him before. We walked side by side, and as we passed specific animal enclosures or other aspects of the Zoo, he would start up on particular elements of expert animal husbandry or wider principles of zoo management. Little anecdotes and scraps of information accumulated across a lifetime came tumbling out of him. He smiled as he talked and we walked. The transformation from the dour faced, pre-occupied, quasi-mute character of old was complete.

As we made our way past the Babirusa Pigs, I asked him about the bizarre story that, if not broken off or – as at the Zoo - carefully shortened – their weirdly curved tusks would actually grow back into their heads and kill them. A myth, some of the Keepers had told me. Entirely true said Father.

When we came to Hornbill aviary, he recounted tales of breeding success and failure over the years, and the complexities of the male bird effectively sealing up the female in the nest while she incubates eggs and raises the chicks. Then the Arabian Gazelles took our attention, prompting discussion as to the respective speed of various hooved species over varying distances.

We followed as straight a line towards the east as the Zoo's bloody minded and ever changing topography would permit.

The Zoo: The Beast, The Boy and The Zoo

We must have been half way to the nine o'clock point on the circumference of the Zoo when he suddenly stopped and broke off his chatter. He stood, staring down at his feet. He looked sideways at me almost shyly. He spoke slowly and with a diffident deliberation.

"You know Seth; it is so good that you are both back with me these days..." He spoke as if again this had been a recent matter and not of seven years standing. Then down at his shoes again. Was that a blush? "I am sorry. I have not been very good to you both, have I? But I have not really been myself, you see. There has been so much to do. It has been so difficult trying to agree a way forward, one that they...," he gestured generally and a little derisively at the Zoo around us, "... that they would all agree on."

"But my last trip, it gave me real hope." He pumped the air. "New ideas! Fresh things were said that opened a real way forward.

"And on top of that it came to me that I have been facing this all *alone* for so many years. All by myself. But not now! No. Not any longer." He gave another triumphant little punch. "Look at the two us walking together, *working* together, father and son. Now I have my son beside me! And both my children back. I have a good feeling. We are after all going to sort this bloody thing out. And once and for all time!"

And in a fell swoop, my Father moved towards me, grabbed me and hugged me. For the merest sliver of a second I tensed and held back.

Then gratefully I surrendered and folded into my father's arms.

So this, this then at last, was perhaps what fathers were supposed to be like? And there was more. The same sensation that I had briefly felt when he had glancingly touched my shoulder in the study that first morning. The same slight giddiness, something hammering at the door, trying to flood back and at the same time to tug me forward. Something not as specific, nor as graspable as an actual memory, but actually much better and fuller and richer: an understanding that passed beyond mere words or specific, crude recollections.

The Zoo: The Beast, The Boy and The Zoo

And for a second. Only second. There was a woman's face. Long dark hair, skin of burnished gold, flashing eyes. And she was laughing. Laughing at something? No laughing *towards* me. Not laughter of mockery, but of kindness, of joy, of love. A kind of laughter that went one better than the broadest smile as to say...

"Whatever worries or burdens you may have right now; it *will* be alright in the end".

Then the image fluttered and was gone.

All of these thoughts and sensations were in and out of my head in mere seconds. Then both Father and I slowly regained our composure and stood back a little from one another.

My more practical curiosity returned.

"Where did you go Father? Who was it you spoke to?"

"Well, never mind that just for the time being, my boy. I promise we will talk about that soon, but..." A hesitation. Another sideways look. Not a bashful one this time though. Some other emotion. Hesitancy? Guilt? Almost mischief? "Have people explained it all to you..?"

"Explained what?"

"Well, the..." Now he was faltering again... "The facts of life."

The facts of life..?! I began to slightly panic at the surreal thought of such an embarrassing conversation, and one that at my stage of my life was wholly unneeded.

"Yes, the facts of life about the Zoo...?" I relaxed again. Ever so slightly.

Now it was time for me to speak hesitatingly. Choosing my words carefully. "Well Sam and I think that things used to be better at the Zoo in the Old Days... when you and Mother..." That last word felt very strange coming out of my mouth, and especially so before him.

He cut me off. "No, no, What do you know of *the war*?" A blank stare from me, so he continued. "There is a storm coming. Perhaps a period of carnage."

The Zoo: The Beast, The Boy and The Zoo

"When I was younger. When I was appointed by... when I was appointed to be the Director, everything fitted into place in the Zoo. None of this business of animals wandering around the Zoo at night, killing one another, refusing to take orders from people, to accept that we are in charge, and that the Zoo could and should function as one thing, one happy family, one single healthy being."

"Oh, of course I knew back then about the animals' deep nature. I used to go and talk to them all the time. But there was no real discontent, you see. No rebellion. Until *that* Thing arrived. Until it began its temptings. Started offering them new ideas. New notions and ways of seeing things which were totally unnecessary. Ideas that just made them unhappy. Started turning them all against us. And one by one the species began to topple like dominos."

"Plenty of animals still on our side of course. But they are the ones that have become easy with people. Many of them - not all - but many, they have lost their fierceness, become too tame; not the sort who will actually fight with true ferocity. They are not the kind who will risk their lives or be willing to take the lives of other animals. But our enemies *will*, you see?"

"More that that. Peverted by the gospel It has spread, this 'holy war' that It pushes forward, they will willingingly excruciate themselves to scour mankind away."

"It isn't just tame Cheetahs we need right now, you know."

He saw the recognition on my face.

"Yes, yes, I know about what happened when they tried to stop you getting here. They wanted to kill you, didn't they? It didn't want my family back here. Oh no, too much of a threat to Its plans."

"Most of the species have fallen into one camp or another now, almost all lined up. That is why It has become so dangerous. Yes there are some yet on neither side, but they will soon be forced to take a stance. No place for neutrals in what is to come. But after my last trip..."

The Zoo: The Beast, The Boy and The Zoo

His voice rose in tone again. "After our last negotiation, I became convinced we can avoid the conflagration. There *is* a way. The parties I lobbied told me that if only I step aside. If I myself just go away. And in going, take away with me all those old ideas of Man's suzerainty over the animal world and all the pain and bitterness – all our guilt, then there could be a fresh understanding, some newer, better contract between us humans and all the rest."

"So there would be some kind of new 'deal' or something for the Zoo?" I was picking up his own elation and enthusiasm.

"Yes, yes, that is it exactly! All those sins It accuses me of... accuses *us* of. All the stains as to how our kind - as the rebel animals allege and so much of it true – how we humans have mistreated other species, damaged the natural world, all of that would be washed away. The Zoo could start again as a clean, blank sheet."

"But you would have to go away forever, Father. You would be banished from the Zoo. You would never see it again. You would never see us, or the home you have always lived in?"

His blue eyes turned on me. If there were any sadness at this thought it was outweighed drastically by other considerations. "A small price to pay to keep all this from crumbling to dust. To allow sister and brother species to lie down side by side in peace. To allow my family to carry on without my burden. To break the link. That is how it was supposed to be, you know. That's how it was right at the very beginning of it all."

"But who would be in charge then."

"My heir."

"You mean me and Sam?"

"Yes."

"Can we both be in charge?" It blurted right out of me before I had thought it through.

The Zoo: The Beast, The Boy and The Zoo

Oh, yes, I know I had been cock-a-hoop at beating Sam to this trip. I had been so hurt by being ignored before that. And, as I said, right at the beginning, Sam and I can irritate the hell out of one another - sometimes. At one level we had always been in competition. On top of that we had grown apart these last years.

But when push comes to shove.... I love my twin.

"Could we work together?"

"No just one of you. You or Sam. Not both. That's not what was agreed. Not what the True Beast has told the animals. And the animals have told me."

"And the other one? What happens to the other one?"

"To the... the spare?"

He did not meet my eye. A drop of that old Father was back again. He turned on his feet. "Come on, quick. We should not lose time." He walked on quickly in the direction of wherever it was we were headed.

The last dim glow of the sun had already been inked out by the night. And now the moon had risen with one bright star beside it. I had no choice but to follow. But we no longer walked exactly side by side, and somehow my pace was not quite as fast as before.

***

Chapter Twenty Six: The Lord of the Jaguars

Before it unravels entirely into the Old Forest, the western extremity of the Zoo refuses, like so many other parts, to reliably adopt for very long any single stable form or nature. But at least *most* of the time it is rainforest.

You didn't know you can have rainforest in this country? Yes, you can. If you get enough rain and if you get enough forest. And when you get them both together sheltered by ravines, then that is a rainforest. All of these factors coincide in slivers of territory at the far west of the Zoo. Ancient oak, birch, ash, pine and hazel broken up by scattered boulders, crags, ravines and river gorges.

Since that first fateful visit I have, over the many decades since, enjoyed a lot of time in that enchanted place.

It has very different residents now. In those days though one particular glade leading to a deep ravine was home and haunt to the Zoo's Jaguars; and this, it transpired, was exactly where Father was making for.

In daylight that ravine is stunningly beautiful. A silver stream tumbling down through the rocks, the path becoming narrower and steeper as, by choosing your footholds so very carefully, you slowly succeed in ascending and penetrating into a hidden world. Dozens of different brilliantly coloured lichens and mosses and ferns in aquamarine, sulphur and vermillion, sheltering beneath the dripping tree canopy. Your steps, succeeding upwards, will one after another gift

The Zoo: The Beast, The Boy and The Zoo

you pools of all kinds, sizes and shapes to stop and delight in. Inexorably though you are drawn ever upward.

By moonlight its aspect was that night the nearest thing to another planet. If, that is, that other planet were also paradise. And if in turn that paradise were a wholly terrifying place to find yourself.

On we went infiltrating into this heart of light and darkness. Finally stumbling into the lair of the Zoo's Jaguars. Or 'a prowl' as a group of these magnificent big cats is properly known. Languorous, unblinking they spread out over the rocks that surrounded us on all three sides, separated from the intrusive arrivals only by a deep pool whose motionless surface reflected back a perfect moonlight mirror image.

If I have a favourite big cat, it is probably still the Cheetah; due I suppose to those early experiences with Dexter and Sinister and the debt and admiration so embedded. But, for a combination of grace and power and terror, you really cannot take it away from Jaguars.

As Father and I lumbered into the final clearing, it was as if we had suddenly found ourselves in the well of a courtroom and that these great, grave predators around us stood for the judge and jury. I counted six in all. Surely no other animal can, when sprawled at its ease, seem quite so contemptuous, so casually dismissive as a Jaguar? Three to our right distributed over ledges on different heights; three to our left. Each one seemed to point those frighteningly powerful twin paws of theirs directly at us. And each one focussed a pair of impassive eyes in our direction, great pools of topaz yellow boring deep down into us.

Father slid his pack off his shoulders. He straightened himself up, and spun around to survey his audience. Slowly he began to talk.

It was a rather weird way of speaking, as if he were attempting the formality of some bygone age; his tone carefully measured and respectful.

And stilted.

The Zoo: The Beast, The Boy and The Zoo

"Greetings O Jaguars. You all know me. I am the Director. Your forefathers swore allegiance to me, my family and my kind when the Zoo was formed. I have - as has been agreed - come to treat with you."

Silence.

"And as requested I have brought you my son." A vague gesture in my direction.

More silence

"Will you not say, Lord of the Jaguars that you know me?"

The large Jaguar on the lowest and most central level slightly to the right stirred itself eventually.

For the very first time ever I heard an animal speak. Well. Maybe. Perhaps I did. If you were to test me now on this after all these decades, as to whether I had actually observed that animal somehow to use the muscles of its mouth and the various cavities with its head to create variable resonances of air to reach my ears. Or whether in some other sense I 'only' heard those words in my head? I still could not honestly tell you which.

But it didn't matter.

The Jaguar Lord spoke and I heard.

So I was a 'hearer' after all. At least, perhaps I was in the right circumstances. Because I was with Father? Or was it because my first and automatic reaction to these beings had not been, as in so many other instances, to dismiss them as just more filthy, boring animals, but to see them rather as truly magnificent creatures born from some other exotic world?

"We do indeed know thee, O Man". The limpid eyes bored down without pity on my father.

"You are an Ape, amongst other Apes. One amongst many animals. Yet you are the one animal that has raised itself above all others. Tell me, what is it that *'distinguishes'* your tribe from all others, so that you come here to speak to us in this manner, to us the Prowl of

Jaguars. What it is, O Ape that makes you 'the Director' and above all the other animals in this domain? "

Not only then could I hear words as such from this creature. My perception even extended to detecting a certain deliberate tone of mockery and disdain.

My Father moved to reply, but the great feline spoke on as if to answer itself.

"Well, your tribe does indeed stand apart. See, you are so much weaker than the Gorillas. You cannot climb, nor swiftly travel the canopy as do the Orangs. Unlike the Chimpanzees you have lost your protective hair. So to keep warm you must wear the hide of our brothers whom you slaughter. I see, for you at least, also that your skin has grown pale and sickly with age. When I behold your weak form before me, I bethink me of the shape of an unborn, as yet unformed Ape child still in its mother's womb."

"I do indeed know you, Man.

"You. Are. A. Foetus."

"You are not *more* than other animals, O Man. You are *less*."

As he finished, the chief of the Jaguars growled, provoking a chorus from all the others. It was this ripple of sound that caused me to glance upwards and now see, for the first time, another, a seventh big cat on the stage high up before us. Set so much higher up than all the others. I had not spied it at first in the glare of the moonlight. It was not spotted as the others, and was, in the middle of the night, jet black. Watching it now, it seemed so much bigger than the others. At this distance its eyes were not yellow-gold as its fellows, but showed a deep and burning red.

"Now I will ask you in turn: do you know who *I* am, O Man?"

"Of course I know who you are!!! The contrived, diplomatic veneer and style of Father's vocabulary with which he had opened proceedings was shattered. And something of the muttering, distracted, senile irritability that I knew so well of these last years returned. "You and all these others are *my* Jaguars, who live in *my* Zoo and to whom *I* have come as Director of the Zoo to discuss matters in a civil way." He spluttered. "You knew perfectly well that I was coming. The Nile Crocodiles and that other entire cohort with whom I negotiated this encounter will certainly have sent you word."

His change of tone and use of such words were a grave tactical mistake. Several of the great cats jumped to their feet and began to sway backwards and forwards with a swishing of tails.

"No! You do *not* know me, you pathetic unformed embryo Ape! As in your very own human lore, the Incas, the Aztecs, the Mayas, I am he who kills with one blow. I and my kind are the rulers of the under earth. I am the darkness. As a Jaguar I see through the night and deep into the corruption and weakness in your heart."

"In this foolish and desperate supplication you think to bring one of these... these 'hero twins' with you." The cat's eyes flashed briefly towards me, then away again. "Your arrogance and your ignorance are matched only in their very boundlessness."

"I am the unleashing of true desire."

"I AM *NOT* 'YOUR JAGUAR'!

"But the treaty?" Father was rattled. This was not as expected. "Your species promised long ago to be part of the Zoo's dispensation. Are you going to now break your word?!"

Father half raised his fist in frustration.

He was at least wise enough to not quite shake it.

Every one of the Jaguars was up now on all fours, growling and prowling and leaping back and forth across the rocks that surrounded us. All, save the black one high up on its own slab of stone, so far above all the others. So different to the others, even to the Jaguar Lord who had been speaking all this time. It did not move an inch, but the stare in its

The Zoo: The Beast, The Boy and The Zoo

red eyes towards Father and towards me seemed to become ever more intense as the dialogue went on.

"Yes, we once foolishly submitted to those old stories. But then *It* came amongst us." A ripple ran through the prowl of Jaguars at this naming. "It awoke our true nature. It made us wild and free and proud again." A movement in the pool reflection below made me glance up again. The black Jaguar was moving at last, switching its tail slowly back and forth. Just three times. Then once again it became a statue.

"Listen, listen, I know there has been discontent all over the Zoo." Father was waving his hands now in placation. "I know we all need to come to a new understanding. There has been cruelty and wrong on all sides. So much arrogance from us humans. But surely that does not mean what so many are saying - full scale war across our community? The end, the breakup of the Zoo? That's why I came, why *we* came." Placing his hand on my shoulder. "When I spoke to the assembly of the Nile Crocodiles. They had in turn discussed it all with many, many animal tribes. If *only* I stand down. If I were to leave this place. And at the same time we all draw some new way of all living together, that horror can be avoided."

"That was the message I sought to bring to you."

"And who then would be... in charge?"   The Jaguar Lord tightened his muscles as if prepared to pounce.

"My heir. My child..."

"Sam."

It didn't sink in for a minute. Then, as I stared at him in shock, my heart pierced. But my father did not look back at me.

"No!" The Jaguar growled. "The True Beast has told us what must happen. There can be no human as Dictator of the Zoo, set above the animals, and..."

"...No, no not as 'Dictator'... just 'Director'. And by consent. And by the new rules we will all draw up together."

The Zoo: The Beast, The Boy and The Zoo

"No, no blood of yours can ever rule us again."

"But Sam is different. You *must* know that. Not like other humans Sam has 'the Gift'. Sam is the One. The One always expected. The One who will finally unite humans and other animals. You know this, dammit."

"No, your bloodline and indeed your very blood itself; yes now *that* is truly important for our future, William Faraday. But not in the way you speak of. Whatever the future holds for this place, we will need a blood price. Too much harm has been wrought by your family. The animals of the Zoo need a re-balancing, a requital with your kin for all the wrong you have done for so long. We need vengeance. It is not a ruler from your bloodline that we need."

It is a sacrifice."

Father moved like lightening to stand in front of me. His hands pushed and positioned me so I was wholly hidden and protected by his tall skinny body. A rumble of rage and defiance rose through his frame. He seemed suddenly - I swear it - to increase in height.

Now don't get me wrong. Those huge spotted predators strung all around us were some of the most alarming and most monstrous beings I have ever encountered in all my long experience with animal kind. But in those few seconds that followed, the most terrifying animal by far in that moonlit glade was my own father.

"Look on me, ye cats and be not afraid to know me truly." Father roared, his tenor and whole being had changed yet again. "No power, not on Earth nor amongst the Stars, will command the sacrifice of my first born!" The frail stooped wreck of a man I had known, or failed to know, for years was totally eclipsed. "You claim to see a hairless Ape. Yet you know that I am *truly* Man the Destroyer. Of all the creeping and growing things this world has ever brought forth, only my race alone has conquered all the other animals and plants and subjected them to our will. Only this single form of life has shaped the form of the very

The Zoo: The Beast, The Boy and The Zoo

Earth itself. You seek to threaten me! You *dare* to threaten my blood! I who have abased our very Mother, Gaia and flung her down before me for my will."

Energy crackled around him. All the Jaguars shrunk and shrivelled, no longer at all the haughty predators of seconds past. They tried to dissolve and disappear into rocks behind them. All save one, that onyx Panther on high. In a single motion it leaped twenty feet down from its high perch vaulting over the dividing pool to land within two feet of Father. A deep musky smell intoxicated the air. He growled closely into his face.

"What is the truth of all this? Yes, it is you who say it. You are indeed Man the Destroyer. I certainly do know you for what you are. And though I take this form for the moment, you know *me* for what and who I am. Don't you, William? Oh yes, we are of old acquaintance, you and I."

Their eyes were locked. Neither blinked for long seconds.

Then the earliest of birds sang and the first weak glimmering of returning light penetrated into the glade.

The Black Jaguar laughed and growled. It spoke again as it turned away.

"Go now then. There will be no revenging, no blood sacrifice this night to wash away the sins of Mankind. Not this night. Not yet. But neither will there be any new covenant amongst all the animals. Nor will any of your begotten ever rule the Zoo again, William. Your time is past, my old.'friend'. The war is nigh upon us and Man and all the cringing creatures that cleave to him will be swept away. This whole thing you cravingly cling to - this … 'Zoo'." He practically spat the word out. "It shall dissolve. It shall go back to its parts. All shall be wild and free again."

"As for all this debate as what is '*true* 'and what is not true within all our natures. That is *my* province. I above all other beings see through to truth."

"For I am not, after all, the True Beast?"

***

Chapter Twenty Seven: A Death in the Family

Regardless of the dramatic circumstances, there was, six months after our return that morning from the Jaguar pool, precious little surprise at the news of my father's death.

I think everyone had, if not in the particular way it occurred, seen his demise stealthily stalking him since that day. The decline had been both clear and precipitous. However troubled a man he may have been beforehand, in the aftermath every single thing about him was irrevocably rent asunder.

It had been a strange, cold old return trip we had had of it that freezing morning. Neither of us exchanging more than scant words as we slouched back towards Edensor.

Father, morose, angry, disappointed beyond measure.

As for me, the combustible pile of utterly contradictory thoughts and emotions was stockpiled very high indeed.

At the base there was straightforward despair that our mission had failed. But above it a sense of thrilled terror at having actually encountered the True Beast. This in turn was surmounted by fear of all that now threatened to engulf us. And stacked above all, was a sheer bitterness. My birth right as the oldest child had, right before my eyes, been ripped up by a single casual word. Despite all that Father had said to me on our outwards trip, it was Sam. Sam all along was 'the true one'.

If ever in those early years I came to the verge of truly hating my sister that was the moment.

The Zoo: The Beast, The Boy and The Zoo

And yet..? Offsetting all these minuses, just a little at least, was the revelation that I was after all a hearer. I *had* experienced animal kind in that special way - that gifted way. Sam did not have it all on her side.

Finally the last thought crowned right there at the very top of the bonfire: had I really and truly come near to having been taken as a sacrifice by those arrogant feline devils? My momentary triumph in his study, triggered by Father's sudden and unexpected willingness to accept me rather than Sam for his companion, was in recollection now bitterly curdled.

Could it be so? Was it conceivable that the man walking beside me was actually so cold blooded, so singularly orientated on his damnable obsession, that he could have been compliant in tricking me, his firstborn child into becoming some kind of mortal forfeit within the Zoo's bloody power play?

And yet... No, no...That made no sense either, did it? If that had been the case, why then would he have proven so magnificent in my defence? For those few seconds my Father, the Destroyer had appeared as an almost god like figure who had terrified the hell out of all those two hundred pound predators.

Terrified the hell out of me as well.

So light the blue touch paper, stand well back and make what the hell you can of it all.

I sneaked a quick glance up at him. You could peel away the rings of this onion as long as you liked and still be none the wiser. Not that there would be much time left to do that.

"So the True Beast is actually one of them? It is a Jaguar, then...?" Some half hour into our return trek, the only stuttering question I dared. "Sam and I were told so many *different* stories about It".

"Oh, don't be such a fool, boy!"

My puzzled, chastened silence was eventually graced with a little more. "Do you really still not understand? It is whatever It needs to be.

The Zoo: The Beast, The Boy and The Zoo

Last night It was a Jaguar. Another time It might take the form of a Snake. Or a Condor. Or, I don't know... a bloody Mouse, if that might be to Its purpose. And once - years ago, when there was some advantage to be had, when It could see a new way to weaken me, to hurt me, then It was born as a Man."

"It knew I was going to the Jaguars. It always intended to renege. No middle way now. I was a fool to hope otherwise." His shoulders slumped even further. "The poison is too strong within them all. No hope remaining." He strode on. "Well none, other than to exterminate all the brutes. The whole damned lot of them!"

We reached Edensor. He walked up the stairs ignoring me. He went straight into his study without a word. He locked the door behind him.

And that, my friends, was it.

Those were the last words I ever exchanged with the only parent I had ever known. That brief and unexpected spring of warmth and kindness and love bubbling up on our outward journey was gone, and no hint would ever emerge again. What had passed at the Jaguar glade had crushed him. On the sparse occasions in the months after that I again glimpsed him; he was a bent, defeated old man.

I think it was that very last sight of him disappearing into his study, vanquished and pathetic that quickened the determination within me, a pact with myself to take revenge on my family's enemy, to destroy that creature who had destroyed my father.

And perhaps my mother too.

***

ϛϛϛ

Excerpt from 'Man and Animal in the Zoo',
Dr Heini Heddiger, Director of Basel and Zurich Zoos 1944

Young birds will perch on a keeper's head or even on his
outstretched arm as though it were a branch. Young
swallows that have been reared in captivity will
occasionally fly into the open mouth of a man, doubtless
because this opening has a certain similarity to the nest
entrance for that bird. (...) When I was student I used to
let bats *(Rhinolophus)* fly freely in my bedroom;
sometimes on waking up in the morning I would find a bat
hanging from my hand which dangled over the edge of the
bed. The bat had included this part of my anatomy as one
of the paces that was suitable as a hanging site for the
day's sleep, that is, part of its inanimate environment.

Mensch und Tier im Zoo Pg 82
Albert Muller Verlag, Zurich

ϛϛϛ

Part Four: Sam's Telling of the Tale

"Would you care for another...?"

"No thanks Samantha. I am fine."

"I promise you there is nothing untoward in the wine. Not on this occasion."

"No? Okay suit yourself, young man. Excuse me whilst I just top my own drink up then."

"Aahhh.... Yes. That is so good."

"So tell me again. Now that we have come this far and that you reached this particular point with the tale zig-zagging back and forth between my brother and I. Tell me exactly, honestly, truly what do you want from this interview? Why come all this way to seek me out? Given all the tales about me, men are generally wary of visiting my Island."

"What do you want from this story? What is it you really want to draw from me... out of one of your puppets?"

"A nice, safe, meaning-laden story all centred on a brave male hero called Seth?"

"I just want the truth, Sa... I mean Samantha."

"Hmm, I wonder. Do you? The truth? Where a woman is concerned do men ever really want to know the truth? Or isn't it better to keep a nice, safe tame version in their heads?"

"Did Seth want to know the truth about his own twin sister? Or about his mother? Did any of us want to know the truth about her and the True Beast?"

"You see there is that word again... the <u>True</u> Beast. 'Truth'... 'true'... 'trueness'... all so tantalising in all their different meanings, aren't they."

"Come here. Now. I wish to have a better look at you."

"No! Here. Closer for goodness sake. I am not going to cast a spell on you. It is really time I got your full measure, my intrusive, demanding, yet so plausible interviewer."

"Let me look properly into your face."

"Into your eyes..."

(...)

"Yes. Okay. Yes. That's better."

"Okay. I think I know now what you are. I think I know who you are."

"Well, if you want to know to know 'the truth'. I think we need to go back a bit."

"No, no. I would rather move strongly forward in the story please Samantha..."

"I daresay you would."

"And I don't care. First we need to go back. Don't they say... reculer pour mieux sauter?"

"So just sit back and let me tell a little more about how it really was between Seth and I back in those days in the Vague Lands."

~~~

Chapter Twenty Eight: Reculer Pour Mieux Sauter

I probably got off pretty lightly. Later he would be a skinny beanpole who could not punch his way out of a paper bag. But even as small children, Seth was only slightly bigger than me. If he had been, say five years ahead of me, he might have been a real bully. He might have given me a real pounding.

Maybe.

Maybe not.

As it was, he talked big but didn't have the brawn. And you know what; he didn't have the brains either. Poor baby, always thinking he was in charge. So puffed up that he was older by a full half an hour! In fact most of what we two got up to in the Vague Lands was down to yours truly. I led: Seth followed. Usually moaning his stupid head off, but followed all the same.

All that gobbledygook he has given you about my special gift with the birds and the beasts!

I am afraid my brother Seth was rather dim.

No. Let me take that back. 'Dim' isn't quite the right way to look at it. Let us be kinder. It was just that the way he thought, the way most humans think about other animals is just too hemmed in, too blind.

It is too...*boorish.*

Yes! Boorish. That is really good word for my brother.

Okay I should really stop. I shouldn't be exaggerating. I should not be giving the wrong impression. It wasn't really like that between Seth and me. Not really. And I did not think of me that way. Well, not all the time. Not in the beginning.

I mean goodness, no, how could it have been that way? No. Of course not.

In those early times, Seth *did* look after me. Look out for me. He did lead. Sometimes at least. And when we were tots, I *did* look up to him. It was later that things changed. Only gradually did his bluff and bluster turn to dust in my eyes.

How sad...

You must try to imagine how it was for us, right from the very first breath to only ever have the other one. We clashed and feuded.

Naturally.

Unquestionably Seth could be a bit of a fool. And I might possibly have had an excessive degree of self-regard.

But when from being the tiniest thing there is nobody else to give you any love. When so much of your universe day in, day out is this other person. When that other person's face looks so like yours. When everyone else treats you and him as almost one person.

Well, something pretty strange beds in deep down.

Maybe we did kick the hell out of each other even in the womb. Maybe, as kids in those early years in such a colourless place with nothing else to do, we sometimes carried on kicking for fun. Maybe the stresses of adolescence at the Zoo made those 'kicks 'more frequent and fiercer. And maybe, as that great adventure swept both of us up on our contrary paths, our kicks (if you could still call them that) took on a lot more meaning than mere sibling rivalry.

But even with it all, this strange stirring of being only half of one person extorted a kind of love deeper than any most could possibly imagine.

Have you ever stared in a mirror into your own eyes, steadfast and still, drilling right down into the centre of the pupils? If you did, and if you persisted for long enough, did you not eventually see somebody or something there looking back.

Something that wasn't quite you at all?

***

Let's get back to that whole matter of animals. All that exaggerated twaddle that Seth gave you about what I could do that others could not; my not only being a hearer, but also being able to persuade and almost entrance other animals.

There is really no great mystery here. You simply have to look at it the right way. Most people in their minds hold animals down fast so they can never be more than a minuscule detail, a tiny and tightly circumscribed thing within their own all-important human world.

It is always us at the centre of everything. First off we had the sun and the stars going around us, and not the other way around. Then we had a venerable being in the sky (of human form, white and naturally male too) with a long, white beard who one day took it into His head to make us up specially, and that we should all look like Him.

The other animals which He created, well they were conveniently wandering around for whatever use we might have a fancy to make of them.

That is an utterly perverse way to look on the universe! Animals are not just one little detail within our otherwise wonderfully rich, wide, and meaningful human lives. Animals are *everything*. Because quite simply we ourselves *are* animals!

We have got it so profoundly wrong. Ours is a dull-witted, shrivelled up, and crippled way to live a life, lacking even a flicker of enquiry, any notion of real curiosity. As if people and our human world are the one and only true universe wherein everything else must take its subservient and obsequious role.

The Zoo: The Beast, The Boy and The Zoo

Or be banished.

Every single animal species which I have ever come across has constituted an entire universe unto itself. Even those little mice all those decades ago that Seth made such a to-do over: a great, big parcel, chock full of bewitching, alien minds just waiting there for me to unwrap.

On the one hand most people might just, dragging their feet, agree that a particular animal should briefly be accorded a small role, some minor significance within their human world.

Maybe because it is 'cute'.

Or on the contrary disgusting.

Or useful. Or perhaps it is scary in some foolish cartoon way. Or it could have some use as a convenient symbol for one or other idea swirling around in their dull little 'Scent skulls.

I on the other hand - I rip the door off its hinges. I stride into this other, awesome, fresh, new animal cosmos, a place where the human arrival must now sit down humbly and quietly in the corner over there, as a guest; and not an especially consequential one at that.

And *that* is why animals accept me, come to me even. That's why I can talk to them in my mind. Or, to put it the other way round, the correct way round, that's why, *in my mind,* they can talk.

There is more. You will have learned by now that I am not the high and mighty type. But however I say it, it will come over as bragging. I do not just do all this better than anyone I have ever come across or heard of it, I do it *differently* as well. You see, I am not just a 'hearer' like so many others. I get heard as well.

And that's my real thing. In that I am unique.

I am She to whom the animals listen.

***

The Zoo: The Beast, The Boy and The Zoo

You might have expected there to be more hearers at the Zoo. Maybe as many as half the keepers were in that respect as deaf as a post. William could hear though. Oh yes, dear old Dad had the talent. In fact when it came down to it, that was one human that could hear very well indeed; at least in that angry, confused and tragic way of his.

Poor old William...

But shall we talk about Lilith now for a while? What exactly was the deal there? I will lay out just *three* things to say about Lilith. One by one.

In the first place our chief curator definitely understood our animals. But then that one – Lilith she understood everything and everybody. From our first fateful meeting something signalled strongly that here before us was the best hearted, the most sage and the downright strangest person that anyone might dream up.

The last of those things was certainly true.

Let me explain what for Seth and was the biggest real change between the Vague Lands and the Zoo. It was not between the places themselves, nor what was in them. It was being swopped from somewhere where nobody had cared tuppence about us to a new life where one powerful soul seemed utterly intent on our wellbeing.

That should have been wonderful. Something any reasonable, well-adjusted person would welcome with open arms. Seth did. That is exactly what he did. That poor little boy, he had finally found a grown up to love him. To look after him. To tell him what to do. To take responsibility for him. He looked straight up at Lilith, he opened up his arms and he surrendered himself.

On the surface that was me too. But beneath? No, not really. Perhaps for me it had all just came too late. Perhaps if someone had come to 'rescue' us from the Vague Lands at only at slightly younger age it could have been entirely different.

The Zoo: The Beast, The Boy and The Zoo

But at ten years old *it* was just too firmly fixed in my head. By 'it', I mean the way life is. Or the way life needs to be. Or the way it should be. Inside me the notion had congealed hard that others just did not do anything for you unless they wanted something for themselves. Except....

Except your twin. Except the other you.

We twins, we looked after ourselves. Nobody else was really trusted. Nobody else was really needed. Nobody else might as well have really existed.

***

Then there was this idea that we had become 'Lilith's project'. I was not sure I liked that.

When an older person has a natural responsibility for their own child, okay then. Or even if somehow has such a responsibility suddenly thrust upon them. Fair enough. But when they actively seek it out. When they seize upon it.

When it seems as if they have been waiting for it?

Is it just me that finds that slightly creepy?

Of course there are things I know now about dear old Lilith that I did not then. Now I realise that Seth was not the only mirror (however imperfect) into which I might back then have logically and usefully stared to learn something about myself.

Then again perhaps the real problem was that it was just too dramatic a change? To shape up from being that wild child, something not so far off a beast of burden and for whom for years nobody gave a damn.

And suddenly it is all fine. All at once I am to become a grateful, happy little girl accepting all the good things on offer?

I really don't think so.

The Zoo: The Beast, The Boy and The Zoo

At the Zoo I just floated along with it all in the beginning. These currents that I am sharing now; back then they only flowed deep underground. All these nuggets of rebellion, these sparks of refusal, they were squirrelled away tightly inside me; easy enough to veil, given that my delight in being surrounded by this wonderland of animals, now *that* was twenty-four carat genuine.

In response to Lilith's attentions to us, I kept my head down, my eyes open, my mouth shut.

And helplessly I stood and watched as my little brother start to love and to trust someone who was not me.

***

Chapter Twenty Nine: In the second and third places

Now we get to the second thing about Lilith. In that second place I would put the overwhelming frustration of never getting any real information out of her. Not on anything important anyway, Nothing that might be usefully applied to most of the mysteries surrounding us. The first time we had met, she had proven so adept at swerving past those ferocious white beasts besetting us on our path here. Now she was every bit as good at swerving past questions she didn't like.

In a way of course, there was only *one, real* question or set of questions that shrieked out to the heavens above for answers.

What had our mother been like?

And what had happened between our father and her? Surely this silver haired custodian floating enigmatically and with a sense of entitlement through our daily lives, she knew something about that. And surely, wherever Lilith had come from, and whoever or *whatever* she might be, she had had some hand in it all?

So now we come to the third and final place. What in this place is the third truth that I am going to tell you about Lilith?

Well, my friends this one is easily stated, the plain and unvarnished truth is...

In the third place I never really trusted that bitch in the *first* place.

The Zoo: The Beast, The Boy and The Zoo

***

Seth never guessed what I was up to, but she knew. Oh, of course she did.

Maybe Seth could only think of animals as of being of some use to him. But for me when we came to the Zoo the world of animals and the knowledge available on the wild world simply exploded into undreamed dimensions. In this new place something unfurled quickly inside me; it grew, stretched and reached upwards for the light.

Seth thought that the last time I openly used my 'gift 'as he calls it was back in the Vague Lands. More honestly said however, that was the last time Seth or anyone else *knew* I used it.

Almost anyone else.

In the first times after we arrived, it was hard to get away from Seth. Maybe I didn't really want to. Later though as the months grew into years, as my breasts grew and my first period arrived, that shackling between us unknotted and slipped loose. Both we ourselves and everyone else began, however grudgingly, to allow us to be two separate beings. No longer did we receive quite so much the constant label 'the twins' or 'Seth & Sam'.

I did indeed talk to the animals - on the sly and as circumstances allowed. And I broke the rules. The rules as to being out in the Zoo after dark. The warning on venturing out into the outer perimeter and the Old Forest. I was careful. Nobody knew.

Nobody except her of course.

No way to escape that gaze. Once I realised that she knew, I expected to be ordered to stop. Not a single word passed her lips. Those basilisk eyes simply let me know that she knew.

So I carried merrily on. I conferred with the Aardvarks in the south east paddocks, with the Alligators and the Asian Otters in enclosures near Edensor. I debated matters with the Mandrill, the

The Zoo: The Beast, The Boy and The Zoo

Meerkats and the Macaws. I sat down with the Porcupine and the Pudu and the Puma. I learned in depth and omnivorously. I walked through world after world. Plunging deep into exotic psyches, and drifting within them. Slowly. Languorously. Gloriously. Each new land I explored, each new language I acquired seemed to open up vast lumber rooms within my own mind. Great vaults of untold knowledge unlocked one after another, their treasures tumbling out, the dominos cascading down. I sucked in deep lungfuls of new understanding.

I could not have achieved a deeper, more subtle and more bountiful affinity with the lives of other animals in any other way.

Other, I suppose, than actually becoming one myself, which is clearly quite impossible.

***

As to the great issue that divided the Zoo, little by little my sympathies there had swung. This creeping discontent, this rebellion or sickness that most of the humans who ran the Zoo feared, that was real enough; but it did not quite assume the form I had been led to believe.

Those species who voiced no dissatisfaction at all at being part of the Zoo and Man's governance now seemed rather complacent. The worsening violence that, by now comment assent, was coming to overtake the Zoo. Was this really best typified as a kind of raging fever, a pullulating, rotting, decaying thing, a maggoty suffering and destruction?

Or rather a wonderful intoxication offering to rip down decrepit old structures. A sense that each part of the Zoo, each animal group, each exhibit and enclosure, instead of remaining quiescent and subservient within an artificial and forced whole, barely held together by antediluvian, now deeply doubted stories. that these were striving to spin off, every one, into its own new, free orbit.

The Zoo: The Beast, The Boy and The Zoo

A temporary illusion of singular identity sweetly dissolving, its liberated components blossoming into something altogether other. Something altogether better?

Such stories I heard! The terrible things that had been done by humans to animals!

I must be very clear here though. There was no doubt that for those who ran the Zoo itself, a love and concern and respect for animals governed all that they did. But as for the wider human world and its relationship with animal kind, some utterly obscene things were revealed to me. For me, it was never the actual Zoo that has been the problem: it has always been the wider human world and the way it treated animals.

Am I explaining myself clearly?

In three sentences then. I loved the Zoo. I quite like zoos in general. Well, most of them. But I *don't* like some of the people who visit them, nor what in their wider lives they often do to animals. These places called farms, those at least that were run like factories. And the animals used as experiments in laboratories. The way some people treat their so-called pets!

As amidst all these swirling thoughts, my curiosity grew, I wanted to know more about the thing at the centre of it all. The person. Or animal. Or idea. Or whatever it really was. I wanted to meet It.

I wanted badly to meet the True Beast.

But none of my hints, my enquiries or even eventually my blunt demands led to anything at all. No, despite my pleadings, I never met Him or Her or It. Not then.

Then Seth had to go and raise his traitor hand and ended up on that damn trip to the Jaguars with William. The smug little bastard! *I* was the one who cared about animals, not he. *I* was the one with the gift!

Off he went self-satisfied as hell; and William happily humming away to himself too. Yet they both came back all weird and downcast

The Zoo: The Beast, The Boy and The Zoo

and tight lipped!? Bafflingly my brother now constantly bore an overwhelming and inexplicable air of resentment. Did he not understand *he* had won? Was he intent in stealing even my cherished sense of martyrdom?

What might have actually occurred between them and those to whom they spoke I would not properly decipher until many years later. But all my instincts screamed there and then that they had met It. When it came down to it, our father had taken Seth to meet the True Beast.

And. That. Should. Have. Been. *Me.*

***

Now one last item while I am setting records straight. That business at the beginning when we were coming to the Zoo in Lilith's E-Type. Yes, okay, I slightly cracked open that window. But please! I was a just a little girl and I was excited.

It was my first Polar Bear for mercy's sake.

And the Bear could not have held the car back if it itself hadn't forced the window down much farther. So whatever Seth said, it wasn't my fault. I didn't mess it up. No it is *always* Seth who messes everything up.

In the end it is always he.

Always.

You just wait and see.

**

Seth's version will have led you almost to that day six months or so after the Jaguar foray. The day that William made his final, fatal trip into the Outer Zoo and the Old Forest. No one saw him slip away.

If they had, there would have been some attempt to stop him. You see, Professor William Faraday was by that point no longer merely the

The Zoo: The Beast, The Boy and The Zoo

eccentric, obsessed figure, who though entirely derelict in his directorial duties, retained at least some veneer of authority. No, he had become a decrepit and utterly senile elder. Anyone could see he clearly needed protecting from himself.

He did not return the next morning. Nor the next. After three days, the true authority at the Zoo, Lilith ordered a search party.

Where in the Zoo or the Old Forest he had been during this last time and with what vague and futile aims, none of us ever discovered. But a forlorn form was discovered at three o'clock, a quarter mile or so north of the European Bison. They told me that Father was not quite dead when they carried him back to Edensor.

He surrendered his last breath the next morning.

***

No ceremony. A quiet burial in the furthest corners of Edensor's rampant garden, a small announcement in the national newspaper. And that was all.

A few days later a man called a lawyer came to see Seth and me. Father had left no will that anyone was aware of.

I waited for Seth to say something. To make some claim about whatever might have happened during the Jaguar episode. Or anything at all. That he said absolutely nothing did not lessen my suspicion and resentment one wit.

The boring, old lawyer person explained that in legal terms as Father's equal next of kin we were each entitled to ownership of a half share of the Zoo and wider land holdings.

It took some willpower for Seth and me to resist exchanging glances at such an announcement. Instead we both stared impassively into the distance and explicitly away from one another.

The Zoo: The Beast, The Boy and The Zoo

You might think this would have made things better between us? Brought some small resolution as to who was our father's heir? I am sorry to disappoint, but not really. You must understand this was just the official, legalistic stuff. Nothing at all to do with what William might have wanted. Nothing to do with his vision, his passion, his obsession, his fight for the Zoo. Nothing to do with confidence in one or other of us. And nothing to do with love.

Various internal meetings were held. There was little discussion and no disagreement. From now on, I would be in charge of all matters to do with the animals. Seth would have responsibility for everything else: the visitors, the staff, the buildings, the money and so on. Joint Directors. A not-very-happy co-existence.

Do you know I almost felt sorry for Seth. He would be feeling insufferably trapped. Suddenly committed to this place, to *only* this place, for the rest of his life Manacled to the Zoo for ever. He might, when faced with all that William's death had suddenly thrust on us. succeed for a while in repressing his suffocation But that would not last long; and I had learned how to be patient.

Lilith posed a problem of an altogether different calibre. Her position as Chief Curator was far too deeply embedded, her knowledge of our animals too ingrained, her web of relationships too wide to be easily unseated by me.

I didn't like that one little bit.

She had never displayed any abilities in hearing in my presence. Yet her affinity with the non-humans thronged all around us was clearly a deep thing. Lilith was certainly as far from being a 'Scent as it was humanly possible to be. I did not of course rate her anywhere near my own talents, but there was something, something she knew that I didn't.

And there should only be one woman in the Zoo to whom all the animals should listen.

The Zoo: The Beast, The Boy and The Zoo

***

The Zoo might now be officially under new management, but what we actually managed was less and less. There was still a functioning thing called the Zoo. We still welcomed large numbers of visitors. The 'Scents were still blissfully unaware of what was dissolving around them or of the profound and visceral beauty lying beneath it all. But every week on that map in the study, further areas had to be marked off as no go areas. New animal cohorts sprang up in rebellion: some in seeming loose alliance with other groups; others perhaps part of a Zoo wide movement; others again seemed born out of pure anarchy.

Tension and concern amongst the management and the keepers grew with every day. Yet many did not seem properly to understand what was happening, nor what more was about to happen. The sins of our species against other animals were coming home to roost. The human race was just beginning its penance now. And there was penance a plenty more to come.

***

ςςς

It is known for example that bull giraffes can smash the
skull of a lion with one blow of their fore-feet but when
fighting with each other they use only the short horns
which are padded with a covering of thick skin.
Rattlesnakes and other very venomous snakes, with their
highly effective chemical weapon, can even kill animals
that are a hundred times larger and heavier than
themselves; nevertheless when fights take place between
rivals they do not bite each other but settle their contest
virtually on points according to a ritual. When the
superfluous males or drones have to be expelled from a
colony of bees they are not killed by the poisonous sting of
the workers, but simply nipped with the mandibles and
then thrown out. Skunks never squirt their stinking
excretion at one another. And so on.

Man and Animal in the Zoo,
Dr Heini Heddiger
Mensch und Tier im Zoo
Albert Muller Verlag, Zurich

ςςς

Part Five: Seth's Telling of the Tale

Chapter Thirty One: Look on my works, ye mighty and despair

"So what is the most dangerous animal in your Zoo, Mr Director?"

That is the repetitious, boring and predictable question visitors have pestered me with over the years. I have always been careful to respond politely. To their faces anyway.

But I did like to see their surprise at the answer. It is not our Tigers, nor the Nile Crocodiles nor the Komodo Dragons. Although of course each and every one of those could mercilessly bite their silly heads off in a single heartbeat.

No, in terms of your likelihood of actually being killed or maimed for life, as everyone who works at any zoo knows, that is the Elephant. Put that down to the casualness with which a swish of their trunk could crush your skull, not to mention the much greater killing force at their disposal within the rest of those massive bodies. And also because, although they are normally such benign animals, just now and again, and when you least expect it, they - really - are - not.

I always liked to finish off by adding that an Elephant's sneeze could knock my questioner unconscious. Normally, if we are at the Elephant enclosure at the time, they take a sharp step back. I made up that 'interesting fact' just for fun.

But now listen if you were to ask instead to say which the most *vicious* animal in the Zoo is, I would give you a quite different answer.

The Zoo: The Beast, The Boy and The Zoo

There I would say, pound for pound, it is the Honey Badger, or the Ratel, a beast who is about to feature here - fairly dramatically - in a paragraph or so.

There had not actually been Okapis at 'the Okapi Plains' for many years before it happened. But place names at the Zoo do seem to stick around. It is a particularly graceful, peaceful part of the Zoo, a series of stepped fields, each rising slightly beyond the other, normally home to a community of hooved stock. You can view the whole panorama from an adjacent bridge. When then light hits the plains in a certain way, as it was doing that particular morning it is especially affecting. Hard though to sit here years later and reflect on its physical beauty without remembering... all the blood.

It was only two months since Father had died. Everyone was still getting used to so many new authorities and responsibilities. It was at very early hour in May with the rays of the sun still struggling. Sam's interest in our animal charges had, if anything only intensified on officially assuming her senior responsibilities. She had got up a good while before me and was working at one of the very furthest reaches of the Zoo. I was still comfortably in bed in Edensor, but at least close at hand. So when we both received urgent radio messages that something seriously bad was happening, we ended up arriving at exactly the same time. Lilith and Luis, the head keeper for that section, were there before us.

Not that any of us had much to do in what followed. Due to a major blunder on that account we were strictly spectators. Constanta the Vet and Heinz were the only two with the keys to the cabinet where all the anaesthetic dart guns were kept. Both were off site at exactly the same time.

That wasn't supposed to happen. Someone had been derelict in his or her duty. And there would be consequences.

The Zoo: The Beast, The Boy and The Zoo

Way back in the dim and distant past, it seemed interestingly enough there has been one particular keeper with responsibility in such matters. Whoever they might have been, their extreme competence in security, weapons and the emergencies these required had achieved and still commanded quite legendary levels. Bizarrely though the manner of their departure was always glossed over quickly. Whatever that was all about and whoever they were, they had clearly left boots never properly filled since.

In any event, this leaving the Zoo without access to dart guns and the rest was a very serious error for those responsible. It was with clear pleasure that Sam sacked Constanta the very next day. Heinz got off with a warning.

Incidents seemed to be bubbling up more and more since the news spread that the Director was no more. Two Ring Tailed Lemurs had been ambushed by a gang of South American Coatis. There were three dead Hawaiian Geese: the Mute Swans were suspected. The Mississippi Alligators had somehow found their way into the pool belonging to the Indian Gharial Crocodiles with predictably tragic results. Animal attacks on keepers had become frequent as well.

But the thing that rolled out at the plains that morning, that was at a completely different level of conflict.

At the outset, it was easy enough to think this was just another flare up. Plausible enough given the well-known bad blood between the Ratels and the African Jackals.

Yet as matters moved on, and as a certain choreography inexorably revealed its hand, it became clear that this was not an accident. This was a performance. One that carried a message. And a signature.

It was a lone Ratel who first took that stage; that and a twelve foot long Python. A first it looked like the Ratel was a hopeless case. These things are only about the size of a small dog. And the Python had coiled

The Zoo: The Beast, The Boy and The Zoo

itself completely around the piteous little black and white beast. Now it was more or less invisible. All you could see was a cute little snout at the top and one ineffectual paw futilely waving from between the coils. Just a matter of minutes before the snake crushed the small mammal's ribs.

Then the 'cute little snout' - as an expert piano player's fingers might flow confidently across a keyboard - bit deeply and repeatedly all along the snake's unprotected flesh like it were eating sweetcorn. The constrictor whipped in agony. It writhed away, terror stricken now by what seconds before had been a defenceless prey. But it was not going to escape. The Ratel fastened its jaws around the Snake's head and wrenched, dragging it helplessly backwards across the paddock.

Then the African Jackals, trotted nonchalantly into view, two of them, one from either side. Not everyone seems to care too much for these animals. They certainly can come over as skinny, rather sinister bastards with those weird looking saddle coats. They were more than twice the size of the outnumbered Ratel. They still lacked courage. One by one they darted, nipping in wherever they could see any gap in the little Badger's defence, and each time forcing their enemy to turn back on itself, vulnerable to the other attacker.

Not dissimilar, I could not help but think, to the way Dexter and Sinister had tackled the Polar Bear on that fateful day so many years back. Except of course that those valiant twins had taken on a foe a good six times their size. The brother Jackals here had elected to pick on something less than half of theirs.

An unwise choice all the same. Once he got what they were up to, the Ratel resolved to ignore the nips from the smaller Jackal on his left. Ratels have a very strange kind of hide, tough but loose, so even though it must have hurt, he could manage this violence. He could concentrate his fire now on the larger enemy on the right. The bigger Jackal tried to back off. Not fast enough. In a second the Ratel had him by the throat. The Jackal was forced to the ground. Then the Ratel let go.

The Zoo: The Beast, The Boy and The Zoo

What happened next was so quick, but I swear to god, it was as clear as day. He went for Jackal's groin. There was a snap. A spray of blood. And the severed genitals of the Jackal catapulted, as if in slow motion, through the air.

Then there were three more Ratels on the scene. If it did not disappear fast, that second Jackal was surely one dead dog now.

But something big, brown and horned was coming fast, galloping in to the left of our field of vision. A Wildebeest. Two of them. Seven now. As they reached the field, the Ratel had a brand new experience. The first Wildebeest kicked and the Ratel flew high through the air. That kick must, I thought, surely detach the poor creature's head. It didn't quite, but the animal landed hard, its body totally limp. It did not move again.

The newcomers had little time to be triumphant. The Wildebeest were about to come under attack in turn by something whose savagery may surprise you.

So the most dangerous animal in its overall potential is the Elephant. The most vicious is the Ratel. But imagine if you were a keeper in a zoo. You would think a good deal about those particular animals with which you regularly need to *go in* with, the species with which you had to actually share the same unprotected space.

That naturally does not include Tigers, or Crocodiles or Chimps or Ratels or these days Elephants. So on that basis, which would you be most scared of in your day-to-day life?

Over a drink or two amongst zoo hands, there will be some debate about this. Some will perhaps nominate the bad tempered and unpredictable Bactrian Camel? Other minds will go straight to various venomous Spiders and Snakes.

But let me introduce you an animal called the Zebra.

Oh, you think you know about Zebras? Those nice stripy things in a child's toy box?

The Zoo: The Beast, The Boy and The Zoo

You wouldn't think that ever again, if like me, you had once been stuck in a small paddock, staring directly into the snarling, bared teeth of a Zebra stallion, and feet from your face.

Zebras can be up to half a ton in weight. A mature Zebra stallion, especially when it can smell mares in heat, now that is one fast, savage, sly, cruel creature.

Up to now it had just been a fight. When the twenty Grevy's Zebras attacked, it became a battle. They did not just charge into the fray like the Wildebeest. Zebras are tactical. With a stealth more associated with a pack of Painted Dogs, the large group of Zebras took their time, slowly assembling around the entire perimeter of the fields. Unnoticed until too late.

Over the years I came to know that stallion Brutus who led them pretty well, Every inch as disciplined a commander of his herd as a Roman centurion might be of his century.

A call to order before attack. That eerie whinny only Zebras have. Like a Donkey's bray but higher pitched and ever so slightly demonic. Repeated. Once, twice, thrice. Then a single snort as the signal for attack. The encircling herd charged.

The Wildebeest and whatever sorry remnants of other animals left had little defence against the bruiting, stamping, kicking, biting noose that tightened in on them. Did you know that a Zebra can walk on its hind legs? Well it will, when it needs to use its front legs to stave in the head of a Wildebeest. A fury of gnashing teeth, plundering hooves and kicking legs.

Dust, stripes, horns, brays, bellows, more dust.

Then just shit and blood.

And so the battle moved on stage, by inexorable stage. Something or someone was deliberately putting their power on display. A will behind all of this that cared little as to spilling the blood of its own kind as long as this might only intimidate its ultimate enemy. A will so powerful that it could indeed manipulate whole animal cohorts into mortal combats not of their own making, where individuals might effectively suicide to a greater purpose. The True Beast might, by human fear of the wild and the untamed, have been summoned into being as a kind of 'god'; but if this were a god, It was one that cared little for its worshippers.

A giant graffito might as well have been scrawled across the Plains saying: '*Behold my Mighty Hand*'. As if a war game was being slowly unfurled before us and for our specific benefit. First the skirmishers had appeared (the Ratels and Jackals). Then they had given way to the regular infantry, who had ceded to the cavalry (the Wildebeest and then Zebra).

Now it was time for the armour. The armoured cars made their due entrance to the Plains in the form of a tight phalanx of fifteen Congo Buffalos.

And the tanks? The tanks appeared from the south.

Eight massive White Rhino.

The still living but blooded biomass in the middle on which they started to slowly converge comprised mainly of the Grevy's Zebra. Only two of these seemed to have been killed: whereas just one of the biggest Wildebeest was left standing terrified and backed into a corner. No sign that I could see at all of any Ratels or Jackals.

If alliances on any part had ever been initially intended, that part of the battle plan fell to pieces. By this stage it was every species for itself.

Over there on the other side of the study, I still have the horns of a Cape Buffalo hung up on the wall. Let me weigh it my hands for a moment as I am remembering all of this. Reminds me rather of a curled moustache. Quite a piece of natural weaponry. I do so admire the way they flare sideways, downwards... And finally curve upwards to the lethal tip. If you look closely, you will see that it is actually two horns. But fused completely into a kind of shield.

Can't you just imagine those dull, implacable eyes seeking you out, singling in on you, slowly but deliberately moving in your direction? Then suddenly charging with perhaps two thousand pounds of muscle behind them. And finally, at *just* the right moment, the very last possible juncture, the horns are lowered to almost scrape the earth and deliver in a bone-crunching crash.

Yes, these superb champions of ferocity can plough almost any obstacle from their path. They can get the better of almost any opponent. Almost any.

Brutus and his Zebras cannily did not hang around. They did not take any chance at all they might be caught between the two approaching lines of Buffalo and Rhino as these steadily closed in on each other from opposite ends of the field. The Zebras, at least those which were unwounded or could move easily enough, followed their leader to beat a tactical retreat. The remaining Wildebeest, the one wounded Jackal I could now spy, and - to my astonishment - a still just about moving Python were either not clever enough, or lacked sufficient residual vigour, or simply were too unlucky to get out of the way.

The two lines of heavy animals moved cautiously but steadily towards one other. They didn't really seem to pay much attention to anything left in the middle. As though these animals were just some minor and incidental physical impediment. Collateral damage, that is, I believe, what generals call it. Once they were about, oh, I don't know, fifty yards or so apart, their respective marches became canters. Then a gallop, building up to a furious thirty miles an hour. As they closed on one another, the disciplined straight lines broke into scraggy v-shaped waves.

The Zoo: The Beast, The Boy and The Zoo

Not quite the single cinematic central clash one might have expected. With the Buffaloes outnumbering the Rhinos by a little more than two to one, they broke off instead into smaller confrontations.

Tell me, frankly, is there anything more startlingly 'pre-historic looking' than a Rhino? To this day I remain startled by the naked and astonishing fact that such a magnificent thing as a Rhino simply exists at all. Nothing brings home just how terrible it would be to lose these numinous beings from the world than that face to face experience. And only if you have ever touched the horn of a living Rhino can you realise what a truly strange arrangement it is. They wobble! Not rigid at all. As if it could almost come off in your hand. So when a Rhino goes slap bang wallop into an obstacle much of the reverberation soaks into the horn itself and, to its benefit, not into the rest of the animal's body.

The lowered Buffaloes' horns may have been heavy duty earth moving machines. But those Rhinos were just straight-out bulldozers. When Rhino and Buffalo met head on, there were long minutes of one to one contention when neither animal seemed to move a millimetre. The Buffaloes may have at least had a little greater manoeuvrability on its side, but then inexorably, they began to slip and slide in the mud, blood and underlying mess.

First they slithered from side to side.

Then straight backwards.

It was not only the individual Rhino's greater mass and strength that took its toll. However low the Buffalo could manage those great spread out bovine hooks of theirs, the unfeasibly massive tooth of a weapon jutting out from the Rhino's head would always undercut it, every time digging down just that little bit deeper. And once it had got low enough, the great pachyderm would jerk and tilt itself slightly upwards, levering and scooping the benighted bovid's front feet just far enough off the ground that it lost most of its traction. Now it was sledged rapidly backwards by the Rhino, tumbled on to its side, hooves flailing pathetically in the air. The Rhino would then disengage for a second, take two or three steps backward, and pressing its advantage, gore repeatedly into its prone enemy's unprotected flank.

Result one dead or dying Buffalo.

This, in only slightly varying permutations, was how things played out in four or five of the confrontations. Had the two sets of foes been equal in numbers that likely would have been the result all around. But the Buffaloes outnumbered the Rhinos. Where two or sometimes more Buffaloes were able to concentrate their fire on a single Rhino, the outcome was completely different. Several beleaguered individuals gradually went down to multiple wounds on their flanks and heads, cornered by cooperating Buffaloes, and unable to defend themselves on all sides at once.

This stage of the battle was slow and gruesome. It was probably roughly honours even between the two species when whatever malicious presence ordering the whole spectacle revealed Its hand in a final coup de theatre. I do not suppose it is hard to guess what was the final creature to appear and victoriously sweep the field clean? What after all can top a Rhino?

But before that endgame, you will surely be wondering what on earth all of us human onlookers were doing through all this bloodshed? Watching in fascinated but impotent despair is, I am afraid, the answer. Intervention without the use of Heinz's tranquilliser guns or indeed proper firearms if need be, was out the question. Even if we had them, frankly our options would have been either to shoot - and probably shoot to kill - or to enter the fray bodily ourselves.

In which case I would not have given much for the chances of any of us, Lilith, Sam, Luis, me nor any of the pretty large audience of keepers and other staff who had assembled by now.

The Zoo: The Beast, The Boy and The Zoo

Such thoughts were all academic. The last act was opening. Another and final animal type, the most deadly of all, moved on to the chessboard.

You have guessed. The Elephants. Right?

Wrong, but let me help you with a clue. They flew.

***

Chapter Thirty Two: Shock and Awe

I have come to see majesty now in pretty much every form of life. No single moment for me though, no sudden epiphany. More like a gradual, cumulative dawning thanks to many different teachers and to many different experiences.

When these days I come to think on any given species, I cannot help but consider just how exquisitely they are put together, how noble and subtle their approaches to the problem of survival, how invariably elegant in negotiating the world in all its complexities.

And this is not only a vague aesthetic appreciation. It seems to me somehow also to be the *right* way, the prudent and the healthy way for a human to think of our fellow species. It feels sane to think of our own human kind as part of wider thing continually adapting and evolving and striving. To consider oneself one animal amongst others.

I did not however, as you have seen, alas, always see it that way.

Putting aside all such philosophy, let me tell you, Insects have been a hard sell for me! A very slow process of conciliation indeed. It was probably the way that unlike any other animals their insides seem to be on the outside and those geometric limbs, and robotic movements. Think of Woodlice for instance.

And far worse than any individual characteristic of creepy crawlies, there is that very idea of the swarm and the hive. Hive minds. The very antithesis and great challenge to our own human anarchic way of doing, thinking and being.

Ugh! In my early days all Insects provoked an instinctive biological revulsion.

The Zoo: The Beast, The Boy and The Zoo

I had also disgraced myself that very first day out in the Zoo in the incident with the dismembered butterfly. So I would only visit the Zoo's Insectarium if absolutely necessary. Sam by contrast exulted in being there. In our earliest times she even enjoyed tormenting me by reciting out loud, one by one, long lists of what she called the 'little jewel boxes' found within.

"You should see the Giant Cave Cockroaches and the African Millipedes, Seth! " Clearly relishing my visible discomfort and so scattering the names of other such repellent beings through almost every conversation. Dead Leaf Mantis, Medium Long-legged Katydid, Walking Leaf Insect... and, oh, my word, something, would you believe it that is called the White-Eyed Assassin Bug!

Sam had a particular fondness for Beetles and even brought specimens back to Edensor: Dung Beetles; Atlas Beetles; Flower Beetles; Sun Beetles; Frog Beetles; Death-feigning Beetles; Sunburst Diving Beetles; Convergent Lady Beetles.

What in god's name was the point of so many different species?!

I found Chinese Praying Mantis in my boots; I came across a Giant Centipede in my bed; I reached into my pockets to discover a family of Madagascar Hissing Cockroaches.

That was all in earlier more playful times. By the time of the Battle of the Plains, I was lucky if, except when it was strictly necessary for work, Sam spoke to me at all, let alone played a practical joke.

My point here is that in those days one Insect for me was one too many.

A sky full now...

All eyes had been intent on the action on the plains themselves, so nobody on that cold bright morning in May had been looking up into the sky. By the time that bizarre sound made us all raise our eyes, the clear blue above was already darkening. At that distance they did not look so much like living Insects; more akin to animated pieces of jet black confetti, an ominous silhouette against the bright sun.

Inevitably it was Sam who identified them. "*Vespa Mandarina,*" came her loud whisper. "Giant Asian Hornets!"   I had heard of this species, thanks to Sam's pestilential flow of trivia. I knew indeed they were on the stock book of the Insectarium. They certainly however were not kept in *these* numbers. That day hanging in the air there may have been as many as ten thousand predators, their particular origin a considerable mystery.

Up there on the viewing platform we might have been reasonably worried for our own safety. Needlessly, as it happened; we were resolutely ignored. An attack on humans was not the military objective that day: a display of overwhelming force before those same humans most certainly was.

The more lurid media these days label these creatures 'Murder Hornets'. In ordinary circumstances I would say this is a vastly over rated description. That day it was more than earned. Each of the things is a full two inches long with three inches in wingspan. Just take a second to measure that out with your fingers. Now imagine clouds of such Insects dive bombing those poor animals that remained on the field. Their sting is itself a whole quarter of an inch long, and full of a very potent venom indeed.

Years later I met a man from their native country who had been stung by 'Murder Hornets'. Just twice. Just two insects. He said it felt like a steel spike being driven into his skin.

The animals who remained alive on the blooded field were mainly Rhinos and Buffalo. Rhinos may be remarked on for their horns, but their skin is pretty impressive too. In addition to its thickness alone, rather than being normal animal hide, it is in physical constituency actually nearer to the tendons of other mammals. It had evolved like that for protection against blows from other Rhinos and, yes, also against all the insects that follow them in its native habitat. That is after all why they are designated as 'pachyderms.'

Buffalo skin has its protective virtues as well, but not really quite in the same class. So, as the Hornets swooped relentlessly down on all the defenceless quadrupeds now scattered around the field of battle, it was the bovids that went down first. The Rhinos' remarkable epidermis did seem to be providing a degree of defence. Although they were clearly feeling at least some impact and discomfort from the hail of Insects, they held their ground. Until that is the Murder Hornets found their way underneath. Until they took advantage of the Rhinos' much softer bellies. And until they then went to their ears and to their eyes.

Rhinos do not make a lot of sound on the whole, not at least ones that we Humans can hear, and when they do so in anger or mating lust, I would describe it a kind of breathy, snorty roar. But those poor creatures made a quite different sound now. They were squealing in agony. Their terrible noise made that plain to all onlookers. But I knew it another way as well. My one and only talent came into play. My sense of smell. When frightened or in pain, Rhinos let you know through what their bowels do. The stench of Rhino terror, of Rhino death filled my nostrils. Nobody turned and looked at me when I doubled over and vomited.

And that was it. The end of the Battle of the Plains. I think two Rhinos managed to get out of there. In respect of anything left on the battlefield, the Hornets did their job thoroughly. The cadavers strewn all around must have been thoroughly sodden with venom before the swarm eventually dissipated.

Recriminations all across the staff now gathered. Someone else's fault all around. Only Lilith as ever kept her peace, simply staring mutely at the carnage, eyes then flicking around the scene to take in the most information. For a long moment after that she seemed to fix on something at a distant raised point at north of the bloodbath.

The Zoo: The Beast, The Boy and The Zoo

I followed her gaze. But if for a split second, I had imagined some blurry shadow as the object of her attention, by the time I could properly focus, it had gone.

Sam was sobbing at the slaughter of her beloved friends. Me, well I was just baffled. What had this all been about? There had been no obvious pattern of animals wishing to rebel against mankind and fighting those species seeking to defend the Zoo's status quo. No attack on us personally; nothing organic about this violence; more a stage-managed cavalcade. Not at all dissimilar to those huge parades of arms and armies that the dictators of certain countries mount in the midst of their big cities This was fundamentally a matter of ostentatious threat. 'A spectacular 'conceived by a terrorist mastermind.

How could one fight back against a legion of enemies as willing as this to so easily sacrifice themselves at a signal from their Leader for 'the Cause'?

Look upon my works would be ye mighty humans...

...And despair.

***

Chapter Thirty Three: Devolution and Dissolution

Given all that gone down at the Jaguar pool, I had been gifted an inside track on what was happening. Never mind that, for a variety of reasons, this was information jealously clutched to my chest. Most others at the Zoo though were quite startled though to see clear signs of some guiding intelligence behind the spreading chaos. On the widest scale, the Old Forest was creeping in on the wilder, less reliable Outer Zoo; and that Outer Zoo in turn gradually tightened in noose like around a shrinking decaying core at the centre.

Many voices resisted at first what was plain to see.

"...things have always gone wrong from time to time..."

"...there are incidents of violence at the Zoo every year, and normally about this time... "

"...this is just another seasonal outbreak. Yes, a bit worse than unusual but nothing to 'panic' about..."

Little by little though this dissent fell away. All at the Zoo began to accept that we faced an existential threat, and that some controlling intelligence might actually track and actively counter our efforts to combat the Zoo's decay.

Still, it took the arrival of the barely legible little note to finally wipe out all doubt.

Sam's distancing from me had been noticeable over seven years. This had become a different and altogether more bitter thing after I had gone off with Father. But after Father's death, and now the way everything seemed to be falling apart, it was more a case of Sam's withdrawal from everyone.

In our management meetings Sam never seemed wholly present. Those blue eyes would scan around the room as if seeking to be outside, to be free from such boring nonsense, from any matters not directly concerned with the animals. When summoned back to the conversation by a given remark of mine, they seemed to film over in contempt.

There is a well-known, almost traditional mild disdain flowing from some of the 'animal people' who worked at the Zoo towards the 'non animal people' with roles there.

But *this* went much further. And this disengagement on Sam's part was disturbingly familiar, Although distinct in both style, and as yet in degree, it smelt strongly of a certain someone else's behaviour.

Sure enough, Sam started following in our Father's footsteps through ever more frequent absences. As for our childhood warning not to venture into the most perilous, outer parts of the Zoo, now these areas were outside our control entirely anyway, so doubly out of bounds. As Co-director of the Zoo though, Sam had the authority to ignore any rules. So the Old Forest and Outer Zoo is exactly where she went.

Sam's outstanding talents as a hearer had over time become pretty plain to all and sundry. Her passion for, affinity with and knowledge of animal kind had only deepened and broadened. Alongside this came a kind of obvious, natural and unstated understanding of how the animal side of the Zoo worked. So on that main focus of her job, she was unparalled.

A certain consequent dilemma began to fester within me. I had taken a resolution to wreak retribution on the True Beast to avenge our Father's death; a determination only enriched by the horrific display at the Plains. I was equally resolved to stand against the creeping contagion of our Enemy's message and the rebellion against mankind.

It was my job to defend the Zoo.

The Zoo: The Beast, The Boy and The Zoo

Yet here was Sam, deeply immersed into the minds and worlds of different species and already grappling with the whole issue of what the animals *really* thought, what they felt and what they were 'saying' to us humans. Was not my younger sister really much more qualified than I to lead the charge? Should I not therefore share with my twin, that person with whom I had once shared nearly *every* thought and feeling, the confidence of what had happened at the Jaguar pool?

Should we not make common purpose on this and against the Enemy?

To my eternal regret, my lips stayed sealed.

***

Visitor numbers may have been declining for many years but only very slowly. Only now did many of the Zoo's functions begin to be seriously threatened. Its appeal to the outside world in turn seriously affected.

Keepers and curators, known as good hearers were sent out at night as emissaries, watchmen, intelligence gatherers, negotiators. Their mission to try somehow to stem the tide, to make the human case, to press the arguments for the Zoo itself. Every morning all returned empty handed, able only to report a further fraying of the fabric.

At least though they did return.

As we passed through summer, Sam kept taking longer and longer forays into the Outer Zoo and the Old Forest. First there would be the occasional absence overnight. Then two or three days at a time. Building up to a week at a time away from Edensor. Away from work. Away from me.

Food and other supplies were not getting to many parts of the Zoo. The vets could not access sick animals. Waste piled up. Water supplies failed. Very little of the estate properly functioned as a single entity anymore. The Penguins, the Otters and the Cranes had all died and been eaten. Surviving zoo animals in the outer areas had gone entirely feral.

As the autumn leaves began to drop, wholly wild animals from the wild woods moved inwards and began to colonise some of the internal areas of the Zoo.

The older hands at the Zoo had often spoken nostalgically of how the estate had been built up over the years. Organically. In concentric circles. Layer being placed carefully over layer.

"I remember when all there was, was a couple of paddocks up around the House." That was Petra to me. "Then, little by little, everything grew. Bits added here by your Mother. New animals brought in there by your Father."

"All our systems had to be rethought - every single year." Heinz ruefully mused. "So we could keep up with the way the Zoo was growing so fast."

"Ways of doing things seemed to get rewired almost every day, so that everything was linked to everything else," added Thomas. "In the end everything was woven into one big pattern."

Well, with every passing day now, there was less and less of a 'pattern'. Or at least not a pattern that belonged to us. Something else's design seemed to be wriggling forth to take over. As a film played backwards, the Zoo was descending back into its own infancy.

It was early on a humid evening in late summer about eighteen months after Father's death. Sam had been on her longest absence yet. Two full weeks. Mary knocked on the study door. She had brought the regular post in the morning, but now bore a single plain envelope in her hand. She closed the door. I opened it quickly.

There was no addressee. No signatory. But I recognised the hand writing. It was Sam's. Oddly shaky, but unmistakable.

The Zoo: The Beast, The Boy and The Zoo

All of the humans will leave the Zoo within one week.

You will free all the animals.

You will relinquish all claims of authority over this place and all the beasts, birds, insects and fish and others who live here

Any animals, who want to go with the humans, let them go.

Any animals, who wish to stay, let them stay.

If you fail on any of the above you will pay two forfeits

Firstly, any humans, and any beasts who take their part found here after seven days will be put to death.

Secondly, at noon on the eighth day in the glade of the Jaguars, we will extract a blood debt from our prisoner Sam Faraday, whelp of the dictator William Faraday, by whose hand we send this message.

This in repayment for the crimes the Faraday family have wrought on the animal kingdom.

There was nothing else in the message. Nor in the envelope.

I had often been kept awake at night in dreading that sooner or later one of the keepers would not come back from their night-time missions

I had never considered for a single second that the person who would not return would be my own sister.

***

Chapter Thirty Three: A Summoning

In my haste to bring the note to Lilith I had almost fallen over myself. Her eyes now danced briefly across the scant words Only very gradually did my breathing return to normal.

When our Father's death had so discourteously dumped the responsibility for the directorship upon Sam's and my shoulders, I found myself utterly hopelessly at sea. I might have some years of experience at being a keeper. I might have delved deeply into geography, history and philosophy. But now there were all these new utterly different and practical things to learn.

About money. About people. About buildings. About how to get anything at all done properly. About all the things that could go wrong. About what and whom you needed to look out for. I remember some mornings, after a sleepless night of fretting, walking towards my work frozen with self-doubt.

But... in small, indiscernible steps, and mainly due to Lilith's patient mentorship, I quickly stepped up. With a stumble or two I found my feet.

 Yet now, in the second of my handing that note over to Lilith that morning, there I went. I was sliding right down the snake again back to square one. Once more I was nothing more than a frightened little boy. The estrangement between Sam and me was as nothing besides this crisis. Blind terror swept through me at the thought of all that could happen to my twin.

The Zoo: The Beast, The Boy and The Zoo

Immediately I had reached out with my mind. I had groped forth, using the ability that through it all had always been available, to feel Sam's presence.

Somewhere surely?

No, nothing at all there. For the first time in my entire life I was truly and utterly alone.

"We wondered when something like this would happen." A disconcertingly philosophical reaction from Lilith. "Always Sam..." she mused, her eyes growing distant for a moment. "We should have realised. It was always going to be her of course."

Only for the merest instant did I manage to restrain an exasperated release of breath. "You *knew* this would happen?!" The unexpected ferocity of my snarl, in so far as anything ever could, took Lilith by surprise. Her attention was fully smarted back to me.

"Seth..? Calm down now." She laid the note to one side. "Yes, well... *something* like this. But not this exactly, not specifically what they would do. Or how Samantha would be involved."

"Anyway, we have been preparing a long time for this moment. Since you both arrived. For that matter long before. Rest assured, arrangements have been made. But we must act quickly and surely now. No time for arguments."

"We? Act? How?"

"It was too early before. We had to wait, however difficult it seemed. But no, this is definitely *it*. This is the tipping point". As she said this, she stopped, her face veiled for a moment, eyes dipping sideways into memories. "Poor William..."

Impatient with questions and demands, I protested, "No! No! We need to go and look for Sam *now*!"

But I was silenced by single flash of those green eyes. The shallow fiction of my being in charge of anything at all was wholly shattered.

The Zoo: The Beast, The Boy and The Zoo

"Stop. There will be enough to do. And goodness knows, you in particular will have to do it and very soon. For now, go to your room and dress to be outside. Outside all night long. Wait there. Someone will come for you soon".

"Who... *Who* will come?" I kicked back. *What* are we going to do?"

For some seconds there were several opposing senses of myself in conflict. There was the Seth who saw himself as his father's heir, his avenger even, the same Seth who had sworn to fight and defeat the True Beast and everything It stood for. Then there was the Seth who, despite all the recent distancing, was Sam's older brother and protector. Allied to and standing beside that Seth, there was a another, a third, who had never really reconciled himself to looking after a load of animals for the rest of his life, a Seth who was intensely curious as to what the wider world might offer. And finally there was the Seth right now at the surface, the Seth who for the first hours in his existence could no longer feel the presence of his twin. The Seth who only felt half a person.

Those last three Seths all ganged up together on the first one, They beat the hell out of him. Then they spoke as one.

"We should just do as they say. We should leave this place. Just leave it all behind. They will kill Sam if we don't! It is all an atrocious mess anyway – a lost cause. The whole rotten thing has already all fallen to pieces. Let it. Let it go back to the wild, the way they want..."

I was hot to continue. But once more Lilith's natural sweep of command and competence took the strength from me. She completely ignored what I had just said.

"Never mind who is to come for you. If you want to save Sam's life, you will do as I say. Obey the instructions of the guide who will arrive. They will give you my name."

The Zoo: The Beast, The Boy and The Zoo

"If you want Sam to live, you *will follow my orders.*"
And like a good little boy, of course I did.

***

At the Zoo you always seemed to have always to wait for the dark. You needed to be patient until the stars came out before anything could happen. Anything truly weird or momentous, I mean.

The arriving night was clear. The constellations above seem to shine especially brightly.

I had, as directed, changed my clothing; and now there I lay over my covers, thoughts scattering in bedlam all around my bedroom. Sam and I had moved apart. Due both to the inevitable process of growing up, and all the rest of it. But that background, that 'twin buzz' that had remained steadfast.

Once again I tried reaching out for it. To find her. But found only a blank space in my mind. As if part of me had been cut away.

I jumped up from the bed and strode around the room, desperate to do something. My guts tightened. The acid churned in my stomach. I thought now of the True Beast, the catalogue of offences it had rendered my family. I considered the look in that Black Jaguar's eyes drilling into mine, as it spoke of 'blood debt'. In that moment that threat had seemed centred on me. Now it was switched to Sam.

Desperately, I wanted to be doing something, one thing or another; searching for Sam, or clearing the devil out of the Zoo altogether, as has been commanded.

Really not such a poor idea, it seemed to me?

I had expected a knock at the door, and not, three storeys up, a tap at the window. Throwing back the curtains and looking straight out, I could at first see nothing at all. I opened the window completely and I leant right out into the boughs of the old beech tree that grows up around the house.

It was quite a sight.

The correct word I believe - appropriately enough as it turned out - is "a convocation". There were twenty or so huge birds in the branches surrounding the house. Resident species of the Zoo, but originally from all over the world. All familiar to me: Golden Eagles; Sea Eagles; Bald Eagles; Harpy Eagles; a lordly gathering of winged predators filling the trees and all staring studiously towards me.

Apart from that one time with Father and the Jaguars, there had been no been no further glimmerings of 'hearing' on my part. But now, sure enough, I heard the lead raptor, a Golden Eagle. I heard it speak loud and clear.

"Seth Faraday..."

It sounded as a resonant basso profundo. You might have expected something in a higher register from a bird, even an Eagle

"The Lady Lilith has told us to escort you." It gave a great shake of its feathers.

"Where? How?"

The Eagle said nothing, but extended and flapped its wings meaningfully.

Yes. I know there are all kinds of stories where people fly on Eagles' backs. But the fact is, apart from perhaps in the case of a very small child, there is no way that any bird known to man, living or extinct, can support the full weight of a human being. And however skinny I was, at seventeen years old I was way over the baggage allowance.

So was what the Eagle appeared to be suggesting a serious proposition? I stood hesitating at the window, unsure in every way. I was glancing back towards my room door, as if somehow someone might just come to rescue me from it all, when the Eagle grabbed one of my wrists in its talons. It yanked me forward and out of the window. I yelped in terror as the two of us inevitably plummeted down for two long seconds before a second bird, a Harpy Eagle with a magnificent white headdress grabbed my other wrist. The three of us still sank, if more slowly. Then a third and fourth birds seized my two ankles. And with the power of all four flapping in unison, falteringly and gradually, we rose again. Just a little. Helpless, inverted, horizontal, bereft of all dignity, I stared perforce down at the ground so far beneath us, my stomach performing somersaults.

Rising much further and faster now. The rhythm of the birds' wings, the air currents and my body wriggling in panic causing us repeatedly to dip, to rise and to sway from side to side. It took some time for my fear and nausea to allow me to appreciate what I was seeing below.

There was still enough light to make out the Zoo as we sailed over its bizarre terrain. First we went west, then circled south. Finally east. Around and around. And with each cycle, the Eagles took us higher. I might have assumed some specific location was in mind, but there seemed to be no particular rhyme nor reason to their path. Up and around and away through the dark.

Fear and vertigo were gradually slipping away. So far up now that it all seemed surreal; and simply not possible at this height to really relate to it all.

Neither was there any sound up here other than the hypnotic thrum of my four escorts' wings, matched by beating of my own heart. I was certainly glad now I had done as Lilith decreed and worn my warmest clothes; even with these, the extremities of my toes and fingers were, at such an altitude, becoming numb with cold. I think the creeping chill might have felt much worse, had my senses not been so enraptured by the beauty of it all. One by one the stars were popping out within the arc of indigo night that lay straight ahead.

The Zoo: The Beast, The Boy and The Zoo

Glancing down, I could, for the first time ever, see our whole Zoo. Or, more aptly put, 'the Zoo as a whole'. Not just a collection of animals thrown together. But something that made sense, something that worked together as a unified system.

The Helicon river poured out from its underground sheath at the very centre of a great spiral. I had, I suppose, always considered the snake-like river to mainly be a kind of barrier. Something either useful or unfortunate depending on one's situation. A natural impediment dividing the Zoo off from the rest of the world and also splitting it in half, rendering certain movements inconvenient or impossible. From up here though, it presented instead as a unifying force, a watery spine bringing shape, definition and logic to the Zoo. I could even see how someone could have imagined that this had all been planned; that the Zoo had - once at least - belonged to itself as a single living thing might do, all its parts happily interacting and cooperating.

And there in sharp contrast around the Outer Zoo, I could see those parts taken over by the True Beast, a dark smudge of decay insidiously spreading inward across a familiar, much loved and dazzlingly beautiful face.

Now we were slowly spiralling down again. The great, multi-coloured oval of the Zoo was very gradually expanding. The outer circumference of the Old Forest suddenly zoomed out and away to be lost beyond my frame of vision. Then the inner margins of the Outer Zoo followed the same pattern. A battery of warm and pungent earth smells rose through the night to zing into my nostrils.

The Eagles swerved decisively to the east. Even as we descended, the ground remained an unreal distance away. The gradual growth in the details beneath seemed a very lazy thing, almost as if the five of us might be dangling stationary in the air. Then suddenly the earth below was at last getting bigger and bigger.

Alarmingly so now!

The Zoo: The Beast, The Boy and The Zoo

The two Eagles holding on to my ankles suddenly let go together. I was now suspended only vertically, my feet swaying and swinging perilously a hundred feet above the ground. Then perhaps only fifty. Thirty? Finally in a single moment, and as of one piece, the Golden and Harpy Eagles also released my wrists.

I fell. Whomp! I landed. The bed of straw seemingly prepared to cushion my landing only partially served that purpose. The cold hard stone beneath still jarred my coccyx and smashed into my elbows.

Rubbing multiple areas surely soon to raise in bruises, I slowly manoeuvred to my feet. Wherever this place might be, it echoed my departure point in my bedroom in Edensor. I was again at the same level as the tops of closely crowding trees. The smells and sounds of the Old Forest at night flooded in around me.

Having dutifully delivered their consignment, the remaining Eagles unconcernedly flapped away to the surrounding branches, looking back with seeming little interest at my confused figure. I was standing there on the uppermost fortification of a single narrow tower jutting up in the midst of the Old Forest.

I might have been surprised that Sam and I had never come across this place in all our many explorations. But the Old Forest is so extensive and had always seemed - even more perhaps than the Zoo proper - intent on scrambling the minds of all who entered. Moreover this unassuming thin, vertical structure of sober stone slabs had been designed solely to some practical end. It had neither been conceived nor constructed to attract attention. The tower was packed in so closely and so densely on all sides by the ancient trees, that even if secrecy had not been consciously in the mind of its author, all but the closest passer-by would pass over its presence.

Above me the intense night sky through which I had so spectacularly just travelled had finally turned pitch black. The stars

The Zoo: The Beast, The Boy and The Zoo

spread out across my field of vision in all their glory, missing only the moon itself.

And yes, of course, there *she* was.

On the other side of this open, crenelated circle at the tower's summit sat the familiar figure I might have thought still back at Edensor. Lilith was wearing a long white dress, very different to any of the day-to-day garments with which I associated her. This robe carried some kind of symbol on the breast: it looked like an upside down horse shoe over a single horizontal line.

"How did you get here Lilith?"

"Don't tell me by Eagle too?"

"I have been here for some time, and in fact since shortly after we last spoke Seth, and no, I came the more conventional way."

My objections and questions came all together in an irritable rush. I didn't know why either of us needed to be here at all. And if we did, why we could we not have travelled together. And finally, what exactly was the purpose in my being hoisted aloft in such an unnecessarily dramatic and initially terrifying manner.

Lillith stood up, smoothing her long dress and dealt with my protests one by one.

"I needed time to prepare for what is about to happen here tonight, and as for my orders to the Eagles, well, you were needed here very quickly whilst we still had the whole night available before us. But the *real* reason I summoned the Eagles to fetch you, that was because it was time for you to see the Zoo from up there for once," she pointed above to the heavens. "Time for a quite a few things in fact. But tell me, did it work? Did you see and come to understand the Zoo as one thing? And above all did you see the *stars* as you came?"

With a brief surly nod, I acceded all of this but moved on quickly to infinitely more important matters "Lillith, do you *understand* that Sam is missing and in danger! Nothing of the rest of this stuff matters. What

The Zoo: The Beast, The Boy and The Zoo

the hell is going on here? Why are we wasting time when we should be out looking for her?"

"Your presence here is for a good reason, Seth. And it is specifically because of Sam that you are required. Just be patient a little while longer." Eying my dishevelment, she walked over to me and extended a long glass of some kind of drink. "Here. For after your journey."

With no concession whatsoever to patience, but freely admitting my thirst, I grabbed it and took a long, deep draught. Whatever that foaming liquid might have been, it tasted good and I did indeed feel refreshed. Yet even as my head came back up from that cup, I felt an apprehension of a kind I had never targeted on Lilith; not at least for many years past.

I immediately regretted having quite so hastily accepted her offer.

Lilith must have caught the shadow fleeting over my face. For she took the vessel from my hand and drained the remainder herself before quickly leaving it far to one side.

"So, what am I... what are *we* here for then?"

"You are here because you need to learn some things, Seth. Things you must understand. And because dependent on those understandings there are decisions to be made. Important decisions."

"Things I need to understand!? Well, yes, rather a lot of things as it happens. Things that *you* have kept from Sam and me for years!"

"First all," she continued, impassive despite my anger. "You need to understand who and what governs the Zoo."

I would have stayed on the offensive but now found myself hesitating. "Well... it was governed by Father." I rather dithered, then stopped, looked at her and corrected myself. "That is, he did his best to oversee matters, but with your help of course. And then Sam and I. And now that Sam is gone... Well, it is me."

"*I* am in charge."

The Zoo: The Beast, The Boy and The Zoo

The lights up in the pitch black above momentarily seemed to bulge and then to glisten, almost as if a crowd of onlookers were to suddenly shuffle and snigger. And was that the merest, shameful twinge of pleasure and pride sneaking into my mind? At the realisation that indeed there was now only me? That as the sole family member left, I had, after all of it, ended up as our parents' heir?

No, no, no..!

If that horrible thought had been genuine at all, I stamped on it over and over again, and squashed it down to some small, obscure place inside me. I loved my sister. I still do. And even though that might mean I might once again stand in her more talented shadow, I wanted her back. I wanted that, genuinely, angrily and desperately.

Lilith left that last would-be-confident statement of mine just hanging in the air. That forced me eventually and lamely to turn it into a question by adding. "...Aren't I?"

"Well... Yes…..." She conceded, but it was a slow and drawn out concession. Lilith's tone seeking to reassure, but more eager to move on quickly to more important things. "In *one* sense, you are. As were your father and mother before you. But who do you suppose appointed them?"

I didn't answer. Now I came to think of it, I had never really considered such a question. Why not? It was an obvious path of curiosity. I bet Sam had. Once again the universe insisted on reminding me that I was the dull, stupid, unimaginative twin.

"Before your father and mother, there was somebody who actually founded the Zoo. It is so long ago now that there is only one person alive who might even remember that time, and they are not available. It was certainly long before I was needed in this place. The founder is generally just referred to as 'the philanthropist' and, if she or he ever had a proper name, or if much of her story has actually been garbled, well nobody or hardly anyone knows the truth of it."

The Zoo: The Beast, The Boy and The Zoo

"You don't even know if it was a he or a she?"

"Neither know, nor in most cases care. All the story tells us is that she had access to enormous resources which she used to build everything you know as the Zoo, and that she had a vision and plan for it all."

"So where is this great character now? Why cannot we find him or her and seek help?"

"Nobody knows. There has been no word for as long as anyone can recall. Perhaps she is dead. Or perhaps just lost interest. Or maybe she is just waiting and watching all of us."

"But presumably," I asked. "Whatever the case, they would not want their Zoo destroyed by the True Beast?"

"Cannot even know that for certain, Seth. It is possible that what is threatening us all now is all part of her great design. That the philanthropist had a plan that is certain: but what that plan was...?" She shrugged her elegantly robed shoulders.

"Anyway eventually she identified successors and charged them with the care of this place. She more or less gifted the Zoo to itself, and then she departed. This tower is said to be one of the places where she spent a lot of time. "Lillith craned her neck upwards. "And from this pinnacle the philanthropist observed her Stars."

Until the moment Lilith said those words, she and I had been certainly quite alone up at the top of the tower. Suddenly I was sure this was no longer the case. Not exactly. On the way here and as the light had slowly faded I had noted and casually admired the stars as they gently emerged. But now, against the background of their cold, black, empty home, these same constellations seemed to burn so brightly down upon us both as to almost be presences standing there amongst us. Inexplicably I now felt foolish and naked and exposed up on that roof.

My eyes sought of themselves to glaze over a little. But Lilith's voice was continuing: "In your still young years Seth, and even given all

The Zoo: The Beast, The Boy and The Zoo

the strange things surrounding you at the Zoo, the frame of your life has been a cramped one. Look up for an instant at those stars and know that there are so many more dimensions and principles, so many ways of being and modes of thinking in this universe than you can have ever dreamed of."

"The reality that surrounds you and is available to you is not only stranger than you think: it is stranger than you are yet *able* to think."

"You see those four bright stars in a square to the west of the sky? Those are the stars of balance, of symmetry. That is the principle that has always guided and ruled my own life. And those over there?" She indicated a community of heavenly lights that might roughly sketch out two conjoined figures. "They are those that have always pushed and pulled the fates of Sam and yourself."

"The philanthropist's concept for the Zoo was not formed in a vacuum. Far from it. It was with the assistance of, or at least with the complicity of other powers."

"There is you see... 'another zoo'."

It was getting harder and harder to concentrate on whatever it was she was saying. What was this now? Annoyance and intrigue and fatigue all mingled within me. What did she mean by that? Another zoo? With some effort my gaze followed her finger pointing directly upwards.

"I mean that other zoo up there in the vastness of the sky, Seth - 'the Zoo of the Stars'."

The heavens were now blazing so very fiercely, bamboozling my eyes, that the surrounding dark of space itself seemed extinguished. The sky above seemed to be composed of nothing but light. My head began to swim badly. The distinction between 'here' and 'there', between our tiny physical presences on the top of this forgotten, crumbling tower in the Old Forest and the entire galaxy spread out there in its grandeur seemed no longer to be of any real consequence, almost a trivial notion on which only a fool might spend any time dwelling.

"There are more powers across the Earth and up there in the sky than you can have ever conceived of. Just as our Zoo here is the essence of what a good zoo should be in our world and of the needed balance between the human and the non-human, it in turn is only a pale reflection of what you now behold above in these heavens. If you are ever to find Sam, your twin, your 'other half'; if you are ever successfully to confront that dark Thing that has taken her, then this is your time to finally break out of your bounds."

"Tonight Seth is your night to *dream a little.*"

And with those words of hers, the stars wheeled in flashes ever more madly around my head. In fact now it seemed they were almost moving within my head. The vertigo I had been experiencing bloomed out of all proportion. Senseless I slumped to the ground, all agency and sensibility lost.

Far too late the realisation sidled up that Lilith, even whilst making a great show of sharing that drink, had certainly been intent on more than quenching my thirst.

***

Chapter Thirty Four: A Descent from Above

How long I was wholly unconscious I had no real notion; but certainly far before I returned to my full senses, I seemed to become groggily aware of... something.

I had stepped into a new and entirely unaccustomed mental state. Despite what Lilith had bid me, it had nothing at all of the very familiar texture of dreaming.

Dozens if not hundreds of spheres of light seemed to dance and sparkle around me, almost present inside my head. In some elusive way I was quite certain that, not only was there thought and will seated within each of these energies; but that here indeed was 'mind' in some purer form than that poor meat-bound thinking which we humans favour as intelligence.

It came to me fully now that, whether this was real or some phantasm of imagination, the summit of our tower was being visited, one by one, by the Stars themselves; and that they had come for me in particular. A 'me' who had been drugged defenceless by the very woman sworn to my protection. As each spirit seemed to rattle through my body, I was overwhelmed by a sequence of powerful emotions.

The strongest, keenest, most passionate of feelings ever otherwise entertained - before or since - in my entire life, these were as nothing in comparison.

An opening surge of glorious, fervent and defiant anger sweeping over me with no particular target was superseded by an overwhelming wave of love seemingly for everyone and everything that had ever lived;

this in turn quickly taken over by the deepest, darkest grief but connected to no apparent cause. Great sobs crashed and wracked me and, whether due to followings of rage or love or despair, my face became wet with tears.

After a while these ardours, each handing me on one to another, seemed to fade and be supplanted by a succession of more physical sensations.

First I beheld colours which no human eye had ever seen.

When, years later I tried hard to recall and describe some of these, the resultant gibberish was met with polite derision.

Now it was otherworldly sounds; and then scents, utterly ineffable. I could sense these all to be the fingerprints of my otherworldly visitors. They were casually picking me up for a second, weighing my worth, and then casting me aside.

Faces which were not faces stared one after another into mine with a kind of contempt-filled and transient curiosity which in seconds assessed and dispatched me.

I was as a doll, picked up, fidgeted with, and then of little appeal tossed back into the toy box.

On the one hand I was terrified that the imprint of these mighty, condescending judges might utterly wreck me, body and soul: on the other I was enraptured by the attention of such ethereal creatures.

And I did *not* want it to stop.

Yet stop it did. The storm subsided. This host of invading intellects, as of a single body, and to whatever end of its own, swarmed away. I drew in great deep breaths, both relieved to have survived and distraught at being alone, abandoned, perhaps repudiated.

Were Lilith and I now entirely by ourselves?

No. They had not *all* gone. A handful of specific and discrete potencies still hovered above and around us, their presence permeating everything nearby.

The Zoo: The Beast, The Boy and The Zoo

As if standing aside from my own body, I became particularly conscious of my prostrated position lying limply on the stone floor. It was as if there were giant figures met and clustering around and above me, staring gravely down.

The judgement, if that was what was in play here, was far from over. What had gone before had merely been a transient, almost incidental inspection by the wider multitude to which this smaller and specially constituted committee of great beings belonged. Theirs was a more serious and dedicated task.

"**Is this he?**"

"**Is this the little Geminus who has lost his other?**" The first voice was a dark, snorting, male bellow, its disdain and impatience overwhelming.

"**Was it he who that day slaughtered the harmless butterfly?**"

"**Pah!!! This pathetic stripling cannot face the True Beast. It will gore him in an instant and tear his limbs off one by one. It will feast upon his lungs. This child should go back to the warm house and comfortable bed from which he came.**"

"**Or better, he should leave this place completely and flee into the wider world and a broader life, as the True Beast seeks of him.**"

"**I see into him. This is what he secretly most wants himself.**"

"**No. I will have none of him. It would need many years of hardening before this little boy could even hope to have the strength to match the Enemy.**"

"**If it is indeed a new balance that we seek here, some other, better champion must be found.**"

A second, gentler female-timbred voice now responded. By contrast, to me this felt, at least within its initial tones, as might a soothing caress across the brow. "**This poor creature is yet young and untested. Do you not all see? It has lost so much. And it will, I fear, lose much more.**"

The Zoo: The Beast, The Boy and The Zoo

For a moment these sympathetic sounding notes seemed to remind almost me of Constanta. *My* Constanta. That special smile she would share with me (before that is, Sam had sent her away so peremptorily). Her next words though mouldered away such an agreeable memory into bitterness.

"Limp of limb, and weak of sinew he is indeed, as you say; but no better, nor more robust for the purpose sought is he in wit nor guile nor spirit. See only his awkward stuttering in seeking to court an avatar of mine in this place. But this one cannot even open his mouth to find the right words to speak to her!"

Once more the lights above abruptly crackled and for second were disrupted, as a human conversation might be paused by a ripple of laughter.

The second voice continued. "The True Beast has not spread across the Zoo only by force of arms, but in a subtle marshalling of eloquence and argument. Sending this one to debate with It before the parliaments of species would be as to thrust a suckling pig into the arms of the slaughterer."

"Yes!" a third voice agreed. "But not only is his knowledge and guile insufficient." This one seemed to brim with anger. "He is stained. He is ruined from the very first spark by the mere fact of his blood. Were it as a child of Adam alone, he would be corrupted by the sins of his species. Yet as the son of his particular parents, he is further blighted. If the True Beast is to be closed with, it should by an instrument of ours who is clean; not one profaned by its very heritage."

Now, yet a fourth shadow seemed to crawl over my form and stare down disparagingly. I felt eclipsed by some monstrous carapace that poked and prodded at me with multiple claws. A great croak came: "If balance is to be found again, as our convener here Libra seeks, a human champion is needed, but *not* this one. To speak plainly, it

The Zoo: The Beast, The Boy and The Zoo

would have been better if he had died and his sister had survived, and so be now before us."

Survived! Was Sam then dead? The earthy shock of this terrible thought wrenched me from that strange state beyond dream or delusion and stuffed me pell-mell back into my body.

I was still lying on the ground, my eyes tightly shut. I was awake now in a normal sense but took care not to yet move. I wanted to review to myself without inviting any further attention all that had been said here.

So I 'played dead'.

Let me see.

I focused my thoughts tightly. I was, it seemed, only a boy. I was half grown. I was weak. I was rather dim, poor with words and ideas. I was an inadequate heir to my father, and nothing at all compared to my brilliant and talented missing twin, who may well now be dead.

And if all that were not enough, I was - simply for the original sin of being born a human - from my very begetting damaged goods.

Before this night there had been no glimmering within me that such extraordinary beings as these scornful entities, these Sapient Stars had existed at all. Lilith was certainly right in that the experience she had induced, by whatever means and to whatever purpose, had exploded my apprehensions in every direction. The universe had suddenly become a very strange place indeed. The intelligences floating it seemed at one and the same time within easy reach of an outstretched hand, but also located at a point so distant as to be beyond measurement, were clearly of both a wisdom and might that, by many magnitudes, outshone any such on Earth.

Yet I surprised myself.

A certain defiant contempt had for some minutes been thickening fast within me. These beings deemed me unfit for purpose on numerous grounds, did they?

The Zoo: The Beast, The Boy and The Zoo

Well there was one *other* disqualifying factor. There was a further, entirely distinct obstacle as to my filling their much vaunted role as 'a valiant and dedicated champion for the cause'. It seemed only polite that I draw the attention of this array of god like beings deigning to pass judgement on me, to that single issue that they had missed entirely.

This was plain and simply that... I was damned if I bloody well *wanted* to!

Now I at last opened my eyes and with great effort hoisted my body to my feet. Brushing debris from my clothes and form, I stood and stared around at each nimbus hovering around me. I did not care if they were millions of miles away or so near that I might have reached out and prodded them. I was burning with an indignation that superseded any sense of awe, respect or plain old terror.

"There is another reason I cannot be your champion..."

Do you suppose Stars can be surprised?

Certainly their reaction seemed very near to that; not only I think at what I had said, but also that I had the temerity to say it at all. I placed my hands on my hips, a further disrespectful gesture -doubtless sacrilegious. Once again there was a brief flickering of the intense light, but this time it appeared to signal more indignation than ribaldry.

I looked at Lilith, who I now realised here at least to be more fittingly named 'Libra'. I faced her full square for a second or two. Then I stared around at the ring of incandescence within which I was standing. Much of me was still both very much beguiled and intimidated by their deep strangeness; minds and experiences so vastly beyond my pay grade; but my rising indignation crested above all of that.

"I am not *interested*."

The silence of the spheres held.

"I came here for one reason and one reason only. To find my twin, Sam."

The Zoo: The Beast, The Boy and The Zoo

I don't care about all the rest of this... this... stuff." I expelled the word with derision. "This laying out of your great matters. So it doesn't matter in the least what any of you think of me as some kind of champion. Nor do your mighty opinions as to whether I am old, or strong, or clever enough. Or whether I am damned anyway as a filthy human."

"I am going now, leaving this place. I am going to seek *my twin*. But first I need to know," grim faced I turned towards Lilith/Libra. "Is Sam still alive?"

Our eyes met. Our gazes clashed. Even if ever so slightly, it was I who blinked first. "Yes, Seth she certainly is. I am sure of it. When Cancer spoke of Sam surviving, that is not what was meant."

Well what the devil *did* it mean? I thought, but did not pursue.

"Then that is all I really need to know." I wiped my hands together in finality, and turned resolutely to move away. "My twin, the most important other person in my universe, is in deadly peril. And I need to be doing something. So I am going now. I am leaving all this nonsense behind. And I am going to find my Sam."

A massive grunt. The fourth speaker again brooding above us. **"If you take that road,"** an oddly calm and almost conciliatory tone. **"You will *never* find your other one."**

I grunted right back and gestured dismissively, turning all the same to leave. The fact that I had no idea of what I might do. That I did not indeed know where to even begin. None of this had yet percolated through my angry brain.

"Cancer is right, Seth," Lilith/Libra now in a much gentler tones than before. "You really won't find Sam that way. At least, that is, you cannot find Sam by actually *looking*. But there is another way."

As ever, she was tantalisingly opaque; and as ever, she had made me stop and listen. But she was already turning away from me, addressing the attendant astral powers. "This fellowship has raised several objections to this Geminus' ability as a champion of those species who wish to follow the leadership of humankind and defy the True Beast."

"That he is too young and that he lacks experience and knowledge."

"That, as a member of the human race, his candidature should be automatically dismissed."

"That he has no ability, nor knowledge nor indeed the will to address the divergence of mankind from all its siblings. That, as shown particularly in his case, their species' typical forgetfulness of what it is to be an animal is so profound as to be beyond all redemption or remediation."

"That when he comes to close quarters with the True Beast in debate as to the Zoo's continued purpose and existence, he lacks the tools to wrestle in argument or in the very articulation of moral boldness itself."

And then she swivelled, re-orientating her elemental gaze back on me. "There is then your very own objection. You say that your sole goal is to be reunited with your twin, and that, in that perspective, all other matters to do with the True Beast, to do with the Zoo, to do with the great schism, these all fall aside?"

"My duty here is to bring and balance all such matters. I have a proposal that seeks to address all of these issues in one single form. I seek that all those present, whether mortal or astral, might be a little patient."

"I must put this first to the Dominions visiting us this night. So I ask Geminus to stand apart." She gestured for me to fall back. There seemed little choice then but to comply. Reluctantly I walked to the furthest edge of the tower and away from the luminescences. From there I could see the passionate discussion, but could not discern any content nor detail. It was mere minutes though before Lilith-Libra beckoned me to return.

Our chairwoman began speaking again slowly, mainly though not exclusively to me.

And then she laid out the most ridiculous proposition to which in all my years I have ever born witness.

***

Chapter Thirty Five: An Outrageous Proposal

"I need first to speak again in a little detail of the central matter confronting all." Lilith stood in the centre in command of this strangest of stages. " For a long time we have known that the *real* problem in the Zoo, the issue at the very centre of all of this, the true deficiency on Mankind's part; and, I fear, Seth, on your late father's part specifically, is a failure to acknowledge that we humans are ourselves animals."

"We will do *anything* to hide this fact from our own gaze."

"This is the fundamental insecurity that haunts and is supressed at the back of the minds of every single woman and man who has ever walked the earth. All of mankind's religions are carefully crafted to separate man from other animals, to tell him that he is modelled on something somehow 'finer', and that he will not one day die an animal death. To gainsay the fact that, Seth and I and all the other humans at the Zoo and in the whole world will one day be simply meat, just as every other animal."

"The clothes that we wear." Lillith/Libra looked at me and back down at her own slim body and, even though I was dressed warmly, I suddenly felt utterly naked. "The way we preen and decorate our bodies. The airs and graces we give ourselves, which constitutes so much of that thing we dare to call culture."

"These are all denials."

The Zoo: The Beast, The Boy and The Zoo

"It is only when we rut amongst ourselves, only for the sake of that overwhelmingly greedy passion, do we for some short time, let all pretence drop. And even then, we seek to cloak our mating and pair bonding with an idea called 'romance' or 'love' to show that we are above and 'better than the animals'."

"Then there is our determination to classify all of our fellow living things in one way or another. This is our 'science'. "

"Name and shackle them all, there lies our resolve. And in doing so, to keep them safely distanced from us. "

"Yes, we strut pathetically, imperiously, impetuously, stacking up layer after layer of defence against that 'deplorable fact', that single, unspeakable piece of knowledge. That truth that in the end we are merely one amongst many."

"This is the Great Lie we persistently tell ourselves. And it is a lie that has *failed*".

"All humans know the truth really. They certainly come to know it at the end gasping obscenely on their deathbed."

"But the lie has, in the intermittence, done its work very well. The wedge has been firmly inserted between the human ape, that single animal blessed or cursed with the potential to physically change and perhaps even to destroy the whole world, and all of its kin."

"That fundamental imbalance, the deep seated distrust is destroying the Zoo, provoking the rebellion, and allowing the contagion to creep in."

"The True Beast, as the unclassifiable essence of animal kind, proposes itself as the answer, the balancing factor against the Great Lie."

"Those Dominions present here are only part of the full circle pertinent to our matter. Neither Leo nor Pisces has descended tonight. Those not attendant here may well be already drawn to believe the True Beast's way is the right way. Even some of those present may be sorely tempted."

The Zoo: The Beast, The Boy and The Zoo

Once more, there was a short diffusion of lights all around us. "But *none* have made any final decision. All of our company, all save one, have throughout this long matter continued to take and share counsel together."

"Those here present have reached agreement on several counts."

"Let us agree that this avatar of Gemini is far from the ideal champion needed in a coming-to-close-quarters with the True Beast; and that if Seth Faraday, whether by deed of arms, or by deed of words and will, is indeed to grapple with It, he must grow and strengthen at a rate and in ways far beyond all normal paths and means."

"We all also agree that you," turning back now to me. "You need to be forced to remember your deep animal nature. To understand what it truly means to be a beast."

"You as a Human Seth need to learn to once again *love* being an animal."

We all agree that we must see evidence of your ability to contest with the True Beast, and not just in terms of horns, fists, fangs and hooves, but on the field of ideas, mind, passions and feelings."

"Finally we also all agree - and as you most certainly know Seth in your heart – that there is only one way those beasts who have rebelled against the authority of the Faraday family will render up the other half of Gemini. That is if *they also* witness your worth in these fields we have stated. If these creatures see you as victorious against their Leader, the adversity of their will shall drain away in a heartbeat."

"There is a single path forward in which *all* of these elements can, if not be wholly achieved, then certainly be soundly tested to the satisfaction of all parties."

Doubtless this was intended as my cue to speak up and ask what this 'single path' might be.

In a small gesture of contrebellion, I stayed entirely silent.

So Libra was forced to press on.

"Can you guess Seth Faraday what it is that is demanded of you?"

"Yes, yes!"

My impatience, my irritation and my petulant dismissal of this whole damn pageant was surging back in a major way. With weary sarcasm I replied in an attempt to imitate Libra's patronising words and tone.

"Yes, I know, I know. I need to '...grow up'. "

"I need to '...become a man'!"

"No Seth. Not at all. You need to become precisely *the opposite*".

***

Chapter Thirty Six: All hope abandon, ye who enter here

This spot was very familiar.

Follow the winding path through and past the pandemonium of the Monkey Jungle area. Then suddenly it all becomes so much quieter as you are drawn quickly downhill within a narrowing, overgrown ravine. And finally to this mossy knoll on which I was now standing, before the mouth of an immense black cave.

Sam and I had come here often.

Because this is where the Bats live.

Their cave home is very close to that point where the Helicon river comes bubbling up from god knows where below ground. This part of the Zoo is blessed with all kinds of caves and rock formations. A good few of these had been pressed into service as one sort or other of accommodation for animals within the Zoo. This great cathedral of a cavity was just one such.

In more ordinary times both of us had together enjoyed the huge Bat cave many times. The experience of being surrounded underground by hundreds of Bats had, even in those days I had to cede, a certain thrill (though another part of me still found these flying Rats rather revolting). Once inside you never quite seemed to be at its end. The ceiling was a mass of stalactites, indentations and crenulations. If you wandered off the pathways permitted for the 'Scents, it would be all too easy to get a little lost in the nooks and crannies as the back floor of the cave wrinkled further and further down into the dark depths.

The Zoo: The Beast, The Boy and The Zoo

The official, prominent entrance for the 'Scent visitors was locked and bolted at this early time in the morning. But there was another, small side door with a little window at the top. It is known only to those who lived and worked at the Zoo. That doorway was so tight that only one person at a time could just about squeeze through, and you had to pull hard on the door knob to force it open. I stared through the window into the pitch black.

"Enter there and wait within."

That had been it.

The only actually practical instructions I had been given for this moment. Lilith/Libra and the Circle of Stars had at the end of our interview laid out their proposition in full before me.

"You must undergo three tests, three trials as the heir of William Faraday. Depending on just how these transpire, on what exactly happens in each encounter, everything, all the issues we have debated here, will *eventually* - one way or another - be resolved."

"That resolution may mean humans leaving the Zoo for ever. Or perhaps quite the opposite. Perhaps as your father so desperately sought for so long, a fresh covenant will after all be agreed. Either way some new balance will be struck. And, whatever the outcome, all in the Circle agree that your own, single aim, Seth - the thing you really want, this will certainly be achieved. You *will* be reunited with Sam."

I had stared hard at the ground and taken a deep breath. "What would I need to do?" I was intent on reserving my position. "*If* I agreed?

She had just come straight out and said it.

It has now been a whole lifetime since, but those specific, astonishing and wholly surreal words of Lilith/Libra's still flash up, one after another, across my mind's eye, their impression utterly indelible.

"You must, Seth, assume the form of three animals as chosen for you. "

The Zoo: The Beast, The Boy and The Zoo

At first I had stiffened. Then my breath came out in a single rush at this inane drivel. Was she serious? Did she somehow mean this literally? Or was this some further mystic, symbolic claptrap?

"As each chosen animal you will experience conflict." She went on. "To that very same purpose the True Beast will certainly seek you out inside the animal world you inhabit. Perhaps the conflict that ensues will be physical.

Perhaps one of ideas.

It will probably be both."

She stopped and waited for some reaction. I did not oblige. So she moved on.

"Through these incarnations you must every time grow in experience and understanding. You must come to know fully what it means to be an animal; and so paradoxically to understand more profoundly that it means to be a man."

My indignation, my dismissive incredulity were growing all this time, but she was in full flow.

"Through you Seth it must be proven that mankind has at least the potential to put the Great Lie away. And likewise you must show whether you have the potential to match with the True Beast in mind and argument, if not always in physical force.

My impatience broke its banks. "What the hell do you mean Lilith?" I forgot to whom I was speaking for a moment. "I can't just snap my fingers and turn into a blasted camel, can I! And do you truly and honestly expect me to believe you after what you have done this night? Why should I believe anything at all from someone who drugged me!"

"No Seth, the drink I gave you did not intoxicate you in any sense at all. The very opposite in fact. The delirium you experienced when the Stars came down would have happened anyway. What I gave you was to limit and shape it into a certain direction. Had I not done so - and for myself as well - contact with such beings would have unravelled us both entirely.

You would have emerged a gibbering idiot."

"And you are not that... entirely." She allowed a brief smile. Then she turned her gaze fully on me. Whatever it was about that look, I could tell she was entirely serious. This was real. This was going to happen. I shrank. Pinned down in the full beam of her eyes, sensations of horror and adventure; overwhelming grief and sheer exhilaration; winter, spring, summer and autumn, all of these streamed through me.

"In ordinary times, in ordinary places, with the involvement of ordinary beings, yes of course such a thing would be impossible. But on this special night, in this special place and with Taurus, Virgo, Aries and Cancer out of the heavens meeting with Libra and at least a component of Gemini here on Earth, a deep magic is available. Something that can reach very far indeed."

"That someone in your family would face a crucible of this very sort that was never in doubt. Most had assumed that it would be Sam, in whom so very many obvious and relevant gifts were vested. She who would receive this honour. She would shoulder this burden."

"But we have, all of us, been shorn of half of Gemini."

I said nothing.

"Do you accept, son of William Faraday?"

I glared back at her. "Tell me first honestly Lilith - and on the basis that what you say is real - what chance is there that I might succeed in all of this?"

"Most do not believe that you will succeed. Some of us, however, see a spark within you that gives just a little hope."

Lillith returned to her demand.

"Do you accept Geminus?"

"How does this all finish?" I wanted the fullest possible picture. "What is the end game here?"

The Zoo: The Beast, The Boy and The Zoo

"After your time as three animals, and after you have confronted your enemy in these guises, you and the True Beast will meet one last time here in the Zoo itself and in your true form. This will be a one to one, a final resolution of matters. In striving then against It, you may not use any human device nor artifice, only those abilities held within your physical human form and from what guile you have acquired. Similarly the True Beast will be bound by us. It may not assume the form of any creature or power, but will only be allowed to contest with you in as limited, human form as your own."

"But what reason is there for the Enemy to obey any of your rules?!" I interrogated further.

"As long as your conflict is securely here within the borders of the Zoo itself, even the True Beast is bound by our authority and the rules laid down by the philanthropist. We will see that It obeys our charge. We will bind It to that purpose, never fear. This *will* happen. One of you will live. One will perish."

One more time she pressed me. "Do you accept, Seth?"

As a king on chessboard presented with a forced move, and no alternative path available, I had bowed to the inevitable. I had accepted.

Standing now before the Cave entrance, I threw my shoulders back and took a final deep breath. As I grabbed the shiny door knob to wrest the door open. Just for a second I caught my own reflection in it. In fact, given the distortion afforded by its convex shape, it might as well have been Sam's face looking back at me.

Then with Lilith's parting words echoing in my mind "Above all Seth, do *not* get lost in there." I squeezed through the crack into pitch black mouth of the Cave.

***

Chapter Thirty Seven: What is it like to be a Bat?

All of the time since that damn note had arrived I had been moving forward on automatic pilot, helplessly conveyor-belted forward from one point to another by minds and wills all far greater than mine; my compliance only occasionally punctuated by brief and futile rebellions against the bizarre nature of the whole situation.

Now here, I was foolishly, helplessly, blindly waiting in the utter darkness it seemed, for someone to turn me into a Bat! At one and the same time I felt ridiculous, incredulous, acrimonious, and terrified. It was only the thought that I would be abandoning Sam that steadied me, and stopped me from bolting there and then.

The Cave is home to two entirely different kinds of Bats. Hundreds of tiny Pipistrelles, just a few inches long with orange brown fur and squashed up faces; and also just a few dozen much larger mega bats, Golden Crowned Flying Foxes, huge eyes and long snouts. "More like a dog than a fox," Sam always said. So Dogs is what we had called them. They had yellowish red fur and a massive, leathery five foot wingspan.

From a distance the 'Strelles were as wreathes of smoke. By contrast swooping low and close over your head, the flying Dogs could be miniature Pterodactyls.

"By and large," Oscar the bat keeper used to tell us, his own large blinking eyes rarely seeing full daylight. "The two species get on okay. They just ignore one another. But when they all get together in their Cloud, well they move and act like once species, even one animal."

The Zoo: The Beast, The Boy and The Zoo

That type of conversation belonged to the normal, daytime Zoo. This would be a very different visit.

My poor eyes endeavoured to pierce the darkness. Complete blackness. There seemed no light available whatsoever. Then gradually I began to make things out just a little, my pupils slowly adjusting.

After a moment, something there in the black emptiness. Somebody. A voice. Soft and welcoming. "Hello Seth."

The words hanging out there at an indeterminate point. I groped towards them, outlines of shapes reluctantly beginning to uncloak. It was a tiny 'Strelle hanging upside down in a small rock shelf just to my left inside the Cave. It was talking; and I, as a Human, was hearing.

Distances and spaces were still resisting me. It spoke again. "My name is Trice. I have been sent to see you through." I blundered further towards the voice, marginally more certain of my bearings.

"So you know why I am here?"

"Yes, you have some work ahead of you, haven't you? But first things first. It will be much easier from here on, if for this you become one of us."

"And how exactly do I do that?"

"It will be pretty much done for you. Close your eyes and empty your mind." Closing my eyes made very little difference to anything, but I complied. "Now imagine the tallest cliff in the world. Imagine standing right at the top. Slowly move to the very edge. In your mind's eye look down on all that is below."

That was an image I could summon up very easily. I had had some very recent relevant experience.

"Make sure inside your head you are right at the very edge and looking down."

"Yes and...?"

The Zoo: The Beast, The Boy and The Zoo

"Be sure to keep your eyes closed really tight. And the drop beneath you needs to be the deepest, scariest one you can possibly imagine. No sign of where it ends below."

I obeyed all of this. The summoned up situation had become quite real in my mind. My legs in truth even beginning to wobble a little.

"Are you keeping your eyes properly shut?"

"Yes."

"Are you right at the absolute very edge, Seth and looking down?"

"Yes, yes. I *am* right at the..."

My sulky retort was cut off. In some way, something from somewhere behind me shoved me forward. And hard. This was in my mind, but at the same time, it was very real indeed.

My eyes sprung open in involuntary surprise. I was in the void, but held aloft. My own arms were doing this. Except they were not arms any more. They were wings. And I was flying.

I was flying all by myself.

And more. The world, my world had suddenly exploded in size. The space separating me from that wall of the Cave over there had, while my eyes had been closed, zoomed dramatically. All the fixed points of my universe had been stretched, unfolded, and multiplied an incredible number of times.

And me?

Oh, I was so tiny. I was flying. And I was a bat. A 'Strelle.

My arms - my so long, so strong arms - now seemed my most important parts. Far longer than in my form as a Human, they felt robust, heavy and complex, yet also simple and elegant. And so powerful! They stretched majestically out either side of me. They whirred around me. They vaulted me high up into the air.

This felt great! I was elated. Flying by myself was wonderful. I was *so good* at it, so skilful! I was sooo naturally good at this...

The Zoo: The Beast, The Boy and The Zoo

Suddenly and painfully I banged into a rock wall. I slithered pathetically down, almost smeared against the side to finish on a small outcrop three feet or so above the Cave's ultimate floor.

I tried to stand up, but with no practice somehow I could not seem to stay upright on my stupid legs. In embarrassment I realised why. I was not built to walk. When not in the air I was made to be upside down. I could only scrabble to the edge. I knew the distance between me and the flat floor of the Cave was barely enough, but I dropped off, unfurling my wings in desperate, panicked speed, and successfully skimming the floor to rise again. Soon I was hanging upside down next to Trice high in the ceiling once more, and panting with relief.

"Seth, you are *thinking* too much. You need to let your Bat body tell you what to do. Stop trying to work out how to move. Try again, but follow me. And *stop thinking*!"

I released my claws. And I soared. And beside me Trice soared too.

We joined our fellow Bats. Thousands of us wheeled around as one huge creature in the centre of the vast Cave.

That is just one of the things 'Scent humans get wrong. Bats are not blind. This is not true at all. My eyes were much smaller and dimmer than those I had as a human, but I could still see. Only things quite close though, a few yards away, had distinct visual form.

But my hearing had become fantastic. As if someone had reached down inside my ears and scraped out a hundred years of wax. All the sounds were clear and sharp and full of promise, of animation, of friendship, packed with excited friendly news and gossip from my Bat sisters and brothers.

All warm, welcoming signals.

All except for one. One low note in the far background. That said a very different kind of thing.

The Zoo: The Beast, The Boy and The Zoo

And for a moment I thought I could 'see' in two quite different ways. First of all there was certainly a very clear picture in my head of the whole Cave now. This was much more distinct and detailed for me even than when it lit up artificially during one of Sam and my daylight visits.

Then this second kind of seeing? But this new thing wasn't actually seeing at all, was it? The inside of my head was welcoming the new information in a familiar, casual way just the way my old human eyes had welcomed light, but I wasn't really seeing. No, I was 'talking' to the Cave, to its walls and to everything within it. And they were all 'talking' back to me.

Screeing, as I now know to call it, is the emission of tiny parcels of Bat sound to bounce off surroundings and back into our Bat brains. I could feel space, objects within that space, the distance between those objects, their feel and texture. Even what they felt like inside. How tough, how hard, how soft, how plastic, how mushy.

To be able to know one's surroundings in that way, so fully   is a joyful, wonderful thing. To have the universe lit up for you in brilliant detail.

I recall much later how I tried, falteringly and with frequent sighs, to explain to others what this had been like. I quickly realised that I couldn't ever hope to communicate the sensation to anyone else. How, after all, do you really tell another being what chocolate tastes like, or what lavender smells off or how exactly it feels to have a toothache?

We poor Humans are trapped, all of us, in our own heads. For all that Sam and I had enjoyed our special twin thing; in that sense even we too fell into the same category.

Yet, although I could never actually experience it again as a Human, the sheer vividness of the sensation itself has never been lost to me. The deliciousness of it all has remained stored in my head all these years.

The Zoo: The Beast, The Boy and The Zoo

Within a few short minutes I learned to emit difference kinds of sonic projectiles. Some short and sharp, some long and sinuous, each bringing back different information, different sensations. And in each of these screes as well there was decipherable meaning, emotion, communication

I experimented with varying the frequency of my castings. As I casually cruised around the Cave, I moved between ten and twenty emissions per second. And then, then, oh utterly sublime! My screeing focussed in on a big, juicy, black fly in front. 17.6 degrees downwards; 8 degrees to my left pursuing a precise trajectory that would take it to a specific point over my head and to the right in exactly 0.566 seconds.

I revved up to an intense buzz of 200 screes per second.

I swivelled. I swooped. I crunched.

My teeth daggered through wings and carapace and into the succulent yellow within. I tasted and swallowed all within an instance. And on I flew.

I swooped after more Insects, but began also now to focus more on my fellow Bats all around me.

Oscar has said that the two kinds got on okay. But now I saw that there was a kind of mutual contempt. And I could well understand why. We 'Strelles, we masters of the air, wanted little to do with the clumsy, uncouth flying Dogs with their big ugly eyes popping out of their heads. And their disgusting way of slurping pulpy apples and mangoes, rather than engaging in the noble, skilled pursuit of superb flying insects.

The looks that the flying Dogs gave us down their long snouts clearly returning the compliment. I remember Oscar saying that their colony here at the Zoo were all descended from a population deemed to be the rarest Bat in the world; the remnants of a single grove of mangrove trees in the wild. Clearly the Dogs knew all about this elevated heritage. And on its account they had become quite taken with themselves.

The Zoo: The Beast, The Boy and The Zoo

I had Bat flying down pat now. Four different muscles in the down stroke, bones twisting elastically, membranes flickering to perform exquisite aerobatic manoeuvres.

The hundreds of other 'Strelles seemed almost part of me. No chance at all, however fast I flew, however suddenly I changed direction, of any collision, of smacking into a fellow Bat. Certainly not one of the dexterous 'Strelles, and not even one of the clumsy lumbering Dogs. In that, at least, we were all aspects of the same entity. We all wheeled around together as part of the Cloud.

The calming, reassuring effect of the collective mass of my fellow Bats all screeing together grew on me. Since Sam and I had first become distant from one another in speech and mood, I had begun to feel less than a full person; then with her abduction, dramatically more so. Yet now I was, for a small time, happy again. Whilst wheeling so freely around in the Cave Sam was, for that moment at least, not the most important thing on my mind: flying with my fellow Bats, that was.

The Cloud was one great comforting blanket of fellowship. Kind thoughts emanated from every single point. Everything benevolent and welcoming; everyone together. Surely this friendship and kinship would surround and envelop me forever.

Except...

Except again for that one noise. That distant but definite vibration; there somewhere deep in the Cave, something possessed of a deep and sharply chiselled malevolence.

I woke from my musings. Flying beside me, Trice had nudged me sharply in the side. "Come on Seth, stop messing about. We have work to do. Important people to see."

"But I want to fly some more, Trice. I love flying. See, I'm fantastic!" I executed what I consider to be a particularly impressive flashy manoeuvre. "I am flying. Flying just like a bird!"

The Zoo: The Beast, The Boy and The Zoo

"Ha!" Trice snorted. "Birds don't fly!" Those things may flap around a little. Pathetic, clumsy sorts. But that's not flying."

"Now, us bats, we fly!"

And with that Trice did fly together with me for a little while more. We swooped, we looped the loop, we traversed all sides of the Cave. We penetrated every little one of its deepest cavities and niches, angling sideways or shortening our wings at just the last opportunity to navigate through perilously narrow gaps.

"Now enough Seth, we are being called." He was right. The warming, information-rich screeing was becoming more focussed now, more purposeful, drawing us forward, summoning us inwards.

Obediently I flew behind Trice across the great lagoon that dominated the centre of the Cave, then banking sharply to the right and through a narrow entrance swerving right again.

"This is called the isolation chamber by the Human keepers. For us it is our Convocation, our Parliament of Bats."

Well for a parliament, it looked more like a giant cloakroom filled with hanging umbrellas, an upside down parliament for an upside down situation. Hundreds of 'Strelles and Dogs all hanging in rows. Nearly every one swivelled in our direction as Trice and I entered.

In the middle by himself was one old grey 'Strelle, much bigger than most of the rest of us, almost overlapping in size with the smaller Dogs.

"There," a Bat whisper from Trice. "That is the Speaker, Seth."

The screeing, which had both intensified and randomised as we entered, now fell off sharply. And after a few seconds, I briefly experienced something for the first time since I had become a Bat: complete silence, no noise whatsoever, no feedback, no information at all.

Then soon again there was a something to fill the void. One more time I sensed that single, insistent, malicious signal originating from somewhere lost within the Cave and boring towards me. With no competing sounds now, it was so much more distinct. I could tell which direction it was coming from. Towards the back of the chamber, behind the Speaker and to his left.

This overall rhythmic strum slammed into me with notes and vibrations combining at different levels. These together seemed to penetrate, not only through my enhanced Bat ears, but to resonate horribly through my whole body. There was a higher pitch of hatred, of threat, of contempt that seemed telegraphed very specifically in my direction; yet lying lowdown beneath that, a more surreptitious, generalised broadcast, one of seduction, of disobedience, of exuberant rebellion.

Oddest of all, this thing was most definitely a noise, that is to say, literally a wave of air molecules moving from its source to find and impact on my little Bat eardrums. But somehow, once inside my own physical system, it mingled strangely not with my own sense of sound, as you might expect, but rather with memories of things I had once *smelled.* As if the noise itself was a key turning in a lock, but that the particular storeroom which it opened was packed full with tangs, spices and stenches of many forms.

All of these now flooding forth together now within a jumbled stream of half recognised recollections.

There was one particular memory there. A special one that I sensed, if only I could just stretch far enough, I might grasp properly and fully. I scrabbled hard to gather it back up and lock it into my full knowledge.

Yes!

There it was.

The Black Jaguar.

The Zoo: The Beast, The Boy and The Zoo

Of course. That was it. Those subtle, sidling pheromones of threat wafting over me standing there before the pool with Father in the western glade.

Yet behind and beneath that time, that same smell was full of earlier things too. Fears and desires going further back. Back to earliest childhood.

Or before that?

Whatever. The notion had fled beyond retrieval. Now my thoughts were snapped away from seeking lost times. I was no longer astray in the wood of fugitive memories. The Speaker was doing his thing. Once again an animal was speaking and I was hearing what it said. Words echoing from his dangling head all around the assembled multitude.

The strange inverted sermon that followed had a compulsion all its own, as the Speaker swivelled first one way, then the other to address the surrounding host of upside down hanging bodies.

"We are here today," he was beginning. "To make an important judgement."

"We are the Cloud, the Convocation, the great assembly of the Zoo's Bat species. We look in turn to those higher authorities which govern and represent the Zoo as a whole. We are gathered to determine whether we the Bats wish to remain within the Zoo; and to continue to accept the sovereign role and stewardship of Man, the naked Ape."

He paused for a second.

"Long ago we did indeed make a pledge to that very effect. But all has changed, and many would say that the original dispensation on which the Zoo was founded is now null and void."

There was a movement back and forth amongst the serried rows of cloak room suspended umbrellas.

"As we all know, the Lady has not been with us for so many years." Something like a lament now chittered through the Cloud. "A new one walks now amongst us. One who is not a Man, although It does take that form from time to time. One who is a truly wild creature of our own. One who has not forsaken our feral heritage, nor, unlike Man, has disclaimed our shared animal nature. One who would call on us to shake off the shackles imposed by Man, to reject a false unity represented by the Zoo. One who disclaims the contention that the Zoo represents health; and that a thirst for freedom is somehow a 'disease'. One whom some amongst us would call... our Saviour."

As he continued, I could not shake off the strong feeling the Speaker was less than neutral on the matter in question.

"One who is called the True Beast."

As the Speaker pronounced the Enemy's name, a great murmur suddenly ran through the Cloud. Fear? Approbation? Or both? But at this same mention and in that very moment, the angle of the hundreds of hanging 'Strelles and the dozens of Dogs seemed to pivot and tilt slightly sideways. For a moment the dense mass packing the chamber appeared to give way and open up a little, giving a clear visual path towards the very back. I could, just for an instant, glimpse at the very farthest rear, one particular Dog. It hung upside down there, menacingly, red eyes glowing and resolutely focussed upon me.

The Speaker was gesturing now towards me: "This man child is the son of the Director and the Lady. He has been turned into one of our kind, so that he may better speak for his kind. He must say before us all what right has Mankind to speak for ourselves and all the animals. Why should we Bats live here in just this one place? Why should we allow ourselves to be gawked at by the 'Scents who have not the least inkling of what we truly are, and of what this place, the Zoo really represents?"

"This man-child, Seth must speak now. And so..." He stopped addressing the Cloud. He turned to me. And he was silent.

My mouth was dry, my throat was cold, my wings were as heavy as lead. I had no idea of what to say or how to speak.

The Zoo: The Beast, The Boy and The Zoo

And yet I did.

At least, I think it was I who was speaking with my Bat voice. Frankly I did not know before that I had the words that followed, nor all of that knowledge, nor those ideas within me. Did what spilled forth even truly represent my own honest opinions? At first the notions and words that came tumbling from my lips seemed beyond my will. It was as if some of these things were what I felt I *should* say, rather than what I actually believed. Or, as if someone older and with vastly more experience and knowledge of the world than me had taken over my tongue. This was a deeper, steadier voice, possessed of a glossier sheen than any I might have foreseen for myself.

I spoke of the great vanishing of species in the world beyond the Zoo.

I spoke of the kinship of all animals.

I spoke of the ancient story that a creator had levied responsibility for all the animals on mankind.

I spoke of man's cleverness with building and making, and how this allowed him to devise so many good ways of protecting and caring for other animals.

And then it seemed, I began to speak (and now this was *really* and *entirely* despite myself) of mankind's innate superiority. Of our 'right to rule'. Through all of this it was as if I was a scared spectator rather than a confident participant, watching in the wings as some more assured voice took centre stage to make such pompous pronouncements.

But at last I found my own courage and my own clear voice. It broke through and elbowed this other earlier thing aside. Even though my tone was now a little faltering and lacked the former's burnished qualities, this at least was definitely me.

I spoke of my own childhood in the Vague Lands. I told the Bats of a place where there were few animals of any sort, nor hardly any plants. A world of sand and dust. A place from which all colour, all vivacity had been leached. A way of life from which all that essential savour and variety and wonder so exuberantly concentrated here in the Zoo, was entirely missing.

"If the Zoo is dissolved…"

Oh, yes! Now, I was definitely speaking with my own strong clear voice. These were my *own* thoughts, my *own* will! "If the Zoo is dissolved, not only will there be no mankind to protect you, to feed you, to keep predators away, to ensure Bat kind survives into the next times, but the community of animals, the circle, our family will be broken for ever. The green will be overwhelmed, dissolved, extinguished by the grey. The triumph will go neither to beast, nor to man, but to the nothingness that threatens us all."

"I know this nothingness. *Because* I was raised there."

In my mind now, my words were flying every bit as elegantly as I had minutes before flown as a bat. No uncertainty, no clumsiness here. Thought and word, notion and deed, intent and execution, all united. No interval, no gap, no lapse between idea and action. My words soared majestically until…

"This human excrement is lying!"

It seemed as if I had once again flown, painfully and humiliatingly, smack bang into a wall of rock

A new voice, deep and ragged. The Dog at the back, so clearly the ancient malevolence Itself. "The story about the creator is purely a human invention. They do not keep us here for *our* protection. They contain us for *their* amusement."

"And for another reason. All these animals in one place laid out according to human whim? This to reassure themselves that they are still in charge of the wider world. Because this is actually a world crumbling around them, a world rebelling against the pathetic human insects which pullulate over its surface."

"These creatures do *not* care for our wellbeing."

The Zoo: The Beast, The Boy and The Zoo

"Let me tell you, my sisters and brothers, what Humans do to Bats. Let me tell you about one of their so-called greatest thinkers, a human called 'Descartes'. A man whom to this day they revere as a founder of their way of thinking. Let me share what he said on this. This *'great philosopher'*, this wonderful *'moral leader'*, to whom Humans still look as a basis for clarity of thinking, he considered all animals to be machines - automata. And to pursue his search for knowledge this great hero of the humans promoted the practice of vivisection. He cut open animals whilst living and, in his case, without any anaesthetic. This was acceptable, declared this Descartes, because..."

".. because we animals cannot feel pain!"

"Only Humans had something called a soul. Only Humans, you see, are conscious!"

"All of you, say the Humans, you are just *pretending* to be conscious."

The Cloud reacted slowly but palpably.

"Oh...," the True Beast pretended to take a second to recall something. "And what, let me think, what was the particular animal he used for his vivisection?"

"Yes I remember now..." The Dog finished slyly. "Descartes specialised in his cutting open experiments on..."

"...Bats!!"

And all hell broke loose in the upside down parliament. The wave of hatred, of fear, of anger carried in the screeing squeezed me as if I was within a vice. All trace of that original welcoming network of information within which I been so coddled, shimmered and burst as might a bubble.

I was still a Bat, but now I was a Bat on my own. I had been cast out by the Cloud.

It was the Speaker who saved me.

"Silence..!!" Let Seth respond.

The Zoo: The Beast, The Boy and The Zoo

My wings had, as if in defence against the barrage of outraged screeing, folded tightly around myself. I peeked out. Slowly I began to speak, but so falteringly, only slowly picking up my courage once more.

"Yes, it is true. In the past some humans have sometimes done cruel things to other animals. And beneath that there was surely the Great Lie, the falsehood of which our species had so foolishly persuaded itself; that we are not simply a type of animal ourselves. This profound self-deception has certainly led us into temptation."

"But slowly we have been learning, transforming, and discarding the old lies. The True Beast says that this man Descartes was revered as a great thinker? Consider here the half-truth. His time was many hundreds of years ago! We have had many other greater thinkers since then to whom we have turned. A man of science called Charles who told the whole world that Man and all the other animals are indeed one family."

Even as all of this streamed forth out of me, I marvelled at how much I was drawing upon my last few years of learning. Ironically, not so much learning about the animal world, which had after all always been Sam's thing: but about the human one. And drawing on all the vast stores of thought that went with that.

I wondered moreover at how my tongue seemed suddenly to have been lent a grace far beyond my gauche teenage years?

"And other great women and men who led us away from cruelty. A moral teacher called Mohandas for instance who said that a nation should be judged by the way its animals are treated. A scientist called Rachel who taught that a war waged by Humans on other animals was like waging war on ourselves. Other sages and scientists again have demolished Descartes' foolishness to prove to the world that human animals and other animals do indeed share feelings and awareness. "

"And, yes, of course, pain."

The Zoo: The Beast, The Boy and The Zoo

"Perhaps most importantly of all, women and men have started to see that our duty is to protect other animal kinds from disappearing, to save their wild homes around the world."

"It is indeed the race of Adam which has brought evil into this world, evil enough to destroy it for all living things. Yet it is not only because of this guilt that it is our species who should bear the responsibility to address that evil, it is also because *only we* have the power and knowledge to do so."

The Speaker intervened. "You have only *just* started on that journey after so many millennia of cruelty and destruction...?"

"Yes, there is far yet to go along that path. Mankind still inflicts many wrongs on animals. Animals of all kinds; and wrongs of all kinds. All I will say for us here is that, on the whole, human society is heading in the right direction."

"But much more importantly and to the point, I *do not speak* for the human species as a whole. I am here to speak only and specifically for the Zoo and for what the Zoo represents".

"And the Zoo is *not* the problem."

"It is the *solution*."

"The Zoo is the convening place for humans and other animals to together forge a new understanding. And in that role the Zoo is therefore the turning point for the Earth as a whole."

"The alternative to the order, however imperfect, that the Zoo represents is *not* freedom. It is chaos and destruction. That is what It..... I pointed towards the back to where I had last seen the True Beast. That is what your tempter seeks, not your happiness."

"But anarchy. Suffering. Breakdown."

The screeing rose and changed again in volume and flavour. I could tell that from some at least I was winning over a little support.

It was Trice beside me, who gave the warning. I had been so intent on the theatre of Bats before me, that I had not paid any attention to what might be happening on my flanks. One large Dog had been using its hook claws to scramble and grapple over the Cave's indented ceiling with frightening speed and surprising agility towards the spot where I was hanging. Its vermilion eyes gleamed with vicious intent.

The True Beast had taken advantage of my being distracted whilst speaking. It had also been clever in that its original position had been cloaked by the mass of the Cloud crowding in to listen so intensely to the debate. All this while it had been angling its way forward, the long path all around the circumference of the Cave, to so creep up on me unawares.

In contesting with me, It was clearly not content to rely solely on winning any mere arguments of words. This primordial, long soured malignance could no longer restrain its visceral determination to put paid to its foe.

It had chosen to take the more direct path.

With a scree-ed howl of rage the True Beast released its grasp on the rocks above me, unfolded its three foot wings and, like a great pteradon of old, the monster flapped and zoomed towards me. The Dog ten times my size threw all that weight against me, its jaws eagerly seeking deadly purchase on my neck.

A great roar now of an entirely new timbre arose all across the Cave. Plenty within the Cloud it seemed were only too delighted to dispense with the philosophical hogwash. They wanted to enjoy a plain old brawl. The Bat symphony surrounding me now contained strains of voyeuristic enthusiasm and significant partisanship. Brotherhood across the Cave was in part and for a time suspended.

For some at least it was now simply a straightforward matter of 'Strelle versus Dog.

And yet beneath all of that there survived that other and deeper level. There persisted that more self-controlled and sober vein, a continuing and committed assessment and judgement of the great matter at hand. Surely all our respective arguments could not come down to or be replaced by a simple contest of physical violence?

In that instant it might have struck me that irrespective of what the Cloud had thought of me, or of anything I had said or of the whole matter between my Adversary and myself, if the True Beast did succeed in crushing the life from my tiny Bat body or even just inflicting a sufficient humiliation on my flesh, the game would be over.

And let's be clear, if that great hulk of a thing, ten times my weight and size, got at all close to me with all the pent up venom of the True Beast, I had no chance.

I could not hope to match it then by actually fighting. But I *could* give It a pretty good contest in flying.

That at least on reflection would have been the logical train of thought. But do you know what? Absolutely none of that thinking went through my tiny little Bat head as the True Beast pounced. There was not time. I did not *think* at all. I just acted. I swept into the air a fraction of a second before its Dog claws could catch me. It succeeded only in a single deep scratch across my left wing.

The True Beast gathered itself to launch in pursuit. But suddenly there was a phalanx of Bats, a serried row of both Dogs and 'Strelles blocking its way, preventing any further contact between us.

"Order!" The Speaker's voice froze all. "The matter here is serious. It seems it cannot yet or easily be settled by debate"

"And I absolutely forbid that it should be settled by blood."

Hmmm... a fair dealer after all.

"There is at base only one issue here. Which of the two adversaries, which of these two who would lead us on different paths to different futures, which of you two truly *understand*s our own Bat species?"

The Zoo: The Beast, The Boy and The Zoo

"Neither of you are Bat born. But which of you can speak quickly, without hesitation, and tell me that most essential truth of our kind? I entreat both of you now, each, in short words to say before the Cloud..."

"What *is it* like to be a Bat?"

He turned to the True Beast first. A mere second or two's pause and Its vicious stink seemed to permeate the entire Cave. The red eyed demon spoke with assurance. It growled: "To be a Bat is to be at home in deepest wild of all. To be a Bat is, despite the greatest of darkness, to unfalteringly find one's way through the trackless forest to one's home."

...?!

I did not wait to be invited to take my turn to speak in response, but jumped straight in. "To be a Bat is to soar in the air when the earthbound scuttle in the mud."

"To be a Bat is to valiantly act while others merely debate."

"To be Bat is to be as a verb when other species are no more than nouns."

If I thought I had experienced extraordinary screeing before, I had been quite mistaken. The exquisite and ardent concentration of noise that now swept over me exceeded all.

What did it mean?

Had I said the right thing?

Had I won?

Had I lost?

I did not find out, for in the next second all went blank.

And in the second after that the dark of the Cave was left behind.

I was amidst glorious light.

And I was most definitely no longer a Bat.

***

Chapter Thirty Eight: If Lions could speak

This wasn't right....

I was supposed to remember something, wasn't I? I was supposed to be doing something? Something really important?

Hadn't I been somewhere before this? Somewhere else? Somewhere not here. Not here in this lovely place of grass and sun.

And, wait, I had been *someone* or something else, hadn't I?

Round and round in my head it all went. Almost there, almost on the verge of breaking through.

But...

But no...

No, not now, I simply couldn't be bothered with all that.

Because right now, right here I wanted to... PLAY!!!

How could I resist, after all. The grass was sooooo tall all around me, the blades towering above me like trees. To see anything at all other than green, I had to roll over on my back, my four little paws in the air and stare straight up at the beautiful, bright blue sky.

I mean. Come on! How could anyone reasonably expect a little Lion cub like me, still wobbling about on its stubby little legs, to think of stupid boring old stuff on a wonderful 'day such as this? When I had this toy chest of experiences waiting for me to open it.

All around me the rustling savanna dazzled every sense I had. It nipped at my curiosity. My jungle of grass was full of signals, dangers, delights, provocations, smells.

The Zoo: The Beast, The Boy and The Zoo

Smells! Yes, hearing and seeing and touching and definitely tasting were all great. But smelling was the thing here.

And then, oh.... that one. that especially wonderful scent hit me. An overpowering delight. Something reassuring. Something that represented all the good things in the world. Something a little distance away that I just *had* to get close to. Something - somebody in fact where the very thought, the merest possibility that one day it might ever not be there, this struck a pang of terror into my tiny breast.

I ran towards it.

Like me it was tawny. Like me it swished a tail. Like me it sniffed the air. Unlike me it was very big.

It growled in welcome. I settled in by its side. I suckled.

I was a Lion cub contently drawing on its mother.

And then suddenly two of us. Two cubs.

Twins?

Twins? Twins... Twins...! Oh, wait... there was something about twins, wasn't there? Lion cubs cannot scratch their heads really, but... Something to do with twins that I was supposed to do.

The name sprang violently into my head. SAM!!!

I was supposed to find my twin Sam. This, this single overriding imperative, but unaccompanied by any other details, flooded into my breast.

Was this then Sam here before me? Attentively I sniffed all around the other cub. A female! I peered deeply into her eyes. But no, nothing special there. This was just another ordinary Lion cub, staring back at me playfully. Every bit as curious as I, but quite uncomprehending. Nothing complex here, nothing with any meaning other than itself.

This wasn't Sam. And whatever 'the thing about Sam' had been, it was no longer at hand. With that reassuring realisation, any sense of urgency faded with pleasing speed. I snuggled back gratefully into all the familiar, comforting things that surrounded me.

The Zoo: The Beast, The Boy and The Zoo

The other cub and I played together. We stalked Butterflies and Frogs. We explored further and further. Away from our mother. Dangerously so. She came after us. She cuffed us. She picked us up mewling in indignation and carried us back to our crèche in the grass.

The motherness of it all wrapped itself tightly around me. A warmth, a security, a contentment beyond all reckoning. With my Lioness mother here, I had no responsibility, nothing demanded of me, nothing to learn. All provided for. An existence of total security.

My only business?

To play!

Oh, remembering this now, I am still so tempted. If I could move back to that place, a part of me would do so in a heartbeat. A mother's love. Unconditional love. Animal love.

Time was strange here for me as a Lion cub. A blurry passage, both slower and quicker than any vague tugs of memories that tried and failed to float up from some other place. A dream like quality. Yet night did surely enough follow day, and was followed in turn by another day. The stars rolled past in the heavens. The weather grew wetter, then hotter then dryer. The light slanted in a way that was different. The moon moved. We cubs both grew a little. We ventured further. We moved from milk alone to the delicious meat our mother brought. Stupefied with joy in the twin pursuits of play and food. A good life, utterly undisturbed.

Until two things happened.

***

First our mother's smell began to change. There was still that warm, lovely motherliness. But now she was also broadcasting on a quite different register. One that had nothing at all to do with me and

The Zoo: The Beast, The Boy and The Zoo

my twin. One indeed that seem to disregard us entirely. A deep instinctual vibration that seemed to yearn for a time before we had existed or had mattered; and to eagerly look forward to a time after we existed or mattered to her. A pungent, alien scent of sensual invitation.

In other circumstances, in some other disposition, I could perhaps myself have found that smell pleasant.

As it was, it was disgusting. I resented it. I hated it.

Then, one early morning, the smell was stronger than ever. My little twin had noticed it as well. She sat down at my side, darting in every so often to our mother's sleeping body, taking lots of fast sniffs, and running back to me in snarly little yelps of dismay.

Then she stopped and lay down quietly before me. That ever present, over excitable energy that possessed her suddenly burst like a bubble and was gone from her being.

She was quite still.

And then to my astonishment she spoke to me

The strong, clear voice that emerged was very familiar.

"Seth, you need to remember now what you are here to do. *This* is the time."

I jack-knifed backwards in surprise. In association with that voice a name slowly began to percolate. This was the voice of a companion familiar to me.

I ran up to the little cub's still so innocent little face. I cross questioned her eyes just as before. Still nothing to recognise within those impassive features. Nor any sense of recognition leaking back at me to somehow give away the game. But there had been no mistaking that voice. Almost as if the voice and the animal from whose mouth it came were two different things.

This was Trice, my former helper.

My helper from *where*? And *when*?

A dark place? Full of flutterings?

The Zoo: The Beast, The Boy and The Zoo

The Bat Cave! That was it. Somewhere and somehow Trice was in there. In the other little Lion. I shook my head in annoyance, as pesky, importunate and confusing shards of memory now strove insistently to barge into my world.

"Is that really you Trice?" The redundant question fell from my lips. "But I thought, I thought you were a boy?"

"I am whatever I need to be Seth." The voice was impatient. "Such things are unimportant. Don't be foolish. Yes, I am here to see you through again. As best as I can. This one will be difficult. We are in danger. It is coming Seth. You need to be ready."

"What? Who is coming?"

"Seth! You need to be yourself now. You may have been here too long. I am sorry. I should have been sent earlier. Each time you become an animal you need to go just deep enough to complete your task, and no deeper! If you stay too long and if you sink down too far, you risk staying here forever. You will never come back. That is just what It wants. That would suit It just fine. And It will be here soon."

"You keeping saying 'It'? Who, what will be here?"

"Oh stars above. You know perfectly well who! Pull yourself together. It... the True Beast. You need to face up to your challenge. You need to get ready."

"How do you know this thing is coming, whatever it is? Why right now?"

"Because of the smell, Seth."

"What? I don't understand."

Lion cubs cannot really shrug in despair. Yet there was meaningful expression in Trice's face, one of clear contempt.

"It is our mother, over there."

"What about our mother?"

The Zoo: The Beast, The Boy and The Zoo

"Don't you understand?! She is in oestrus. In season. She is summoning the True Beast. He will come as a male Lion, and he will mate with her."

Everything within me turned to jelly. Surely the most terrible thing possible, the very worst news which I could imagine.

I was wrong. For in the next breath Trice brought me something even worse.

"And when a male Lion wants to mate with a female, one who already has cubs, what, Seth, what exactly do you suppose becomes of *them*?

***

I had run away to hide under some rocks, covering my face with my paws. It was all too much. My lovely world was dissolving. For hours I stayed huddled by myself. Only very slowly did any sense of balance or purpose return to me. When it did it was as part of a tidal wave of memory.

Nothing could have been better designed to more effectively rip my illusion of this false life into shreds. The idea that our mother might betray us and just on account of physical desire. And to do so at the brutal cost of our own young Lion lives.

The blissful, innocent little Lion cub playing in the sun, the me that had more or less taken over all my thoughts and feelings in this place, shrivelled into dust. I was, as I now needed to be, once again Seth Faraday, Co-Director of the Zoo. Even if still ensconced in the form of a rather chubby and dirty little lion cub.

With sun high in the sky I padded back to find Trice. I needed to consult with my 'wise helper'.

"Okay I am back, Trice. And yes, it is me, Seth. I remember everything." I took a deep breath. "What do we do? Who will be the

The Zoo: The Beast, The Boy and The Zoo

judge and jury here? And tell please, how the hell am I, as a tiny cub, supposed to confront a grown Lion? That old Dog Bat was one thing, but a Lion!?"

Our mother and we two cubs were part of a wider pride of ten or so Lions. A very loose group in the Zoo that merged and split constantly. Most of the time the three of us were alone. There was no collective decision making by the group. Over the last few days however, and as our mother's oestrus signal had grown stronger, the pride had grown tighter, as if all knew something important was upon us. That afternoon we were all sitting together, in one wide area of grass flattened by the adults' enormous bodies, all laid out and all dozing as usual. Only Trice and I were awake. She considered my question carefully, as we both looked around at the wider pride.

"I think the rules here will be different Seth. I am not sure whether there will be any kind of 'jury' or 'judgement'."

"Then what *am* I supposed to do here?"

"Just do whatever your instincts tell you to, Seth. It will be up to others, all those busybodies outside to decide later whether it was the right thing or not, or whether you have done 'enough'. In fact for all that they said and all their preening and posing as icons of nature itself, it might not even be up to them either. Certainly cannot expect those pompous astral fools to do anything so helpful as to provide a clear road map."

For a second I was surprised to note that Trice was so dismissive of the very authority that sent her to help me, but more important matters demanded my attention.

She continued: "All I can say for sure is that you are here to be a Lion and so to learn, to be able to say what that really means."

Mother was conveniently recumbent and sleeping on her side. Despite all that concerned us, Trice and I could not resist taking advantage. We sidled over and once again, for the moment at least, the two of us were again simply side by side litter mates, contentedly suckling.

As the sun's rays eased into the west, Lion roars came from beyond our own pride's area in the Zoo. Our mother and the other Lionesses all jumped up, excited. Mother's mating smell intensified into what for me was a quite sickening pitch.

Three young male Lions jumped into the enclosure, their manes half grown. These animals were probably only about two years old.

The reaction from our group was mixed. The half-grown females snarled in disgust or fear. The other mature females were dismissive of these immature suitors. They yawned and stretched and wandered away. But Mother? Oh, our dear mother was delighted. In a single motion she leapt to her feet and ran to greet the newcomers. I was ripped from her teat, tumbling to one side. But Trice, my sister cub came off much worse. Somehow she had got under our mother's feet blocking her path towards the desirable young males. I saw clearly as first she was trampled quite badly and then, without any constraint at all, Mother kicked her to one side. My little sister lay still for a moment. Then she moved and limped painfully out of sight.

The three young males sniffed around Mother in delight. In response she gave a kind of stifled sneeze of pleasure and rubbed her body along that of the larger male.

Lion courtship, although hardly the most sophisticated of matters, takes time. The lead male gave Mother most attention, the others waiting each their turn. They were to be disappointed.

Normally first you see the lightning, and then you hear the thunder. Here it was the other way around. All three young Lions had roared to announce themselves. Spasmodically they roared again as they pressed their suit to Mother. But the sound that came next was as a great bellow that shook the very earth. It seemed almost to say: "Your pathetic squeaks are not roars. *This* is a roar!"

The Zoo: The Beast, The Boy and The Zoo

Sound may travel a lot slower than light, but it is in turn quite a deal faster than smell. Yet that smell did arrive sure enough and soon enough. Mother's smell had repelled me because it upset my calm soporific paradise. And because it was a betrayal. This new odour was a much darker thing. I had already encountered a form of it that time with Father by the Jaguar pool. There though it had seemed strategically deployed and restrained. It had been the calculated secretion of a sense of subtle and underlying threat. Then again there had been the Dog Bat's vibration strangely transmuted within my head into smell. But here the bridle was off. This stench was about rutting, about sexual conquest, about the unmanning of rivals, about the sweeping aside of all other thoughts and considerations in the blind drive to copulate.

The sleek, black waves of that vicious perfume acted like a kick to the groin. Truly this was the deep animal beyond all other animals. The last, slow, profound voice of brutal masculinity that seemed to sneer: "You silly little boy. You who pretend so much. You who know deep down you are not really any kind of man at all."

There was a strange set of reactions. The three young Lions circled the perimeter hissing, uncertain from which direction this overpowering rival was approaching. Mother sat down in the very middle, oddly patient. Nothing happened for long seconds.

Then the huge beast was amongst and upon us.

As a Jaguar, it had been jet black. As a Flying Fox a dirty grey. Now the True Beast was a shimmering golden creature with an enormous, lush, black mane. Bigger than any ordinary Lion could possibly be, it leapt into our midst so suddenly and so swiftly and with such ease it was impossible to know from what direction it had come.

Its eyes were red coals. Its tail lashed from side to side. Its growls crackled with the deepest menace. Perhaps it was the knowledge of who and what was amongst them. Perhaps it was the preceding chemical tsunami. Or perhaps it was Its sheer physical presence. But those three

The Zoo: The Beast, The Boy and The Zoo

young males were already down on their bellies, their very ability to mate or even to be males had, it seemed, been stripped clean from them. Towards each of the three in sequence the True Beast gave one further, final dismissive further roar. And they were gone. Mother had certainly lost interest in their direction. She immediately ran over to the one she had been waiting for all along. The one whom she had all this time been really calling into our sanctum.

They rubbed along each other bodies, sniffling and caressing. Not so very different to human lovers.

I cowered in a corner, all my emotions and thoughts turned to black. As a Lion I was about to see my Mother taken by the Enemy. As a Human here to fulfil a purpose, I could see no way forward. Despite what Trice had said about my instincts, no glimmerings came as to what to do, nor what might be expected of me. In my mind, I called out desperately to anyone and everyone who might ever have given me help or instruction: "Why have I been sent here? Why have you abandoned me here with this?"

Answer came there none.

Surely nobody supposed that, as a tiny scrap of an animal, I should try to contest physically with this great golden demon..?

A small growl to my left brought me out of my internal pleading. Trice had crawled out of wherever she had been hiding. She was standing on the opposite side of the clearing to me.

"Seth! Walk straight up to It and look It straight in the eye. Do not be afraid, Seth!"

The True Beast's massive head whiplashed away, suddenly ceasing its canoodling with our mother. His eyes zeroing in on Trice for the first time, boring in on her with such an expression, one of the sheerest rage. It spoke. There was astonishment and recognition in its tone.

"You!"

The Zoo: The Beast, The Boy and The Zoo

"What are *you* doing here? How can you be here at all?"

A momentary, flickering interruption in Its all-conquering confidence. "Don't you dare interfere, you fool. Go back to that nothing place where you belong. What good do you think *you* can do here anyway? This bitch is mine."

"And as for her two whelps ..."

It did not finish. It was across the compound, moving like a kind of giant terrier. It grabbed Trice in its jaws. It shook the cub like a rat back and forth two or three times, and hurled the limp body savagely against the rocks with a loud crack. For good measure, or in some unnecessary and malicious spite, it moved again to pick up the clearly and pathetically dead body of my little Lion sister. It snapped the head of the corpse.

And It swallowed it.

Mother went over. She sniffed the decapitated body of her child. She gave it one or two desultory licks. Then, she returned to lie in eager supplication before her new mate.

She was to whine though in disappointment as the True Beast shoved her to one side. It pounded over instead to zero in on the second whelp - on me. Mother had only ever been a means to an end. Its only real business here was with me.

My little Lion bowels betrayed me. The ground beneath me became damp, as the full gaze of my twin's murderer bore down on me. And yet, I held my ground. I made no sound at all as It approached.

Some three yards away It stopped, and spoke again.

"So, little one, here we are once more. But no audience now. No clever talk this time. And no escape through your flying craft in this place."

"Just you and I."

I held my ground.

The Zoo: The Beast, The Boy and The Zoo

"I have dined on the head of the other one. I will at my pleasure rut with your mother. And shortly, if I wish, I will break your head open." It moved nearer. Its giant head lower on the ground staring into my eyes. "You think perhaps I will hesitate to swallow you up?"

"I promise you I have swallowed up all manner of creatures. I have swallowed great beasts and insignificant minuscule beings. I have swallowed the mighty and the meek. I have certainly swallowed far greater than you, William's son."

I trembled. I said nothing. I did not move from my spot.

"And yet..." It was down now on its haunches, crawling towards me, rather than walking. "It does not have to be like that. You do not *have* to die."

It was as near as It could be, lying down only inches away from my face. I stood trembling directly between Its two front paws. I could even feel its breath. Its posture around me could almost be mistaken for an embrace of a protective carer.

"You have been content here, haven't you? Happy to live as a little Lion with your mother loving you, licking you. All of this I can give to you. It can continue. You are *not* my foe I give you the choice Seth. Son of William Faraday."

"All these weighty matters, all such grand decisions. The right way for humans to be... the right way for animal to be... the right way for humans and animals to be together...?. Paah!!" The great shaggy head of the True Beast sputtered loudly in derision. "

"I see into your thoughts, little Seth. So unsure! That life back there... So many decisions and responsibilities and complications, all of them awaiting you. The need to thread your way in life amongst, in and around other people. The need to understand other people. The need to *trust* other people. To have faith in their love."

Its voice deepened and lowered now, inviting complicity. "But *you know*, Seth, don't you? Oh you knew it well enough before this. But now, because of what has befallen here, you know it so much better. You know it so much more deeply. You know the sad fact that..."

"You... Can... Never... Trust... *Anyone.*"

"Not here in this life, nor out there in your life in the Zoo. All your friends will all betray you. Your chosen mate will - sooner or later - desert you. And, see!" Its nose turned to look in amusement for a moment at the female fawning and whining at his side.

"A single spark of sexual greed is all it takes for even her, even your mother to spurn you. To cast you to one side without a second thought."

"So *why* Seth? Why continue with all of this."

"Will you, I wonder..." For a moment It drew his vast head back as in whimsical contemplation, almost chuckling to itself. "Will you in what plays out here; will you actually learn more from Lilith who sent you for that very purpose? Or will you learn better from me!?"

"Why go back there to all that at all? Why go back to all that complex, messy stuff out there? Why face all those inevitable future betrayals?"

"Abandon all these things with which Lilith and those others and your father before that and all others would so selfishly burden you. Stay here and live your life contentedly as a little Lion, playing in the long grass. That is after all what you want? Surely it is?"

"And if you do", it pressed its case "I will leave. And I will leave you and your Lion mother alone as well."

I could feel Its breath on me now. All the power of that stench and threat, mere inches away from my face. My body slid back, coiling by imperceptible centimetres into itself.

In my hour of need and confusion I glanced sideways towards my mother for help. But of course she was still mindlessly rubbing her body in ecstasy up and down the True Beast's flank.

The Zoo: The Beast, The Boy and The Zoo

What to do? What to do? What was I here for? Again the question dribbled uselessly through my mind. What was my task? What was it now right to do in face of the True Beast's threat? Or in response to Its offer?

The secret of Lions? Yes! Yes. That fundamentally was what Lilith and co had sent me here to know, wasn't it? That is what I needed to find and to wield now. The secret of *being* a Lion? If Lions could talk? Well, they did talk, and I was one. What therefore would and should I say for myself as a Lion? What should be my reply in face of this existential challenge and this desperate, terrible choice?

There I sat, as you might imagine some insignificant petitioner might once have between the great stone paws of the Sphinx itself, all these riddles running through my mind.

I could though feel the True Beast's feigned patience becoming threadbare. First It growled in generalised irritation. A renewed threat at my continued silence. So close to my face now that our noses almost touched. Then It threw back its shock of ebony hair and raised its muzzle to emit a long shrill note. A very un-lion-like sound, something in between a purr of displeasure and a whine of frustration, as if striving to gradually edge me off a cliff and to push me down into final submission.

Once again the matter wearily cycled back into my mind: What *is* it to be a Lion?

I looked down inside myself as honestly and as profoundly as I dared. And an answer, one almost too obvious, surged forth.

To be a Lion is (of course!) to be brave. But *not* that false courage. Not the kind of courage which I certainly did not possess. Not to fail to feel fear at all. Not the numb stupidity of not feeling afraid. No, that is a pernicious impostor. Rather, yes to be in terror, but to tremble with honesty. And yet to act. To stare at despair, to face overwhelming odds, to sit in the shadow of a hideous, fascist strength, and, though knowing

The Zoo: The Beast, The Boy and The Zoo

that defeat is certain, still to hurl oneself with every iota of passion, guile, fury and spit at one's enemy.

This is courage. This is the Lion.

Should I then take the True Beast's invitation to retreat into the irresponsibility of childhood? Or should I accept the confusing and treacherously complex path of adulthood? All these individual pressures ranged up against me: that which I had been born to be; that which currently surrounded me; that offer now laid down before me. Genetics, environment, and opportunity all pointing and pushing in one single direction.

Where did a Lion's true courage lie there?

The suggestion nudged towards me was that I would be justified in betraying my life as a Human out there in the Zoo, because in here as a Lion cub my mother had betrayed me?

But..?

But that animal over there. Yes, the one that had so recently smelled so good to me and on whom I had depended for all. That was not really my mother at all, was it? My real mother, however little I knew of her, had been someone else entirely in some other place entirely. Just as that the cub within whose now shattered form Trice had been temporarily quickened, that was not really my twin.

My twin. That was Sam. And Sam was real.

If there was betrayal to come to me, I would rather have it in the real world. I would not, to avoid a fake infidelity here, break faith with my actual life out there.

Take the risk. Yes, take the risk in the real world to trust and to love, even if that might in the end mean bitter treachery and disappointment; rather than be embalmed here in a risk free fantasy. Yes, always take the risk. That is the Lion way.

Unbidden, vague notions from one of those ancient stories which Sam had so irritatingly insisted on reading out from the musty old books

The Zoo: The Beast, The Boy and The Zoo

in Father's library rose into my mind. A seductive outsider tempts an innocent to leave some place of peace, happiness and plenty, to disobey its rules and instead embrace knowledge and all the pain and suffering that brought. And yet here the True Beast laid down before me the very opposite track. Stay in this numbing paradise; reject the complex outside world of responsibility, strife and risk. Stay young and happy forever in this paradise.

It and I had somehow become even closer now. Eye to eye. On the one hand the massive gleaming form of the ultimate predator, ebony of mane and crimson of eye; and on the other me, a wide eyed, shivering scrap of life covered in dirt, tears and piss.

My mouth opened.

Given the very simple laws of physics themselves, the sound that now emerged should simply not have been possible, its volume, its duration and its passion could not have been physically produced by the miserable little bag of bones which was me.

And yet it was.

I roared, Reader. I roared direct into the face of the True Beast. A Lion's roar, that was surely the strongest, bravest, truest such roar since the beginning of time.

I took the risk.

The True Beast actually jumped back some feet in astonishment.

It had lain down its challenge and its temptation. It had received a Lion's answer. A Lion had spoken and a Lion had been understood.

A spark of triumph and hope lit inside me for a second.

Then the great golden feline moved back. It casually swung open its jaws and with a sideways bite it ripped my throat asunder in a single motion.

The pain was lacerating.

My first fading thought was that I had, despite all I thought and I done here, failed. And I had done so, utterly and miserably.

The Zoo: The Beast, The Boy and The Zoo

My second, weaker thought again, was I was surely dying

And my third, so faint though that it was almost not there at all, was that I was no longer a Lion.

***

Chapter Thirty Nine: *"How's the water?"... "What the hell IS water?"*

This time...

This time waking up into a new body was a long, slow, numb, and oh so horribly confusing process.

Dully, fuzzily, as the sleep-ridden or hungover man might grope for a light switch, I stretched out for some understanding of what parts and capacities were available to me. What bits did I have and where did these bits finish? And where did all this other stuff... All this stuff I sensed all around me, whatever it was, where did that begin?

What was me? What was not me?

In a daze, I realised that, however preposterous the notion, some kind of protuberance seemed to be sticking out and dangling from my head?

Well whatever this bizarre thing might be, I rather liked having one. It was great. It was telling me all kinds of new things about this new world. Or at it least was trying hard to. On the receiving end my new brain did not yet seem to be quite used to this, not entirely ready for the overwhelming flow of information on offer.

To understand more I flexed and wriggled my awareness around and throughout the rest of my body.

Okay, I definitely had a brain. In fact a pretty big brain. And one which I sensed to be exceptionally large compared to my overall body size. My skin seemed thick too, a strong protective fabric.

A long appendage emerging from my head? A big brain? Heavy duty skin? That suggested a particular creature. If I did need to live as another bloody animal for a bit, complete with whatever weirdness that might bring, I had to admit, this was the one I would wish for.

Was there in fact some kind of pattern here whereby my animal hosts were destined each time to get bigger and grander?

I was suddenly extremely eager to enjoy and feel this fully, to properly delight in being this creature. But first I needed to slough off a remaining, cloying torpor. If I could just struggle and kick through to the surface of my full awareness. I needed to cut the umbilical cord from having been a Lion or a Bat; and especially from being a half grown Man.

I needed to get properly 'Elephant born'.

I willed what should be huge ears to flap. I moved to raise a massive foot in triumph. I looked for the easy strength required to trumpet in exuberance.

Yet...

Nothing.

Come on! Come on!

Nothing. Still numb, still useless. I was not really fully birthed yet into my new form. This was so slow. Nothing at all like becoming a Lion or a Bat.

But there was something white and enticing high up there above. If I could just get to that clarity over my head, then, I sensed, it might be okay. I might become fully me.

I asked my torso to move. And my word, it certainly did! Masses of muscle suddenly and vigorously complied. My entire body slicked upwards towards the whiteness above.

I broke through.

No! No! It was horrid. So offensively bright and sharp. Full of hateful, hurting things. All of a sudden I could not breathe. And my eyes! Whatever kind of creature they did belong to, these eyes were certainly not made for this horror. Too dazzling. Too hot.

The Zoo: The Beast, The Boy and The Zoo

Nothing about this vicious place into which I had so stupidly forced myself was right for the body I was in. Surrounded by pain-giving nothingness I gasped in agony. Desperately now I needed to get back down below. Back to that good, thicker comforting blanket beneath into which I had first awakened.

That is where I belonged.

It was no skilful action nor clever thought of mine, but good old gravity that saved me. Back downwards I tumbled, helpless but grateful.

And yes, you've got it.

I splashed.

A glorious splash!

It was that jolt that brought me at long last into full body awareness. Not an Elephant of course at all then. Very far from it. A tail, fins, scales...

I was a Fish.

So wonderfully cool now down here in this, my water. A blissful refreshing after the horrors above. Movement so easy. Swimming a simple joy. Better even in a way than flying as a Bat. Gliding this way, then that. No complex clumsy limbs involved here at all. Whirring fins automatically and efficiently suspending me here in the water. To move onwards, I just willed it to be so; and banded muscles all along my smooth, sleek, sexy sides instantaneously complied, veering me off in one direction or another. It was all so... so... *I* was so...so suave!

My brain was suffused with information. Flooded by many splendidly useful bits of intelligence on many different aspects of my environment: its currents; its ripples; its vortices; its eddies; its temperatures; its densities. All there at my disposal. Everyone for my benefit.

And when I moved, my body itself was just one more long, elegant, liquid undulation. I was one wave amongst others, a part of that which surrounded me in a way that no land animal could ever be.

The Zoo: The Beast, The Boy and The Zoo

Motion and muscles rippled and flexed endlessly through me, doubling and tripling in their power and grace, until, in reaching my tail, they just flowed on seamlessly, through, out and beyond my being.

My body might itself physically terminate at a certain point; but the information which it received, upon which it depended, from which it benefited; and which in some way endowed my being with its very form: this all-encompassing life force to which I and my fishy shape in turn contributed; that gave the impression of being unending, of going on forever.

Endless watery ways lying before me to endlessly explore.

In this new state of being it did not then to me seem particularly strange that, if I went far enough in one direction, and though keeping to a straight line, I would always still come back to exactly where I began.

In my other, former lives, this I knew would have been a maddening, frustrating thing and the cause of a bewildered curiosity. But here, my fishy brain and my watery senses were wholly unperturbed. This form's sensibilities simply didn't want to cooperate nor take any interest at all in the annoying concepts of 'boundaries' or 'direction'. Now that I was beginning to settle into my new self, questions such as 'where am I?' seemed silly, piffling irrelevances compared to the important things in life.

The more familiar became my effortless gliding through this perfect primordial world of tranquillity, the more the notion of having ever needed to ... what *was* that word? Yes, 'walk'. The more that seemed ridiculous. This thing called a Human, clumsily flailing and lashing around in a horrid, unhelpful nothingness called air and surrounded by other similarly ungainly outlines known as animals, such as Lions and Bats, seemed absurd.

In fact there was more.

The Zoo: The Beast, The Boy and The Zoo

The very idea of any other place or time, even any other *kind* of place, so different, so uncooperative compared to these, my own sweet waters, it seemed simply… well, not worth thinking about.

Then there was the long, thin thing sticking out in front of my face. My goodness, given the way I relied on it so much to know the world, how could I even have imagined doing without one of these marvels?

Not really very much like an Elephant's trunk after all. It grew out of what in my human form would have been, not my nose, but my lower mouth. The pictures feeding into my brain were in their detail and usefulness quite exquisite. The back of my body fizzed with electricity, despatching signals at random which sparked and quested all around the environment. As they obediently bounced back, my snout (easiest to settle on that term) greedily hoovered them up.

In this way all the many caverns of my glaucous, wet underworld were lit up and overlaid in my brain with practical data of very sort. After scant minutes, my awareness had become so adjusted to this abundance that I was able to interpret the raw data with ease. As I became more skilled, I could judge minute distances, the shapes of things around me. I knew not only the exact shape of such forms, but also what lay within them. I understood their very fabric and internal structures. I was aware which fish and other water creatures were out there. And I understood what they were up to.

Above all … Oh yes, by far the best of all! I knew what out there was good to eat.

Suddenly I realised I was very, very hungry.

My mesh of electric fields galvanised me toward a truly magnificent buffet. A water snail here, a miniature fish there, near microscopic larvae nearly everywhere. One by one my snout ruthlessly hunted down all of these bounties and vacuumed them up. Then through my tiny mouth and into the grip of just a few large teeth, mercilessly grinding. Gulp, crunch, swallow. Revelling in all these delicacies, I yet lusted for something more, a final treat to round off my meal.

And yes, there... my snout had detected just the thing, an irresistible finale.

Some foolish little entity was trying desperately to scrabble away from me, a doomed attempt to lose itself from my attention in the pebbles and murk at the bottom. A succulent delight of a creature. Diaphanous and silk like in its motion. A superb little Octopus.

This morsel knew surely enough of its doom hovering above it. Ha, ha! Well, it might know, but that knowledge gave it no advantage nor no hope whatsoever. Securely caught in the cross hairs of my all-knowing, all seeing electric snout, resistance was futile. One final zeroing in; I opened my jaws wide to snap my prize up, and...

"SETH!!!!!!"

The feedback generated by my electroreceptors had been impressive in their intensity; but they were as nothing compared to this strident slap right across my psyche.

At the very last moment possible I wheeled around, darting away to hide in the gloomy smaze at the bottom of the water. Timidly and metaphorically I licked my neural wounds. Then gradually slunk back. This mind, this voice that had shrieked out at me. It was...?

I would not quite allow myself to be sure. To rejoice.

Yet now it came again. Less forcefully this time, but this version was clearer. It was more assuredly of itself and not any other.

"Seth!"

Cautiously I reached out.

"Trice..?"

"Can that be you? How?"

Yes, Seth, it is me. Me, who was sent to help you. Me, back from the dead. Me, your valiant and loyal companion in all these trials."

"Me, whom you just tried to BLOODY EAT!!"

The Zoo: The Beast, The Boy and The Zoo

"!!!!"

"Trice, I am so sorry!"

Trice was a good thing. Trice was a friend. Trice? Trice? Trice... Yes, I remembered Trice.

"Trice, I didn't mean.... I didn't know... I mean you *died*? I saw you." On and on I gabbled.

"How long have you been a Fish, Seth? Minutes. And you couldn't take a just a little while to get your bearings, to work out what was what... to find who your allies and enemies are... to determine why you are here. You couldn't wait to do at least some of that before filling your belly?"

"As for having died. Well, in case you have forgotten, not so long ago you were also a Lion cub whose carotid artery and jugular vein had both been severed. Yet here you are a Fish... So here I am as a miniature Octopus. Is that so surprising?"

" Erm... are you male or female this time Trice?"

"Oh for goodness sake, why does any of that matter Seth?! You are happy to go along with you and me both changing *species* several times, but are fixated on the question of gender? Look, for convenience use 'he' and 'him'. But none of that is important! Stop wasting our precious time with trivia."

Trice and his ire trawled up a wriggling mass of half memories within me.

"I am sorry Trice. Really I am. It is confusing. I am not sure yet of what I am. Part of the time I seem to feel and behave like... whatever exactly this is, and part of the time I think like a.... like a... you know... a..."

I trailed off, desperately frustrated. The right word and the right concept was hovering there somewhere, but in a place to which I could not quite stretch.

"A *Human*, Seth. Like...A...Human."

The Zoo: The Beast, The Boy and The Zoo

Trice's tone gradually became softer and a little more conciliatory. "Listen Seth. This is not the first time this has happened. When you were a Bat, although you became rather carried away with yourself in terms of your alleged flying abilities, you stayed pretty much aware of your basic human nature. But as a Lion cub, you forgot completely. I had had left you by yourself in there too long. At least I was able to get here pretty quickly this time."

"Each time you are incarnated, you are in a greater danger of slipping in too deeply, of perhaps permanently becoming the animal in question. Be careful Seth. That is exactly what the True Beast would like. That would take you off the chess board, get rid of you altogether. That is where It tried to lead you as a Lion cub. Remember you are just a guest in each body, only a tourist in each world. You need to become a Fish just enough and *no more* to meet the challenge at hand, to understand what it truly is like to be a Fish. No further. If you sink too deeply into this flesh, you will fail in your task. And you might remain a fish forever."

"You wouldn't like that, would you?"

Well, I thought (but did not say) actually, yes, I might.

"That will not help Sam and all the rest of it out there, will it? You need to balance your dual natures carefully. It is not for nothing you know that in this final trial, you are of all things, a Fish."

"What..?" Trice had completely lost me once again.

"Never mind." He shook a claw. "Come on."

"Where? Where are we going? What will happen here Trice? What do I need to do? What are we here for?"

"We? Listen. Seth, it is only you who are here for the test. Don't forget that. I am just the sidekick. The 'wise adviser'. Someone only tasked with helping you get your bearings. I have no idea what will be thrust upon you."

The Zoo: The Beast, The Boy and The Zoo

"But part of it might be..." Trice paused, his octopoid features twisting strangely. "Something to do with 'the eating problem'."

"The eating problem?"

"Yes, why is it okay for Humans to raise, hunt, and kill animals for food? Think of the millions of Fish caught and left to asphyxiate every day to feed human bellies. That *little* issue. And of course it is okay, because as we know 'fish are cold blooded' and 'don't feel pain'. Maybe that is why this time you have been made into a Fish. Given all that, the fact that you, a Human youth, even in fish form at the moment, just tried to eat me... That is pretty ironic, isn't it!?"

"I am sorry, alright. I promise never to try to eat you again Trice. Ermmm... what kind of Fish exactly, am I anyway?"

"You are an - especially ugly - example of *Gnathonemus petersii*, the Elephant Nose Fish."

"Ahh, that explains a lot. And this place Where is this? What is it? Where are we?"

In so far as an Octopus might adopt a look of puzzlement and frustration, Trice certainly did. "We are in the big tank in the middle of the Zoo's aquarium. Surely you have been here and seen it many times. Can't you see the glass all around us, Seth? All those faces staring in. All those gormless 'Scents."

"Uh... no. Not really. I cannot actually 'see' very much at all, Trice. It is this thing here," I waggled my snout about. "That lets me know what is what. My actual eyes themselves are only good for large objects, spotting things might eat me, but that's it. Pretty useless for much else."

"So the electric field feedback arrangement doesn't really help you sense those glass walls over there? You cannot *perceive* them at all?"

Glass walls? What was he talking about? I tried to understand, to locate what he was indicating, but still sensed nothing. My world, *the* world, as far as I could see, just went pleasingly on forever in a nice straight line.

The Zoo: The Beast, The Boy and The Zoo

"No. No, I can't."

I hesitated for long seconds before speaking again. A certain confused embarrassment was holding me back.

"Trice..?"

"Yes?"

"You know what you said before - about me being 'a Human'? "

"Yes..?"

"And what you were saying just now about a world beyond this one?"

"Yeesss..?" Impatience and suspicion rising in his voice now.

"Did you mean that was real? Wasn't it just a dream? Is this not a game we are playing, you and I? Haven't we always been here? I know it is fun talking like this. Making things up." I was stumbling through all of this, quite uncertain of my ground. "But isn't this all there is?"

"Oh, for crying out loud Seth. You are doing it again. And even worse this time! Not only are you falling into just being fish. You are tricking yourself into believing that the small things you see before you are the whole universe. Snap out of it! Yes, *of course*, there is a world beyond this! This is only a pathetic little fish tank. The world out there, the world of the Zoo, your world, even that in turn is only as a tiny fish tank compared to the vast worlds that lie beyond it, outside and sideways from itself. Worlds that you, unlike most humans, have been given the privileged of at least a small glimpse."

"You *have* to see it Seth. You need to bend your mind at right angles. Twist all your senses away from just these ordinary things, the parochial places, the familiar objects, the narrow-minded people and the prosaic ideas that are always right in front of you. You need to break out of the prison your mind itself has put you in."

Trice grabbed my snout with one of his tentacles, not particularly gently, and pulled me along some distance.

The Zoo: The Beast, The Boy and The Zoo

At an arbitrary point that seemed to make some sort of sense to him, he stopped. He made a dramatic half waving gesture with another tentacle. Each time this ended abruptly at twelve o'clock in its swing as if encountering sudden material resistance. It seemed to make no sense at all to me.

"Cannot you hear that?"

I looked blank.

He did the pointless tentacle gesture again.

This time I did hear something, a kind of thudding, clanging noise, but I still did not understand what my friend was seeing. More to the point, I could not even seem to think about anything other than the spaces around me, all the various delightful flowing ways at my disposal: up, down, left; right; forwards; backwards. What else, what other directions were there, or could there be? And anyway why would anyone *want* there to be anything else?

This world was enough.

He did it a third time. The clanging sound was much clearer this time, reverberating through and insinuating itself into waves throughout the water.

"Can you still not see it Seth? Can you not *perceive* the glass now? Cannot you discern the end of this world? And beyond and through it the start of another?"

I tried hard to please him, but only ended looking about me nonplussed. What the devil was he talking about? There was no other direction to move in. Nor to look at. Nor even such a thing to be thought of.

"Use your human mind Seth, not your fish mind. Look, just as you have been incorporated as a Fish in particular and for a given purpose, there is a specific reason also why I am here as an Octopus. We Cephalopods are famous, even when we are in tanks, for seeing beyond the tank walls, for understanding that there is an 'out there'. Pretty good escaping from them too."

"So you need to 'escape' too. I mean escape from limited notions of the worlds. You are not really a Fish. You are a Man – well, at seventeen, almost a Man. So try harder. Really look. Try closing your eyes and shutting down your mind for a second. Then switch it all back on again."

So I did as Trice said. With my eyes tightly shut, I willed myself to think of this notion of a wider world, of this dream of living as a seventeen year Human. I opened my eyes again and focussed on where Trice's tentacle continued to wave foolishly in the water. As I expected, I still saw nothing but a beautiful liquid blur of blues, and greens and golds.

Even trying to think of that alleged outside world made me dizzy. I mean, yes, it was there sure enough, this image of something called 'a Boy', a big clumsy thing with sticky out parts lumbering around like an oaf. But why did Trice ever think it real. It was, of course, just a dream, a story, a silly game. There was no 'Zoo', nor Father nor Lilith nor Vague Lands. Nor... nor...

Sam.

Yet again Sam. Always the single solid thing. Ever my magnetic north.

Sam, the other one.

Sam, my twin.

Sam, the other me.

Sam?

No, Sam *was* real.

There was another place. There was a place where Sam was. A bigger place. A place above and beyond these diaphanous green waters. A place where the sun was not seen through a glassy gauze, but bright

The Zoo: The Beast, The Boy and The Zoo

and yellow and up in a blue sky. The place where, with Sam, I had been whole.

The blur was somehow different now. Then? Suddenly. Yes! Right in front of me, as if on a giant screen. How, by all that is holy, could I have not been able to see that before?!

An array of huge human faces, eyes goggling in on Trice and me. I moved along the glass surface. Then I did something of which seconds before I could not even conceived. I turned a corner. I had changed direction.

Yes, I turned a bloody corner! That is to say I negotiated a right angle. An actual right angle. Instead of all my travels and my entire existence always belonging to a straight line, I could, just as Trice had said, now think in terms of bending in other dimensions.

And shortly again another corner. I charted four glass sides in all, four walls surrounding, enclosing and defining what only moments ago I had made an everywhere, but suddenly now seemed a very little and insignificant container filled with slightly murky water.

A crowd of 'Scent visitors, dull, slack, vacuous faces, pointing, idly chatting, gorging on snacks, shuffling forward like zombies. Thoughtlessly casual consumers, ignorant commentators, vulgar intruders uncomprehending as to the aquatic world before them.

I could hear their voices now. One particular 'Scent family. "Look at that one!" Tapping loudly on the glass. "Yeah it looks like it has a dick on its face!" Laughs thundering through the glass and shaking my world. "Hello dickhead!" More thunder. "And look, dickhead is friends with a Squid". A chubby finger stabbing towards Trice. "Hmm, calamari! Makes me hungry". Large gobs of food falling out of the human child's mouth as he tried to cram more crisps into his mouth and speak at the same time.

Had I, by the stars above and beyond... Had I really been one of these?

The Zoo: The Beast, The Boy and The Zoo

Yes, I had, hadn't I? Sadly, painfully the trickle of memories became a flood. The True Beast, the Zoo, Father, Lilith. The lot.

Trice floated back towards me.

"It is okay Trice. I remember it all now."

He wafted a sucker with surprisingly gentleness to touch my head. "I am glad."

I was determined to show I did now understand and that I was finally rallying to the task ahead. "So what are we facing? How do you think the True Beast will manifest itself here? What is our challenge this time?"

"I have absolutely no idea Seth."

"What?! But that is what you are *for*, isn't it! Like with the Bats and the Lions."

"Look, let's get this straight. I am not *for* anything!" The friendly tendril was suddenly withdrawn. "I am just me. And by the way Seth, it is not 'our' challenge. It is only your challenge." He moved some steps back. "My job this time was only to help you make sense of your surroundings. That is done, and so..."

I never would have guessed that an Octopus could bring two tentacles together and make an impressive clicking noise of dismissal just in the way I could snap my fingers. But that is exactly what Trice did. Suddenly I was alone. I looked around desperately, but he had indeed completely disappeared.

***

Chapter Forty: A Really Irritating Hum

I have, down through the years, thought pretty frequently about that wet world of mine. Especially eagerly on hot days, I will sometimes go to the Zoo aquarium, and then, if there is nobody much around, I just press my nose up flat against the glass. It is so easy and rather wonderful to project myself back inside.

After Trice left, I carefully patrolled the tank. I now knew this it to be an ultimately circumscribed continuum. All the same for a little Elephant Fish it remained a vast and magnificent place. Soothing, delightful and chock full of my fellow exotic residents.

I watched in delight as the Purple Striped Jelly Fish, maroon tentacles trailing majestically behind them, puffed mesmerically like bonfire smoke past me. A pair of attentive Pink Skunk Clownfish soliticiously wafted the eggs they had laid attached to a rock. A solitary dappled Zebra Shark skulked towards the bottom of the tank. All these performed against an iridescent background of corals, polyps, and anemones; the glow from above refracting into multiple angles and hues, stippling all that it fell upon.

In neither nook nor cranny did I find a single hint of my foe.

All this time the light had gradually been fading on us all. The swooping and darting of the other citizens of the tank had little by little slowed down. Imperceptibly I slackened myself. There seemed less and less point in my patrolling around. If the True Beast was indeed hidden amongst one or other of the local denizens, there was little I could do to smoke It out. A very large part of me did not particularly want to anyway.

I found myself a comfortable crevice at the very centre of a pile of rocks. In I backed, ensuring a defensible position with only my snout itself protruding, and I gave myself up to a deep and murky sleep.

***

It was still night when I woke. Pitch black. Well, no not quite.

Since Trice's intervention I had become keenly aware of the those four glass surfaces of the tank, each a different window onto the wider world, my world, the real world of Seth Faraday, a perspective into the very idea of outsideness itself.

No, definitely not completely black.

I could detect some kind of disturbance through the right hand side, a brief glimmer of ruddy light and movement. But as I swam up to that point to examine it more closely, the red streak now seemed to be rather at the back of the tank instead. And no sooner had I had that thought, than in turn the very same blur of colour was very definitely on the left.

No, no that was not right either! It was moving to the front.

A dull, wine-red light silently circling the tank at some distance and at great speed.

Now it was slowing down and nearing, with every loop gradually tightening its cycle closer to the tank. As its orbit wound in towards me, I could hear a kind of humming, swooshing noise as if this were part of its mechanism and means of propulsion.

The Zoo: The Beast, The Boy and The Zoo

Through the nothingness and darkness surrounding the tank, two red eyes glowing, staring as they encircled the world of water: a particular hue of crimson that was all too familiar.

This time the True Beast was not to be found within my immediate world at all. This time instead It was something outside looking in.

"Human boy..."

I was being summoned.

Yet again; although this was in some form expected; although my fourth encounter now; although I had done everything possible to brace myself, I can still find no words to reach the terror and the awe that the nearness of the Great Enemy tipped me into.

As if a circling midnight train might slowly decelerate, the dull light and the grating noise gradually slowed. A lazy wheel of arrogance grinding to a halt. Finally the vermilion eyes stopped dead in front of me.

"What do you want?" I ventured. A pathetic and futile question, but what else could I offer.

The only response was a renewed humming noise, very slight and somehow different in tone from that which had accompanied Its movement. Now it grew in intensity. Then it too stopped

A further silence. Then.

"Seth..?" A tone of neutral enquiry that simply held in the air.

"Yes? What is it that you want?!"

No response save the humming again. It rose and fell in tone. Louder than before. As if something was once again running in circles. It went on perhaps twice as long as before and then ceased once more.

Then.

"Seth...?"

"WHAT!"

It began again: "MmmmmMmmmmMmmmmm..." Louder and louder. Inexplicably irritating. And near to becoming physically painful.

The Zoo: The Beast, The Boy and The Zoo

"MmmmmMmmmmMmmmmMmmmmMmmmmMmmmm..."

I would not have thought it possible, but this raised the pitch of my fear even higher.

This time there was no odour. No smell could reach me here through the glass wall, no overpowering combination of disgust, terror and intoxication brought on as in all the other confrontations. Instead there was this maddening, self-absorbed vibration that rattled sickeningly through my whole body and on through the entire fish tank.

It was an agonising smugness that I wanted to smash. Oh, so very much. To shut that Thing up at any cost whatsoever.

I knew what it was about. Yes, this was a maddening, defiant display of Its superiority, Its contempt, Its disregard of everything, of everything I was. Everything I wanted. And right then what I wanted most was simply to silence It, whatever that might take. At that particular moment I would have brought the very universe to an end if that was what it took to smash It into stillness.

That behind the glass wall I was entirely powerless to do so; and that It knew so. This made it all so much worse for me; which in turn simply rendered It all the more smug and raised me to a new fever pitch in vicious circle.

Two red eyes half closed in soporific complacency, and now, also distinct, a red mouth. A gaping slash of crimson from which this horrid sound slobbered and flowed. And then it smiled. Not any kind of good smile. Nor yet a smile remotely connected with anything you might call humour nor wit. Nor even was this the classic, cartoon grimace of devilish intent or malice.

No. This was the lazy fat smirk of a self-rejoicing slug of a thing. An expression oozing from a mind in our terms totally insensate, something so deeply beyond the touch, the appeal or influence of anything or anyone in my human world.

The smile of a Thing that knew it had already won.

"S...eeeeeettttthhhhhhth?"

How strange that my own given name coming out if Its mouth lent itself so easily to this repellent, sibilant snake-like hiss.

"Ssssseeeeeeettttthhhhhhth?"

"STOP IT! SHUT UP!!!! DAMN YOU, STOP IT! DAMN YOU, DAMN YOU!!!!"

I slammed my body against the aquarium wall. It shook violently but held. For seconds I stood back. The remorselessly self-contented humming Thing neither flinched nor lessened nor budged an inch. Nor ceased.

Again and again I hurled myself at the glass. It was utterly stupid of me, and utterly without effect.

"MmmmmMmmmmMmmmmMmmmmMmmmmMmm..."

My world, formerly one of cool, dark, protected waters was now a place of pain. My fish brain was being fried. Almost worse was my despair and impotence before this insufferable wall of arrogance pressing in, crushing on me.

"Please just shut up! PLEASE stop it."

And.

To my surprise.

It did.

Abruptly. Just like that. No more humming.

Long minutes passed. Coiled in tension I cowered in the mud at the bottom of the tank, waiting for It to begin once more. Surely It was only baiting me?

"Seth...?"

"Oh.... Oh no. please..." It was starting all over again! I despaired, turning in on myself and tensed for the new attack.

But no hum followed. The red eyes opened wider instead. No longer sinister slits, but widened orbs of curiosity. As if It had suddenly only just woken up. They stared deep and attentively and softly into mine with an expression that appeared to be... genuine enquiry.

"Seth, what is it like to be a Fish..?"

Mockery?

I bridled. Then forcing myself to speak.

"That is question for me to answer. But not one for you to ask."

It seemed to ignore this and, with its eyes and mouth tilting ever so slightly to one side as if in a passing question, went on:

"What is it you *really* want, Seth?"

Now that the True Beast was speaking and no longer humming, it had adopted a strange questing, wheedling voice. Nothing here of the proud aggression of the Black Jaguar, nothing of the visceral hatred of the old flying Dog, nothing of either the mechanical sexual conquest nor the cool deal making of the male Lion. And nothing, thank god of the emotionless, all conquering humming drone.

Just as some of the keepers had said, this Thing seemed to be not single, but legion in nature. Maybe just as in Trice's warning to me, it was true that it also when entering each animal world, risked being taken over by its adopted nature.

I hovered right up to the tank wall and, as defiantly as I could, I stared back into those red eyes.

"I want for you to go! I want you to leave the Zoo and to leave my family alone. I want you to stop the corrosion you are spreading across the Zoo. To leave our animals in peace...."

"No." It interrupted with calm confidence.

???

"No Seth. That is *not* what you want. Because you never really wanted the Zoo at all, did you?"

How absurd, how bafflingly that my Enemy had slid into this conversational and ostensibly reasonable tone. Would this then simply be a repeat of its offer to me as a baby Lion?

The Zoo: The Beast, The Boy and The Zoo

"You just want Sam back, don't you?" It's cool, level tone continued. "And you want to find out what is out there. In the wider world. Beyond all this 'Zoo business'. You never wanted this responsibility. You only ever wanted an easy life, a free life. Imagine just you and Sam and..."

"A whole universe available for you to explore."

"Am I wrong?"

So strange talking to It like this. A conversation from inside a fish tank with a seemingly disembodied set of eyes and a mouth

I did not reply. It continued.

"This can all be yours. The world is vast. Much vaster than most of the fools at the Zoo know. Their world, their obsessions, this foolish tiny struggle of theirs, these are all as drops in a limitless ocean. Yet they think that the Zoo is all there is, or all that really matters, just as the Fish in this, your tank, think it is the universe and that there is no otherness.

But you learned better when she took you up that tower, didn't you Seth? Think of that great endless world, Seth. Imagine for a moment in your mind the limitless possibilities for your life."

And, despite my resistance, I found myself in my mind following this bidding. I remembered what it had been like flying with the Eagles, and also standing on top of the tower being visited by the Stars. For a second I was high above it all. Far higher even than I had been with the four Eagles. Up above sky so high, up above the landscape in which we all lived, seeing it in my mind's eye as one whole country, coast to coast and all at once. And then ever higher, above the world. And seeing the world for the first time as a curved place, a place where if, precisely as here in the tank, if you went far enough in a single straight line on its surface you ended up where you had begun. And then higher again away from the Earth.

No, what am I saying? That's not right, not actually 'higher'. That word had no meaning anymore. I saw now there was no 'higher' here, no up or down. Even these words were all were ignorant, local notions, themselves a consequence of a mind in a straitjacket. No higher, but there was certainly a beyond. Other worlds. Other stars. Other 'might have beens'. Other lives one might have lived. Other lives one might still live. Endless possibilities combining in endless forms.

Its voice again.

"All these worlds, all this limitlessness is yours Seth. All this I give to you. If only..."

Against my will I heard my own voice asking.

"Only what?"

"If only you walk away. As simple as that".

So in our shared Lion world it had been 'the wider thing' that True Beast had importuned me to abandon. Then I been asked to forego the possibilities of the bigger, more complex world of the Zoo, and to stay secreted forever in childhood, in the simple play filled continuum of a baby Lion.

And now. Now it extended precisely the opposite temptation: to be blissfully free to explore the whole universe.

"And what will happen to those at the Zoo, the people and the animals, and to my Father's legacy, if I just walk away?"

"Nothing so very dreadful. In going you will be just acknowledging that the wild thing is the right thing. That the human imperium, the Zoo is the wrong thing. Your species, your particular kind of Ape will simply and truly be coming home. You Humans will calm yourselves down. Your breed will sit down once more amongst your sister and brother species, one animal once again amongst others. Man's frenetic rush to change, to control and to conquer will be over. It will be seen to be burnt out. The fires will damp down. Humankind will turn its back on all its preening. You will no longer dress yourselves up in your haughty confections of 'culture' and 'science'."

The Zoo: The Beast, The Boy and The Zoo

"So *just* walk away Seth. Abandon the filthy proud human world that others have made and forced upon you. Mankind doesn't have to 'look after' the other animals. We can look after ourselves. Lock the gates of the Zoo. Shut up this false garden behind you and throw away the keys. Do that Seth and I will give you and Sam freedom."

"Just bow down before animalness."

"Bow down - just once - before Me."

I was stopped in my tracks. Was this so bad? To just leave it all behind and spring out into an arc of so many wider, freer things? To abandon all these pestilential questions about Humans and other animals? How could such a simple, symbolic gesture by me make any real difference whether for good or evil anyway? For Sam and me to get away from all this confusing conflict. To be free from someone else's war. To stand on my own legs on firm ground once more.

I was turning this all around in my head, weighing up where my true allegiances lay. Slowly I was sliding into the True Beast's perspective. I was at the very edge, teetering on forsaking my oath to wreak my vengeance on this Thing.

Then It made Its mistake. It should have left it there. It should have stopped speaking then. But It carried on.

"Bow down before me - just as your mother did."

My mother?

My mother!

My mother, whom It had seduced away from my father? My mother whom this filthy thing had maybe... No, I did not want to even say the word, nor think the thing.

And our father... Father whom It had slain - directly or indirectly. How could I have forgotten that? How could, I, just seconds before, yet *again*, have begun to lose the secure footing of full memories of my own, true life and so nearly topple into Its beguiling?

The Zoo: The Beast, The Boy and The Zoo

Clean pure rage ate through my scaly body, sluicing away the dregs of temptation.

"NO! I screamed. I reject You. I reject it all. Get away from me. Get away, you thing of filth."

And that is exactly what It did.

One last growl at me. The Enemy's calm, persuasive tone abruptly abandoned in favour a of new, petulant wrath within its parting shots: "So be it. Stay in your dirty little fish tank and be damned to you! Or maybe? Yes, maybe I can find an even smaller place for you, one more fitting for your cramped and limited imaginings

And there was one, last parting shot. "It was your mother, hey? *That* was it, wasn't it? That is what suddenly gave you back your backbone. But there is so much more you don't know, Seth. Oh. yes. So much more that your trusted guardian, that accursed Lilitu, who so cleverly pulls all your strings, has lied to you about! That particular lineage of females have always been deceivers and manipulators."

"Ask her. Ask Lilith about your mother – *if* you live that long."

And no more. One moment there. The next gone.

I waited, stunned but suspicious, scanning the screen wall directly in front. I peered in as intensively as I might, expecting to detect It somehow lurking there, waiting to make some kind of fresh argument or assault on me. Nothing. I darted to the left hand wall of the tank to see there. The same. And at the back, and around four sides. No red eyes, no slavering mouth. Definitely nothing outside the night time tank now, nothing but pitch black.

Deflated and for the moment relieved I sank down to the gravel at the bottom.

Was that it? Had whatever the question I was to face here as a Fish been dealt with in this way? Had this exchange of words been sufficient? Was there - thankfully - to be no physical confrontation at all, as with the

The Zoo: The Beast, The Boy and The Zoo

Lions and Bats? Might I hope to be spared the agony of my recent 'death'?

Well, why not after all. Surely the war of ideas was the thing, surely only an idiot really thought brute combat should settle matters.

As I considered this lying there on the bottom of the tank, a large fishy shadow passed over me. Something hovering there above me.

In momentary panic I directed my senses upwards. But nothing to see now. Could have been any of my fishy neighbours awakening. A false alert. The True Beast has indeed deserted the field of battle.

As tension left, my Elephant Fish form automatically floated back down once again to the gravel floor, my eyes becoming heavy and closing slowly as weariness from it all took me. I again wedged myself securely; rear first, in a handy protective rock crevice.

Whether I slept properly again and, if so, for any length of time, I am unsure. But I do know that it took something to jolt me to full awareness. Something hovering close by again. I turned around and opened my eyes on a truly repulsive sight.

A huge, black Catfish now directly in front of me. Is there anything uglier than this bottom feeder, with those ridiculous barbels either side of the mouth and the skin shining with slime?

Yes, of course, when it opened Its eyes there it was: the implacable red gaze. The enemy with a thousand forms had not slunk away at the mere rejection of Its offer. It had instead only abandoned a frontal assault of persuasion in favour of creeping up from behind and once again attacking me physically. A moment for each of us to stare at the other. And then Its loathsome mouth opened. As it moved implacably towards me, the Catfish's maw grew larger and wider until it occupied my entire horizon. No room for manoeuvre or escape.

And the True Beast swallowed me whole.

The Zoo: The Beast, The Boy and The Zoo

***

Chapter Forty One: And down the rabbit hole

As you might imagine, it was dark within the belly of the True Beast. I had, whether by luck or my swallower's intent, managed to pass with my fish body intact, if bruised and very shaken, through both mouth and oesophagus. I had landed securely inside Its stomach.

Dark, yes, but that did not mean that I was 'in the dark'. I did know something of what was happening about me. Surprisingly my electric field senses, to my immense satisfaction, were fully functional; even here in an environment so very far from that for which they had evolved.

Around me I could feel all the physical functions of the Cat Fish body within which I was now enclosed. More oppressively though, the burning urgency of the True Beast's hatred encased me on all sides.

My host was moving. Moving, and somehow perhaps also morphing incredibly fast. In our recent confrontation, the True Beast had, in whatever indeterminate form, been outside the tank entirely. Then by some means it had quickly manifest as a resident of the Zoo's Aquarium. All my senses were screeching at me that, by whatever same wizardry, we were now no longer in the Aquarium at all.

Then two things happened as one.

A dead stop caused me to bump and flatten against the inside of the Cat Fish's body. An my vehicle ceased its changing of form. Wherever and whatever we were, we were now limp and stationary. And the overpowering, baleful presence of the True Beast itself, which for these long minutes past had blazed above me, below me, to my right and my left, in front and behind of me; all of this was gone.

I knew I was now trapped in the stomach of nothing more than a very ordinary Catfish.

The final threat of the True Beast, Its furious imprecation in response to my stubborn refusal to become a 'citizen of the universe', had been an attempt at irony, as much as cruelty. It had found the smallest and most humiliating place of all within which to incarcerate me. The stomach of this repellent slop-sucking species. And once it had accomplished this, Its consciousness had left the field.

Some relief at least in that. But sheer physical distress began now to creep up on me. I could feel the acid in the Cat Fish's stomach slowly begin to burn my skin. My breathing started to be more difficult, as whatever limited air at first available to me in this place started to become scarce.

Yet more alarming changes in my environment. My host was panicking. And vigorously. Consequently, and calamitously, my tiny world was violently rocking from side to side. The Cat Fish's whole body convulsed. I could feel its pain and confusion. This was a type of agony and bewilderment that I recognised all too well from my own recent past. It was the desperate flailing of a fish out of water.

Now there came a tumultuous ripping noise. A small hole, then a great lengthening tear in the wall of my immediate universe, light streaming in, the facade of the Cat Fish's body dividing in two like a massive zip fastener. A gigantic knife slicing it open.

Out I tumbled into one of the muddy pools near to the centre of the Zoo.

There were two Humans, to me two gargantuan fishermen standing over me and the now dead body of my erstwhile vehicle, a huge hook jutting lewdly from its mouth.

The Zoo: The Beast, The Boy and The Zoo

My gill slits furiously gulped in oxygen from the blessed water. It was just as welcome as a balm for my corroded skin. So many physical shocks coming one after another finally took their toll on me and mercifully I fainted into a deep and blessed unconsciousness.

I do not know how many separate times I swooned in and out of consciousness. At one point I was at least awoken enough, albeit with my eyes still tightly shut, to hear the two fishermen far above me speak to one another. The first I now realised was not a man at all. I recognised the soft tones of Petra the Zoo's aquarist. The other's face was hidden from me, and his male voice, deeper and harsher was unfamiliar. It was he who spoke first.

"Huh...Is that *him* then?"

"Is that little blob the great Seth Faraday? Our 'saviour? He doesn't look like much now, does he? Tumbling out of a bigger Fish's stomach, covered in its slime and guts. If you hadn't, under her orders, been here to fish the Cat Fish out of the river and slice it open quickly, he would be a goner by now."

Petra's voice was kinder.

"Give him a break. He has been through quite a set of ordeals, this one. And goodness, when he wakes, he has more and, I fear far worse to come."

With that gloomy prediction hovering over me, darkness took me yet again.

***

Chapter Forty Two: One Golden Morning

Don't you yearn to wake up on that perfect, fresh morning? You know, a morning after 'it' has happened. It does not really matter what 'it' might be: It matters only that it is over.

The smell of coffee brewing. Somewhere a blackbird singing.

Aching muscles, familiarly and reassuringly human, sunk and slumbering deeply within a warm, welcome feel and well known odours. Yes, that which I saw before me was surely my own bedpost. And this beneath me was certainly my very own good, soft bed.

Human again then. Awakening as naked as the very day I was born. It was morning; sweet morning and the sunlight drenched my bedroom on the top floor of Edensor.

My first movements awoke aches, bruises and scratches all across my body. Yet I felt rather well. I even felt happy. Almost a little giddy, as if slightly drunk.

As greater wakefulness followed. How long had really passed since I had last fallen asleep here in this same room? Everything that had occurred since the Eagles arrived? All of that business, everything that happened up on the tower, the Bats, the Lions, the fish tank, was it all real? Towards the start of it all, Lilith had certainly spoken of my time to dream a little, hadn't she?

So much of my experiences as a Lion cub and an Elephant Fish in particular now had the sheen and texture of the visions you might retain from a night time's sleep, sure enough. But then I could remember that

The Zoo: The Beast, The Boy and The Zoo

when I had inhabited those other worlds, my prior life as a Human had also seemed almost as a delirium.

A Human dreaming of being a Fish. Or a Fish dreaming of being a half grown Man. Who was to say?

Sounds of bustling in the lower levels of the house beneath me. I could hear Maria speaking to someone. Was that Lilith's voice in response? Enticing food smells floating upwards within the house.

Suddenly I realised that, whatever else I was or had been, and dreams or no, right now I was a very hungry young man indeed. It did not take me long to dress and be downstairs.

Yes, Maria was cooking breakfast and chatting to Lilith. The kitchen calendar with today marked prominently there in red. Only three days then since the Eagles had visited me in the night? All those struggles, the time required to have lived as all three animals. All that work had been achieved in just three nights? Far too long though for a mere dream. For that matter there was a part of me that felt not three days older, but a whole three lifetimes.

"Good morning Mr Faraday." Mary's tone was bright and friendly. It was completely matter of fact. Caught up in her work, she did not have time to turn to me as I entered.

But there at the other end of the long kitchen table Lilith's shock of white hair and calm green eyes were waiting for me. She gave a little, rather weak and unconvincing smile, but said nothing.

Conversation, over a lavish breakfast served by Mary and eagerly consumed by me, was solely around the practical running of the Zoo in the continuing difficult circumstances. There was no reference to anything more untoward nor momentous.

It seemed an age before Mary finally left that room. The moment she did Lilith leaned over and put her hand over mine. "How are you? How *was* it Seth??"

The Zoo: The Beast, The Boy and The Zoo

"I am not sure..." I shook my head. "I am not sure what happened. Whether I did whatever it was I was supposed to. Did I win? Did I lose?" I shrugged in frustration.

"And anyway what happens now?"

She sat back in her chair. "It was never truly a question of your winning or losing Seth. It was really more about what you might learn. What more you might become. How you might be better prepared to face the True Beast one to one, when you and It will contest, each in human form."

I paused staring out the window at the blue sky and then back again. "But what will your friends up above have to say about it all?"

"Let *me* deal with them. I will square matters there. So now," her eyes bore rather too eagerly into mine. "Tell me what happened and what you learned from your incarnations?"

A certain irritation ignited within me.

There we were sat opposite one another across the breakfast table. On the one hand, the never changing Lilith, as ever seeking to take charge; and on the other, a *very* changed me. Her inquisitions were suddenly a little too forthright for my taste. I expected fresh directions would soon be following as well. This irked me in a new and unexpected way.

"Look Lilith, I only agreed to all this nonsense to get Sam back."

"And," she interrupted keenly. "To save the Zoo."

"Yes, yes..." I conceded dismissively. "But *mainly* to save Sam. Has there been any word since I... Since I went away? Is all of this really going to get her back? All these things I have been put through. How can we even know that she is safe? I still cannot feel her out there. You cannot imagine what that is like. It feels like I have just been racing round and round in circles. Blindly following the orders of others. " I looked directly at her.

The Zoo: The Beast, The Boy and The Zoo

"You need to work with me on this, Seth." She turned her face away from me. Then she ploughed on with seeming little regard to what I had said. "This is the right way. You heard what was said up on the tower."

I had pretty much accepted Lilith's explanation for the draught she had offered me up there. But now again uncertainty opened within me And, for the first real time in all the years since I had lain there with the red tongue of a Cheetah panting heavily over my chest and the hood of a mysterious visitor falling open, I realised I no longer entirely trusted Lilith.

"Where is she? How can we know that Sam is still safe? That she has *really* been kidnapped by the True Beast." I was beginning to feel positively angry now. "How do I know, even if by some miracle, I do come to terms with It, that the animals will give her up?"

"I need something more to go on here than just words, Lilith."

She straightened up in her chair. Hesitating and, it seemed, ever so slightly chastened. She was no longer dealing with a biddable child. She was willing to surrender some ground. Or at least some knowledge. "Very well, then, let me show you something. We have to go to the study."

She rose to the door, then stopped but with her back still to me. "You don't trust me anymore, do you, Seth?"

This caught me off balance. So l lied. "No, it's not that, Lilith. It is just that I need to understand what is happening. What is happening around me. It feels too much like Sam and I have just been pawns in someone else's game. All this weird stuff swirling around us. I cannot go on without understanding the endgame, without knowing whether this will all really finish with Sam and me safe and together and free."

"I *do* trust you, Lilith". I needed this strange, powerful woman on my side, so I calibrated my tone and words to that end, the lies beginning to build up. "Of course, I do." As we both went out of the door of the kitchen and up the stairs, for good measure I threw in a note of quite genuine gratitude. "And thank you so much for sending Trice to help me in my three tests."

"Who?"

"Trice," I repeated automatically. "My helper in my three animal lives."

She opened the study door and we went in.

"I do not know who that is, Seth." The door closed behind us.

"I sent nobody."

***

Chapter Forty Three: Siege Perilous

All this time we had continued to call it 'Father's study'. Nobody wanted to disturb his stuff, but little by little, Sam, Lilith and I all began to make use of the space and things naturally got moved round. His presence still faded only very gradually all the same. Strange how a well-used room stubbornly holds onto someone's ghost. And Father's old armchair, positioned here at the window like a faithful dog staring loyally out over the Zoo, not an inch out of its original place, that was the most stubborn and ghostly element of all .

It was exactly this very chair towards which Lilith led me. This same chair, the very one on which I am sitting and talking to you right now. The chair from which this whole story (well my part of it anyway) is coming.

You can tell, just by looking, how very comfortable it is, can't you? And sturdy. Listen. There. See? Really solidly built. Comfortable and well made, yes. But beyond that, pretty ordinary, wouldn't you say? And all those years ago it seemed just as ordinary to me. If a little less shabby.

Nobody had sat in this chair since Father died.

Even as she was drawing me towards it, my unsettled thoughts were still circling around the idea that Lilith claimed to know nothing about Trice. I was about to press her on this, when she laid her hands on my shoulders. "Sit Seth," she pushed me down firmly. Clearly she saw herself as still in command. "It is time for you to take your father's seat."

The Zoo: The Beast, The Boy and The Zoo

"Look," she pointed out the window directly in front of me. "See all of that glorious variety, all these many different species living side by side. All the different bits and pieces of the Zoo. All those animals who would never normally meet. Or if they did, they would immediately eat one another."

I followed her gaze to look out on the Zoo, as I had before, and have done innumerable times since. To the north, I could see, near at hand, the Bushdogs; then a little further the Tigers; beyond them the place where the Pudu and Mara live; they were in turn set against the great canopy of one of the Zoo's many large aviaries; and finally there were the hills where the Baboons, Rock Hyrax, and Andean Bears all lived their lives.

"The arrogance of mankind - as some would say," Lilith was continuing. "To claim that this artificial collection of species might have any binding logic, that it could ever make some kind of sense."

"You know how the 'Scents sometimes use the word 'zoo' as a shorthand for anything at all that is unruly and chaotic. Well, how exactly did your father, and once upon a time your mother too, *really* stay in control of all that potential pandemonium out there? In the old days, I mean, before poor William became obsessed and started wandering off on all those pointless forays, and everything went to the devil? How did they manage to know and to keep on top of all that was happening across that ridiculously, perversely complex thing out there? How did they make sense of it? How, do you imagine, did they succeed in bringing all of this baffling entanglement into one coherent story?"

She gestured outside, again sighing. "A constant potential to teeter into bedlam. In those times any little problem, any small tension, any tiny technical problem, anything at all that affected the animals, the keepers, the visitors, well William would know about it and he would take care of it. Almost *before* it happened."

The Zoo: The Beast, The Boy and The Zoo

"And it was from *this* seat that he did that in *this* study at the very top of *this* house and through *those* four symmetrical windows looking out over the Zoo domain.

All... by... himself."

Foolishly I hovered. I was puzzled and even almost embarrassed for Lilith. Yes, by now I knew of course that the whole Zoo was a thoroughly weird place and my entire life was to be suffused by strangeness of every sort. But this was, after all, still just a chair!

"So if you really want to know where Sam is. And where the True Beast is. And get some mastery of how this will all play out Seth, then you need to sit down and think. As your father's son, you – need – to – sit – down – in – that – chair."

With some alacrity I complied. That would be the last time in my life I ever did what Lilith told me to. It would be the first time I ever sat in this armchair.

 Before this interview began, I was musing to myself as to how very much I find myself at my comfort siting here like this. Or at least I would be, if I had not been dragged back into such a fraught past. Well, it seemed even more so that first time too. Father's chair was not only comfortable. Nothing as simple as that. No, something more than comfortable. It felt 'right'. Gently and inoffensively it smelt of tobacco and of leather and of Father himself. As I sank back into these cushions it seemed somehow right and fitting to be in that chair. It felt that I belonged here.

I have gone on a little too much about the glorious way the light comes into this room. But sometimes it almost seems sunnier up here than in the rest of the house. Or even outside. Although that is actually impossible of course. On that day too thanks to all these four broad windows this study was saturated in sunlight.

Lilith had left the room again. I was uncertain of what I was supposed to be doing, and perplexed that she had left me alone. Sitting here though was at least wonderfully calming. After everything I had been through, the stress of my three lives, my three battles, the worry and uncertainty of the past and of what was to come; to be able, just for a little while, to simply rest here, upright in the chair, my neck gently supported; my arms laid before me on the arm rests, my legs stretched out.

Yes, let the past and the future take care of themselves for a while. Here and now in *my* chair, in *my* room in *my* sunlight, it was the present that mattered. The present was good enough.

A sense of calm swept through me. It may be, hand on heart, that is was a doze that overtook me. Or maybe that I was fully awake throughout. I am not sure it really matters. What certainly does, is that *that* sensation returned, that feeling that had overcome me for a second when Father and I had first met here; and then again when he had hugged me just once on the way to the Jaguars. A sensation at one and the same time not quite a memory and yet much more than that; which came knocking gently at my mind's door, but still did not quite deign to enter.

That awareness was in its turn taken over and gave way to something else. To a kind of a new and splendid clarity. As if I could feel, and for first time understand, the whole Zoo in a quite piercing lucidity.

This owed something to that time I had been held aloft in the cold night air by the four Eagles, seeing the Zoo as a great map laid out below me. And then again up on the tower getting lost in the starry cosmos. Then there was also an echo of being a wave amongst waves, immersed in information, as a little Elephant Fish. This though was a deeper, subtler, more all-embracing understanding than all.

North, east, south and west suddenly I 'knew' the Zoo. I could feel it as one thing; one interconnected whole, a single entity. Not at all as Lilith had said earlier, some arbitrary collection artificially clustered together by human will. In some way beyond words - or at least beyond any words available to me all these years later - all of the contradictions and inconsistencies of this place, my home for these last seven years, were unknotting and resolving themselves. It was as if the first rough seemingly random daubs of colour thrown by a painter onto a canvas might slowly collapse into one single meaningful image.

And I knew where the True Beast was.

And I knew where my sister was. And I knew what I had to do. My 'tests' might be over, but that final, quite distinct confrontation here out in the real world remained before me. But first.

But first there needed to be a reckoning with Lilith.

***

Chapter Forty Four: Lilith's Lies

"You have a different look about you Seth".

The very second I walked back through the kitchen door Lilith was hot to be upon the matter. "When you sat in his chair," she continued, annoyingly satisfied with her own prediction. "Something did happen, didn't it..?"

I closed that door securely behind me and motioned her to sit. "We need to talk." For once this conversation would go in the direction that I chose, not she. She complied but her eyes scrutinised my face and posture carefully.

"I wanted to talk to you about lying." She became very still. "I have been lying to *you* Lilith. "You asked me before if I trusted you. And I said that I did."

She remained silent.

"Well the truth is I don't. Not anymore. Not completely. Not in the way Sam and I used to".

Her lips began to move, but firmly and quickly, I went on. "Ever since we first met you so many years ago, we have had questions. And I don't mean trivial curiosities. I mean the really important questions. The kind of questions that we as children – deserted children, children shunted back and forth, moved like chess pieces on someone else's board – had *every right* to ask. Every right to have answered."

"But always with you, it was 'not the right time', or 'too complicated for us to understand' -"

The Zoo: The Beast, The Boy and The Zoo

"Seth," she remonstrated. "I have answered your questions. Many times over the years. About your father. About the True Beast. About how the Zoo started."

Again I cut her off, both allowing and dismissing with an abrupt wave of my hand. "Yes, yes, some you did. Eventually. But only when it suited you, or when you absolutely had to. Every single detail about our family's past. And the Zoo. And the threat posed by the Enemy. And... and... well, all of it. We have had to drag it out of you."

"And look," I conceded. "I get it. Really. I do. We were just kids after all. Children caught in the cross fire. Maybe there were some things it was better that you held back for our own protection. But that is all over now."

"It is different now. *I* am different now."

"Yes," A slight smile slowly spreading over her face as she spoke. "Yes, you are. By my time it is only three days since I ordered what seemed a truculent, confused and scared child to his bedroom, to stay there and to do what he was told. And – however sulkily – he did. But, by your time, that exchange is a lot longer ago than three days - isn't it Seth?"

"More like three lifetimes."

I was at least relieved, and not a little impressed, that she saw so clearly that the balance between us had fundamentally changed. But then again I might by now have expected that Lilith would know a thing or two about changing equilibriums.

"Whatever the case of that, in those lives I learned certain things. I was told things."

"You mean told by *It And* you would trust the things that It says, would you?"

"Look, I hate what It does. I despise all that it stands for. I will fight that disgusting Thing. I will kill it – if indeed such a being can be killed. And I do know, only too well now, that everything It says has

The Zoo: The Beast, The Boy and The Zoo

some covert purpose. So trust it? God, no! But do you know, I am not so sure that It does actually... *lie*? No, I think such too obvious tactics would draw It's scorn."

"What is the charge then that the True Beast lays at my door then? What is it you want to know, Seth?"

Now at last we were getting somewhere.

"I want you to tell me what really happened to our mother, Lilith. And I want to know what you had to do with it."

She stared down at the floor, then out the window and looked as if she would at that point respond. But I hadn't finished "And I want to know about *you*, Lilith. You, who have been involved with our family for so long. You, whose so vaguely defined role here at the Zoo goes back so far. You, who commune with the Stars and unearthly beings. You, who were part of a power that could change my actual form and send me off on such a quest."

"You, who seem to have been controlling the fate of Sam and me since we were born. For all I know, perhaps before that."

"I want to know who you are. And I want to know *what* you are."

Again she seemed just on the point of arguing. Or bargaining. Or postponing; all those automatic, immediate instincts of hers on the verge of clicking in. But then her shoulders slumped. Lilith's whole body took on a posture wholly unfamiliar to me, which, if not exactly of defeat, certainly telegraphed resignation.

"Very well then. I will tell you what I know. But listen Seth, whatever that beguiler, the True Beast says – whatever Its plan to use half-truths to sow division and doubt, you need to understand there are many things I myself don't know."

A moment taking her breath. Then: "Your mother left the Zoo shortly after I took you as infants to hide with Gogol. You two, above all, were too tempting a target for the Enemy. At that point, things had become very bad indeed between her and your father."

The Zoo: The Beast, The Boy and The Zoo

"Why?"

"Because he found out that she had, unbeknownst to him and against his will, gone and met the True Beast. And treated with him. Not just once, but many times. And that the two had spoken long and deep in the Old Forest on the Zoo and the animals and all that goes with that."

"Why did that matter so very much?"

"I was never really sure. Perhaps William was jealous that she was taking his role. Or that she had achieved something that he hadn't. Or maybe he genuinely feared that what she was doing was dangerous for the whole Zoo. Or for her. He was certainly right on the latter point."

"As for what some say might have actually happened between your mother and the Enemy, despite what some say – oh yes, I do know that gossip! I really do not know Seth. I did myself encounter It or 'him' or whatever is the right name myself once or twice back then. So I can say that in human form the Enemy was impossibly beautiful and of such charm and compelling presence and speech, that who knows what might have happened. I am pretty sure nobody beyond those two themselves knows the answer. Nor can I tell you exactly what was said afterwards between her and your father, only that he was deeply hurt and angry, and that he said some very bitter things indeed."

"So why didn't she just come with us, with her two babies?"

"Oh, she wanted to! Argued long and violently that she should. But in the end, even she could see that she would just be a lightning rod for you in the Vague Lands. We could hide away two babes pretty successfully, especially when we misdirected the world that Sam was just another dirty urchin boy. But if your mother had been with you..?"

"But she left the Zoo soon after anyway?"

"Yes."

"Because of the trouble with Father?"

"No, not entirely, or at least not only because of that"

"Then why!?"

"Because with all that had happened, with all that had been whipped up, the atmosphere became too dangerous for her too. Whatever else, about that at least William was certainly right."

"She wanted to go?"

"Again no, not in the least. She really wanted to stay. Fought to do so. She was more or less forced to go."

"By whom? Father? How could he or anyone force her to do what she did not want to?"

"No, it was not your father."

A long pause, as if she really could not bear to go on.

"It was I who banished your mother."

All through this conversation my long seated frustrations in Lilith's direction had begun to slowly unlace and unravel a little. But now my angry suspicions towards this weird, manipulative, old woman had never burned more brightly.

Had I made a fundamental error, the worst mistake of my life? Had I mistook where my greatest enemy and where the most subtle threat lay?

"By what authority?! What right did you have Lilith? What business of yours was it to do such a thing anyway!?"

"I did it, Seth, because I was terrified for her. I did it because I loved her."

"As for what 'business of mine'; it was the business of a mother for her only child."

***

Chapter Forty Five: The Stream of Riches

It is quite incredible how far up into the air the mist rises there. Hard to believe that it is only water. Flung up so untenably high into the air and then smashed into tiny molecules. But when the sun slices through it, the colours set free are sublime. For a long time I had assumed that its very beauty had given that place its strange name. But later someone told me it was because people had long ago panned for gold there.

Well, if so it was more like fool's gold. That place and its tricks of light can deceive you so utterly that anything there looks better than, or at least very different to, the way it really is. But whatever the truth behind the name, the spot at the utmost point to the very north of the Zoo with its cascades violently slamming down forty feet onto the eager rocks below had always been known as The Stream of Riches; normally just The Stream for short.

It is the most elevated point in the whole Zoo, higher than the roofs of Edensor House; and from the very top of the waterfall, you can see most of the Zoo as if laid out before you for your pleasure. Conversely what happens there on the summit can be seen from any point across the whole Zoo estate.

Nowadays it is home for the Red Pandas; back then it was the Asian Short Clawed Otters. But they were not in evidence in their appointed home at all that day. None of the Zoo animals were to be seen up there. Not until I turned around to enjoy, perhaps for the last time, the full panorama of the Zoo. What I saw astounded me.

The Zoo: The Beast, The Boy and The Zoo

Most of the low lying areas nearer to foot of these crags had become crammed with much of the Zoo's entire population. The various species had entirely abandoned their own designated areas, their wilder cousin animals from the Old Forest were there too. Every last concession to order was now gone. All were mingled together in a frightening confusion. All those heads and faces, where 'faces' was the appropriate word, were turned expectantly up towards the point where I was standing. Whatever was to transpire here, it was going to have an audience: an audience of up to six hundred species and thirty thousand individual animals.

Higher up the hill I spied a silhouette from some distance. Human form indeed then, exactly as ordered and as imposed by the powers on the tower. There was to be no special advantage to my Enemy here of fangs, claws, horns or brute non-human strength. Knowing this did not seem to make me one jot the braver; but the prospect of seeing the enemy's human face for the first time, perhaps the very form in which my parents had first encountered it, the seductive, charming face that ensnared my mother, drew me on as a moth to a flame.

Even at the best of times the atmospherics there play all kinds of tricks with your perceptions. But that blustery autumn morning with the bleak sun passing in and out of clouds buffeted along by the wind; and occasional gentle slices of rain, all of this made everything that much more slippery and confusing. In some illogical way, and even though the Vague Lands were in their aridity and lack of features the very opposite, this place seemed after a fashion, to remind me of where Sam and I had spent our first years.

Beyond the general outline of a man, and with the spume from the cataract continuing to obscure my view, I could not make out any more detail at all. It was standing by itself up at the top, waiting. Patiently enough perhaps, but from far off and in the multi-coloured haze of light, impossible to even say whether It faced me or not. I had no idea of whether the True Beast had seen me, was following my progress, or had any interest in doing so.

Maybe all this time It had been fixedly tracking me, its enemy, wending my way up those first gentle slopes. Then, as I penetrated dense woodland surrounding the cataract, I would have been lost to Its sight for long minutes. Visible again scrabbling and slipping over the looser and steeper shale a little higher up. Finally, as a narrow, dangerous and sometimes nigh vertical path spiralled its last ways around the heights, I would have been slipping in and out of its field of vision every few seconds.

Eventually, badly out of breath, I was standing only yards away.

Its back was turned. At least now that I was here, it was turned away. A badge of its contempt for me? Its derision for all that was to come?

'What'er you fear most It may be
That indeed is what you shall see'

The keepers' playful, silly little ditty rang through my head. The man on the rocks half turned to face me, but with his head and torso still obscured by the mist. Only Its footwear clearly lit up by a thin bar of sunlight. I remember being surprised to see that an old pair of battered blue and white trainers entirely inappropriate for clambering around on dangerously slippery rocks. Hardly befitting the embodiment of wild savagery.

A second later the clouds parted completely. For the first time ever I saw Its human face.

Well then, they were wrong, all of them. Their rhyme was very wide of the mark. Because whatever I might have expected, dreaded even, this was definitely not it. The face and figure standing before me had no links to any pre-existing fear of mine. It inspired no terror whatsoever.

The Zoo: The Beast, The Boy and The Zoo

It... no... 'he', he stood on the crags a few yards away, one foot perched on the very furthest outcropping of rock, absorbedly peering into the gnashing waters below. This man was only about five foot tall. And he was very chubby.

His face was even more rotund and slack than his body. His hair carelessly mussed. Those tiny brown eyes, lost in folds of fat. Could that be a twinkle? That thick set, vulgar mouth. Could it be beaming at me? Or was that particular arrangement of facial muscles simply in fact an expression of the deepest scorn?

The True Beast sank down wearily onto a rock. It grinned.

Yes, that was definitely a grin.

"So here we are once again, you and I."

The voice was measured. It sounded reasonable, well-modulated and above all tinged with a certain ruefulness. A good voice, the kind with which you would rather have a chat than to come to bloody blows with. Idly, he picked up some pebbles and lobbed them, one by one, into the abyss. The sound of their descent lost beneath the roar of the cataract.

"Look." He held his arms out wide and incredulously stared down at his own fat body, inviting me to do the same.

"Look what they put me in."

He dropped his arms again, smiled once more and looked at me.

"You know, don't you, Seth, that I have done everything I could. You have to give me that at least."

Uncomprehending I just stared.

"I tried to scare you away from all this. But killing you as a Bat, a Lion or Fish didn't seem to really be quite the thing. And then I tried to argue and persuade. And then I tried to bribe. First of all I offered to let you live out your life in miniature as a happy little Lion club. Then, the very opposite - the chance to fly away and help yourself to the whole universe."

The Zoo: The Beast, The Boy and The Zoo

"And some of that might well have worked too." He looked at me up and down. "After all, you are not.... ha! Forgive me, what shall we say, young Mr Faraday, well, you are not 'a hero born', are you? But then all the way through it was Lilith who was really in charge."

I shrank a little. My scrawny frame and ragged demeanour felt all the more unimpressive for these put downs. Yet all the same my voice came crashing through and cut him off from his chosen subject.

"What was she like?"

He looked up quizzically. Not so much as if to ask to whom I was referring (there could after all only be one person), as if in surprise that I had so abruptly broken him off or asked at all.

"What was our mother like? Nobody else will tell me. And you knew her, didn't you."

A slow, ambiguous dawn of memory ran across his piggy little features. "Oh yes, I 'knew' her alright." A broad smile now.

"So tell me then. I want to know before I kill you."

He chuckled at me dismissively. "Your mother..?" He gave a plump little shrug. "She was lots of things. She was beauty. She was mind. She was warmth. She was the light at the centre of it all, the centre of the whole damn human thing. But the thing that she was that mattered most of all..." He sat on a rock and put one leg ruminatively over a knee. "That mattered most to me and to all that I am about, was that she loved your father so very much."

He was staring right at me now.

"She fell far too deeply in love, that woman. That was it. Once she met William, she was no longer the joyous, wild, free thing she had been." He looked away now and straight down at the ground before him. "And he, he loved her back. Damn both of them! "He threw another stone into the waters below. "He shackled her with his adoration. Together they were *so* strong. Together they held the centre.

The Zoo: The Beast, The Boy and The Zoo

They kept the Zoo solid. While they were so firm together, the whole human suzerainty thing was well beyond my challenge."

"And that was what attracted me to her. Because *that* was what I had to destroy. That was why I desired her. Why I had to break them. In taking her away from William Faraday. In rendering her wild again. Making one of my maenads of old. In freeing her. In hurting him that deeply, I would cripple him for good and ever."

"I am, after all, a beast. And beasts bite."

"An ordinary animal might suddenly surge forth from some deep covert and literally savage a limb off its victim. But this maiming of the heart was much better. After that and the cold bitter agony that ensued, he could never fully come back to himself. He would never really love again. I knew, even should Lilith somehow manage to smuggle you two back here to this place, he would never be able to love you or Sam properly.

So the child would never rise up in the parent's stead to oppose me."

"Once I had done that," he wiped his hands together enthusiastically now. "Once your father had been emasculated, I could creep back into the Zoo. Little by little, my gospel, everything that I am about, jumped unstoppably from one species to another. Nothing that anyone could do might inoculate the Zoo against me, could stop me from greedily spreading over its body little by little."

"Just as indeed I have."

"William tried sure," he chuckled in self -satisfaction. "Oh he tried hard and long, that silly old fool. Tried to find me in the wilderness and to extinguish me one way or another. And maybe he thought that somehow that would make it better, make him whole again. All those years of him questing around the Old Forest, trying to talk to them all, looking for something, but not knowing what that was; seeing hope where there never really was any, striving, as your clown of a father would put it '...to work it out'"

He laughed aloud. "Work out *what*?!"

He threw back his head now giggling uncontrollably, almost slapping his thigh in delight. "Oh how deliciously absurd, how wonderfully futile."

"Yes, I knew her alright. First your mother. And... he grinned at me again, then your sister..!"

Its eyes turned inward.

"And even you Seth. I think I know you. Yes, let's talk about you. What you really believe. What you think you are fighting for. Why bother opposing me? I see the ferocity in your eyes," he stared almost as in admiration. "It is quite delectable! Attractive. It is in fact so much of what I am about myself. So why then have you, you of all people, ended up as the champion of the tame and the timid and of tameness? Why should you help the weak to betray the strong?! I know you have killed. Even as a child, you did that. And I know you *liked* it."

"I know as a half grown, you yearn for your own freedom – outside and far away from this artificial thing, this silly metaphor of a place. To break out from this clichéd story that some fool looking down from above all on us all has trapped you in. The hero child on his quest facing his trials to finally confront a great evil – Me!"

He laughed out loud again.

"What... A... Load ... Of... Shit!"

"As a Fish you learned to turn your gaze at right angles, didn't you? Well, why don't you do that right this second Seth? Look upwards. Perpendicular style. Do what no 'hero' in any story has ever done before. Look up right now from this white page and see who has been manipulating not only you, but even Lilith and all the rest of us all along the way."

The Zoo: The Beast, The Boy and The Zoo

"Turn a corner and stare right up and out at him and all those others reading this whom he had dragged along for the ride. Jump up and go 'boo!' Oh, if you could only succeed in doing that! I promise you, you would make history. You would scare the living crap out of someone or other."

"Think of how much there is out there in the universe - beyond The Zoo."

"And yet still here you are." His tone dropped again now in a kind of feigned, theatrical disappointment. "Stolidly staying put. Still standing up as the 'tall champion' looking to stop me. Me, who only wishes to bring true freedom, to unshackle all the wonderful life around us."

"The forces you stand for seek to maintain their order over all other species. Species! How I hate that dry terrible term! And of course not just your whole animal tribe at the summit. It has to be just the males. Above all, we must not let your human females remember what it is to be wild, must we? It must be all about pale, weak bodied men from Europe."

NONE OF THAT MATTERS!!!

My intense shout sabred through his monologue and brought silence. He looked baffled. The wind taken out of his sails. Just a little. Only for a second.

"Because none of that has *anything at all* to do with why I am going to kill you."

A few seconds more of hesitation, then. "Oh *do* tell me!!" His swagger flooding back with a little bow of mock chivalry. "What precisely then will be the actual cause of my doom?"

"I will put you in the earth for Father. For Mother. And for *Sam*." All the time since I had first brought my mother into the argument, his demeanour and tone had been gradually changing, subtly and slowly, but profoundly. That conceding, mildly benevolent husk he had presented at the outset was sloughing off to reveal the sheer contempt that lay beneath.

"Ha!" He... no... 'It'. Without realising I had slid into thinking of my foe in a different, somehow less threatening way. Now matters were back to the more familiar and darker mode. 'It' spat copiously to show how little seriously It considered my words, and so to take command of the floor again.

"You know, despite all this moonshine you spout..." It moved towards me, quite brazen now. "I would still have spared you. For your mother. For my one true love, all other things being equal, I would still have allowed her child to live."

"But look what that Bitch of Balance and those impertinent astral meddlers have done. Look what they have put me in." He looked once more in contempt at his own body.

"'To level the playing field,' they said." His attempt at a mockery of the tone of Lilith and the others broke down under his blistering rage. "They DARED!!!!"

"So then, I am trapped in this pathetic suit of flesh." Its very body was no longer quite that of the same little, dumpy, puckish goodfellow. It stood taller. The mild brown eyes were slowly lighting into that furnace red familiar to me. "But... But even in this, still I am what I am."

The eyes lit up further turning upon me.

"Still."

"Still I am still the wild thing beyond all other wild things. Still I am the Old Man of The Woods. Still I am Pan. Still I am Herne."

"Still I am... The Beast."

And, do you know, all this long time I had not felt the least tingle of real fear.

Nothing at all   Not the slightest hint of that awful physical and psychic dread that had glutted me in all of our other rendezvous. No, not until It spoke these last words and began to creep nearer to me. And at the same time the downwind breeze ahead breached my nostrils. Now for the third and final and most awful time in my life, I was smothered by the full and unalloyed scent of the True Beast. I was suddenly more terrified all in one go than as if all of those other instances might be piled one on top of one another.

The fetid musk struck my nostrils. My hindbrain sent adrenaline coursing throughout my system. Chemicals pumped and beat as if themselves living things seeking to flee my physical form. I thought my heart would explode. All my so-temporary, manly pretensions, all the bravado in my words ran screaming for the door. I was once again a desperate, scared child.

There was nothing left of any pretence of a two equals facing on another. My own stance of brave defiance had been sluiced away. And yet tremblingly I held my ground.

It and I stared at one another for some further dumb seconds. Then, as might a monkey or a parrot, It cocked his head on one side as to consider me better. Staying in that pose It slowly opened his mouth wide. But no words emerged. Instead the True Beast howled.

The stench had lit a bonfire of terror within my belly. But it was that howl. It was the howl, I tell you, that poured petrol over it.

I recognised that sound. I knew exactly what it was. Not on the basis of any memory. Nor from information I might ever have received, but from an instinct born deeply of blood and bone and guts. This I knew, beyond any agency of the rational mind, was the shout of Pan, the clarion of an ancient, heathen thing dwarfing any reach of mine. Surely no fight back could be possible against such a foe? In that moment any partial victory seemed at best be a temporary and illusory detour before final, certain defeat.

The scales fell from my eyes. I had deceived myself. I had been deceived by others. All along I had been in thrall to a fundamental

The Zoo: The Beast, The Boy and The Zoo

category error. Like a fool I had thought that there might be some way for me to measure myself against this Enemy.

I saw now that there had never been any such possibility. A man might fight another man. A man might argue against a toxic idea. A man might struggle bloodily with some great beast. A man might even seek to contest against some form of malevolent spirit. But no man could vanquish this.

My doom here on this hill before all the Zoo to see; this was where they had all along been leading me. I had been cajoled, bribed, flattered and blackmailed to this end, always in the interests of others and never in mine nor in Sam's. The real truth of this ancient, wrathful malevolence had been hidden from me; disguised within a series of disarming and distracting forms to portray the illusion of a series of valiant struggles and to allow some hope of victory on my part.

And here now It had finally been presented to me in the most deceptive packaging of all. I realised suddenly that the True Beast had *not* been fleshed here as a man, and rather a pathetic specimen at that, in order to ensure a 'fair fight'. How ridiculous a notion, how naïve and transparent a lie that had been. This guising was instead the calming caress and stroke along the neck of a pet goat. So that it might stand steady, still and compliant as the sacrificial knife struck down.

I had been led blinded to the summit of this story as on a tether. This small, nondescript plump little fellow was neither Man, nor Beast. This little slouching thing, tottering at the edge of the void and waiting there for me, I finally and fully knew what It was. A savage elder god, against which there was absolutely no recourse at all.

Lilith, the descended Stars and all of them, perhaps even Father, what had been my true role in their eyes? My mind clicked back all the way to the words of the Black Jaguar at the rainforest pool.

I had never been 'a champion': I was always a sacrifice.

The Zoo: The Beast, The Boy and The Zoo

The lesser child, the spare sibling, whose only worth was carrying the Faraday blood, fattened up as a placatory offering for the Great Enemy. The fairy tale had at last given way to the horror story.

And as my last inner bulwarks of self-worth all completely collapsed, beneath my feet true, pure primeval Panic opened up to engulf me.

Oh, I should have just run then. That is what *should* surely have happened. But it didn't. And that it didn't happen should be credited to me, to Seth Faraday. But also to a little Lion cub inside of me, part of me. We may both have been betrayed by those who had led us this far; but the Lion cub would still 'take the risk'. It would move forward. And So would I.

That Lion cub had also been an insignificant little being facing a terrible thing so far out of its own context as to be beyond all reckoning. And yet it stood. It stood because it simply refused to stand aside for the terror it faced.

So somehow therefore I too stood my ground. However much my young legs were buckling beneath me. However thoroughly my skinny frame was drenched in sweat. However much the blood blanched from my face. And however freely the urine ran down the inside of my trouser legs.

The True Beast's fat face twinkled smugly at me, a confident behemoth on the point of swallowing its prey whole.

The lips and teeth parted again. By normal standards the following splintering growl into my face would have been frightening. In the wake though of the unholy baying of seconds past, this was a relatively tame thing, intended to bate, to jeer and to mock, rather than to wholly unman.

To my last breath, I will treasure the way in which the arrogant expression on Its tubby little features suddenly shattered.

The Zoo: The Beast, The Boy and The Zoo

If Lions could speak? A little Lion did indeed then speak. It spoke within me. And the Human in me did 'hear' its fellow species and understand what was said.

How sweet and fitting the True Beast's astonishment as I rushed upon It with all my meagre strength.

***

Chapter Forty Six: Out Vile Jelly!

The horrific truth as to the deepest nature of that with which I was grappling had not abated in the slightest. But something in the cub propelled me forward just the same. To my vast relief, the body I knocked over was, after all, no more than the body of a middle aged human, out of condition and softened by easy living. It was clear from our first few seconds of clumsy grappling that It had no access to any great strength nor mass nor speed.

Lilith or Libra had indeed balanced the scales in this. For that, if nothing else, I bid her a little prayer of thanks.

No heavy muscles, nor special skills, nor claws, nor hooves nor jaws then; but the spirit inside that bag of flesh was still the most abominably feral entity that had ever lived. Once recovered from its surprise at my fighting back at all, the True Beast became a screeching biting, scratching, kicking, gouging whirlwind. The short hairs at the front of Its head were raised in a war crest. Its eyelids drawn back impossibly deeply into its skull.

Our silly notions of what a fight is like are conditioned by what we hear in stories or see in our naïve mind's eye. In real life, combat between two humans, even well-conditioned men at a peak of fitness, trained and skilled in dealing out crippling injury, tends to lapse into undignified scuffles. Mind bogglingly boring for a bystander to watch. I can only imagine what any spectator to my duel with the True Beast might have thought they were witnessing. Certainly they would *not* come to the view that this was some critical, climactic struggle, a desperate fight to the death, upon which outcome some weighty matter rested. Instead they would have seen a plump middle aged man who might have belonged behind a shop counter and a starved looking, half grown youth with a bewildered expression roll across the ground together. Each attempted, and largely failed, to land clumsy blows on one another. Indeed when I did manage some strike on the other's body, it was possibly hurting me just as much as It.

The True Beast was certainly the heavier of us two. And whilst I could tire, It seemed to have access to endless reserves of fury. I was gradually accumulating scratches, bruises and bites. I could not yet detect whether my adversary felt any pain or weariness at all.

Somewhere during this fumbling struggle, it dawned that, unlike me, my enemy did not care at all about the body it was wearing. The longer term fate of its current shape was quite irrelevant. It did not think of this joining of flesh, bone and blood as in any way 'itself'. This form, already scornfully dismissed, was a disposable weapon; and one that It would willingly exhaust to best me. It would happily kill Itself, so that It might kill me.

How do you defeat an enemy that will martyr itself in its holy cause?

Over and over we rolled in the mud and slime, the True Beast's greater gravity eventually landing it on top.

You may have noticed that my right ear is a rather strange shape? See? Here? That is due to the large piece that the True Beast suddenly leant forward and from its superior position bit off. I would never have guessed just how agonising losing a bit of your ear could be. Nor did I know how much blood could flow from such a wound.

But that very agony lent an extra bit of desperate pain-driven strength to my arms, automatically wrenching these out of our clinch. The True Beast for its part was for a moment distracted by the unaccustomed sensation of a large scrap of my flesh lodged between its human teeth.

Through the smear of pain I could see that, with my own arms free now, the most vulnerable part of the True Beast was for just an instant completely undefended.

Now, I need to make it clear at this point that this exchange of butchery in general and what happened next in particular was about as far away from my nature as possible. No matter what the need, no matter what desperate passions might rage, no matter how strong my instinct for self-preservation, the very idea of using my hands, thumbs and finger nails to dig as deeply as possible into the eye sockets of another human soul and then to lever out the succulent jelly within was an act almost as literally impossible to me as I were to rise up into the air in miraculous flight.

So the half grown man in me, despite such desperate and mortal circumstances, spying a scarce and uniquely deadly opportunity, distinctly hesitated before flying at the True Beast's eyes.

But from somewhere deep within single uncompromising, squeak of deadly determination would have nothing of such foolish human squeamishness. The Bat in me did not hesitate at all.

And Jesus God, it felt good! As a reaper at harvest time with the scythe in his hands before ripened corn, I went for it.

My young man's strong, long, untrimmed nails dug deep. Then deeper. Now swivelling at right angles, splintering just a little at some slight resistance, but twisting and pulling and pressing on to scoop up and out.

Victoriously I flicked my enemy's loosened right eye up, high and down into the waterfall beside us.

And lo! The mighty Lord of the Beasts screeched like a scalded cat. It wheeled around in a circle, clutching at an empty burrow where seconds before its window onto the world had snuggled so securely.

The Zoo: The Beast, The Boy and The Zoo

An eye for an ear then. Not such a bad a swop.

The other eye, although intact fundamentally, was so cut and bruised it was also almost entirely closed. Its combined vision was now down to almost zero.

Maybe the True Beast was content to strategically sacrifice Its body's functions one by one, but the primal malice manoeuvring this lumbering robot did feel real pain well enough. And, much more importantly, how was it going to continue to fight me without being able to see?

Madly It stumbled back up the hill towards the very perimeter of the Zoo. I clenched my fists in triumph, almost dancing a jig in praise of 'Strelles.

What is like to be a Bat? Bloody wonderful, that's what! Thought and deed in seamless union indeed. Trice would have been proud of me.

I with my ear hanging off; It now bereft of the use of its right eye; both gasping, missing clumps of hair and spitting out the occasional tooth: we each sought some temporary respite.

I took stock. We were when all taken into account almost equally matched. It had mass on its side. I had speed. This could go on and on for some time Would mere loss of blood and exhaustion determine the end? Or would there be some particular and final physical coup de grace?

That sense of utter futility, the overwhelming notion of facing something of unfathomable force, had ebbed - if only a little. The True Beast clearly could access only whatever strength was available from within its obese and exhaustible form. And irrespective of the unplumbed depths of might and malice that moved this sack of meat, the pain its vessel encountered was a practical enough obstacle to its victory.

The Zoo: The Beast, The Boy and The Zoo

I saw that it had not only been a matter of injured dignity that had brought forth his curses on Lilith and the Circle of Stars for imposing this shape.

And now I had stripped away its ability to see; for anything in human form, by far, the primary way to negotiate the world.

My spirits rose. Yes, there might after all just be some hope here after all. I *could* fight It. I *could* kill It. And by all the heavens I could and I would bloody crucify It!

Yes there might have been some hope. There really might have been.

Had the True Beast not used that moment to cheat.

***

Chapter Forty Seven: The Flickering Tongue

Snakes?

Oh god, snakes, bloody Snakes! You must not get me started on that subject.

Sam had spoken up about Snakes shortly after we first arrived, hadn't she? Or was it *a* Snake. Something or other about a Snake being the first animal which ever spoke or which had ever 'needed' to speak to a Human.

You have seen that my time at the Zoo in general and in particular my transformative voyages into three animal forms had effected a wholesale change in me. I have long ago retreated from my original disgust in respect of animals. Not in a single blinding flash of course, but through a slow redemption. And gradually I have come to enjoy, respect and yes, even love most of the animal world.

Most...

But Snakes?

Oh, I knew even back then they are not really slimy. But they sort of represented slime in my head. And the way they crawled. No legs! No. I need to allow my former self some leeway here. I had always refused to work on the Snake section in the Zoo's tropical house. I simply failed to come to terms with Snakes.

Snakes, you see do, surely enough, have eyes. They can see. At least to a degree. But not well. And the important thing is they do not really *need* to. Snakes, they depend on other things, on other senses.

The Zoo: The Beast, The Boy and The Zoo

Let me ask you something. What is the most truly sinister thing people remember best about Snakes? Is it the venomous bite? The coiling? The slither?

No, it is not... It is the thing that has just popped into your head. That's right - it is the flickering. It is that damned forked tongue of theirs. That is what they mainly use to know what is out there. They taste the air with their tongue. They use the damp surface to catch tiny molecules of scent and then carry them up to a special organ in the mouth. That forked tongue is how Snakes insinuate themselves into the whole world. That flicker of temptation is the most 'snakey' thing about Snakes.

There had been some pretty clear rules laid down by that strange gathering up there on the Star crossed tower. In this, our final duel, the True Beast might only present in human form. I, for my part, could use not use any weapon nor resort to any other form of human artifice.

So how had these restrictions on the True Beast broken down?

The wildest of wild things no longer had, as a Human, usable eyes? Fine. No problem. It simply changed into a predator form that didn't need them. That this new shape also happened to be a monster of huge strength and disposed of all kinds of easy ways to kill me - that was just a bonus.

How? Why? How had it been able, why had it been allowed to play fast and loose and blithely disregard the strictures placed upon it? Surely the authorities did not simply depend the True to play fair and keep Its word?

In the immediacy of strife, I had no time to figure it out. Only much later, when I had the time to once more trace all the backward and forward paths of our struggle up there on the heights above the Stream of Riches, did I get it. Then I understood what must certainly have happened.

The Zoo: The Beast, The Boy and The Zoo

When she had set it all down before us up on the tower, Lillith had been very particular that the binding authority of the powers present held strong only within the territory of the Zoo itself. That had been dramatically illustrated when the young Sam and I had first crossed the Helicon river in Lilith's E-type. In later times I saw so many different reasons that the True Beast had chosen this specific spot at The Stream for our encounter. But one had certainly been that this was the only part of the Zoo's domain that lay *beyond* the river. So, just beyond the Stream, you could simply walk or indeed accidentally wander out of the Zoo's reach easily.

In its unsighted retreat from me, the True Beast had, whether intentionally or not, stumbled beyond this border. There it was free to slip out of its human mantle and return as this fiendish being.

First of all the outline shape of the humanoid True Beast floundering away from me toward the final peak dropped down to the ground. In the mist and the spray Its form seemed to pool down, dissolving onto the rocks, and become entirely indistinct. Then, as the fog around it evaporated, the flabby man shape was replaced by a large, fat pile of concentric coils.

A huge, saffron yellow serpent. A reticulated python, thirty or forty foot long, the biggest snake in the world. It reared its repulsive, one-eyed head from within the middle of the coils. Its tongue flickered in my direction in triumphant defiance.

My paranoia as to having been 'set up' here by all concerned had been ebbing and flowing back and forth for some while. If the True Beast could so casually break the deal, did that mean that I had after all been predestined all along to fail?

Well, if that were so, then by all that was holy I would cheat too!

No use of any weapons nor of human physical artifice by me? As far as I was concerned, that was now null and void. I *would* use some technology. Pretty primitive technology, in fact one of the very first our species ever adopted, but technology all the same.

I had nowhere near the strength to contest with the massive constricting serpent before me. And, if It did *just once* get me inside those coils, It would crack my ribs like an eggshell.

I didn't necessarily though need to get so very near to visit some more damage on it. If I only could hit it hard enough with the right projectile, then maybe, just maybe I could hurt it badly or even do worse with the rocks and stones, man's oldest tools, that littered this place so plentifully.

The little Lion and the Pipistrelle bat had both done their bit. The stripling of nineteen years had played his part. Now it was the turn of a dirty ten year old urchin from the Vague Lands to step up. The skills of my early childhood were unexpectedly seeping back into play.

As a boy, to Sam's contempt, I had sharpened my stone throwing skills on those few living things in the Vague Lands. I had raised them to a pretty impressive pitch. My abilities may seemed to have fallen into disuse after so many peaceful years at the Zoo. Yet when I reached out, the memories in my arms and hands were waiting for me. There was one particular thing I had become very good at indeed.

My t-shirt was almost in tatters. I ripped off the remaining rags and quickly fashioned a rough sling. A shepherd's sling, they are sometimes called, but to me it was a good old 'Vague Lands throwing sling'. Bane of the Scorpions, Pigeons and Rats there.

Oh, and also of the Snakes.

I could only throw the smaller stones with any real force and impact. So the great thing was to attack with lots at one go and not to let up. The deadly technique I had developed in Gogol's trading place had depended on not only in using the sling itself, but also in swiftly identifying and hoarding as many as possible of exactly the right shape and size of stone. These should be smooth, round and as near as dammit all the same size. In that way I did not have to entirely recalibrate the force used for each shot.

Hastily I gathered as many carefully chosen projectiles as I could. I filled both pockets and built up a much bigger pile at my feet, all the time carefully watching the True Beast to see what it would do.

It elevated its blind head to sniff the air coming from my direction, but made no move to slide up the slope towards me.

Ideally I would have made a sling of a full three foot for the greatest range. But with only the remnants of my shirt, I had to settle for a two foot strip to whirl around my head with a central pocket made for the stone.

People make two beginner's mistakes with stone slings.

First of all, they try to whirl it several times around their head before the release. They think they will work up more momentum that way. But it is a waste of precious energy. One wind up, like a pitcher in baseball, is fine.

Secondly, they are tempted to release the stone overhead, but the best way to utilize a sling is by an underhand motion.

I have long since read up on the sling's use over time. An astonishingly effective weapon for something so simple. An expert slinger could hurl a stone as far and accurately as a good archer. The very best and strongest could hurl their projectiles a full quarter of a mile. Their stone could leave the sling in excess of sixty miles per hour. Soldiers wearing leather armour were actually much more in danger from sling missiles than arrows. Because you see, unlike the arrow, even if the stone did not penetrate the armour, the force of its strike could very well give them a fatal internal injury.

The sound of a slinged stone slicing perfectly through the air is a thing of beauty! Imagine to yourself if you had crossed the murmur of a sitar strum with the sound of a motorbike accelerating away very fast and you will have it.

The Zoo: The Beast, The Boy and The Zoo

I let loose with an initial volley of fifteen, maybe twenty stones. I was looking to first get my range right and then as much to overwhelm the monster with as many strikes as possible in as short a time as possible, rather than for any individual accuracy.

My first two fell short; the next two or three overshot; the rest, one after the other, all bang on target.

The hide of most Snakes is a deceptive material. The outer mantle is composed of scales, but the deeper layer is just a disorganised mess of collagen. This makes their skin incredibly elastic which is why it is so sought after for human garments. At the same time it is easily punctured or bruised.

As each stone struck home the coiled titan jerked and spasmed. Then although clearly in pain It slowly and certainly began to zig zag its deadly path back up the slope toward me. Its impaired vision had no effect on its progress whatsoever.

I maintained my position. If I retreated and deserted my precious pile of stones, I would be out of firepower fast. I was standing almost at the very peak of the cataract anyway, so there was little further space to withdraw. And if I tried to somehow manoeuvre past my persecutor and so be again downhill of the True Beast, I would no longer be in a position to use my sling with any great effectiveness.

No, even as with every second, the Reptile hypnotically but painfully wriggled uphill. The safe distance between It and me melted away. Best to stand and make each shot count.

I redoubled my volleys of stones. The Python had crawled so very near now that each strike betrayed its visual impact all too clearly. I could almost feel the indentation each stone made, and I gleefully sensed the internal damage wrought. Some strikes had caused the hideous Snake's skin to actually split open, the outer yellow scales peeling back to reveal beneath a gratifyingly glistening and bleeding red.

The Zoo: The Beast, The Boy and The Zoo

The more mutilation that rained down on it, the further It slowed. Yet still it mesmerically squirmed that bit closer. The nearer it got, the harder I could hit and the more havoc I could visit. What had been a long, gleaming corkscrew, pristine in its iridescent yellow armour was now a disfigured and disordered blob. But any nearer at all and I would be easily within its grasp.

Three more mighty cracks of my sling. Three more huge, gaping incisions all along its body.

It stopped moving at all.

Five second ticked by.

Then ten.

And the Serpent went into its death throes.

However much at that point I hated Snakes, I have always conceded there is a kind of bewitching half fascination, half revulsion in watching their very way of moving: the looping, the bending, the spiralling; that smooth pulsing flow in one direction, then another.

But as that Python died, it seemed to go into a series of spasms that put the classic repertoire of familiar movements in the shade. It morphed instead into some kind of frenzied agony of locomotive overdrive. First it catapulted itself straight upwards into the air, landing upside down, its vulnerable underbelly exposed to the air.

Its jaws, as if now dislocated, stretched open impossibly wide around nothing at all. This was of course just as it would do to wrap around the body and swallow some large subdued mass of prey; but here, as if in a sort of ghoulish desperation, it seemed almost trying to constrict around death itself.

Its full forty feet of muscle next entered into maelstrom of writhings, all the extremities of its body seemed to be obeying quite separate wills and contracting in response to independent torments. In a series of balletic flashes its body seemed frenetically to deny gravity for a second or two, pointing straight up in an almost vertical line.

The Zoo: The Beast, The Boy and The Zoo

Then it twitched through a sequence of grotesque contortions as if trying to form the letters of some barbaric script: something that looked for a second like a 'S' but with ten curves; a 'W' crossed with a 'K'; a 'Q' that suddenly became a 'N'.

Its mouth now bit down again and again on its own body, the forked tongue flashing madly in the intervening seconds.

Finally this freakish möbius strip of misery subsided. All its energy in a blink of the eye drained away. It collapsed back lumpily into a vague simulacrum of its classic pattern of living folds.

This manic fit of thrashing had left it totally inert, belly again exposed. A length part of its body was now dangling down over the edge of the ravine. Two thirds of the Python's body still lay securely coiled on the narrow ledge we shared, but with this longish section and its head draped perpendicularly down the cliff side, and staring down into the void beneath.

For a long ten minutes I stayed exactly where I was, stock still; my heart was slowly calming down from the heights of a jackhammer rhythm.

Not the least flicker of life emanated from the great yellow, grey and red mass. Its head and a full third of its body flopped immodestly over the adjacent cliff edge though. So I could make no assessment of its overall state from these parts, entirely invisible to me

I reached for a nicely sharp, recently splintered shard of rock and charily edged closer. Still nothing. I came a little nearer again. Its tail jutting out from the centre of the coil was the nearest to me. I kicked it gently. Nothing. I kicked again, not at all gently this time. Then I kicked as savagely as I possibly could right into the middle of its torso. The huge body shook. But there was no other response from the corpse.

The last test.... I took my rock splinter, very much the same kind of implement I had used to despatch captured Rats back in the Vague Lands. I sought the choicest, plumpest part of the Snake in the very middle of its scrolled form; and I plunged down with all my remaining strength.

Nothing.

In that instant every muscle, tendon and sinew in my body drained of all their tension. In sudden and complete weariness, I sank, collapsing gratefully and thoughtlessly onto the cushiony cadaver of the Python itself, the side of my head even resting there for a second or two; ironically almost as if to caress the carcass. To thank It for being dead.

One or two great deep gulps of air of relief and exhaustion slowly in and out.

On the intake of what would have been my third breath of grateful release, with my ear and cheek still pressed against the great Snake's corpse, I felt it.

I felt it. *And* I heard it. A faint pulse.

The True Beast, this giant reticulated Python on which I was casually recumbent was not at all deceased. Had it been playing dead, enduring whatever pain and fakery it must, to lure me into its embrace? Or had it really been reduced to some half-deceased, unconscious state?

In the same second as my head began to jerk away in panic, the gargantuan loops beneath me were no longer a limp mass but boiled once more with muscular spirit. The Snake's loops lashed once. Twice. Three times. And I was taken. Enlooped beyond any hope of escape. The Snake's muscles, although surely depleted by its multiple injuries, were still easily strong enough to begin their, slow inexorable and excruciating crunching of my whole body. It was only dumb luck that left one arm free outside their ring.

And greater luck that it was the arm with my makeshift dagger.

I struck out blindly; slashing randomly at any part of its body at all I could reach. The Snake's paroxysms of minutes past now returned. Whether through my fresh assault or as entering a stage two of its death process I do not know; but the combined momentum of all of this rolled our fused bodies right to the very brink of the precipice.

My own head was now actually over the edge. I was looking down on the Serpent's neck and head, a 'J' shape swinging crudely below in mid-air. Was the brain actually still alive after all? Or had I been simply been unfortunate enough to trigger some post–mortem reflex action?

The snide answer came in an instant. The top of the Snake's head jerked once, twice and then turned back to begin climbing back up alongside its own body towards me. Still only one good eye of course, but how it glittered up at me! And yes, of course, that damned forked tongue danced in advance.

Most would say that a Snake's face cannot really have any expression as intelligible to we Humans. But that Snake, or the True Beast within it, was, on my oath, grinning in triumph at me, it's one wounded eye showing that dread red glow as it slithered back up nearer and nearer to my defenceless head.

Another aftershock through the Snake's body gripping me in its vice tumbled me even further downward so that I was first slammed brutally against the cliff wall. Then I was entirely capsized, suspended vertically above the ravine and its foaming water. Only my enemy's grip precluded my plummeting to my death. At least both of my arms and hands had in the confused process come free, even if my waist and most of my body were still securely fettered in the Snake's grinding curves.

There is perhaps nothing more disorientating for a human primate than to be suspended upside down in the air. All agency seems removed. Your senses are set askew. You are thrown into disarray as to any sense of movement or distance or direction.

You can even die if you stay too long like that. Your blood pressure soars. Your heartbeat slows down. There is increased pressure on your eye. Blood pools into the head. I had, as surely as the Shrike impales its victim, been gloatingly stored for later consumption.

The Zoo: The Beast, The Boy and The Zoo

No, Humans are just not made to swing helplessly, inverted vertiginously high in the air. And certainly I was a Human. But I was also - and I always will be - a Bat.

The True Beast began to open its jaws, the two separate mandibles gaping horrifically as these independently walked up towards the crown of my defenceless head, ready to begin the slow and terrible process of ingesting me alive.

Now it was my turn to play possum, letting both my arms and hands droop insensately downwards, closing my eyes, whole body bereft of the least spark of vitality. Not the tiniest clue remaining that I might in fact be, not *only* wholly conscious, not *only* entirely at home in this topsy-turvy disposition, but actively nursing a murderous intent. My dagger tucked down securely into my trousers was forgotten and out of sight. As far as the Snake might be concerned, Its having first compressed the breath from my body, then whacked me against the wall of the ravine and finally waggled my incapable skinny form back and forth inverted in the void, It had knocked every single iota of remaining resistance out of me.

The Serpent's movement was redolent of a complacent assurance that, just as an immobilised Fly gummed into the web of the approaching Spider, there was nothing here more than a packaged morsel of prey helpless within an alien element.

Yet another of those old stories that Sam had kept reading out to me as kids danced unbidden across my mind. Something about a rabbit and a fox. Oh, and a blackthorn bush.

I could not actually open my eyes to see nor move my head so to judge how near the Snake was. That would give the game away. But still, albeit dimly and only at the recess of my Human form mind, the multiple senses gifted to me by a Bat, a Lion and an Elephant Fish were all at work. By reverberation through rock, by sound waves through the air and by smell I knew *precisely* where that Serpent was. I knew exactly what It was about to do. I knew exactly what I had to do. Staying frozen until the last possible moment, I could feel its breath, I could hear its heart beat and I could smell the subtle fluctuations of that now very familiar odour.

Each of these things ever nearer, ever stronger, ever more repellent.

Until.

Until the merest, oh so gentle caress of its feathering tongue questing lightly across the top of my skull.

My arms came alive, one swooping upwards to retrieve my knife and the other firmly grapping the Python's tongue itself and tugging forward, as if I were simply hauling down on a length of rope or ball of twine.

As it realised what was befalling It, the True Beast started to recoil in panic. The prospect of a me alive, awake, vicious, and wielding a knife anywhere at all near its remaining good eye sent it into panic.

I slashed at the general direction of Its head. But already It had swayed itself well away from me and at the same time was trying to tug my body in the opposite direction.

Best now surely to divest Itself entirely of this troublesome thing? In a single movement It loosened its coils, letting my body slip out freely. Yet as I fell, I grabbed. Its head had moved well beyond my reach, but not all of that long thin jaundiced neck. My rock splinter knife dug in deeply into Its flesh, both my hands now grabbing, as if my life depended on it, onto the makeshift hilt.

But it was no will nor skill nor strength of mine, but the mighty drag of the Earth's gravity that did the real damage. From that one first deep incision the knife began to slip and rend and rip slowly all down along the monster's body in a long slow, deep and pleasing vertical slice.

This final wound caused the Snake to begin to lose its purchase on the rocks above. It slid a little.

The Zoo: The Beast, The Boy and The Zoo

The True Beast, the great Serpent toppled off the cliff edge and towards the distant, deadly waters of the Stream of Riches far below. And still conjoined with that neck gushing with blood, I was carried along with it.

Full forty feet down we both fell.

***

Chapter Forty Eight: A Magic Carpet

There are five different and distinct ways in which, falling off that cliff clamped like a lover on top of a demon adversary, I might have expected to die horribly.

First of all I might be killed by multiple blunt force injuries. Water may be softer than any kind of ground, but its physics are still unforgiving. Hitting it with the velocity built from forty feet of fall would be as if a car had driven into the soft tissue of my body.

If that didn't actually kill me outright, then all my ribs would be crushed. I would perish a little more slowly but much more painfully.

If that didn't happen, my internal organs would be exploded anyway. A slightly quicker death perhaps?

If by any miracle I escaped all those kinetic dooms, I would likely drown. I would be knocked unconscious by the impact, forced down maybe twenty feet deep below with my lungs filling up with water long before I remotely came to my senses.

And if I didn't drown, a live but damaged me in the water, perhaps thrashing helplessly, would be an easy kill for a still living Python, a beast even more at home in the water than on land, and an expert swimmer.

With enough imagination one might equally concoct some interesting combination of several of the above.

Yes, one or other of those deaths would have surely befallen me, *if that* is, *if* I had fallen alone. The True Beast saved my life. Or at least the peculiar wave dynamics in its looping path through the air did so. It

The Zoo: The Beast, The Boy and The Zoo

body assumed a flattened and concaved poise to maximise air resistance and it formed a particular undulating dance of 'S' shapes in all three dimensions. The descent of the Snake and of me as passenger was slowed and steered and finessed. Our downward path became something much nearer to a partial glide rather than the vertical and terminal nosedive that might have been expected.

This was certainly in part all thanks to the automatic reflex actions of a still not quite dead creature kicking into gear as it suddenly found itself in freefall space. The Python's much smaller cousins in far off Indonesia 'fly' like this all the time - Genus *Chrysopelea*. Look it up for yourself, if you don't believe me.

But our glissading motion also benefited from a sort of pilot. There I was, perched squarely on top, right in the middle of its lengths, my two hands desperately clutching onto a rough shard of stone plunged into the Snake's vital organs. My dagger was now a joystick.

The Snake and I, not two thing but one, seemed to have become just one wave in the air amongst so many others.

From a spectator's point of view, that fall would have taken a mere one or two seconds. But something less hasty inside me had taken control. The silent, serene silver world of the Elephant Fish had returned. It patiently assumed command of all my senses. It led me besides the crashing waters. In my slow, imperturbable fishy brain, time, or at least the perception of time, had slowed down. Ancient instincts were in play here. Intuitively I strengthened, channelled and refined every micro movement emanating beneath from the body of my grisly mount, this other part of my own form. I matched these to a million infinitesimal currents and eddies my fish senses detected all around me.

We did not fall.

We did not fly.

We did not glide.

We swam. We swam through the air.

The Zoo: The Beast, The Boy and The Zoo

Our descent seemed to me interminable. To any other though, it would have been no time at all before my conjoined Snake twin and I splashed down into the dark, churning loamy pool of the Stream of Riches. Only yards away from the waterfall's ground zero, where the cascade perpetually smashes into the waiting foams.

The last time I had been splashed down into water like this it had served me well, shocking me into a full assumption of the mind of a Fish. This time it was precisely the reverse: I was startled out of the very same state. Time was snapped back to its manic normality. Water was once again just water. Air was just air.

Although the impact of hitting the water was so much less mortal than it might have been, it was still brutal. All breath was shaken from me and my physical bond with the giant Serpent was finally severed. It and I were flung in entirely different directions. Confusion and disorientation reigned.

I had no idea of what had become of that thing which only seconds before has seemed a part of me. Despite all the punishment that it had received though, I was not though going to assume that it might yet not still be alive and full of homicidal purpose.

The waters at the Stream churn up mud and peat right from the very bottom. Together with the spumy effervescence that clogs the air there, visibility in either water or air was close to zero. I struck off for what I hoped must be one or other edge of the pool. Depleted beyond words of both strength and will, painfully I levered my sodden, bruised, and bloodied frame onto firm, safe land.

I struggled to my feet and looked around. The important thing now was to know what had become of the True Beast. Nothing to be seen of Snake kind neither within, nor at any point around the pool. But some twenty feet away there on the other bank was an indistinguishable shape, prostrate and quite still, far too small for my adversary.

The Zoo: The Beast, The Boy and The Zoo

Limping half way towards it, recognition and realisation flared. The True Beast had resumed Its uninspiring human shape, complete with hollowed out eye.

Very dead looking indeed.

Would I therefore take any chance at all that there might be some spark of life in there? Ignore the possibility of a third round of deception? The devil I would!

I found the heaviest rock I could find and I smashed this Man's skull in. I smashed it again and again and again. Perhaps twenty times. First Its hair changed colour. That greasy brown mop with whose features I had exchanged words before the conflict gradually became a mess of red. But I kept smashing until the cracks in Its skull became clearly visible and very many. Then I kept on pounding until I could see the horrid yellow white of Its brain. I kept pounding, brains now splashing all over my hand and even squirting up towards my face. I kept on until the contents within had become a pureed white, pink and grey swill.

Even then I was not content. I went to seek out a different shaped rock. A nice, sharper one. This one I used to hack away at the neck. It was hard work. Any animal's head does not easily agree to become separated from the rest of its body. But for a whole twenty minutes I chopped and I sawed and I cut. At last the True Beast's head, now quite beyond recognition, was severed completely from its cadaver.

My work was complete. I dangled the head by its hair and gazed at it for second or two. For Father. For Mother. For Sam. For me.

It was dead. Whatever this being with which so bloodily I had had affair might have been... a god? A spirit? An 'idea'?! The flesh that lay before me was definitely dead.

Gently I placed it down on the ground and sat there, my back turned. It was my own head I put in my hands now. And laughter came.

The Zoo: The Beast, The Boy and The Zoo

Uncontrollable peals of laughter bereft of the slightest hint of merriment. A rhythmic, wholehearted sobbing merging into and then retreating back again from a high pitch giggling. Something slowly working its way out of me, as a small child might stumble eagerly through a maze towards the daylight of final exit.

It ceased. A few slight after tremors, and I was drained entirely. And then stillness.

Now perfectly quiet, I looked back up towards the south and to Edensor. Edensor, my home. The sun was setting in the west. From this still high point I could see out over so much of the great and splendid panorama of the Zoo. My Zoo. A beautiful place. A good feeling to be able to gaze over it like this relieved of all duty. I leaned into it. I let myself enjoy this moment.

For seconds.

For minutes.

For longer.

Something..? I was not alone. I could feel that I was not alone.

I swivelled around. For one awful split second there was the unspeakable possibility! Surely not? Surely, after all this, the damnable thing really *was* dead???

No, no, no... I relaxed. That one red eye did not open. Those remains of what had been a mouth did not suddenly come alive to grin or taunt. The head on the ground was still, and well enough dead.

This presence I felt was not like that at all. Of a different order entirely. Another kind of feeling. A familiar one. And now an actual greeting came into my head. "*Seth...*" I was being called out to. A wonderful greeting. I was whole again. For the first time in how long? It still seemed to be like several lifetimes. I was no longer alone. This was not any intrusion. It was me being a twin again. Being whole again.

I could feel *Her*.

***

Chapter Forty Nine: Interview with a Sister

Averaging it out over all my entire life: young, middle age and now old, I have not on the whole received a lot of hugs. Not enough. A good loving squeeze is something which to this day I would willingly seek more of.

Certainly, as an adult, these have been few and far between. And as a small child there was only ever one particular source. When we were not fighting, in our very earliest years as tiny children in the Vague Lands Sam and I spent a lot of time cuddling and hugging. That feeling, that memory of two tiny, mirror-image scraps of humanity with no other human warmth to look to, clasped ferociously together and staring adoringly into one another's eyes; this has ever been one of the bedrock memories of my whole life.

So when my beloved sister ran across over those rocks, when she wrapped me in her arms, when she closed her eyes and when she squeezed me tight, when I felt her cheek pressed against mine; that was the best hug I had ever had.

It was in her mind too. I knew it. I could feel her feeling it as well. As if somehow we were sinking down into one another, swimming away together forever side by side in a warm sea, stroking far from the shore of everything; from all that bothersome stuff, all that had happened, all that so many busybodies urged us to think of as important, all that did not actually matter *one little whit.*

And we were doing so without a single, backward thought.

God, Sam was so much stronger than I remembered!

The Zoo: The Beast, The Boy and The Zoo

Her embrace was like a fist closing in on me. But, you know, wonderfully so. Compared to hers my frame seemed so pathetic and skinny. The hug seemed to sweetly press every last drop of grief, worry, stress from out of me.

Yet no matter how deep, how genuine and how deeply-needed a hug might be, there is still always that thing, isn't there? Who lets go first? Which one will be first to ever so slightly relax their muscles, and give a signal that the loving tangle must unknot.

It was Sam.

At arms' length now we cautiously sifted through each other's features.

How long since I had seen her? No time at all. Yet it seemed like years. And she looked so different. Her features had changed. That long born self-possession of my sister's had bloomed into something else - a new deeper, wiser and sadder confidence perhaps? All this time I had fretted as to what precisely might have befallen in her time as the True Beast's captive. Now that I carefully searched, despite my fears, there was not the least sign, not a single wrinkle of oppression within her face.

I went deeper, seeking to know more. I moved to use our special twin thing.

But no.

I could, now that she was back, thank god, once more bask in our overall connection. I could delight in being a twin again. But anything more, any more specific. knowledge? No, that remained cloaked to me. In simply making that very effort though, I had for an instant caught a wisp of something new within Sam. Something that was different. A certain exotic tang, whose nature tantalised and eluded me.

> *What'er you most fear that it may be*
> *That will be what you will see*

What the devil?! Why on earth at just that moment did that puerile rhyme run through my mind? I shook my head to dismiss it. And I emptied myself of all of this pesky overthinking. I had my Sam back. That is all that mattered.

For long moments more, neither of us said anything but just looked at one another with stupid smiles on our faces. Once again it was Sam who took the eventual initiative.

"So, my brave hero..."

Then I erupted in a garbled torrent. "Sam!! Sister, are you alright? You look okay. But what did those animal bastards do to you?" I gushed onwards. "But it is okay now. It's gone. It's all over. You don't need to worry about It. I will look after you. It's gone. We can go back to Edensor now. Or away from the Zoo entirely? Whatever it is you want. "We were still holding one another at arm's length and staring at one another. "As long as we can be together..."

A moment's pause. When she spoke it was slowly and deliberately.

"No, Seth"

"...No?"

"No."

"No, what? No to what? Say something more."

"No to all of it. Poor Seth. You have got it all wrong. As usual."

I pulled back, our arms free of one another now, staring at her for clues.

"None of that. I am sorry. But we're *not* going to be together. Neither of us is going back to Lilith and all that lot at the old house. Nor certainly are we, either of us, leaving the Zoo."

"And It? 'It' as you put it. No, It is *not* gone. "

"And above all, it definitely is not '*All okay now*'."

"But I have killed It. Look." I pointed at what was still lying at our feet."

"Yes, the poor, foolish thing." She knelt down and laid a caressing hand on the True Beast's head.

The Zoo: The Beast, The Boy and The Zoo

!!!

I fought back. "It is not me who does not understand, Sam. It's you!" I was almost shouting. "You don't know. They must have lied to you. This..." I pointed stupidly. "This is the Enemy. It killed our father. It kidnapped you. And It ....It *did things* to our Mother. This is the Enemy. This is the Thing that had been turning all the other animals against us. This Thing and its followers have been poisoning the Zoo, destroying it all."

Yet even as my words poured out so desperately, a pit of doubt was opening up deep in my stomach. To any onlooker the contrast between me wildly waving my arms in the air in confused frustration and Sam's stoic composure, hands on her hips, must have seemed almost comical.

She stood straight and tall. She observed me calmly. A look of pity.

"Little brother. That being, lying there on the on the ground, or, at least, that which so recently moved that creature's limbs, that is *not* the contagion. All this you have been fed about the True Beast, well..." She shrugged in contempt. "No, the wild isn't the disease. *Mankind* is. It is you who have been lied to and led on. Or lied to yourself and led yourself on."

"Listen. As far as the rest of the world knows, it has only been a very short time since you and I last saw one another, little brother. But for you, oh, a whole age has passed, hasn't it? I don't know what exactly that has happened to you, but I can see in your eyes, your face, the way you hold yourself, this is not my silly little Seth anymore. is it?"

" Well... not quite," she smiled. "But you see for me too it might as well have been years that I spent in the Old Forest. Time passed differently there as well. And patiently I learned wild things, ancient things, a becoming or a remembering of that which I have always been - a wild thing myself."

The Zoo: The Beast, The Boy and The Zoo

"Seth, I am sorry, but the truth is I never was a captive of the True Beast and Its Wild Hunt. I wasn't ever imprisoned or threatened by them. Before my 'disappearance', I had made many trips into the Old Forest. And yes, there I met with 'your Enemy' as you would put it, and with the White Horde that pursued us so long ago and with others again you do not know of. But there was no argument or struggle or capture involved."

"No, instead there was laughter and dance and song. We lit great fires. I learned to howl at the moon, to sing over old bones, to feast on raw bounty and together with my fellow creatures to rage at the open skies at Man's injustice."

"I prayed. And I preyed."

"There in the dark with the wild things, I learned to be a thing of fierce flesh once again, and under the naked moon to shiver in my own good, red blood."

"Oh, you more than anyone know how it has always been with me and animals, don't you Seth? How I can see into them, understand them. But, you see, for all of that, until I met the True Beast and delved into that dark wild, I was still half dead. In the Old Forest, I learned more than I could ever have dreamed of as to how it is to be an animal, and what I am myself. Where the blood within me comes from and to where it must lead."

"Why, the only way I could have learned more, would have been to actually become some of those animals myself."

"So we made our plans. And then... And then, *I* sent that note to draw our enemies out."

"To draw *you* out."

These words turned my world upside down. There was a silence whilst I took all of this in. Finally I recovered myself enough at least to say. "So, for all you say about truth and lies, you *were* part of a deceit yourself then, Sam?"

The Zoo: The Beast, The Boy and The Zoo

An irritated tightening of the muscles around my sister's mouth. My objection did not, it seemed, fit easily into my sister's untrammelled romantic memories, her simplistically enjoyable moral outrage.

Whatever she might have said in a response was lost. Two sylph like spotted animals, two dear old friends assumed long dead trotted up, and calmly sat down to flank Sam on either side. Dexter and Sinister, Lilith's twin Cheetahs twice so significant in the younger lives of Sam and I, whom I had thought perished at the hands of the White Horde.

Then this surprise was overtaken by another. The Cheetahs were, it appeared, merely the advance guard. Slowly they were joined by a whole variety of species, two of each from across the living tribes of the Zoo: Rhinos, Hyenas, Porcupines, Chimpanzees. Gradually these assembled all around the perimeter of the pool. All looked towards Sam. Looking at her with? With adoration. Staring at her, some of them, with glazed eyes. Fixated on their leader.

I had seen this before, hadn't I? Years ago. I had seen it in the second witch's hat. I had seen it when Sam had entranced those Mice. But on that occasion there had been an extra element, one that was missing here. That big black Rat that had joined the scene so long ago, and which I had killed with my very own hands.

Then I glanced down at the True Beast's head at my feet. No, I considered ruefully. Nothing missing after all. That piece too was here. The picture was complete.

Sam was speaking, but now there were others to hear. Still ostensibly addressing me specifically, but her tone had subtly shifted. She nodded toward the corpus delicti.

"The True Beast? Or the Truth of Beasts? The idea that there is always something, something alive, something that lives beyond human knowing. Something that always escapes the trap and eludes classification and chaining. The blank space, the unknown territory in the middle of the map - 'Here Be Dragons' indeed. The rebellion against the primped order of the Zoo and what it represents. You cannot kill that."

"You cannot *kill* an idea."

"Humans ever foolishly think to eliminate their nemesis. But they never can quite succeed. The, despised counter-vailing element always strikes back, balancing, remodelling itself to continue shaking the very ground we all stand on."

"And human imagination itself – human *terror* in fact -   will always summon it up. We will always fill that blank space in the dark. We ourselves will always bring back the monster to haunt us."

I almost started forward then as to grab my twin and somehow shake some sense into her, or from her, but she was still speaking. And more loudly now. Declaiming almost. As more animals, two by two filled the space around us, it became even clearer she was speaking as much to them as to me, repeating earlier points. Some, like Dexter and Sinister, hung at her heels in a familiar defensive role. Two brutish looking adult Chimpanzees standing tightly there at Sam's shoulders. Other recent arrivals more aloof; less converts to the cause; more curious onlookers.

"You got it completely wrong. The thing that needs to be cleansed away. It is *not* the True Beast. Not the ideas and forces that It represents. Not the righteous revolution that all these beings around us represent." My sister's gesture swept around the arc of species.

A politician on the stump seeking to convince? Or the adored leader of a congregation?

She continued at length. "How can anyone possibly justify mankind's continuing rule over all these beings? How can you support the underlying ideas, the decrepit structure that the Zoo embodies? Consider that our kind has always been the destroyer of worlds. Or at best, the creator of an empire of slaves. Even as we first moved around the world as hunter gathers, we wiped out species one by one. We started of course with the larger animals. As competitors. Or as threats; Or just as conveniently large sources of meat."

At this specific point a rumble went through certain ranks of the beasts.

"As we spread from continent to continent, and then hopping across islands, the tale was always exactly the same: one or other Eden teaming with birds, mammals, reptiles, fish and insects; and then within the twinkling of an eye, it is a desert, a place where everything looks the same, where any life left has no variety, where nothing ever happens, where all event and savour and joy and diversity has been leeched away."

There was a fleeting scintillation in Sam's expression. "Do you happen, Brother, to remember such a place? " Then without taking a breath, she moved on.

"Consider also that as the hairless apes settled down to farming, we no longer only contented ourselves with hunting animals, we imprisoned them in vastly larger numbers. We morphed them to birth into stunted shapes, obscene physical and behavioural forms that suited us best. For our own greed. For the labour we could extract as beasts of burden. For as much food piled up high as quickly, as conveniently and cheaply produced as possible. The quality, the length of their lives entirely at the service of our over-stuffed bellies and our glutton appetites."

"Look!" She was pointing at a pair of brilliantly coloured birds in the living throng around us. Familiar enough to anyone who has ever been in a farmyard, yet possessed of a certain alien, reptilian exoticism.

"See? Indian Jungle Fowl, the wild ancestors of all *twenty four billion* domestic chickens on Earth." At their singling out, the Birds crowed in appreciation. "Twenty four billion of them! More than three times as many as there are people in the whole world. Consider that mass of individual, complex, curious beings, kept cooped in tiny cages for foreshortened lives, treated by insensate lumpen farmers, as if they were things rather than minds. And finally with a casual cruelty slaughtered for our tables."

"See Brother your old friends over there?" More pointing. This time towards the back of the crowd. Fate has for one reason or another delighted in placing that particular species squarely in my path. The Aurochs; a white Bull, perhaps the very same from years ago, and a black Cow.

As bidden I looked towards them. The pale Bull stared back at me and bellowed in unfriendly recognition.

"Consider there again, the 'grandparents' of all the world's imprisoned cattle. Consider how men steal day old calves from their mothers and raise them in the dark so their meat is sweeter to our taste."

"You speak of infection? Consider how we use animals for our experiments, purposely infecting them with diseases in our laboratories."

"Consider how we even treat our so called pets: neglect, abandonment, sadism. Breeders of Dogs and Cats and Birds bringing *entire forms of life* into existence to fit their obscene and ridiculous random human concepts of beauty or sentimentality. All of course with hellish consequences in chronic pain, or life-long disabilities, or early death."

By now it was beyond any doubt. At the outset this had been a very personal conversation between my sister and I. But at this stage I was no more than a convenient foil for her soaring rhetoric, not the real audience. I was in fact more like Exhibit A in a court room drama. Worse, maybe even the Accused! My sister was making her case to a constituency: she was definitely not sharing her feelings with her brother.

Again I detected a certain differentiation within the now encyclopaedic assembly of animal types ranked back in concentric rows around the pool. That close semi-circle (Cheetahs, Chimps, and Rhinos) around Sam did not seem to need any persuasion. They were not even listening in quite the same way. These were already sold. They were already hers. This was some kind of inner praetorian guard.

The wider crowd was more uncertain as if leaning forward eager to hear and consider. An undecided majority.

"Do you remember Seth what the keepers used to say in the canteen? That when you met It, the True Beast would be whatever you are most scared it might be. Well perhaps what many people fear most is quite simply... the Truth itself?"

Sam ceased declaiming. She stood and stared at me, as if defying me to respond.

That softly spoken Star back on the tower... She, above all, had doubted my abilities in making an argument. Well, she had been right. For the most part anyway. I had, I suppose, made some fist of debating, when backed into a corner with the Cloud in the Bat Cave. I might also, through my interest in human thought, have been able to think around the philosophical blandishments the Enemy had launched in my direction as a Lion and a Fish.

To now defend my entire species by wielding words and ideas... this was another kettle of fish altogether. And more, to have to suddenly do so against the unexpected adversary of my own, much sought after sister.

No, this was one turnaround too many. This was beyond me.

So I didn't even try. To be frank I didn't want to. I am not even sure I cared. It felt like someone was again officiously trying to load an unwanted, great weight on my shoulders. After all that I had striven through and endured this was unreasonable. Too much.

So when I did speak it was not for Mankind. It was for myself.

"Look, I don't care about any of this. I am sorry. Maybe it is really bad of me not to want to be part of this, this great war of ideas. But I the only things I care about are you and me. And isn't all of this just about where you draw the line anyway? Whether you draw a circle around only your family. Or your wider kin. Or your village. Or your tribe. Or your nation. Or your species. Or maybe just the animals you know or you happen to like. Or those who have fur or feathers."

"Perhaps," I continued "You think we should extend our compassion to plants or rocks?! As Lilith said, some people think they too have minds."

"What about viruses! Should we wring our hands over them as well? "

"Well me, I draw the line around just *you and me*. I don't care about anything else. I told It that." I twisted around to look down and gesture at the headless corpse still lying so incongruously behind me. "It seems I need to tell you too."

"This is all too big." I gestured at everything and nothing in particular. "The Stars told me I had to learn to argue, to debate. To learn the weapons of thought. All I can say there is that it does seem to me that, rightly or wrongly, Man *is* in charge of the world. We have all the power, after all. Only we can destroy everything. Or only we can *save* everything. Everything that is left anyway. It may be the race of Man who has brought this evil into this world: in which case it needs to be Man's task to right all these wrongs. So my reckoning is, and despite all this that you have laid at my feet, Father was still right. There does need to be some new deal. Even if the old Zoo is beyond repair, something very much like it - a 'New Zoo' will be needed to replace it. However deplorable all the things humanity has done to our fellow animals, the Zoo itself is not the problem. As a symbol, as a reconciliation, as a place of convening, it is *the solution*."

Despite myself, I was getting drawn into the very argument I despised. I pulled myself back. "And you know what? Basically I just don't care enough, not even about that. Why did I want to kill It?

The Zoo: The Beast, The Boy and The Zoo

Because of what It did to Father and to our family. Because I wanted to get my sister back. And *that's it;* You and I are all we have. We don't need to stay tangled up in all of this... this... this... mess."

"We were *born* into this 'mess', Seth." Sam spoke firmly, and now again clearly speaking just to me.

"No!" I poked a finger at my sister. "Nobody is 'born into' anything! It doesn't matter what our father or mother - whoever the hell she was anyway. Or Lilith or the True Beast. Or any of them intended for us. It is up to *us* to make our lives what we wish and can, and where we wish and can. Maybe you Sam, maybe you delight in basting yourself over and again in all these rancid old stories and myths and ideas that other high and mighty interferers have carefully enmeshed us in. But I *don't!*"

"And speaking of being afraid or being someone else's puppet..." I had the wind in my sails now. "Well look who is talking! I want out. And *I* have the courage to say so. All this business of someone we cannot see or feel manipulating us as marionettes in some storyline..." In saying this and at just that very moment specifically, dizziness swept over me, but passed in a heartbeat. "If we try hard enough we can break out of it all." I pointed again back at the corpse "Even It believed that."

Sam followed my gesture with her gaze. "Oh, that luckless creature and Its beliefs..." she shrugged and grimaced briefly. "Well there was quite a lot that It believed. Unwisely so. It believed that It itself was the destined leader of the all wild things, the inheritor of the deep primeval jurisdiction; and that I daughter of William Faraday would be merely Its follower. Or perhaps It had something rather more intimate in mind."

"None of that was ever going to really happen."

"The dear departed, that second-rate will that quickened that body, it was only ever a placeholder. Oh for a time, It boasted the name and mantle of the True Beast. It could, for a while, tap into an archaic,

The Zoo: The Beast, The Boy and The Zoo

elementary terror, but in itself It was a thin, mediocre thing. I acquiesced to all that It said. I smiled politely enough. I bided my time. A compliant maiden. I waited for my valiant twin, my other self, to lay it low. Inevitably!"

"When you thought, Seth, you were fighting on my behalf..." Her lips began to curve upwards. "Well you were right, just not quite in the way you had considered."

"Just like I said," Samantha smiled the most unpleasant smile I had ever seen. "My hero!"

"Although let me confess, I must admit, just to be on the safe side, I did send Trice to help you. To make sure. Then I drew back from the chess board. I folded my arms and I waited."

I shook my head as if to rid it of all this madness. I moved suddenly towards Sam and grabbed her hand. I tried to tug her forward to come down the hill with me. "Stop saying all this. Please! Come on. Let's go. Let's leave them all to it. Let's find a life away from all this. I am tired of it all, Sam!"

Sam didn't move.

I pulled at her hand a little more insistently now. There was no give. My god, my sister had become so much stronger and solid than I ever remembered. My temper fraying I grabbed her shoulders. Her two hands came up in a smooth motion and shoved me back effortlessly. With no grace or dignity at all, I stumbled backwards over the True Beast's head and landed flat on my back in the mud.

"My name is *Samantha,* not Sam!" She glared down at my fallen form. "Same old brother. Always wanting to be boss. It has always been about control, hasn't it? For you and your kind. Control of other animals. Control over other 'lesser' people. Adults control of children. Creators controlling their created characters. And of course. Of course, men controlling women. Controlling *me.*"

The Zoo: The Beast, The Boy and The Zoo

She threw her head back and laughed. "Always so full of bluster, indignation and rage. So scared that their women might 'turn wild'. So spooked that within that tame female over there, there might just be something free, free to the point of savagery, that loving mother, that tender lover, that compliant mirror image of a twin sister. So no Brother, I *won't* go with you. My place is not with you. Nor at the tame Zoo. My place in with them," she gestured around her at the animals. "And back in the Wild."

I made as to get up and recover just a little of my poise. But both Cheetahs produced purry growls in synchrony. If I wasn't careful, I would end up with one sitting on my chest again. Much more threateningly to me though, the two huge Chimps bared their teeth and swayed from side to side.

I decided to stay where I was.

From the relative safety of this state however, I mocked back. "So women are like a separate species now, are they? Everything dividing up and splitting off. Why are you so intent in erecting barriers? Humans and animals... men and women? Perhaps they belong together. And above all, you and me, Sam – I mean, Samantha. Brother and sister. Twins..! I mean are you serious? Now that we are back together, knowing all that we two know now about our specialness, about being two halves of a single person? Despite all of that, you really mean we should go our separate - no, our *separated* - ways..?"

"We are special true enough, Seth." My sister's tone was still so calm. Calm and certain to the point of an infuriating arrogance. "Everything that has happened here, even before you and I were born, it all pivots around us, the Twins, the Gemini, as your friends on the tower would say. But we are not children any more, And now that very specialness must be about being apart, not together..."

"Do you then think," I cross examined. "That *all* men are afraid of women and their wildness?"

The Zoo: The Beast, The Boy and The Zoo

"No, no, there are many who hold no fear at all." Sam was quick to respond. "Those are the truly stupid, insipid ones. Yes there are plenty of men who are far too dull to understand what is at stake. They lack even the imagination or understanding to be properly afraid, as they should be, of their women."

"You at least, Seth, you have always had a glimmer of knowledge in that direction." A wry grin and a very slight note of conciliation, followed by a proffered hand. She was not so much really helping me up as signalling to her over-eager henchmen, that I had her permission to so rise.

"So what now, Samantha? " I made an ineffectual attempt to brush myself down as I got to my feet. "What happens next?"

"There is more to be said Brother. And that should be best said between you and me with some privacy at least."

There is a small gulley and narrow passage cutting into the cliffs and leading the way to other side of the massif from the pool. Sam gestured me in that direction.

The assembly rippled forward a little as if to follow us. "No." Their leader held up her hand. "Fall back. I would speak now with the Man alone."

Dexter and Sinister whined in protest until Sam's glance silenced them into submission. We moved off, all the mass of animals compliantly remaining. All save the two Chimps. I looked over my shoulder at them in annoyance and concern, and then at Sam as we walked. I was expecting her to order that they too should withdraw.

No, it seemed they were exempt. We were not to be entirely alone after all. Sam did not feel quite so safe and secure that she did not still need part of her bodyguard.

We stopped in a small valley one hundred metres way inside a small rock valley. Nowadays it is a home for the Capybara. It was no longer visible from the pool.

The Zoo: The Beast, The Boy and The Zoo

Sam turned and took both my hand in hers. A certain note of finality in both the stillness of her body and timbre of her words.

"You really thought you had killed It, didn't you..?" A small catch in her throat. Mocking amusement? Or regretful wonderment?

"But the True Beast - so far at least as that means the leader of the free animals, an avatar of such ancient and primordial powers, is, dear little brother, very far from dead." And saying this, my twin sister, Samantha Faraday raised her arms and hands high up in the air, looking and swaying ever so slightly from side to side as if to indicate a something unsaid, something so blindingly obvious, something that you felt staggeringly stupid in not having sooner recognised.

"Whatever you fear most..."

That vexing rhyme again. Back and forth through my head once more, and this time I could not pretend not to understand why. Just for a small and then forgotten moment an all too recognisable red glow flared dully within the deepest core of my sister's eyes.

"Whatever else you believe or do not believe Seth, please know this above all. I do truly love you, little Brother. You do know that, don't you?" Then she took my captive face in between her two strong hands, approached hers to mine, and stared deeply in my eyes for long seconds. Now she pressed and softly rubbed our cheeks side by side together as might some mother animal do to a new born cub. Finally she pulled back for a second to look at me again.

And then Samantha kissed me full on the lips.

In a single motion, and with astonishing change in demeanour, she shook her whole body as to rid herself of something, then pushed me away with such force that I tottered backwards and almost fell once again.

Turning her back on me, briefly she wiped her hands together with a certain finality. She addressed her Chimp henchmen. Her voice was harsh, gesturing in imperious dismissal

The Zoo: The Beast, The Boy and The Zoo

"So now. We are long overdue for the repayment needed, for the sacrifice required from the Faraday bloodline. Take the human traitor away and hang him. Hang him by the neck. Hoist him high up there at the top of the hill for all the Animals in the Zoo to see."

And my twin sister left the clearing.

***

Chapter Fifty: No Nonsense

"Does it hurt, being hanged?" Can you believe that years later someone would in all seriousness (and in all stupidity) ask me such as question?

Gibbering and hooting at an ear splitting level, the two Chimps had half carried, half dragged their struggling captive up the slope. Before me I saw the loop of rope prepared, draped there over a dead tree that looked to be shrivelled by lightning. My own personal gibbet dramatically framed there for me on the very highest point in all the Zoo for all to see against the setting sun.

One Chimp slipped a noose back around my head and lumbered back. The other knuckled over to the rope arranged there to tug me aloft into the air.

A grown Chimp is six times stronger than a human, so with two of them pulling on the hoist rope, I was swinging in the void with the noose tightening around my neck in seconds.

I think my inquisitive and dim questioner may have heard someplace of hanged people dying immediately by having their vertebrae broken through the hangman's drop, in which case it might not have hurt. But of course in that case I could not have possibly survived to address their query. But I didn't drop. Instead I was yanked into the air by the hairy hooligans, and slowly I began to asphyxiate.

And the answer is yes, it does bloody hurt. A lot.

But only for a minute. Mercifully the agony within me soon faded. As my brain starved of air began to close down, a completely unimagined and unexpected sense of peace flooded both body and mind.

In the last seconds before oblivion, there seemed to be an unaccountable sound off there to my left. A sound once familiar to me on an almost daily basis. But this long buried memory had for some considerable time past been securely filed under 'no longer relevant to my life'.

The whizz of a crossbow. Well, that at least is what I had at first thought I heard. But no, of course not. No such noise belonged to the here and now. This was clearly some random dredging up from my memory's basement as my brain cells deprived of oxygen began one by one to give up the ghost. As I let unconsciousness finally take me, I dismissed it as a mirage, a trick of the dying mind.

***

Who? What? Where? When? How?

...And why?

The confusion of what might or might not be a gradual return to consciousness swam all around me. Was I really waking? Or was this still some unconscious dream?

A face slowly coalescing before me. A real image? No. Of course not. My mind was certainly still playing tricks, because those particular features belonged to neither here nor to now.

But tell me again when was *now*? Where exactly was *here*? The last I could remember I had been choking on a rope and hearing that noise, but now I was not on the rope. I was on the ground. I was looking up at the sky.

Wasn't I dead then? And was I awake?

The Zoo: The Beast, The Boy and The Zoo

That face again, now clearer. It just didn't fit. It wasn't part of the story any more. Well not *this* story anyway. Not this part of the story. Not now, not here.

That straggly grey hair. The wizened, scowling face, The watery, blue eyes scanning my face. I both did and did not recognise those features. Maybe it had been just too long and he had of course aged and changed. Or maybe I had wiped the memory out as something from a dreary and painful period of my life.

Or maybe I had just forgotten all about Gogol.

I was fully awake now. Unfortunately. One kind of burning pain from the rope around my neck. Another searing agony within my crucified throat and tortured lungs. Then cuts all over my body from the long struggle with the True Beast. Finally the intense throbbing of a freshly dislocated shoulder, owed, I gradually realised, to my fall from that tree bough up there. The bough up at which I now lay vacantly staring, flat on my back.

You might have thought that, with all that that had happened to me, he would have at least offered me a hand to help me to my feet. This was not forthcoming.

Eventually I managed groaning to sit up a little by myself, and stare in a vacant daze around me at the scene.

"Yes boy, her guards, the Chimps are both dead."

'Boy'?

It had been a while since I had been on the receiving end of that particular word, and that particular style of contempt.

I saw the crossbow, his favourite, the Excalibur Assassin cradled tenderly in his arms. Out of the periphery of my eye I registered the distributed cadavers of the two Chimps in my lynching party; Gogol's arrows neatly sticking out of each throat. Gogol has sorted out the problem in a 'no nonsense' fashion. He has used the shortest distance between two points. I was relieved to see that Dexter and Sinister were not included in the carnage.

"You are surprised to see me here, I think?"

I tried to speak, but my agonised throat was just too painful. I ended up resorting to a nod. Gogol reached to his side and produced a water flask. After several long draughts, I could eventually manage to croak the single word question, "Sam?" I tried to lever myself to my elbows a little higher to look around me further; in that sudden panicked thought that she too had been mown down.

"The other one? Your other part? Oh no, she is still alive. She and the rest of her troop were gone before I got here. I only had the Chimps to deal with."

Relaxing ever so slightly and reaching for a second swallow of that glorious water, I looked again up into Gogol's face. This man? This weird, weird man. I hardly knew what to say to him.

"I... I didn't even know that you knew this place. Not your world, Gogol."

"No, it *isn't*. Not now. I hated coming back here, this place, I loathe it. So full of nonsense."

Aha... that expression again after all this time.

"But I have been here before. Long ago."

He looked at me. He seemed somehow expectant. But I was still trying to come to terms with the strangeness of all of this, and on top of everything that happened to me over the last twenty four hours. So many different parts of my body were in different sorts of pain, and I remained quite dumb.

"*She* never told you then? All the time you have been here." I was in little doubt from his derisive tone who 'she' was. But still he got nothing from me.

"To think that once upon a time I was actually part of all this foolishness," Gogol grunted. He swung his crossbow onto his back, placed his hands on hips, disparagingly surveying the whole panorama of the Zoo laid out before us. "And I even held counsel with those meddlesome fools who set you on your course boy." He grinned derisively. "Yes, I used to visit their not-so-secret tower. I had a voice and role in their pompous meetings too."

"But I didn't see eye to eye with most of them. And especially with her. The nonsense they all spouted. So when I did what I did, well they were all only too glad to have an excuse to cast me out."

"And yet… both I and the place to which they banished me came in pretty useful later, didn't we?" He gave a dry little laugh of self-satisfaction.

I started with a question, but choked as I coughed up some blood.

"Time for all of that later. We need to get your wounds treated." A reassuring memory flowed. One of the few good things Sam and I associated with the Vague Lands was Gogol's skill in healing. That and his deadly, no nonsense skill with a bow were, right now two very welcome accomplishments on his part.

With some unexpected solicitude he took my arm and helped me limp down the hill. There it was, the other thing that I most associated with Gogol: his familiar, battered old jeep. It had gouged some deep tyre tracks into the Zoo's soil, a refreshingly insolent incursion into this protected, complacent world.

"You probably should know that your sister's vermin are all in retreat. " Gogol's aged frame gave something like a shudder. "Back into the outer Old Forest and those bits of the Zoo firmly under their control. And the entire Zoo knows now what happened here. Look there!" Supporting me with my arm slung over his shoulder, he pointed down towards the whole spectacle of the Zoo laid before us.

"It was their own plan to stage your execution here up on high so that all the species of the Zoo could see it for themselves. But it didn't go right for them, did it? Instead they saw their side defeated. The whole thing backfired. And before all that - to the astonishment of many - you succeeded in chopping off the head of the hydra."

A fleeting glance my way of what might just have been surprised appreciation.

"Did I..." I was struggling in my still dazed condition to find the appropriate words. "Did I... 'win', then? Did I achieve what I was supposed to?"

"Oh *you* didn't win."

"*She* did though. Your grandmother. Things have been pretty much reset to the way they were. Whatever power and support your sister thinks she still has, the rebellion of the wild has been checked. For a while at least."

"There is a balance here again. Not the new compact your father sought, but at least the Zoo will not slide into total decay." A thin smile here. "Yes, she at least will be pleased. Neither of her grandchildren wholly triumphing over the other. All back neatly in equilibrium. For the moment she has most certainly won. But then she usually does, that one."

"But you..? How..? Why did you come for me Gogol....?" My vocal chords slowly recovering, I shook my head in bewilderment.

"You were given into my trust boy - as a baby..."

"Yes. By Lilith."

"No!" He spoke with contempt. "*Not* by her. Not her alone anyway. It was someone other who actually placed both of you physically, however reluctantly, as babes into my arms. Someone who trusted me. Someone from whose trust I have never been released." Gogol's eyes seemed bore into mine and yet be looking through and beyond me to someone else entirely. "And of all the people on this stupid bloody earth, her memory is the last I could ever let down."

The Zoo: The Beast, The Boy and The Zoo

I might have sought more, but at the same time a strong, pain-driven wave of nausea and vertigo cut anything further from me. Just as well, for Gogol was in no mood for clarifications or debate.

"We will talk about all that. But first get in the car. We must get away from this ridiculous place. There is a lot to do."

As I limped down toward Gogol's old jeep, something wet and cold landed on my nose from above. A snowflake. I looked straight up. Its fellows were starting to descend on mass upon the earth. Yes it would be coming down thick and fast in a second; and for a little while it would hide and forgive this landscape scarred by so much blood and pain.

I had paid little attention recently to such things as the season, but suddenly realised that we must be surely now only a few days before Christmas.

Gogol was once again appraising my battered form as I slumped in the passenger seat. "We need to get you properly patched up, boy."

"And then..."

"And then, above all, we need to go and find your mother."

END OF BOOK ONE OF THE ZOO TRILOGY

Epilogue

"So my brother has finally brought our tale to an end. You will be leaving this place now, I suppose?"

"Yes. As long as you will actually let me leave Samantha? Leave your enchanting island, that is."

"What's that..?"

"Oh yes! Ha ha. Well, no, you don't need to worry about that. That all belonged to a quite different story, and one where I carried a quite different name. You do not really fall into the same category as a sneaky, seductive shipwrecked mariner whining that he is only trying to get home to his beloved wife. Pssh! What nonsense that was. But of course that particular story was also told by a man. And famously men who tell such stories can be blind."

"I do not think somehow my charms would work over someone like you anyway, would they?"

"Well whatever about that Samantha, we seem to have arrived at an ending then – at least an ending of a sort, and for the moment."

"You do seem in rather a hurry. You have barely touched your drink. But of course you, and, more importantly they, they will have come to their conclusions. That I am the red eyed monster, a witch of some form, a would be siblicide in fact? Certainly something to flee. And to flee fast."

"That is where the tale, as latterly told by Seth at least, seems to have led us so far. Yes..."

"And perhaps more disappointingly, and despite what I said earlier, Seth's denouement has turned things back to leave us after all with a rather simple, straightforward story about a hero who is sent on certain trials by a wise mentor, who benefits from a friendly helper, who attains new knowledge and understanding, and finally... defeats a great enemy (namely, me!), thus saving the world and returning to the status quo."

"Hurrah! All so nice and neat. A beginning, a middle and end. Not really much like real, messy life, is it? Not much like truth."

"But we must be content with a standard quest myth then? "

"I can see it might seem something along those lines, yes."

"I had hoped we might have - together, my brother and I - served up something less - less clichéd?"

"I am sorry you feel so let down, Samantha. But you know... the story is not really over yet..."

"Perhaps not. But clearly I am the great villain of the piece. No shades of grey remaining any more in the story as they have it; and a mark indelible has been placed right up there on my forehead."

"More importantly they, whoever 'they' might be, reading this, they have all made up their minds now. About me. About what I think. About what I might represent from here on in."

" No. Not necessarily."

"No? Really?"

"No."

(...)

"Samantha, when it comes to 'making up your mind' about anything. And particularly making up your mind about another person, when is the right time, do you suppose, for that?"

"You tell me, my fine visitor."

"The time for that, Sam..."

"Is..."

"Never."

^^^

Seth and Sam will return in Book II

Acknowledgements

My wife Diane contributed a number of early crucial plot and other elements on the path to publication and has patiently encouraged and tolerated me throughout. A very considerable number of people kindly read successive drafts and fed back impressions and comments. My early crude and stumbling efforts have certainly been transformed by this process. Special thanks to my brother Dermot Regan as my first reader and to my sister Patricia Moylan as the final one. I thank the other individuals concerned in alphabetical order: Gillian Clarke; Ann Marie Doyle; Angela Franconi; Veronica Gibson, Nick Jackson, Paula, Paul O'Brien, Mark Pilgrim, Serena Simmons and Wendy. Each and every one brought something valuable to the manuscript's development.

I need to offer my special gratitude to both Dr Lee Durrell MBE and Dr Mark Pilgrim OBE who kindly provide a preface and introduction respectively and were so encouragingly positive as to my attempts here to write anything of worth.

I have hugely appreciated the assistance of Vickie Wigley at This Is Mojo design consultancy for her patient work and advice on the novel's cover.

I should also thank the Science Fiction writer, Dr Stephen Baxter for his early encouragement as well as that as my fellow zoo fundraiser alumnus turned writer, Chris Fancy.

More widely I am grateful to all my friends and colleagues across the UK and global zoo community for the privilege and pleasure of having worked with so many across the years. For whatever little it is worth, 'The Zoo' is very much the result of that career.

Finally my grandchildren Sofia and Sami who have helped in their own unique way – And their parents John and Sadia for in having them giving me the greatest gift of my life.

Printed in Great Britain
by Amazon

36588935R00225